Cupcakes
and
CROOKED SPOONS

Sweet Treats
Book Three

CHARITY B.

Editor: Joanne LaRe Thompson
Cover Design: Murphy Hopkins
Formatting: Champagne Formats

Author's Note

This is the final book in a Trilogy and should be read after Sweetened Suffering. If you've read the previous books in the series, thank you so much for continuing to read. You mean more to me than you know. This book contains very dark subject matter. It is by far the most triggering book in the series and the characters are children for a large portion of the story.

To those who have stuck by me to the end, I wish I could hug each and every one of you. When I began writing this story, I had no idea it would impact me like it has. This was an intense journey for me and I hope you feel the same. I love these characters and this world so much more than I ever could have prepared myself for. The love and responses you have given me, touches me all the way to my soul, and I mean that. I truly do love you guys and it's because of you, my dreams have come true.

Trigger Warning
This novel contains heavy drug use, explicit sexual content, violence, extreme child abuse, and sensitive subject matter which may be triggering to some readers.

Dedication

To Alycia: I wish you could be here for this. You were so supportive of me, ALWAYS. You were truly one of the kindest and most beautiful people I have and ever will know. You understood me and knew things that no one else does. You will always be one of my closest friends. I love you, girl, and miss you like crazy.

We are crooked souls trying to stand up straight,
dry eyes in the pouring rain.
—*Switchfoot*

CHAPTER ONE
Beginning

October, 2001

Tavin

SHE'S SLEEPING AGAIN. SHE DOESN'T MOVE, EVEN when I poke her with the fork.

"Mommy, wake up!" I yell it in her face, but she stays still. My stomach twists; I'm so hungry.

There're voices. My head whips to the door. Uh-oh. Daddy's home and he's with someone.

I better go hide.

I jump off Mommy, rip open my door, and run downstairs to my room. Crawling under the stairs, I hold my lips together so I don't make sounds with my breathing. I hug myself tight as the door creaks open from the top of the stairs.

BOOM. BOOM. BOOM. BOOM.

Someone's coming.

"Stay down there, you little fucker. I'll get you when I'm done."

That isn't Daddy's voice.

A loud pounding above my head makes me try to shrink smaller, and a big thump lets me know whatever was just thrown down here, has made it to the bottom.

The door slams.

I hear moaning and grumbling. Someone's here. I stay perfectly still as the source of the noise comes into my view.

"Bastard," he mumbles.

It's a boy, and I don't know who he's talking to because he doesn't know I'm here. I think he is close to the same age as me. His brown hair falls into his face while he kicks at the floor on his way to my bed. I make sure I stay under the stairs as I move out a little further for a better look. He sits down and bounces a few times before he looks up and sees me.

"Ahh!" He yells and falls back a little. "What are you doing, freak?"

I crawl out. "My name is Tavin."

"I didn't ask you your name, freak, I asked you what you're doing, creepin' under the stairs."

Why is he still calling me 'freak'?

"I was hiding. Why are you in my room?"

"Because my dad wants to get high with yours." He rolls his eyes. "I don't even know why he brought me."

I've never met another kid before. I see them all the time, I've just never talked to one.

"What's your name?"

I stand up and walk to the bed to meet him and look at his clothes. He's wearing a long sleeve, black shirt and he has a black hat on.

"Toben."

I like his name, it kind of sounds like mine. The sharp pain turns over. My tummy hurts so badly, I hope I don't throw up in front of him.

"Do you have food?"

He shifts awkwardly. "Uh, no. Sorry."

"Oh, it's okay. You can play with me if you want."

His eyebrows scrunch and he frowns at me. "I don't want."

Oh…dang.

I look at his hands and he's holding a notebook! Maybe he likes to draw, like me. He sets it down on my bed before reaching into his jeans, pulling out two long wires that are attached to a little shiny, black box. It lights up when he touches it.

"What is that?" I point to it.

"It's an iPod, duh."

Then he does something so funny, he puts the wires in his ears!

"Why did you do that?"

He raises one of his eyebrows and I can see his eyes. They're as dark as night. I bet he's good at drawing.

He takes one of the wires out and hands it to me. "Listen."

I put the wire in my ear like he did. Instantly, loud screaming and banging music fills my head. I rip it back out.

"What is that?!"

"It's Behemoth." He sort of smiles. I wonder what a bee-hee-moth is.

"Why is he yelling?"

"I guess because he's mad."

"Why?"

He shrugs. "Maybe because there's no God."

That's the first time he looks at my eyes and I hope he does it again. I like it.

"Oh."

He takes the wires out of the black box. The bee-hee-moth starts coming out of it and I can hear it all over my room.

"I've never seen you at lunch or anything, where do you go to school?"

I shake my head. "I don't go anywhere."

He frowns at me. "Everybody has to go to school. You're lying."

"Hey! I'm not lying."

Why would I lie to him?

He crosses his arms. "Then how did you learn to read, and tell time, and write your name?"

I climb off my bed to show him my wall.

"I don't know how to do any of that stuff. Here, stand up, I want to show you my pictures." He gets off the bed so I can move it. "I like to draw."

When my bed is out of the way, I look at him and his eyebrows are lifted.

"Obviously."

I kneel by my drawings. "Do you want to help?"

He walks around my room. "Uh, no I'm good." Shoving his hands in his pockets, he blows his hair out of his eyes. "All you have is that little TV and old radio? You don't have an Xbox or anything?"

What is this silly boy talking about? "I don't think so."

He stomps to my bed and falls back onto it. "Great."

I crawl to him and prop my arms on the sheets. I rest my head in my hands as I watch him.

"How old are you?"

He lifts his head. "I turned ten last week. How old are you?"

I want to know so badly! "I don't know, I think I might be nine, but maybe I'm ten too!"

"How do you not know how old you are, freak?"

This boy is making me mad now, he knows my name. I point my finger at him, so he can see I'm serious.

"Hey! My name is Tavin."

He gets off the bed and sits on the floor with me. "Okay, *Tavin*. What's your deal? You're filthy, you aren't even try-ing to cover up your bruises, you say you've never been to school, and now you don't even know how old you are?"

I guess I have worn this dress a long time. I don't have very many, though, and the others are just like this. I didn't know it was bad.

"I'm filthy?"

"God, yes. When was the last time you had a bath?"

I close my eyes and try to remember. "I don't know, I think Mommy gave me one when there were still kids playing outside all day."

"You haven't had a bath since summer vacation? That was over a month ago!" He brings his knees to his chest. "You're too old for your mom to still be washing you. Why don't you clean yourself?"

I shrug. "I didn't know I was supposed to." I look at the purple marks on my arm. "Why should I hide them?"

I can't help that I get them. Should I be embarrassed? He keeps looking at me funny. Oh, I hope he doesn't think I'm stupid.

"Because then people will know. If they know, then they will call the cops, and you don't want to meet a cop."

I know about police. Daddy says if they find me, they will lock me away in jail and I'll never get out. I've never actually seen them, I just know they are bad.

"Why would they do that?"

"Because people don't know how to mind their own damn business."

"I don't ever see people, though. I never leave the house."

"What? What about the dentist and the doctor?"

"Daddy says I don't need a doctor because I should be dead anyway."

I think I did something wrong because he looks mad at me.

"You never leave? Will your parents not let you?"

I'm always too scared to leave. Daddy says there are a lot

of people who will hurt little girls. I don't want him to know I get scared, though.

"They don't care if I leave, I just don't. I like to watch all the people through my window."

He turns his head and points his thumb. "That's a window well, the only thing outside there is a concrete wall."

"You have to climb the ladder, silly."

"Wow, really?" He stands up and hurries to my window. When he opens it, he looks at the ladder. "Well I'll be damned." He turns to me and smiles. His whole face changes when he smiles. "You're weird, but I like you. See you around, Tavin." He climbs out and is gone.

Why did he leave? He said he liked me.

He left his eye pad I think he called it, and his notebook, on my bed. I bet he will come back for it. Oh, I hope he does!

Toben

Damn it. I left my lyric book and iPod in her room. I'll need to go back to get them, just not tonight. I still don't know why he dragged me over there in the first place, he normally can't wait to get me out of his sight. Is he trying to be an actual parent and punish me for getting suspended today? Why doesn't he just punch me in the stomach like usual and be done with it? Whatever. I don't give a shit. I thought he was bad when he was drinking, now that he has been using, it's as if his hate has become a creature of its own.

That Tavin girl is the oddest person I've ever met. I wonder if she's telling the truth about all that stuff. I've lived two houses down from her my whole life, and I've never seen her before. She doesn't act like she's nine, and she's smaller than the girls in my class. She's covered in dirt and her hair needs washing, but she's interesting. I think I was kind of mean to her, and it's not normal that I care.

I found myself constantly looking at her pretty, purple eyes that were out of place with her ragged clothes and tangled hair. I don't understand how her parents have been able to keep her locked up and out of sight for so long, or why they'd want to. Maybe I can ask my dad, if I can catch him on one of his good days.

I'm gonna get the crap beat out of me for leaving. What else is new? At least I don't have to stay in the room that time forgot.

I run back to my house, get my bike, and begin to ride the two blocks to Christopher's, as I breathe in the perfect air.

I love the fall. It's calming to watch the grass and flowers dying. It's the end of stupid pool parties and getting crazy-ass looks from people for wearing long sleeved shirts. It smells cleaner, and the air feels better than any other time of the year.

Christopher is the closest thing to a best friend that I have. His parents think I'm a bad influence on their perfect, little boy because my dad's a dick and I listen to metal. If they only knew their angel introduced me to pot, and I'm about to get drunk off the vodka he stole from their liquor cabinet.

I almost told him about my dad, the last time we drank, and I have wanted to tell him on a few other occasions, but then I remind myself of the possible outcomes.

He could try to help by telling his parents, which would most likely mean I'd go into foster care. I definitely don't want that, at least now I pretty much do whatever I want. He could keep quiet, but always pity me and get all weird which would cost me my only real friend. He could ask why my dad does what he does, and when I tell him it's because I killed my mother, he could end up agreeing that I deserve the beatings. The odds of him staying my friend and staying quiet are pretty damn slim, so I keep it to myself.

The thought occurs to me that I could tell Tavin. Just from what I saw, her arms, neck, side of her face, and legs are all covered in either new or healing bruises. I feel bad for her, she's so small. I don't think she can take too much. Her dad is a decent sized guy, nothing like my dad, but he could definitely inflict some damage. She doesn't even act like it's a secret. She probably wouldn't bat an eye if I took off my shirt so she could see my bruises. It would be so nice to just say it aloud. To tell someone.

I'll go see her tomorrow to get my stuff.

I drop my bike in Christopher's yard and knock on his front door. His mom answers, which is better than his dad. I try to be as polite as I can, and they still don't like me. At least she tries to hide it.

She sighs in greeting, "Hello, Toben. Christopher is in his room."

"Thank you, Mrs. Reed."

I give her a big smile and she makes a sad attempt to return it. I pound down the stairs and take the left into Christopher's room. Some top forty shit is playing, and he's propped in bed pounding buttons on his Gameboy.

He turns his head and when he sees me, a huge grin crosses his face.

"Dude, that was seriously legendary. I swear you didn't even look at him the first time, your fist was just punching his face out of nowhere." He starts laughing, "Then you lost it." Shaking his head, he adds, "You're crazy."

He reaches under his bed, recovers a bottle, and takes a drink. He hands it to me, and after a burning swig, I tell him why Thomas asked for everything he got.

"He deserved it. He's a dick. He was kicking Michelle Andrews in the shin and I've seen him pick on other girls before, too. So, I thought, if he wants to fight, he can fight me."

"Yeah, well, just give me a chance to explain things if I ever make you mad."

We drink a few more drinks and soon my head is fuzzy. I better stop or I won't be able to make it home.

"Hey, do you have any weed? I can pay you." I reach for the twenty I ripped off from my dad, this morning.

"No, but you can get it from the high school kids. Just make sure whoever you ask looks cool."

I'm able to walk up the stairs fairly straight and I only fall off my bike once on my way to the high school. I think the ride clears my head because I can focus better once I get there. Even though they're already out for the day, there are always a few who stay for clubs, or practices, or whatever else they do in senior high.

I ride by the football field, to the parking lot. Sure enough, there's a group of them heading to their cars. I scan them, and my eyes land on a kid with dreadlocks. There's no way someone that doesn't smoke weed, would do that to their hair.

I park my bike in the rack and try to hurry without being obvious about it. I catch up to him just as he's getting into his car.

He raises his eyebrows. "Do you need something, little man?"

I reach in my pocket and pull out the twenty, showing it to him, while keeping it in my fist. "I need a quarter."

He laughs at me. "A quarter of what?"

"Of weed."

"Jesus, you're a little young, yeah?" He looks me up and down, sighs, and then nods toward his car. "Fine, get in."

I think for sure he'll rip me off, but he's cool. His name is Cory Ridge and he tells me to hit him up any time.

When I get back to my house, I still have a great buzz. Thankfully, my dad isn't back yet. Getting some papers from my desk drawer, I roll a joint and light up. The high is calm and relaxing. I feel my heart rate slow and I close my eyes.

I know that I would want to see Tavin again even if I hadn't left my crap there. I don't have school for three days on account of my suspension, and she apparently doesn't have it at all. I think I'll try to get her to leave tomorrow and take her to the beach. It's the best time of year to go, in my opinion. If she's never left, then maybe I can show her some new things. I've never had a girl for a friend before.

I wonder what it will be like.

CHAPTER TWO
Allies

Tavin

MY HEAD AND STOMACH STILL HURT FROM when Daddy kicked me yesterday. I turn the pages in Toben's notebook and there isn't a single picture, only a bunch of squiggles. I hid his eye pad yesterday, so his daddy wouldn't find it. It just took me a long time to make it be quiet. I hope I didn't break it.

I need food. I feel sick. Daddy's already gone to work, so I walk up the stairs to see if there's anything in the kitchen to eat today.

I hear Mommy before I even open the basement door. She's getting fucked again. Dang it! I'm so hungry and she hates it when I interrupt her with the men.

Maybe if I'm extra quiet, they won't notice me.

Creaking open the door, I peek out. Mommy is on her hands and knees and she's naked just like the man kneeling behind her. Since they're facing away from me, I open the door the rest of the way and tip-toe to the kitchen.

You're a princess hiding from an evil sorcerer. You have to find the magic fairy dust to beat him and return to your castle.

Mommy is still making noises. There are times that I

think the men are hurting her, until she asks them to keep going or do it harder.

I hold my breath as I open the cabinet that sometimes has bread or crackers. It's still empty. The refrigerator has beer, but that just makes my stomach hurt more if I don't eat with it. I don't know if they have ever gone this long without having food in the house and this is the hungriest I think I've ever been. Looking in the trash, I find a wrapper that has ketchup still on it, so I lick it off. Since there isn't anything else, I sneak back into the living room to go back downstairs.

"That's right, skank, you like my fat cock?"

The man pulls Mommy's hair and she yells, "Oh, yes, baby."

They're still turned away from me, so I quietly pass them to open my bedroom door. As I do, someone is standing there! Even though I jump, I'm able to keep myself from making noise with my surprise.

Once I focus, I see it's Toben. He came back! He smiles at me before his gaze moves into the living room to watch Mommy, and his eyes go wide.

"Whoa!"

Too loud. His voice is way too loud.

I turn as the naked man jumps from the couch. "What the hell?"

Mommy lifts her head and glares at me. "Goddamn it, Tavin! Get downstairs. I'm working."

"I'm sorry, Mommy."

She doesn't answer me, she just spreads her legs apart and touches herself between them. "Come on, baby, it's just my kid."

I shove by Toben to get on the steps and shut the basement door. I hear Mommy's moaning, so I know the man has started again.

Taking Toben's hand, I pull him down the stairs. Once

we're in my room, I smile at him.

"You came back. So, you really do like me?"

He laughs and it is such a nice sound. I can't stop myself from smiling even bigger.

"Yes, freak, I like you." My cheeks go flat as my mouth drops into a frown. "Oh, Tavin, I'm kidding. I'm sorry, I won't call you that again."

That makes me feel better as I walk to my nightstand. "Good." Wrapping my fingers around the handle I pull the drawer open. "I have your notebook and eye pad."

He grins and that makes me happy. "It's called an iPod. There's no such thing as an iPad." He looks at my ceiling, "So…your mom's a hooker?"

"Yes." I hand him his things.

"Well that's uh…different. So, whatcha you doin' today?" He seems happier than yesterday.

"I don't know. I don't feel well. I'm hungry." My stomach lurches at the mention of it. He frowns and I feel bad because my complaining took his smile away.

"You were hungry last night too, when was the last time you've eaten?"

We need to stop talking about food, my head hurts.

"Six days I think."

He grasps my arm. Uh-oh, I think I made him mad.

"You haven't eaten in a week?! What the hell? Grab a sweater, we're going to get you some food."

He wants me to leave? I can't do that! I've never been further than the yard. He did say we would eat though…

"I don't know, I don't want you to be mad at me, I just-"

"You need food and you need to see more than this room. Your mom won't even know. She's obviously preoccupied." I'm really scared, I'm just hungrier. My stomach jumps when he whispers, "You can trust me."

And I do.

My lips stretch into a smile when he takes my hand. His dark eyes sparkle as I say, "Okay."

We climb out of my window and he points to the front of his bicycle. "Sit up there."

My heart is thumping and I'm getting sweaty. For the first time in my entire life, I'm leaving my house. He climbs on behind me, and when we begin to move, the wind blows my hair back and my stomach tickles in a good way. I feel like laughing, so I do. It's a short ride, and before long, he pulls into a driveway where he stops the bike.

"Come on." He waves his hand for me to follow him.

His house is kind of tall, like mine, but instead of blue, it's white. The keys jangle as he unlocks the door and we step inside. There is tan carpet on the floor and it's much cleaner than my house. It smells better too. Passing through an entryway, we walk across his living room. His house is so pretty! The couches match the chairs and the curtains. There are pictures of all sorts of people on the wall and the carpet is spotless. We come to an archway that leads to the kitchen. He starts opening cabinets and I can't believe what I see. They are full of cans, bags, and boxes of food!

He sits in a chair by the table and crosses his arms. "You can have whatever you want. There's some juice and soda in the fridge, and I think there are some frozen dinners in the freezer."

I don't know where to start. I've never seen so much food before and my stomach turns simply from looking. I go to the cabinet and when I reach up, my arms are too short.

He doesn't even make me ask as he walks up next to me. "What looks good?"

All of it.

I recognize the cookies so I point to them. "Those, in the blue bag."

He gives them to me and I am so relieved at having food, that I rip open the bag and start shoving as many into my mouth as I can. I wish I could chew and swallow faster.

"Whoa! Tavin," he laughs. "You can have as much as you want, just slow down. If you eat too fast you'll get sick."

I nod, making myself slow down my chewing and only eat one at a time.

I have cookies, chips, an apple, two glasses of orange juice and a few chicken nuggets. I eat so much that I can't eat anymore and I *always* want more. Having a full belly is the most wonderful feeling. When I finish, I march over to him and hug him.

"Thank you, Toben."

At first, he's stiff, but he soon relaxes and hugs me back. "You're welcome." Smiling, he waves for me to follow. "Come on, I got to see your room, now you can see mine."

I trail behind him, back across the living room. We walk down a hallway to the left of the entryway and climb a set of stairs until he stops at a door. He opens it and there are more steps leading up to an attic.

I climb up behind him and I can't believe how it looks! The walls are painted black with a bunch of posters covering them and the ceiling. There's a big TV with chords everywhere and a large, black box with a green circle on it lying on the floor. A lot of other stuff is around it too, I just don't know what it all is. I look over to his desk and there's another TV sitting next to a rectangle covered in square buttons.

"Why do you need two TVs?"

He shakes his head. "You really don't know what a computer is?"

I shake mine back. "Does that make me stupid?"

"It makes you deprived, not stupid." He turns on his big radio, falls down on his bed and rolls over to his night stand.

"Have you ever smoked pot?"

I took one of Daddy's cigarettes to try it once, it made me cough and my throat hurt. I don't want him to think I'm a baby though, so I won't tell him that part. "I smoked a cigarette once, is that the same thing?"

He shows me something that looks like a cigarette. "You smoke it the same way, except you hold the smoke in for a minute."

Lighting it with a lighter, he puffs on it and it smells good. I sit next to him as he hands it to me. The smoke tastes better than the cigarettes. It still chokes me though and I start coughing so hard I think I might throw up.

Toben laughs. "Don't take such a big hit next time, I bet that'll fuck you up."

We pass it back and forth, and by the time it's halfway gone, my head feels blurry, my body is warm, and I'm smiling more than I think I ever have. I'm so happy that he came back that I could cry, and I am so excited that I'm actually inside someone else's house. When we finish the 'joint' he says it's called, he gets up, picks up a funny looking marker and hands it to me.

"You're going to love this." He walks over to his desk, flips a switch, and the room is pitch-black. Just as I begin to get nervous, a long, skinny, purple light comes on. His teeth, fingernails, and shoelaces are all glowing. Suddenly, writing and pictures appear all over the walls. It's like magic!

"Pick a spot and write your name."

Disappointment pokes my heart. "I…I don't know how."

I can't see his face clearly, but he sounds sad when he says, "Shit, I'm sorry." He takes my hand, leads me to the wall, and points to some writing. "Look, see this? It's a *T*, it makes the *ta* sound in Tavin. It's easy. Can you copy it?"

He's right, it is easy. It's just two lines touching. He does the same thing for each letter, and before I know it, I have written my name for the first time ever. I feel so big and important.

"There, you signed my wall, so now it's official: we're friends."

"You're my first." Even though it's embarrassing, I want him to know.

"And I'll be the best." His glowing smile makes me laugh. He goes back to his desk and turns on his bedroom light before shutting off the purple one. "Hey, I was thinking we could go to the beach today. Do you want to?"

I will go anywhere he wants me to. I catch his excitement and I can feel happiness in my voice when I tell him, "Yes."

Toben

My dad may be an asshole, but Tavin's parents make me feel like I might not have it so bad. At least I'm clean and fed. Sometimes, he will even give me money and buy me stuff so he can keep up the appearance of a normal, even good, dad.

Six days without food. I can't imagine what that must be like. I've always felt alone in this, I never understand why I'm the only one with a dad who hates them. Everyone else's dad is teaching them how to fix cars or play football, telling them they love them, and showing up to parent/teacher conferences. I see now that I'm not alone. If a girl like Tavin has parents that don't love her, then it can happen to anybody.

I like it when she smiles, and her laugh is like a lullaby. I make it my personal mission to see that she does both as much as possible. She rides on the front of my bike on our way to the beach and her joy causes my grin to be a permanent fixture, as I watch her enthusiasm. When we arrive, I chain my bike to the rack and lead her to the shoreline, by holding her hand. We take off our shoes and bury our toes in the sand. I can feel the mist from the ocean on my face and taste the salt on my tongue. When the first tide rushes over our toes, she squeals with delight, and when I laugh, I feel it in the deepest part of me.

"This is the best day of my life," she sighs, as she lies back into the sand and looks to the sky.

At first it makes me feel wonderful that I can do that for her. Then I realize that I can't think of a single day, other than maybe when I found the letter from my mom, that was better than this. I lie on my side next to her, propping my head in my hand.

"You know what? I think it might be mine, too."

She turns to me and grins. She makes me want to help her, to give her the things her crazy parents deny her. I will do whatever I can to make sure she never goes another day without some type of food. I will be her friend and I'm excited for her to be mine.

We pick out clouds that look like an elephant and a turtle and make up a story about them. Her laugh is contagious and before I know it, we are in our own world of Tavin and Toben, unaware of anyone else on the beach.

My stomach growls. "Hey, do you want to get some food?"

"Again?"

"Yeah, most people eat three times a day."

"Three times?! Do you eat that much?"

I try not to chuckle, she just gets so stunned by such basic information. "Yes, silly." I sit up and stretch my arms. "Come on, there are lots of shops on The Walk." Standing up, I hold out my hand to her.

Once we make it to the concrete, Tavin throws her head back and groans, "It's so hot! I can't wear this anymore."

Ripping off her sweater, she exposes her bruised arms and they are worse than yesterday. I feel a pang of fear in my gut that she had been hit because of me skipping out last night.

I don't even get the chance to ask her when a woman comes up to her. "Sweetheart, are you alright? Where are your parents?"

Adults and their questions. I have to think fast. "They're right over there," pointing toward a large group of people huddling by the glass shop, I add, "and we're more than alright! We were in a car crash a couple days ago and are lucky to be alive. See?" I lift my shirt to show her my bruises that are as fresh as Tavin's.

The woman covers her mouth in shock. "Oh my…"

That's good enough for me, so I nod to her, clutch Tavin's hand and skirt around the nosey bitch.

When we are far away from the lady, I stop and turn to her. "Look, I'm sorry that you're hot, but you have to wear the sweater. You'll draw the wrong attention. Please put it back on."

She gives me a sad look, but still pulls it back over her arms.

"You have bruises, too."

"Looks like our dads have a lot in common." She doesn't respond, she just scrunches her eyebrows and jerks her head. I nudge her shoulder with mine before leading her to the ice cream parlor. "How about burgers and milkshakes?"

Her smile is so big when she nods, that it makes me laugh.

We're eating our food on the curb when a woman with a Polaroid camera around her neck approaches us.

"Hey, do you guys care if I snap a picture? I'll give you one." I shrug in response and she obviously takes that as a yes, with the click of a button. A blank photo prints out, and the woman removes it before snapping another picture. When she retrieves that one, she hands it to me. "Thanks, guys." She waves to us and is on her way.

Tavin leans over to look. "There's nothing there."

"You have to shake it." I show her and her face lights up as the photo comes into view. "See?" I give it to her.

"Wow! It's just like magic."

That makes me laugh, and I realize that I've been doing that a lot today. "It's like dated technology is what it is." I stand and hold out my hand. "We better get back. If my dad gets home and I'm not there, I'm as good as dead."

She pulls her stare from the photo to look up at me. "Okay."

After she gets back on my bike, I ride back to our neighborhood and across her lawn. She jumps off the handlebars and smiles at me before wrapping her skinny arms around my neck.

"Will you come over tomorrow?"

I grin at her. "Promise."

She turns and runs to the side of the house to climb down the ladder into her window well. I watch her waving until she disappears, and I smile the whole way home.

Tavin

What a wonderful day! The ocean is the prettiest thing that I've ever seen. I think it's a creature, even if Toben did laugh at me for saying it. It moves in the most amazing way and it makes powerful sounds. You don't know what it's going to do until it does it and it smells so good. I've never had that much fun before. Never. He's so nice and his eyes make me happy, and when he holds my hand, it's the only time I've ever felt safe. Ever.

He promises he will come back tomorrow.

I look at the photograph the lady took and I hug it. Now I won't ever forget today. I look at it again and I see that Toben is right. I'm covered in dirt and he's so clean. Maybe I can ask Mommy to give me a bath, so that I won't be dirty when I see him again, and maybe he'll like me even more.

I decide to go see if she's awake and alone. After I climb the stairs, I peek out of the door to see her by herself on the big chair. I creep towards her, nice and slow. She says I am too loud and too rowdy, so I try to not be either.

"Mommy?"

She's tying herself off, so I better hurry and ask or it won't be until later tonight that I will get another chance.

"Oh, good, Tavin!" My heart jumps because she's happy to see me. I just knew she loved me. "I'm having a hard time finding a vein, come over here and help."

Oh.

"Mommy, can I have a bath?"

"I just gave you one." Her strap is falling down her arm, so I push it up. "Now, shut up and get this in."

She hands me her syringe. Even though the veins are all blown out on her left arm, I'm able to find a good one on the right. I tap her and get the needle into her vein before I pull back on the plunger. Once I see the blood, I take off the tourniquet and push down, making sure to get it all into her. Moments later, her body is limp as she slumps into the chair.

Dang! Now I probably won't get one at all because she will be useless for a long time and I don't like to come up here when Daddy is home. If he sees me, he hits me. That's just the way it is.

I'll just wait until it gets dark outside to check if she's awake. Maybe Daddy will already be on the nod by then.

I turn on my radio and the music leaks into my skin. I like to dance, it makes me feel like I can be whatever I want, and when I grow up I am going to be a singer. I can make the music that I want to dance to. I like to pretend that when I grow up and people look at me, they will think I'm the prettiest girl they've ever seen. I want people to like me. Even though Mommy and Daddy don't, Toben does. I wonder if he knows other kids. Maybe he will let me meet them if he isn't too embarrassed.

Oh, I hope I get a bath.

I look outside and the moon is up, so I climb the stairs quietly, and when I get to the top, I take a big breath and slowly open the door. Mommy is smoking a cigarette on the couch, so I peek my head out further and try to look into the kitchen. Even though I don't see him, he could be upstairs.

Quietly, I sneak over to her, and when she sees me, she groans, "What do you want?"

I sit on the couch next to her. "I want a bath."

She flicks her ash on me. "I already fucking told you, I just gave you one."

I don't mean to, really, but my foot stomps against the floor. She's so frustrating!

"No, you didn't! That was a long time ago. I need another one."

"Seriously, Tavin, shut the hell up about the bath." She draws in another drag of her cigarette.

"But Toben says-" A throbbing tightness comes around my head and I can feel my body in the air before my back shatters into something, causing the familiar pain to creep around to my chest.

"You want a bath? I'll give you a Goddamn bath."

Daddy.

"I just don't want to be dirty anymore!"

He brings his fist into my tummy, taking away my breath

and voice. He pulls me by my hair, to the hall, causing the uneven wood floors to cut and scrape me. He yanks me up the stairs and pushes me into the bathroom, slamming my head against the toilet, making my ears ring.

There's water running.

He kneels down in front of me, grips my chin and makes me look at him.

"Every day I pray I'll find your little dead body in that basement and every fucking day you're still breathing." He pulls my hair again to get me to stand. He smells like coffee and it usually makes me sick. I'm not hungry, though, so it's not so bad. His rough hands start ripping the buttons off my dress. I won't be able to wear it again, and now I only have three. When I am completely undressed, he screams at me, "You don't want to be dirty? Well then let's get you mother-fucking clean."

He picks me up and throws me into the tub. The hard porcelain sends a sharp jolt through my body when my spine hits the side. He flips me over so that I'm on my stomach and I feel his hand grip my head to push it down beneath the water. I'm not very good at holding my breath. I keep thinking he will let me up. He doesn't. My throat and my chest are on fire, it hurts and I'm so scared. I need to breathe! I try to kick and get away while he holds my body down. I think my head is going to explode. I wonder what will happen once I am dead. Where will I go? Maybe it will be pretty...

Air. Air rushes into my lungs. It burns and I welcome it with big gulps. I try to get all the oxygen I can. The water splashes around me and I can't hear anything besides the rushing in my ears.

"Damn it, why do you always push him?" My eyes burn and tears start falling from the relief of being able to breathe again. "One of these days I won't be here to stop him."

"Why do you?" I'm able to yell at her, even though it

takes all the air I have gained.

She starts putting shampoo in my hair when she chuckles, "God, I really don't know." Silently she scrubs until eventually, she breathes out, "I should have listened to him and had you vacuumed out. It would have saved us all loads of trouble." Her nails feel good as they scratch my scalp. "I should have, I was just too scared that they'd know about the drugs and send me to jail. And I hadn't even tried tar yet, I was just on a lot of coke. Besides, I got more business the further along I got, so I talked him into letting nature run its course." She rinses my hair by pouring a cup of water over my head. "You've always been a stubborn and defiant little shit, and you just refuse to die."

"Why don't you just give me away?" I like it when she talks to me, even if what she says is mean. She usually just wants me to go away or shut up.

She shrugs. "You can come in useful sometimes." She starts looking at me funny, right in the eyes. "When you were first born, the hormones made me...feel things. I thought I wanted you." She stops looking at me and picks up the loofah to put some soap on. "Brian was so angry. He knew it wouldn't last though, so he left us alone. You were a happy baby at first and I thought you might grow on him. There was one day though, you began to cry constantly. I almost killed you, myself, it was so maddening." She scrubs under my arms and across my back. "I remember coming into the living room and Brian had you on the floor. He was smothering you with a couch pillow and I almost let him. I don't know why, I just couldn't. It's like that every time. I guess I just don't want you to die..." Her voice trails off before she shakes her head and smiles at me. "I mean, no one else can find a vein like you do."

"Do you love me, Mommy?"

She sighs and shakes her head. "I can't, baby."

"Well, I love you." She puts some conditioner in my hair. "Can I wash myself from now on? All I need is soap."

"Jesus, I don't know. Here, start by rinsing yourself off." She gets up to get a towel from the cabinet. Once I have all the soap off, she holds it open. "Stand up." She wraps the towel around me and I pretend she's hugging me.

"Daddy ripped my dress and all the ones I have are dirty."

Her eyes narrow as she snaps, "You're such a stupid bitch sometimes, Tavin. This is what I mean, you push him. You know he doesn't want you to call him that."

"He is my daddy."

When she's finished drying me off, she ties the towel around me. "He doesn't want to be." She looks at me and frowns. "I'll see about getting you some new clothes okay? For now though, just deal with what you have."

⟨⟨⟨

"Wake up, lazy bones." I feel myself smile even before I open my eyes. It's Toben! I throw my arms above me to stretch out, rolling a little to get all loosened up and reach as far as I can with my toes. "That's quite the stretch," he laughs.

I open my eyes and sit up. He's sitting on the edge of my bed in a gray sweater and his hat. "Hi."

His face is bright with a grin. "Hey." He looks at me and tilts his head. "Did you take a bath?" I can't stop my smile from covering my face and I nod my head. He lies back on my bed. "So, what do you want to do today?"

I push off the blankets and sit on my knees looking down at him, "Can we get food again?"

His eyes sparkle when he says, "Of course." Then he looks at my dress and frowns. "Wait, they gave you a bath and didn't wash your clothes?" He sits up and puts his arm around me. "Come on, all I have are boy clothes, but at least they're clean."

I want to clap my hands and jump up and down. Two days in a row with food, two days in a row leaving my house, and best of all: two days in a row with Toben.

CHAPTER THREE
Play

Two months later—December, 2001

I HOPE HE CAN COME TODAY. I LOOK OUT AT THE STREET and I shiver because it's so cold. I keep my eyes peeled for the big, yellow bus. Even though he doesn't ride it, he usually comes over soon after it leaves.

He's been teaching me so many things. I can write my name, his name, and a few other words, all by myself. I can count all the way to one hundred, I know the days of the week, and I'm learning months. He says he's going to teach me to tell time and to read. He is my best and only friend. He has other friends, but he says that I am his favorite. I met some of the kids he goes to school with, once, and I don't think they liked me. He yelled at one of the other boys for calling me 'retarded' and made him apologize.

I hate that he has to go to school all week. I spend the whole time waiting for the weekend because we get to spend it together going to the park, the beach, or to the pier to watch the boats. Oh, how I wish I could ride on one of them! He brings me something to eat every time he comes over, so I haven't gone more than two days without food, since I met him.

Once, on a Sunday, we had been gone all day, and while

we were out, Daddy wanted help with his needle and I wasn't there to do it. He was so mad by the time I got back, he was waiting in my room and immediately started to hit me. I don't know why Toben came back. I'm glad he did though. He used one of the electrical cords to wrap around Daddy's neck. I couldn't believe it. Daddy told him that he would pay for that and I think he did because when he came over the next day, he even had bruises on his face and that never happens. I cried and cried because he got hit because of me. Ever since then, though, Daddy always leaves me alone when he's here.

Toben's daddy's name is Jarod. He and my daddy have been spending loads of time together. They don't shoot tar anymore, though. Recently, they've started using 'white'- that's what they call it. It's not really much different to make, it's just a powder instead of sticky goo.

The yellow bus comes and leaves and he still isn't here. My feet are cold and hurting from standing on the ladder because I didn't put on shoes. My shoes scrunch up my toes, so I don't like to wear them. Even though I know he can't come every single day, I still get so sad when he doesn't. I try to wait a little while longer, I'm freezing, though, and can't wait anymore. I climb down the ladder and back inside, through my window. I lie down on my bed. I don't feel like drawing or dancing right now.

Suddenly, stomping footsteps are coming down the stairs, so I run and hide behind the wall by the bathroom. I bet Daddy just got home.

"Tavin? Where are you?"

It's Toben!

I run out from behind the wall to hug him. "I didn't think you were coming today, you always come to my window."

He walks over to my bed and throws his backpack down on it before he sits. "I know, my dad picked me up from school today. I think he is trying to look good for Mr. James, his boss. He never gets me from school and he was being weirdly nice the whole drive here. For some reason, he brought Mr. James over here to meet your dad. They're upstairs right now."

"Your dad doesn't hit you when Mr. James is around?"

Toben shakes his head. "He won't hit me around anyone, except your dad."

I wonder if Daddy will be nice to me around this man. He has never been nice to me. I wonder what it would be like.

"Let's go meet him."

He gives me a funny look. "Why?"

"Because I want to feel it." I turn around and run up the stairs.

I hear Toben chasing me. "Wait, Tavin! Feel what?"

When I open the door, Mommy, Daddy, Mr. Michaels, and a man who has to be Mr. James, are all sitting around the dining room table. I slow my pace and hear Toben's footsteps behind me. My heart is thumping so hard it hurts. What if Daddy doesn't care about this man? He will be so mad that I interrupted them. Then I will really get it. They still don't notice me, so I take a deep breath and close my eyes before I finally work up the courage to speak.

"Daddy?"

They all turn to look at me and I'm only watching him. His blue eyes are filled with hatred when he stands so fast the chair falls backwards. He's on me in one big stride.

"What did you just call me?"

I'm shrinking. He brings his hand across my face so hard I feel my neck pop, before I hit the floor. I scream from pain when he brings his boot against my spine.

A voice that is slow and steady seems to still the entire room.

"Is this completely necessary?"

I hear a chair scrape against the floor and when I pull myself to my knees, I'm staring at a pair of shiny, black shoes. My eyes slowly follow a long pair of gray pants all the way up to the face that matches the calm voice. His hair is brown and he looks a little bit older than Daddy and he's dressed up nice. He holds his hand out to me. "Come now, it's alright."

I put my hand in his and he pulls me up. When I raise my head toward him, I meet his golden eyes, and my stomach feels queasy. He lets go of my grasp and brings his hand to my cheek. He softly runs his thumb across my skin and lets out a low groan before turning back to his seat. Daddy looks livid and I am frozen in place.

Mommy breaks the silence. She's angry too. "Go back to your room, Tavin."

Toben's fingers lace with mine as he pulls me back to the basement. Once we get to the bottom of the stairs, he lifts my chin to look at my face.

"Are you okay?" I nod. There's sharp throbbing in my back, but he doesn't need to know about that. "I want to stick his precious needle right into his fucking throat. I hate that he treats you like that, it's just, my dad…he was glaring at me." His fists ball up as he turns on his heel. Hunching his shoulders, he lets out a snarl. "I hate that he can control me and make me feel so scared! So small! I want so badly to kill the bastard in his sleep and I still can't bring myself to do it. I want to kill your dad, too!" He's starting to get too loud.

"Shhh, Toben you have to be quiet."

My heart starts racing, I can't let Daddy hear him.

His shoulders slump and he lets out a breath as he whispers, "He makes me feel so weak. All he had to do was stare at me and I couldn't protect you, but someone has to or that asshole is going to kill you!"

I smile at him to calm him down. "You don't need to

protect me, Toben. I just want you with me. That's it."

He smiles as he hugs me. "Who would have thought my best friend would be a girl?"

Toben

We are listening to System of a Down on my iPod when my dad yells down the stairs, "Toben, we're leaving, let's go." His voice is so fake I want to barf.

"Okay," I yell back. "What he really wants to say is: hurry your ass up, you little fucktard." I horribly mimic my dad in a whisper, so I can hear her giggle before I leave, and I'm not let down. I jump off the bed with a smile and a wink before I run up the stairs.

I glare at Mr. Winters before I follow my dad and Mr. James. Once we are in the car, I put my headphones in and lay my head against the back seat. I don't have any music playing though because I want to hear what they talk about. My dad turns the car around to go back to the plant where he works.

"Sir, I want to apologize for the episode back there. I never imagined he wouldn't keep himself under control in front of you."

Mr. James waves his hand and lights a cigarette. "No matter. We were guests in his home."

"I know that you're selective about who you sell to. Just know, he'll be a loyal customer and he's trustworthy. He keeps his mouth shut, his head down, and he's a hard work-er. He's just not much of a parent."

"Yes, you've mentioned all this before, Jarod. No need for more gushing." I can't decide if he's bored or irritated.

We drop Mr. James back at the factory, and I make no attempt to get in the front seat. I keep my headphones in so my dad doesn't talk to me, and he still reaches back and yanks them from my ears.

"Don't think I didn't see you getting all pissy over Brian's little bitch." He turns back to take me to my bike at the school. "What kind of fucking pussy spends all of his time with a retarded little girl anyway?"

I hate when people say that about her. "She's not retarded! She has the worst parents in the world who don't even let her go to school! She's actually smart. She picks things up pretty fast." I meet his eyes in the rearview mirror. "Why do they hate her so much?"

"Because she fucked up their life just like you fucked up mine. Make no mistake, you dumb shit, you killed the only person I have ever loved, and I'll never forgive you for it. If I could throw you in a basement and forget your fucking face, I would."

I don't say that I believe him. I just keep my mouth shut for the short drive to my elementary school. He barely lets me get out of the car before peeling out.

I don't know what to think about Mr. James. He has a way about him that makes me feel weird, like there is something off or not right. He helped Tavin, though, and that earns him some points in my book. I just don't understand why a guy that owns a huge company like Rissa, would be a heroin dealer. I know that's what they were talking about. That was the purpose of him coming to Tavin's house; he was deciding if he was going to sell to Mr. Winters. Apparently, beating the shit out of a little girl isn't bad enough to fail the test.

Two months later—February, 2002

Tavin

I am able to get up early enough to see Toben on his way to school. He tells me he has a surprise for me and he will give it to me tonight. I don't know how I'm going to make it the whole day! I'm too excited to see what it is.

As I climb back down the ladder, I hear the quietest little purr. I look around to see where the sound is coming from, and my eyes land on an orange cat, blinking at me. I reach out and he lets me grab him, so I take him into my room.

His name is Mr. Tickles.

It's such a wonderful day! Mr. Tickles cuddles with me on my bed and lets me pet him. I wish I had food to give him. I get him some water and put it in a tea cup. He doesn't drink it though. I draw a picture of him and dance with him while we listen to the music on the radio. I know all the words because they play this song a lot. The day is going by so fast with him here to keep me company. I can't wait to show him to Toben. I hope he likes the name I picked.

I hear footsteps and I can't believe it is already time for him to be out of school. I pick up Mr. Tickles and carry him to the stairs, but by the time I see that it isn't Toben, it's too late.

"What the fuck are you holding?"

He will hurt him. I just know it. I don't answer him, I just turn to run to my window so I can set Mr. Tickles free and away from Daddy. I'm not fast enough, though, Daddy grabs a fist full of my hair and pulls me back hard, causing me to land hard on the concrete floor. I am able to keep ahold of Mr. Tickles and I think that he's okay until Daddy rips him away from me. I'm not able to close my eyes fast enough to miss him twisting his head.

I can feel my scream roll up my throat. "No!"

Please let it not be true! I just got him, he can't be dead! I can't stop myself from crying so hard. How can he kill an innocent creature? Mr. Tickles didn't do anything!

He hates me? Well I hate him! I have always hated him. I can't stop him, though, I'm too little and I'm not strong enough. I wish more than anything that Toben was here. He would have saved him, I know it. I keep crying and Daddy just drops him on my floor and leaves. Why did he even come down here? I reach out to pet him and fresh tears pour out. I lie on the floor as I hold my precious baby to my chest.

"Tavin?" Hearing Toben's voice makes me cry harder as I hold Mr. Tickles tighter. I feel him kneel next to me, "Oh no, what happened?"

My words don't come out right through my sobs. "He killed him."

"Oh, Tav, come here." He lifts me up by my arms, pulls me next to him, wraps me in the biggest hug, and lets me cry all over him. He's the only one who has ever hugged me. I don't know how long he holds me before his throaty voice says, "We need to bury him."

He picks up Mr. Tickles and carries him out my window. I can't follow him, I don't want to watch. I just lie down and let my pillow soak up my tears. How can I already love him so much after only one day? He had loved me back, I know that he did. Toben seems to be gone a long time, but he comes back eventually. He crawls into bed with me and when his arm drapes over me, I can feel his breath on the back of my neck. When I open my eyes, I see he has a red box in his hand that's shaped like a heart.

"What's that?" My voice is scratchy from crying.

"It's your surprise. Happy Valentine's Day."

I roll over to face him. "Another holiday? I thought you said that they aren't every month?"

He smiles, even if it's sad. "I guess this time of year it seems like they are." He fidgets with the box. "Open your mouth." I do and he plops something inside. A smile that is more sincere, peeks out when he urges, "Chew it, silly."

I do and it is the most delicious thing that I have ever tasted. It's sweet, crunchy, and chewy. Without even meaning to, I hear myself saying, "Mmmm."

He laughs. A sound I need to hear terribly. "It's a chocolate," he says.

I haven't swallowed it all yet when I tell him, "I like chocolate."

His cute grin makes his eyes sparkle.

"Obviously."

He's so wonderful for trying to make me feel better, because I've never felt like this before. I'm so sad that my chest hurts and I let more tears fall. He holds me as I cry for a long time. He's never stayed this late and when he gets up to leave, my heart jumps into my throat. I miss Mr. Tickles and I don't want to be by myself.

"Please don't leave."

He sighs and takes off his shoes. "Okay, I just can't be late for school tomorrow."

When he lies down next to me, I don't know why, I guess I am just so happy with how nice he is to me, I softly put my lips against his.

"You kissed me," he whispers.

I just nod and lay my head against his chest.

Toben

My first kiss. Tavin Winters gave me my first kiss. She's different from everyone else. She's her own color, her own song, and she's my best friend. My lips tingle where hers had been. I can hear her steady breathing and I know she's already asleep.

I can't believe that waste of oxygen killed her cat, and I truly fear for her life. The thought of telling someone about her situation has crossed my mind, but if our parents are like this, how much worse is it out there? I hate myself for being selfish and keeping my mouth shut, because if anyone knows and they take her away, I'll never see her again. While the thought of running away with her jumps into my mind again, so do the questions of how I will feed her and make sure we have a place to sleep. I'm just a kid.

I have to make sure that I'm awake in time for school so I set the alarm on my watch. It feels like I just closed my eyes when I hear the beeping. I try to be extremely careful as I slip out of bed so I don't wake Tavin. Too bad I didn't set the alarm for earlier, then I could run home to shower. Well, it's too late now. I hope my dad never realizes I was gone all night. He'd be pissed.

Watching her sleep for a moment, I put on my backpack and slip out the window. Once I'm on the lawn, I throw on my beanie and jump on my bike to head to school.

Lately, I have been separating myself from my friends. I just can't listen to what great movie they saw, or video game level they beat, or concert they have tickets to. It's all pointless, meaningless shit. They talk all the time, they just never say a damn thing. Even Christopher and I rarely hang out at all, anymore. I put more effort into my school work and intently listen to the lessons because I will be teaching them to Tavin and I have to make sure I explain them right. I spend my days wondering if she's okay, and I'm scared that one day I will go to her house and she'll be gone and buried like her cat.

After school, I head home for a shower. As I ride by Tavin's, I don't see her little head poking out of the window. What I do see is Mr. James' dark gray Mercedes parked outside her house. He's been over a couple of times and he never speaks to me.

I feel better after my shower and I'm pedaling fast, back to Tavin's, when I see Mr. James and another man I don't know, leaving her house. I drop my bike in her yard and climb down the old metal ladder, open her window, and jump through. I can hear her soft voice humming, I just don't see her. Suddenly, her head pops up by her bed and her face brightens when she sees me.

"Toben!" She pushes to her feet. "You didn't wake me up this morning, and I was hoping to see you before you left."

I sit on her bed as I pull out the books. She doesn't even realize she's already learning to read, and today I am going to show her. She knows all of the letters. It was like once I sang the ABC song to her, she had it down. I am shocked at how quickly she picks things up. She struggles with math, but I focus mostly on teaching her to read. Even though it took her a little longer to learn the sounds, she knows them now, as well.

I've noticed that every once in a while, her head kind of twitches, a small, jerky movement. The first couple times I didn't even think about it, it's just when she gets frustrated it becomes a little bit more noticeable. Since I have been trying to teach her things, I've noticed when she doesn't know what the answer is or she just doesn't know what to say, she does it.

I think Sesame Street has helped. I know she's technically too old for it, but I think it's been a part of her picking up the letters so fast.

"You looked so peaceful and relaxed. You don't get to be that way very often."

She sits next to me and I see that she's dirty again. Her whore mom had actually given her some shampoo and soap and she has been cleaning herself every day. She's obviously out of the soap now.

Her breath is shaky. "I'm sorry, Toben. You left your chocolates and I got hungry and ate them all."

Her face looks so ashamed like she's committed some horrible crime. A laugh jumps from my mouth. "I brought them for you, silly. They were your Valentine chocolates."

She perks right up with a smile. "Oh. Thank you."

I pull out the book I got from the lower grade library, a notebook, and a pen, from my bag. "Are you ready to read?"

She smiles and nods. I open the book and the first damn word is cat. I turn the page-we will just skip that. The next word is hat. I have her sound out the *h* and *a*, then I explain that since the *h* comes first, you say that sound before the others. Once we get to the *t*, I tell her to put all the sounds together.

"H—ha-t. H-a-t. Hat! It says hat!" Her eyes are so bright against her pale skin.

"Good job! See it's easy, you just have to practice."

I've read the letter my mother wrote to me a million times-always alone and always to myself. I will never tell my dad about it, there's no way he would let me keep something like that. It's the single most important thing I own and I have wanted to share it with someone for a long time. I almost told Christopher about it, I was just scared he would call me a pussy. I want someone to read it to me so I can imagine her voice. To have a girl do it would be great; to have Tavin do it would be perfect. I can't wait until she's able to.

"I have the book for a month so keep it for a while and practice when you can."

"I will, I promise." She's already turning to the next page.

I smile at her. "I am proud of you, Tavin."

"I'm proud of you, too."

I chuckle. "For what?"

With a shrug she giggles. "I don't know, it sounded nice."

One month later—March, 2002

Tavin

I am so glad the weather is getting warmer. That means it's getting closer to summer and Toben won't have to go to school for a long time. There was food in the kitchen, yesterday. I found cheese and a package of noodles. I broke the noodles apart and sucked on each one so they would last me a long time. I ate the cheese fast, though. I'm getting hungry again. It seems like the more I eat, the hungrier I get.

I sneak up the stairs and don't even have to get halfway to the top and I know she's with a man. Dang, now I have to be super quiet. When I open the door, I see Mommy on her knees, on the floor, in front of a blond man, sitting on the couch.

The man is pushing her head down, "Yeah, that's it. Suck it, whore."

As I tip toe across the living room, I pretend that I am sneaking past a sleeping dragon and if he wakes up, he will burn me to bits. Once I'm in the kitchen, I climb up on the counter. There are still noodle packages! I grab one and climb down to open the fridge. There are a couple of slices of cheese and some beer; I get one of each.

They are having sex now so it's much easier to sneak past the dragon.

I eat the cheese and chew on the noodles while I draw on my wall. After a while, I look at the clock on my radio and it shows two zero three. Toben will be out of school soon. I go upstairs. Maybe Mommy will talk to me instead of telling me to go away.

She's still on the couch and is smoking a cigarette.

"Hi, Mommy."

"What?" She snaps at me. She doesn't want me around, so I turn to go back downstairs. "Well, since you're here, you might as well fix me up."

I walk over to the coffee table and pick up the spoon with the crooked handle. There's still a glass of water next to her, so after I sprinkle the powder into the spoon, I stick the needle into the cup and pull up on the plunger to get enough to mix with.

"Do you like what those men do?"

She snorts. "They sure think I do."

I think that means she doesn't. I don't think Daddy likes his job either. I'm very careful not to spill and when I lift the spoon, I use Mommy's lighter to heat it up until it starts bubbling. I put the cotton ball in and watch it swell up before I stick the needle inside of it.

"Straighten your arm, Mommy."

I clean the inside of her elbow with a wet nap and flick the syringe before I push up to get all of the air out. After tying her arm off with a tourniquet, I search for a good vein and tap her arm. When the blue line rises, I slide the needle in, pull back for blood, remove the tie, and inject her.

I've learned that TV makes time pass faster, when I'm waiting for Toben, so I turn it on and sit on my bed. I see a commercial for a princess doll with long blonde hair and a prince doll who also has pretty blond hair. I don't know how to get them though. Maybe I can make my own! I decide I want to draw, so I turn off the TV and I reach under my bed to get my pencils and pens. I have a lot because I always take them whenever I see them, and ever since I've been leaving the house with Toben, I find them everywhere.

There is a song that plays on the radio that I like so much. It makes me think of him and I hum it to myself as I draw the blonde prince and princess dolls. I don't realize how much time has passed, because I jump when I hear Daddy yelling.

Uh-oh.

He is home and he's coming to get me. I drop my pencil and move my bed to cover up my drawing. I don't think-I just hide. There are some boxes by my bathroom so I run and crouch down behind them. My chest is sore from the hammering of my heart. Maybe he will think I left and go away. The *BOOM BOOM BOOM* of his shoes pounds the stairs and vibrates in my ears before the sound softens as he steps onto the concrete.

"Tavin! If I have to look for you things will be worse!" I squeeze my eyes shut and try to get further behind the boxes. He has something in his hand. I don't know what it is, but I bet it will hurt. He shoves open my closet doors and I can't see what he's doing, I can just hear his mumbles and grunts as he reaches high inside. It gets so quiet, I cover my mouth so my breathing won't be too loud. He walks away from the closet and the black thing he was holding is gone so he isn't going to hit me with it. He's pacing around my room, so I close my eyes because it makes me feel invisible.

"Goddammit, Tavin! Get the fuck out here!"

I jump at his yelling and bump one of the boxes, making it fall. Oh no, no, no! His hateful blue eyes meet mine for a split second before his hand comes down and yanks me into the air by my dress. I am able to catch myself with my hands, so my face doesn't hit the floor. "Every time with this, you stupid, little cunt."

I feel a hard slam against my back and the pain vibrates around me. Tears fly from my eyes as the sounds of my crying pour from my throat. I just don't want it to hurt anymore. Rolling toward him, I plead without thinking.

"Daddy, please! Stop!"

"I swear you like getting the shit beat out of you!" My ribs explode, the sting from my back meets up with the hot pulsing in my side. "How many times do I have to fucking repeat myself?" He's on the floor with me when he hits me in the tummy. "Do." He brings his fist back and hits my chest. "Not." Then my arm. "Call." Each blow seems harder than the last. "Me." He finally backhands me and my entire face shakes, burning from the force. "Daddy!" He must have stood back up because I feel his hard shoe kick my ribs again. I need it to stop.

"I'm sorry!"

My head hurts as he pulls me to my feet by my hair and drags me to my bed. The blanket presses against my face when he shoves me down. He throws his kit at me and it hits me in the chest. Sharp pain shoots through me when I sniff and unzip the kit.

"Make it fucking quick," he barks.

I will. I want him on the nod as fast as possible. He sits down next to me and rolls up his sleeve, as I prepare his fix. By the time I'm done, he's already tied himself off, so I push it into him. I have a little while before he will be awake enough to go upstairs. I look at the clock and it shows four zero eight.

Oh. That's way after Toben is usually here, so he must not be coming today.

My body hums with the constant ache that I ignore and I pretend that Toben and I are at a fancy ball, and I have a long, puffy, pink dress on. We dance around the ballroom and everyone watches us because we are so beautiful. Nobody hates us, they all love us and cheer at how well we dance together.

Daddy moves around and he's always angry when he wakes up, so I run to my window and climb the ladder. Once I am safe at the top, I look toward Toben's house. I can almost see it. I've never gone to his house alone before, and his daddy scares me, but I want to see him. Besides, he says I am big enough to do most things by myself, I just have to do it, so I am going to go over there and see if he wants to talk to me.

When I skip onto his lawn, I see his window is really high. Maybe I can climb up the tree and jump. It's not that far. As I grab a branch and pull my way up, I feel the tree scraping my feet and the throbbing pain from my Daddy's beating jabs at me. When I climb high enough, I break off a stick and throw it at his window. I make it on the first try and nothing happens. I try it two more times. Dang! He isn't home. I'm about to climb back down and go home when he finally shows up in his window. I feel myself grin, while he barely smiles. He lifts his window and his shirt is off. I see all the red, and the agony on his face. He's hurt!

"Toben! What happened?!" I climb to the edge of the branch to leap to him.

"Tavin, don't you dare jump." His voice is strained.

"Well, I'm going to, so you better move out of the way."

I push with my legs and stretch out my arms. The distance looks shorter than it really is. I thought I could jump right through, but I'm not going to make it, so I just reach. My arms wrap over the edge of his window sill as I dangle against the shingles. My body screams when the sharpness shoots to my toes and I hang on tight.

The ground is further down than I thought.

Toben

I pedal fast. For some reason, all my teachers decide to pile on the homework for tonight. Before I met Tavin, I would have just said screw it, now, though, I'll be teaching her this stuff, so I have to make sure I know it.

When I get home, I head to the kitchen for a soda. My dad is already home and he's opening up a box on the kitchen table. Even though I find it odd that he doesn't talk some kind of shit, I get my cola and try to rush past him. Just as I pass by, his open hand smacks my chest and he shoves me against the wall, making my shoulder blades stab at the contact. When I focus, he's staring deep into me. His blue eyes darken with his fury and are rimmed in tears. I can smell the alcohol as I glance over to the open bottle of whiskey next to the box.

"She was my world. The only one to make me feel anything…ever." His hand wraps around my throat as his other is in a fist, punching my gut. I involuntarily double over, but he won't allow it. "For nine motherfucking months you were all I heard about. It didn't matter though, because she was happy and her happiness was the only thing that ever mattered. The day you ripped her apart was the day you killed us both." He lets me go while I gasp for breath. I don't get much before he hits me. "Every fucking day you look at me with her Goddamn eyes!"

I hear his sobs as he kicks and punches all over until I can't really tell where he's hitting me, my entire body just pulses with agony. I try to fight back, I always do, I just can't ever stop him. He's too strong. I'm somehow able to get to my feet and I see the box is full of wedding stuff.

He's vulnerable and I'm going to use it.

"You think she would be happy if she could see how you treat me? She would hate you as much as I do! Do you do this because it's my fault she died or because she loved me more than you?!"

It happens so fast. He snatches the box cutter off the table, spins, and lunges at me as he swipes the blade across my torso. The cold sting quickly bursts into hot pain. It feels like my entire chest is wide open. I look down and see the blood in the shreds of fabric, leaking through my shirt. When my eyes match his, I see no remorse and no regret, simply disgust.

"Take off your shirt, and I swear to God, Toben, I better not have to take you to the fucking hospital." Even though it hurts something awful, I won't let him see it as I lift my shirt over my head. He must be satisfied because he barks, "Get out of my sight."

The stairs hurt the worst, but once I lie on my bed, I feel better. Damn it, I don't think I'll be able to see Tavin tonight. The thought of riding my bike sounds like torture. The idea of getting out of this bed is inconceivable, yet the blood is starting to get everywhere, so with a loud groan, I lift myself to go get a washcloth. In the back of my mind I think I hear a tapping sound, but I disregard it. I hear it again when I return to my room, yet it's not until I try to clean myself that I hear it's coming from my window. I look up and want to laugh because Tavin is sitting in the tree outside my bedroom, wearing a cheesy grin. When I open the window, her face falls as she stares at my chest.

"Toben! What happened?!"

Her concern warms my heart until it's quickly overrun by fear as I watch her climb to the edge of the branch. The crazy girl is going to kill herself.

"Tavin, don't you dare jump."

Her body prepares for her to push. "Well, I am going to, so you better move out of the way." She shoots off and there's no way she is going to make it. My heart falls right before her bony little arms grasp on to the window sill.

I try to pull her up, but my body just hurts so badly.

"Damn it, Tavin, I just got the shit beat out of me, I am too sore for this," I groan out. Finally, I'm able to pull her into my room and we both fall to the floor. Her eyes are so sad when she reaches out to touch the damage, pulling back at the last second.

"What did he do?"

I stand, dabbing it with the cloth. "I made the mistake of talking about my mom, so he cut me."

She gets to her feet and hurries to me. "Here, lie down and let me try to clean it up." She takes the towel and dabs it. I think the bleeding is finally starting to slow.

"You shouldn't have jumped, Tavin. If you hurt yourself, we can't take you to the hospital. You need to be more careful."

"You're hurt." She says it like it is a full explanation as she tries to get all the blood.

She stays with me the rest of the night. I have her try to read the words off my poster and let her draw on my wall. She falls asleep on my floor and even though it hurts like hell, I pick her up and carry her to the bed. I get in behind her, hug her close, and thank whatever power may exist, that I found her.

I drop her off at her house on my way to school. My cut is bothering me, so I just have to be careful not to bump it.

While Christopher and I still talk at school, I think he's hurt that I never hang out anymore. I don't know what makes me decide it, I just really want to ask if I can come over. I always feel bad when I don't go to Tav's house. I do want to see her, it's just, for some reason I feel like I need to spend some time with Christopher. She'll understand.

"Hey, do you want to kick it after school?"

Christopher raises an eyebrow. "Really?"

"I know I haven't been around for the last couple months…"

He smiles like all is forgiven. "It's okay. We can ride our bikes to my house, together."

He's so understanding that it makes me feel worse for not making more time for him. I know Tavin needs me, but I can be there for both. I could have all of us hang out together, I just don't think that they will exactly mesh. They met each other once when that prick Thomas called her retarded, and Christopher laughed along with him. I hated the way Tavin's face had looked. Even if I can't really tell him much about Tavin's parents, maybe if I try to explain a little bit he will give her a chance.

I have a tight feeling in my stomach since this morning. It's like I'm scared or worried, I don't really know what about, though. It doesn't ease up until I cross the threshold into the comfort of Christopher's familiar room. We play video games and I realize that I haven't picked up a controller in over two months. It's a nice break and it does seem to settle my stomach. I stay as long as I can because I know once I am through my door the feeling will more than likely return. I don't even make it to my house before the anxiety claws its way back over me.

I'm barely able to sleep, tossing and turning all night, I keep going hot or cold, and simply can't get comfortable. I am out of bed before my alarm goes off and in the shower. With a stroke of luck, I'm able to leave the house without seeing my dad.

The day goes in slow motion. Not in a bad way, just like everything is going at a leisurely pace. When the school bell rings, I tell Christopher that we'll hang out tomorrow, before I ride to Tavin's.

Mr. James' car is parked outside of her house again and I abandon my bike to climb down to her room. I can see her dancing through the window and I feel my cheeks lift in a grin as I push it open. She twirls around and her eyes light up when they meet mine.

"Toben!" She runs up to me and hugs my neck tight before skipping away. Following her, I throw my backpack on the bed and sit while she digs around under it. "Look what I made!" She tries to hand me a wad of torn cloth, I just have no idea what it's supposed to be. "A prince doll for you and a princess one for me!"

Oh, jeez.

"Tavin, boys don't play with dolls."

She holds it in her lap and looks like I told her she was the stupidest girl in the world.

"Oh."

It's the saddest *oh* I've ever heard. I feel like a jerk when I give her a side hug, "Ah, come on, don't be sad. You need to practice reading first, anyway. Then I will play with the dolls, just don't tell anyone." I wink at her.

With her big, sad eyes, she frowns at me. "I don't want to read."

She has been fighting me on reading the last week or

so. Even though she's getting burnt out, I think she needs to know this stuff.

"And I don't want to play with dolls, but I'll do it for you if you read for me."

She still objects with an exaggerated fall, back onto her bed. "Okay, fine."

I open the first book and she starts off great. Then she gets stuck on the word chair, "C-h-caha-a"

"Okay, hold on. Remember when I told you that when *c* and *h* are next to each other they sound like *ch-ch*? Words like chip, chew, change, and-"

"Chair!" Her arms are thrown up in victory and a low chuckle climbs up my throat.

"That's right!"

I think about the letter from my mother in my pocket and I almost have her read it, before I decide since she has already read through two books, that it's good enough for today. Besides, she is starting to get restless.

"Alright, Tav, you did great. Do you want to play with your dolls now?"

Her face completely brightens when she smiles. I can practically see her bouncing with pride when she gives me the one that's apparently the prince. It's bunched up, so I stretch it out and see that it actually does resemble a doll. It has a head, body, arms, and legs. She's drawn a face and hair on it, and I realize it's made partially from her sheets. She found rubber bands and twist ties to separate the head and limbs and left hers without legs. She wants to pretend that they are a fairy prince and princess ruling over the forest. Even though I feel like a major idiot, when she's happy and laughing, that's when I feel good.

The door to her room opens and I hear footsteps. Oh, hell no, just let her dad try to beat her ass while I'm here. I'll smash his head in with her TV. Mine isn't here to stop me this time.

That's when I realize there are two sets of feet coming down the stairs: Mr. James and the man I had seen him with before. They are both in casual clothing. That's strange—I've never seen Mr. James in anything besides a suit. Why are they coming down here? Mr. James is carrying a black bag and the other man has a large dog cage. What the hell? Are they giving her a dog? Well, it won't live long in this house.

The man I don't know puts the cage and a tin can on the floor as Mr. James drops the bag and strides to the bed, his sights clearly on Tavin. Unease rises within me like a storm. Something is wrong, something is terribly wrong. I can feel it beneath my skin.

Bending forward, he gets down to eye level with her and ignores me all together, when he asks, "Do you remember me?"

"Yes."

"Do you know what it means to buy something, Tavin?"

Her head barely jerks, just enough for me to know she's nervous. "It means it's yours."

He laughs and I don't know why because what she said is true, and it sends shivers through my whole body.

"That's exactly right." His large hand envelops her face as he holds her jaw and runs his thumb over her cheek before he taps her nose with his finger. "And you are my newest purchase."

Quick as a flash, his hand goes to her hair and he clutches a large fist full, using it to throw her to the floor.

What is he doing?! Nobody else is going to hurt her! I have to stop him, I don't know what to do, I just go for him. The next thing I know, my face is bursting and my back is cracking against the concrete. I don't care. Ignoring the pain, I try to lunge for him again. All of a sudden, Mr. James' hand is lifting me in the air by my throat. I can't breathe and even though I hear Tavin scream in the distance, I'm not able to see.

I think the other man hit her because Mr. James' face is angry when he barks out, "Not the Goddamn face, Kyle!"

She's getting hurt and I can't help her! I still try to kick him and loosen his grasp around my neck until I think the back of my head cracks open when he slams me against something hard. My vision is blurred and the buzzing is all that I hear, until his gravelly, calm voice fills my head.

"If you do not do everything I say, I will kill her. Defy me and I will slit her throat. Her living through this is completely up to you." Finally, he releases his grip and I crumble to the floor. I gulp in large breaths as my throat burns and my eyes blur through unwelcome tears.

Mr. James is back on Tavin. "Your life is about to change, my little Lotus." He pulls her to a kneeling position. "Put your hands on your thighs." With a shaky body, she obeys. His voice holds sick humor when he says, "You will become well accustomed to this position." What does he mean by that? Crouching down to her, I see him squeeze her chin to make sure she is looking up at him. "If you comply, things will be much easier for you. Now take off your clothes."

"W-why?"

I feel all the air rush out of me. I may only be ten, but I know exactly what that means. Even with her scared voice making more tears threaten to fall, I can't be weak right now.

Amusement laces his steady voice. "Because you are my new toy and I want to play."

CHAPTER FOUR
Toys

T AVIN IS TERRIFIED. SHE MAKES NO ATTEMPT TO DO what he says, and he doesn't really give her a chance to. He throws her back on the floor and tears open her dress. How am I supposed to just watch this? She's fighting him and I am proud of her, she's just never going to do enough to stop him. She bites down on his arm and he yells as he brings his knee into her stomach. The man named Kyle is grasping at my arm; his nails nearly breaking the skin beneath them.

"Tavin!" I scream for her.

I don't understand why they're doing this…he's always been kind to her.

Upon hearing my voice, Mr. James turns and snarls, "Come here." Kyle has a strong grip, so when he lets go, I almost fall, as Mr. James adds, "Hold her down."

What?!

I can't contain the tears any longer as the fear of what is going to happen consumes me. I promised to protect her, but I'm too weak. The only thing I can do is make sure she lives. I get down on the floor and hold her arms above her head.

"Please forgive me, Tavin," I whisper through tears as

Mr. James gets up to go to the black bag.

Her eyes are wild as they dart around in fear and her chest is heaving in quick spurts. Even though I'm shaking, I can feel her vibrating beneath me. As Mr. James returns, I glance up at him to see he's holding a stethoscope. Small relief causes a breath to whoosh from my mouth, until he presses it to her skin. The smile that spreads across his lips freezes my blood.

He turns to Kyle with a shake of his head. "This shit gets me so fucking hard."

I just know I'm going to be sick as he unzips his fly and licks his hand. In my head, I'm aware of what's going to happen, and still, when he rips her body apart with his, it's so much more horrible than I could have ever imagined. Her screams are the soundtrack to our nightmare as her body revolts against the torture he inflicts on her. Why is he doing this?! The bile keeps rising, and every time, I swallow it back.

The only thing I know to do is try to comfort her with my words, I'm just not sure if she can hear my whispers over her wails.

"Remember the first time you wrote your name? How proud of yourself you were? The first time you saw the beach and felt the sand on your toes? When you first tasted chocolate and read your first words? Remember our first kiss? Think of happy things. Go to the happy things." I don't know if this is helping and I don't think she's listening. I squeeze my eyes shut letting the tears pour, as I continue. "Someday, you will be a princess. You will have a long, pretty dress and we will dance in our castle, every day. Please imagine it, Tavin."

"Look at me!" Mr. James' voice booms through my veins. My eyes shoot open, and he's glaring at Tavin. "Look at me!" He keeps screaming it in her face. He wants her to see what he's doing to her. My heart shatters when Tavin's pleas break from her lips.

"Toben! Please, Toben! Why won't you help me?!" I want to scream. I wonder if I was an adult if I could stop them. Mr. James brings his elbow to her ribs momentarily causing a break in her cries. "Toben!"

She keeps calling for me, and every time he hits her. She can't possibly think I'm purposely not trying to stop this, not protect her…can she? The thought chills me to the core, that in this moment, all she knows is that I'm not saving her.

I whisper around my sobs, "Please, Tavin, I don't know what to do. I'm scared. I don't know how to make them stop."

After what seems like an eternity of listening to her innocence die, Mr. James turns to Kyle; I almost forgot he was still here.

"Get it ready, but not too fucking much, this time."

Kyle walks behind me, so I can't see what he is doing. I'm using all my focus to hold her tight and try to get her body to stop shaking. She loves the song *Black Balloon* by the Goo Goo Dolls and because of that, I know every word. Softly, I sing into her ear. The lyrics take on a deeper meaning causing the tears to pour from my eyes.

A thousand other boys could never reach you.

How could I have been the one?

I saw the world spin beneath you, and scatter like ice from the spoon…

Soon, Kyle returns and I'm horrified to see what he's holding. I've seen my dad shove it into his arm too many times to not know what it is. He ties her off, cleans inside her elbow, and taps her. Her eyes get big and she doesn't have time to do anything other than cry, before Kyle removes the tie and begins to push it into her vein. Her body heaves and she throws up onto Mr. James' shirt. He looks down and his hazel eyes blaze before he smashes her head against the concrete.

"Fucking bitch!" He finally gets off of her and she lies still with empty eyes.

"Tavin," I whisper.

All she gives me is a small mumble in return. I wish I believed in God because I would be praying that the drugs take her away from here so she doesn't know what's happening.

Mr. James pulls out a cigarette and lights it while Kyle returns to her body. His dark eyes reveal no emotion, and when I see the knife I want to scream!

I AM HELPLESS!

What am I supposed to do?! He drags the blade over her body, deciding where to inflict the damage. Above her elbow, on the inside of her upper arm he presses the sharp steel. Slowly, he cuts as the blood drips down her arm in streams of scarlet. I keep wanting to be sick, but I'm able to keep the contents inside my stomach. That ability is tested when he traces his tongue along the trail of blood. She isn't moving. She isn't here at all. I close my eyes and imagine our souls floating away from here, leaving our bodies with the demons.

I refuse to open my eyes as I try to block out the atrocious sounds. Her body keeps rocking into me again and again. I don't have any sense of time, it seems endless and my hands are wet from sweat. How long my eyes are shut I don't know, I just know I don't open them until I feel her stirring.

When I look through the slits in my eyes, what I see threatens my stomach again. She's covered in blood and it's all over me. It's on my hands and arms. Mr. James is painted in red as well, and when he stands, he fastens his fly. More tears fall as the knowledge that he's finished, trickles over me.

"We're almost done for today, little Lotus. Now it's time to exchange gifts." He returns to his bag and I actually can feel the blood drain from my face when he pulls out a long piece of iron. From the corner of my eye, I see Kyle go into her bathroom and I don't know if my heart can beat any harder, when Mr. James heats the end of the iron with a blowtorch. He's going to burn her! Why can't I be stronger and bigger?! WHY IS THIS HAPPENING?!

Kyle appears out of nowhere and rips her dress even more, cleaning her sternum with the disinfectant wipe and drying it with the towel. My voice screams in my own head as Mr. James comes toward us, smiling at me like the Cheshire Cat from *Alice in Wonderland*.

"Hold her tight."

He presses the hot metal into her flesh and the sizzling sound pierces my ears. I can smell the pungent burning of skin. I wish I could trade places with her. I wish it was me. I will hate myself until I die for letting this happen.

His gaze is back on me when he barks, "Take off your shirt and get on your knees with your hands behind your head."

My fear shifts to myself. I'm terrified of what they plan to do to me. Kyle comes around behind me and my back feels cold from the wipe, but is soon followed by the softness of the towel patting me dry. The *shhhh* of the blowtorch sounds in my ear and I actually almost laugh with relief. I'll take a branding over rape any day of the week. Mr. James circles behind me and I'm barely able to grit my teeth before a hole is burning into my back below my right shoulder. The pain is difficult to explain, because 'hot' is way too small of a word to describe the excruciating burn overtaking the right side of my body.

"AHHH! MOTHERFUCKER!"

The smell mixed with the pain is nauseating. I bite the inside of my mouth as I release my arms from my head so I can use them to support me as I lean forward.

He points at me. "Stay."

After lying the iron rod on the floor to cool, he retrieves a small knife from the bag, turning his attention back to Tavin.

"You will always have a part of me. Now it's my turn to keep a part of you."

Hasn't he taken enough of her? What else can he do?! I can barely focus. My back is on fire causing my mind to fantasize about being submerged in ice water.

Dropping to one knee, he yanks her foot onto his leg. I see the blade just as he digs the knife into the inside of her left ankle. He takes the piece of flesh he has just cut off of her body and holds it up in the light.

My eyes widen in horror as I look upon true, real-life evil. Reaching into his pocket, he takes out a locket and puts the piece of skin inside. I may not believe in God, at least not in the sense most people do, but I can't deny the devil when he is standing right in front of me.

His gaze lifts to meet my eyes. "Get in the cage."

I did what he asked with her, and now I'm done with this. He can kill me if he wants, there's no way I am getting into a damn dog cage.

"Fuck you!" There's so much more about to jump from my mouth when he pushes her legs open and holds the knife in a horrifying threat.

NO!

"You want to say that to me again?" I keep my mouth shut and shake my head. "Then get in the fucking cage!"

I crawl inside when I feel a shoe against my lower spine lurching me forward into the cage. I hear a *clank,* and when I'm able to turn around, Kyle is locking me inside. What are they planning on doing? How long are they going to leave me in here? Kyle returns everything to the black bag of horrors as Mr. James carries Tavin to her bed.

"You were a very good girl today," he murmurs. He runs his hand over her hair and kisses her forehead. Without another glance toward me, he picks up the bag and both men finally leave.

I need her to talk to me, I need her to know I wanted to stop them.

"Tavin! I'm sorry, Tavin. I'm so sorry." I shake the cage door. We need to get out of here! I need to hold her and try to help her. What if she never forgives me? "Please talk to me." She won't move or speak. "I didn't know what to do!" I go hoarse calling for her. I need her and I need to be there for her, but I can't because I'm in this cage covered in her blood.

"Tavin…I'm so sorry."

Tavin

I've never felt like this before. It's like my body has been flipped inside out. Sharp pain radiates all over and I wish I didn't have to breathe. Two very different memories fight each other in my mind.

One I think was an extremely real dream, because in that dream, I touched magic. I *was* magic. For the first time ever, I was perfect, safe, and untouchable. The other memory, though, I know was real, and from it, one fact rings out: Toben helped them and not me.

He didn't try to protect me or save me and I don't understand why. I heard the things he said, I heard him sing, but then he held me down for them! How could he do that? Mr. James was always so nice to me before. I don't know what I did to make him hurt me so horribly and I don't even know the man named Kyle. Daddy has *never* done the things they did.

The skin on my chest is burning. It's so hot; it feels like my skin is melted, and I think they cut off my foot. Everything is blurry, I know I'm in my bed, though. Toben called my name for hours last night. I didn't know what to say to him and I couldn't make myself speak anyway.

He helped them. I wonder if he went home.

I don't want to open my eyes, but I have to potty and I've held it as long as I can. Tears fall in response to the stabbing that starts at my shoulders and reaches to my toes. I'm able to push myself up and I still have both feet, even though one is wrapped up and bleeding. I'm used to the bruises on my arms, and now there are bloody cuts, too. I look down to see the blood on my sheets, and I cry as the fabric of my dress rubs over the heat on my chest. My whole body is so much more banged up and bruised than I'm used to. It aches every time I move. Putting a little bit of weight on my bandaged foot proves that I can walk on it, I just need to be careful. Once I am standing, I'm able to begin the journey to the bathroom, but I'm limping.

"Tavin?" Even though it's hoarse, Toben's voice glues me to the floor.

He's still here.

Slowly, I turn my pounding head toward him. I'm so angry, and still, what I see breaks my heart.

"You're in a cage." My voice is messed up, too.

"Tavin, please, come here." His hand is sticking out of one of the square holes. I go to him and carefully kneel down in front of him. I won't touch him, though. I'm so mad at him! How could he do that? He's the only one who has ever been nice to me, he's supposed to be safe.

"You helped them!"

I try to scream. I've never yelled at him before. It hurts and I don't care. He's my best friend and he didn't try to rescue me.

Tears wet his face as he shakes his head. I've never seen him cry. "No, Tav. Mr. James, he… he said if I didn't obey him, then he would…kill you." His fingers grip the cage, "I'm sorry I couldn't save you. I just didn't want you to die. Please, don't hate me."

Mr. James was going to kill me? Why? What did I do to him?

I'm in pain, confused, frightened, and sad. What would I have done if it was me? Hurt is not dead. I don't want to be alone or mad at Toben anymore. I want to hug him, but I can't.

"I have to go pee, I'll be right back."

Cracks in the dried blood on my thighs remind me of the veins in Mommy's arm. I wonder if she will care if I tell her what they did. I'm careful as I wipe and I flush the toilet.

I feel different. I don't exactly know how, all I know is why. My dress is ripped, and when I look down, I can see part of something below my chest. Looking in the mirror, I pull apart the torn fabric to see angry, bright red lines dug deep into my skin, and it looks like…a flower? I don't dare touch it, and somehow looking at it makes it hurt worse.

When I go back out to help Toben, I try to cover up the flower wound, even though I know he's already seen it.

Shaking the cage in frustration, he says, "I can't open it." The sound of his voice is so sad. "Go upstairs and try to find a wire or something that I can pick the lock with," he says.

I nod, and even that hurts. Climbing the stairs takes a while. I don't know why I can't just ignore the pain like usual. I make it to the top, but the knob won't turn…it's locked. It has never ever been locked before. I knock softly because I don't know what time it is and Daddy might be home. I don't think I can handle him right now.

"Mommy?" Holding my ear against the door, I listen

for her and I can hear the TV, just not her. "Mommy, we're locked in." I wait for a little while before I make the journey back down the stairs, to Toben.

"It's locked, so I'm going to go outside."

It must still be night time because the sun isn't shining, and the clock shows eleven one five. When I get to the window and open it, the first thing I see is that my ladder is missing. Turning my head, I look up and my stomach twists.

We're trapped.

Something is covering the top of the hole. Maybe we can build a ladder and try to push it off? Oh…that won't work. Toben is in a cage.

I slowly make my way to my bed, pull off a blanket, and pick up my pillow as something falls to the floor. I look down and it's a lollipop! I remove the wrapper and put it in my mouth.

"Thank you for the sucker." I tell him as I lay the blankets down.

He shakes his head. "That's not from me."

"Do you want some?" I hold it out for him.

He looks so grossed out when he rasps, "God, no. It must be from him." I continue making my bed. "What are you doing?" His no-voice is shaky when he pushes his hand through one of the squares.

I hold it this time. "We're stuck down here. The window is blocked off."

Toben lies down in his prison to face me, as he whispers, "He said he bought you, but you can't buy a person."

I hate hearing him like this. "Please, stop talking, Toben, your voice is broken."

I doze in and out of sleep as I keep hold of his hand and he keeps hold of mine.

"Tavin, come on, wake up."

When I flip open my eyelids, he looks pained. "What's wrong? Are you okay?"

I sit up and he looks away from me toward the tin coffee can on the floor. "I need to take a piss." I've never seen him look so embarrassed. "I need you to hand me the can." Reaching too quickly causes a stabbing pain to shoot through me to my fingertips. I cry out and Toben clutches the metal of his cage. There's a hole in the cage the perfect size to slide in the coffee can, so I push it in for him.

"Will you close your eyes?"

Humming to myself as I lie down, I shut my eyes, and I try to give him as much privacy as I can without moving from this spot. When he's finished, his embarrassment gets worse as we realize I will have to dispose of it in the bathroom. I don't care other than the effort it takes to trudge there and back. I tell him so, and he still keeps apologizing.

We fall back asleep until I wake up to the sound of the basement door being unlocked and opened. "Toben!" I whisper as best as I can, with my voice still missing. His body stirs. "Toben! Wake up, someone's coming."

Jumping up, his eyes go wide. "What? Go hide!" I shake my head and immediately regret it because it causes the pounding to return. "Please, Tav!"

He's begging me, but I don't want to leave him out here alone. Footsteps begin their decent and his eyes are frantic. My heart beats wildly, and soon, my fear wins out and I run to my closet.

I'm suddenly not in as much pain as I try to silence my breathing.

Shoes are hitting the pavement when the voice that makes me want to shrivel up into nothing says, "Good afternoon, Toben."

I wish I would have left the closet door open a crack

so I could see. My stomach twists. I'm so scared, I think I might puke. I don't ever want it to happen again, and I don't understand how Mommy could want that. My leg gets really warm. I look down and I'm peeing, I'm just much too frightened to be able to stop it. My body won't stop shaking as I realize his footsteps are getting louder. My closet door swings open and I look up into the face of my boogeyman.

"Oh, come now, little Lotus." Kneeling down, he looks right into my eyes. "I'm not here for that today."

Holding out his hand, he helps me to my feet. He glares down at the wet spot and his nostrils flare, but he says nothing about it. He leads me into my room and we stop at my bed. My blanket from the floor has been picked up and he's put a bunch of bags on top of my mattress. He's still holding my hand as he picks up a bag and leads us to my bathroom. I glance at Toben to see him gripping the metal, with fear etched all over his face.

Turning on the bathroom light, Mr. James lets go of my hand and starts the bath. He's back in nice clothes, except he isn't wearing his jacket and his sleeves are rolled up a little above his wrists. Reaching into the paper bag, he takes out a toothbrush and toothpaste. After spreading the paste across the bristles, he hands it to me and I begin brushing my teeth. He places the toothpaste in the cabinet and continues removing the contents of the bag. A towel is hung on the rack before he lines the edge of the tub with a wash rag, body wash, shampoo, and conditioner. He puts a bottle of lotion on the sink and places floss with two sticks of deodorant in the cabinet, before adding a pile of clothes to the table.

I finish brushing my teeth, and he takes the toothbrush, placing it in a case before putting it in the cabinet. I can already feel the steam coming from the bath.

"Take off your dress."

He promised he wouldn't do that! I cry when I shake my

head and hug my arms.

"No."

His shadow eats my whole body and I vibrate from the force of his fury.

"I want to let you heal, but disobey me again, and your brooding little friend in there will be cleaning up pieces of you off the floor. Now. Take. Off. The. Dress."

I have to consciously make myself breathe again as I pull my dress over my head. My body screams, and I hear myself cry as he stares at me. Wrapping his hands around my ribs he lifts me up and carries me to the tub. He lowers me in and as soon as the water hits me, I scream. It's so hot that it almost feels cold at first. He forces me into the boiling water causing my skin to instantly turn red from the scald. I try to fight and get out because if I don't, my skin will melt from my bones.

"It's too hot!"

The heat of the water getting into my cuts is excruciating, even if I'm momentarily thankful he hasn't pushed me far enough in to reach the burn on my chest.

He holds me down without any effort. "It needs to be hot to clean your filth. You are a very disgusting girl, Tavin."

Hey! I'm not disgusting!

I'm too scared to say that, though, so I frown at him. I can't stop myself from whimpering even when I calm down.

Either the water is beginning to cool or I am getting used to it, because it doesn't feel quite as bad, anymore. He leans me back so my hair is submerged and I think he's trying to avoid getting the flower on my chest wet. When he lifts me back up, he rolls his sleeves up higher and shows me his arm. He has a tattoo and it is identical to the burn.

"Do you know what this is?"

I nod. "Yes, it's a flower."

He doesn't smile, but his eyebrows relax when he puts

the shampoo in my hair. "It's called a lotus. It's a symbol and a reminder that you are my property." He doesn't speak to me again until he is putting in the conditioner. "I know that you're confused. Once you're both clean, I'll explain everything, okay?"

I nod. He's right, I am confused. He's nice one minute and a scary monster the next.

He sighs. "When I speak to you, I want you to respond with words. Do you understand?"

Staring at the pink in the water, I tell him, "Yes, Mr. James."

"My name is Logan." He begins to soap up the wash rag and the water feels quite comfortable now.

"Hi, Logan."

He chuckles at me as he lifts my arms to wash beneath them. After he washes me everywhere, he completely submerges me and the water touches the bloody flower and somehow makes it burn worse. I can't yell because I am underwater, so when he pulls me up, I cry.

"It needs to be cleaned, Lotus. Don't touch it or mess with it, okay? It will take a long time to heal, so just leave it the fuck alone."

"Okay."

He washes it, and I can see he is trying to be gentle. I don't know why he's being so nice after what he did yesterday. It doesn't make any sense.

After he's done, he pulls me up to a standing position and picks up the towel. He pats me dry and wraps my hair up. All of the cuts and wounds look much better now that the blood has been washed away.

Squirting lotion into his hands, he rubs them together and massages it into my skin. Even though it stings a little on the cut parts, mostly it just feels good. He gives me the deodorant before he hands me clean panties. When I finish and look up, I see the dress he is holding. It's a brand new, purple dress. I don't think any of my dresses have ever been new! It's sleeveless with a white bow, and ruffles on the bottom. It's so pretty! Just like a princess would wear, I bet. When he puts it on me, it lands at my knees and it feels so good to be all clean. In fact, I think the bath helped my soreness because that seems much better also. I feel pretty and I've never felt pretty before.

"Do you like it?"

The smile on my face stretches my cheeks when I say, "Yes."

He takes my hand and we go back into my room. Toben slumps into his cage with a sigh of relief as he sees me. Logan orders me to sit on the bed while he lets Toben out of his cage. He gives him a towel, a stack of clothes, and a toothbrush.

"Go get cleaned up. Make sure to get the brand. Be gentle with it."

When Toben passes by, I see that he has a Lotus on his shoulder, just like mine…why didn't he tell me? He gives me an uneasy glance while obeying Logan.

While he's in the bathroom, Logan cleans the wet spot in the closet before returning to the bed. He removes Toben's backpack, all of the blankets, and the sheets, when our dolls fall from the bloody fabric. Leaning down, he picks them up and I want to yell for him to leave them alone, but I get scared. A squeak gets out before I can stop it and he flips his eyes to me, then back to the dolls. I want to cry with joy when he hands them to me.

"Thank you."

"You are welcome, Lotus."

I shove them in my drawer while he empties all the bags on my bed. Boy and girl clothes, along with towels, underwear, socks and shoes, all fall from the bags. There are also new sheets and blankets that are pale cream and yellow. He tells me to make the bed while he puts away our clothes.

Toben is quick, and within a few short minutes, he's walking out of the bathroom in jeans and a baby blue T-shirt. He always wears long sleeves. I think he looks nice in that shirt.

"Toben, come here and sit on the floor." Logan sits on the bed next to me while Toben obeys and hugs his knees. Taking a deep breath and removing the towel from my head, Logan speaks gently. "You no longer have the freedom to leave this room." I feel his hands gather my hair as he begins to comb through the strands. "You will receive everything you need to survive and I expect you both to keep clean. Next week, I'll bring down a washer and dryer. You will then be responsible for washing your own clothes." He's careful not to pull while he brushes my hair. His steady speaking is somehow calming when it had nearly caused my heart to blow up not that long ago. "You need to understand that you will never see your parents again because they are no longer your parents. They sold that right to me." He finishes brushing my hair and he stands up to light a cigarette. "The best way to think of this relationship, is to imagine yourselves equivalent to one of my planes or yachts. I will maintain you and play with you, ultimately though, you are nothing more than toys."

Just then, the door to the basement opens and Kyle comes down the stairs just far enough to see Logan. "The fridge is here." Logan nods before following him up the stairs.

I smile at Toben. "Do you like my dress?"

From the look on his face, I don't think he does. "Did you hear what he just said?!"

Of course I did, what a silly question. "Yes. He's going to take care of us."

I'm worried he's going to cry, as his eyebrows knit together. "Tavin! What do you think he means by *play*? He will do what he did to you yesterday, over and over!"

I shake my head. "Not if we do what he asks."

I'm making him angry. I can tell by the way he clenches his jaw and scrunches his eyebrows.

"We did what he asked yesterday! This is very bad. He's worse than both of our parents combined!"

"Why are you yelling at me? I can't change it! At least now I will have food and be clean. Besides, he's being nice today."

He stands up and bunches up his fists as he leans toward me. "How can you not see the severity of this? All because he gave you a new dress?!"

Now I feel guilty for thinking I am pretty in it. I guess I'm not supposed to like it. I'm not sad that I won't see Daddy again. I maybe am a little bit sad that I won't see Mommy, though. I will miss being able to go outside, but I have only been doing that for a few months. Maybe if I am good, stay clean, and do everything he asks, then he won't do that stuff to me.

"No! Because I have clean clothes and clean skin at the same time, for the first time. Ever. Because they are bringing in a refrigerator. Refrigerators mean food. Food that I can eat whenever I get hungry. Because he is being nice to me today! Daddy is NEVER nice to me!" I am screaming and it's hurting my throat. I don't even know why I'm yelling at him. He's right. I am scared that Logan will do that again, it's just, he isn't doing anything bad right now so I want to enjoy it.

Toben holds out his hands and I take them before he sighs and sits next to me.

"Tavin I-"

He is interrupted by a loud scraping noise by my window. We glance at each other before running to see what's causing the scratchy sound. The sun shines through as Kyle and Logan move a large piece of wood from the well opening. Kyle lowers down a ladder for Logan to climb down and open the window. Kyle lowers a small refrigerator to Logan, before climbing down himself. They lift and carry the little appliance to the wall, opposite my bed, and plug it in. When they climb back out, Logan removes the ladder, but doesn't close the window or cover up the well. I can hear their voices, I just can't make out what they're saying, as they trail off, getting further away.

I climb up into the well and so does Toben, even though we'll never be able to get out without something to climb on. We sit and face each other as the sunrays shine down on us. It isn't long before we hear them coming back down the stairs. They are both carrying a bunch of grocery bags, and I climb back into my room as they unload them. I wasn't aware of my hunger until watching them put away juice, cheese, and grapes. They have chips, bread, cereal, applesauce, and so much more. I lurch toward the food. I'm not going for any item in particular, but before I can get there, Kyle takes ahold of me. He bends my finger back toward my wrist and the tearing sensation is so intense that I'm scared it's going to rip apart from my hand and I cry out.

"Kyle, it's Acclimation Day. Leave her be," Logan murmurs as he lights another cigarette.

"Acclimation Day." Kyle shakes his head and grumbles, "Fucking ridiculous." He gives me one final push before he releases me, and quickly grips my wrist as he whispers, "You should be thanking God you aren't mine. I would be de-fleshing each one of these grabby, little fingers right now."

"Kyle!" Logan barks, as he walks over to us.

Kyle tosses my hand towards my chest and I back up to Toben.

After all the food is put away, he and Logan speak in

hushed tones for a few minutes. Finally, Kyle leaves as Logan's gaze shifts back to us.

"Go on, you can eat."

That's all I need to hear. There are plastic cups with paper plates and I fill them quickly before I sit on my bed. Toben is hesitant until he sees me piling grapes into my mouth, which is already full of peanut butter and jelly, so he gets some too.

Logan leans against the bed as we eat.

"There's plenty of food for the both of you, to last the week, just be sure you don't go through it too quickly, because you won't be getting anymore until our next playdate."

"Mr. James?" Toben's scratchy voice comes out, while he sits beside me.

"Call me Logan. You are not my employees or my associates. You are my possessions. Which brings up an important point: whenever you address me, you are to use my name."

"How long are you going to keep us here, Logan?" Toben sounds like he isn't scared, even though his hand is shaking next to mine.

"For as long as you are fun."

"Wow. You really are a psychotic fuck," my heart jumps into my throat and I glare at Toben as he adds his name with petulance, "*Logan.*"

Please stop talking.

Logan's fingers are clutching the wire footboard of my bed when he hunches his shoulders for momentum and pushes off the frame. He towers over Toben.

"You can't say I didn't try."

Logan's eyes blaze to mine as he grabs my ankle and pulls me so I'm dangling half way off the bed. Fingers fly to the buckle of his belt. NO! I try to pull away and scramble to the other side, as his big hand covers half of my leg. He's holding on too tight for me to get free.

"No! Please, Logan! You promised!"

Tears gush and I instantly feel sweaty. I'm scared my heart might blow up, it's beating too fast. He can hit me and cut me all he wants, but please! I don't want that ever again. How do I get him to stop?! He takes my face and jerks my head to look at Toben.

"This is his fault," he bellows.

Toben's head shakes frantically.

"I'm sorry, Logan! I'm sorry, please don't."

This is going to hurt so bad. I'm still sore and my thighs are already bruised from yesterday. He pushes up my pretty dress while I scream and fight to get away from him.

"Hold her down!" Logan barks.

I fight as hard as I can before I feel Toben's clammy hands on my arms.

No, no, no.

Toben is about to cry when he begs, "Please, Logan. I made a mistake, please just punish me instead of her."

Logan's golden eyes are terrifying when he releases me. Dragging Toben off the bed to the floor, he pushes his shoe against Toben's chest and slams him against the concrete.

He's getting hurt because of me! If I try to stop Logan, then he will have sex with me again, and that thought scares me so bad I can't move.

Logan's eyes are scanning my room.

"I didn't expect to need my tools today. Now I have to get creative." He cocks his head and all irritation evaporates from his tone, when his gaze lands on a broom. "That will do." He pulls Toben up by his shirt so that he's on his knees. "Take off your shirt and put your hands behind your head."

He walks to the far wall, and I'm still frozen. All I can see is Toben's back so I have no idea if he is scared or angry at me.

"Tavin, look at me."

My head snaps up in obedience. Logan is already back. If I do what he says, things will be better.

"This is a one-time favor because it's Acclimation Day. From this moment on, if either of you disobey or disrespect me, the other will pay the price." Rolling his neck and shoulders he continues, "Never forget, my playthings: it can always get worse."

With that, he holds the end closest to the bristles while he swings the handle against Toben's back and it arches from the force. Howling in pain, he falls forward. My tears fall uncontrollably, and still I stay in my place.

"Get up!" He assaults his body twice more until Toben is struggling to get himself off the floor. I'm a horrible friend. How can I even call myself his friend when I just let him get beaten and all I did was watch? I nearly jump off the bed when Logan's voice thunders, "Get in the cage."

My heart falls apart like petals from a rose as I watch Toben try to drag himself to the wire box. He keeps falling and I am finally able to lift myself off the bed. At the very least, I can help him into the cage.

"Toben, I'm so sorry," I whisper. My apology does nothing to help his battered back.

"What do you think you're doing, little Lotus?" Logan asks with raised eyebrows. The slight upturn of his lips, along with the amusement in his voice, leaves me unsure.

"He needs help." My voice is so small.

He waves his hand to proceed as he lights another cigarette. "It's Acclimation Day."

I'm trying to be careful, while Toben keeps gasping in pain. Finally, I help him inside his jail and Logan kneels beside me to lock it. The smoke is burning my eyes when I feel Logan's hand around mine pulling me up.

"Finish your food." When he releases me, I go to my bed. "If you both simply accept your fates, you will realize it's not as bad as you think. In fact, you may even find your-selves grateful for the things I do for you." Toben lets out a groan and Logan ignores it. "Once a week, I will bring you supplies, we will play, and if you are good, you will get your treat."

He pulls a small box out of the last bag and hands it to me. Then, reaching into his pocket, he takes out a cell phone and flips it open. "All you have to do is press this button," he shows me the one with a little green phone on it, "and it will call me." He holds my chin hard to make sure I look at him. "Do not ever call unless it is an emergency. Do you understand?"

I shake my head yes, and then remember he wants a ver-bal answer.

"Yes, Logan."

"Good." He nods and places the phone on the night-stand. "Welcome to your new lives, my playthings." Then, just like that, he turns to leave.

"Wait!" Toben yells and rattles his cage. "You can't leave me in here for a week!"

Logan tilts his head and laughs. "You aren't the brightest star in the sky, are you?" He straightens and all traces of his smile disappear. "I can do whatever I want. I. Own. You."

Neither one of us say a word or move a muscle as we listen to him climb the stairs. As soon as I hear the lock click, his words ring through my head.

Welcome to your new lives, my playthings.

CHAPTER FIVE
Normal

Toben

A DARK SHADOW OF UNDERSTANDING SOAKS INTO my pores. He's so much worse than simply evil… he's insane. Certifiable. My father sold me to a psychopathic child rapist. I keep thinking I'm dreaming because of too many nights watching *Unsolved Mysteries*, yet the nightmare refuses to end.

I wonder how much I went for. Knowing my father, he probably paid Logan to take me.

Logan gives me the impression that he thinks what he's doing is acceptable, even normal. Then Tavin, oh my sweet Tavin, she's the perfect prey for this sicko. She's so starved for basic needs and affection that she eats up his crap. I wanted to vomit at the way he held her hand, regarding her as a loving father would, within hours of slicing her up and taking her innocence. As if she can sense me thinking of her, she's next to the cage with her fingers grasping the wire.

Tears are in her eyes as her head jerks. "I just let you take a beating for me. I'm sorry! I got scared, I thought if I did anything, he would…"

Her gaze shifts to the floor. Damn it. I can't hold her

and I'm supposed to be the one to do that. Be the one she leans on. I can't give her what she needs because I'm in this GODDAMN CAGE!

"That was what I wanted, Tav. I would have been pissed if you would have done anything other than what you did. We need to focus on staying alive and keeping him off of you as much as we can. I need you to promise me that."

"You can't say things like you did, to him. He wasn't going to hurt us today, and maybe you could have been spending the week with me. Out here."

She's right, I should have kept my mouth shut.

"I know, but you see it, right? Tell me you know he's crazy."

"All adults are crazy."

She spouts it like it is the oldest known fact of all time. I surprise myself when a deep laugh bursts from my mouth, instantly feeling it in my back and I suck in air. "You've got that right."

"Are you going to be okay?"

"Come on, Tav, my dad was a boxer in high school. It'll take more than a broom to do any real damage." I wink at her, trying to add some light to our dreary new world.

She stands up, picks up the box from Logan, and sits down next to the cage so I can see. When she opens it, I am surprised to see it's an actual treat. It's a large cupcake with pink frosting and little blue hard candies sprinkled on top.

She gasps, "Oh! It's so pretty I almost don't want to eat it."

She barely gets the word 'it' out of her mouth before she takes a big-ass bite.

I snort, "Not that pretty, apparently."

"I ted ah mos."

I laugh again and even though it physically hurts, it warms by body with a much-needed moment of normal.

When she swallows her bite, she holds it out to me.

"Do you want some?

I don't want anything from that possessed pedophile, even though at this point, everything is from him. I didn't finish my food and the cupcake does look delicious...

"Sure, I'll have a piece." She breaks off a chunk that has hard candy on it. I snort at the fact that his twisted sickness knows no bounds, not even the cliché ones. I shake my head at the cupcake. "He's a child molester that gives us actual candy. I wonder if his rape van is an ice cream truck."

I laugh at my little joke as Tavin's eyes widen with her mouth full of her sugary snack. When she swallows, her excitement is apparent. "You think he has an ice cream truck?!"

That's what she picks up from my statement: the damn ice cream truck.

"No—God, Tav-do you know what rape means?" She shakes her head as she licks her fingers. "It's forcing someone to have sex that doesn't want to. That's what they did, they raped you."

Her eyes fill up with tears and she pushes herself off the ground. She's moving much easier now.

"I don't want to talk about that," she sobs.

Damn it. I made her cry. I should be the one person who doesn't do that. "I'm sorry, I don't want to upset you, you just seem to think he is an okay guy. He isn't. He's bad. Very, very bad."

"Aren't they all? You are the only person who has ever been nice to me, but today, there were times Logan was nice to me too!"

Even though I tried, I know there were days I wasn't able to come over and she probably didn't eat those days. While I made the effort to wash the dresses she had, I didn't do that as much as I could have either. I want to be understanding, I just don't see how she can just overlook him brutally abusing her, for a few moments of kindness and some clean clothes.

"He will keep doing it, Tavin. Do you understand that? No matter what we say, no matter what we do, he will *play*." I use his term hoping it will help things sink in, that the worst isn't over. It's just beginning.

She exhales and looks to the ceiling as her teary voice whispers, "Do you think my parents are up there?"

"I don't know, but I've wondered, too."

This whole situation is surreal. I mean, how did he happen to find the two parents who hated their children so much that they would sell them to a monster? Not to mention, he's keeping us in her house. Wouldn't he take us to some cabin in the woods or something? What's the end game? That's the biggest question of all. What happens when this is all over?

She shrugs, stands up, and starts getting blankets from her bed. I don't want her to sleep on the floor again while she's still hurt.

"Will you sleep in your bed tonight? You need to heal and the bed would be better."

She opens her drawer and takes something out. "Maybe you should have thought about that before you called him a 'psychotic fuck.'"

Her tone catches me off guard, she rarely snaps at me. "Are you mad at me?"

She kneels by my cage to make her bed and brings her eyes up to mine. "I need you out here with me."

I know she's right. I need to bite my tongue because she'll end up paying for it one way or another. What she doesn't know is, I need to hug her as much as she needs me to.

"I'm sorry. It was stupid and not worth the moment of satisfaction. I promise I'll be out there with you next week. Okay?"

I put my hand through the cage to hold her hand, and when she grasps it, my breathing takes on the calm it always does when I touch her.

She nods and reaches down with her free hand to push my prince rag doll through a hole in the cage, while hers stays in her lap.

"He let us keep them."

She smiles, yet it isn't a happy one. I look down at the rags and the smudged blood mocks me. These dolls are our last memory of before. Our last taste of freedom.

I'm scared. I'm scared for her and I'm scared for me. While our fate is uncertain, it's also terrifying, and I cringe when I think of what's in store for us. We have to make a plan before next week. We can't let him tear us apart no matter what he does or makes us do. We are all each other has.

It's us against him.

Tavin

"Please, look at me, it's not a big deal."

His eyes flicker to mine, darker somehow, as his face twists in self-disgust and humiliation.

"You had to clean up my shit, Tavin."

He shakes his head and looks away. I hate that he feels like he has to be embarrassed around me. He held it for two days before he couldn't anymore. I went into the bathroom to give him some privacy, but it still had to be disposed of when he was finished.

Blowing air through my closed mouth causes my lips to vibrate as I turn on the music.

"Are you hungry?"

"God no, I'm not eating for the rest of the week."

He's being a baby.

"Stop it, Toben. Don't you think I hate that you've seen… everything?" I gesture up and down my body so he knows what I mean. "It is what it is, so being embarrassed and not trusting each other only hurts us."

He slumps against the side of his cage. "I trust you, Tavin, there's just something dehumanizing about having someone clean up your crap, and I hate that it was you."

"Well I'm glad that you were with me when they…did that."

I know I'm a bad person because I am grateful he's here.

He lets out a groan. "That's not what I meant." His face softens and I feel relief at the appearance of a small smile. "There is no one I would rather be traumatized and trapped with, other than you."

I grin before I lie down on my floor-bed. "Will you sing me one of your songs?"

His smile is full now. "Of course, my book is in my backpack."

All of his songs and poems are so pretty. His voice sounds so different when he sings, and the words fit together perfectly. I close my eyes as his words sprinkle over me.

<hr>

I find his hat under the bed. It must have fallen off when everything happened. I hand it to him and it seems to make him more like himself, when he puts it on.

Then he brings up reading.

"Why don't you go get the books you want to read, from my bag. It's been a while since you've practiced."

What does reading matter now? "Why should I? Besides, I don't want to. Let's eat some of the food."

"Being held prisoner in your own basement by a lunatic is no excuse to stop learning to read."

He grins as he says it. His smiles are connected to mine

and I think mine are connected to his. Reaching into his pocket, he pulls out his iPod, keys, and a folded piece of paper. "Here," He gives me the iPod and the keys through the cage. "You can throw away the keys…literally. They're to my house and I'm never going back there." He points to my nightstand. "Put the iPod in the drawer, I don't know how much of your constant alternative music I can stand, so I don't want it to get broken."

After doing what he tells me, I sit back down as he starts unfolding the piece of paper, his hands are a little shaky and he seems nervous.

"I've never shown this to anyone." His eyes scan the worn paper before folding it back up and slipping it to me through the cage. "I found it in my old baby book, a couple of years ago. I think the only reason my dad kept it is because it has her writing in it. She wrote it when I was still in her stomach. This is how mothers are supposed to be."

I take the paper and it's so flimsy and soft; it doesn't even crinkle. I am very careful, and when I look at the first word at the top of the page, I know it instantly.

Toben,

I begin sounding out each letter for each word, and even though Toben has to help me with a couple of words, I am able to read most of them.

Each sun that sets brings me closer to the day that I will be able to hold you in my arms. I feel you move and it fills me with so much overwhelming joy that I weep. I dream of the man you will become. Will you have my blonde hair and dark brown eyes or your father's blue eyes and dark hair? I dream of your voice and how it will sound the first time you say 'mommy'. I love you with everything I have and it comes from so deep inside of me that I didn't even know it was there until your soul made its way into my womb. I think of what I want for you, and at first, all I wanted was your happiness, and though I do want that, I quickly found that I desire so much more for you. I want you to be strong, kind, and confident. Be brave, love, and always see the sunshine. I know your father is a hard man, though he does have love in him. I see it every time he looks at me and I feel it in his touch. Be patient with him, for he loves you as well, even if he struggles with how to show it. You are my perfect little man and I cannot wait to finally meet you. I may not be able to give you everything, but I will always protect and take care of you, my Love. You are part of me, the best part.

-Mommy

My eyes are rimmed with tears while I read the most beautiful thing in the world. Toben's mommy had loved him more than I knew was possible. The letter makes me sad. It makes me sad because his mother had been an angel and he never got to meet her or hear her voice. It makes me sad because my mommy doesn't love me like that. When I look up to Toben he is smiling as a tear rolls over his cheek.

"That was nice, thank you, Tavin."

Logan never told us exactly what day or what time he would be back, so the tension grows thicker with each passing day. Last night, as we held hands to go to sleep, we promised that no matter what happens, we will never hold it against each other. We will obey his every order and try to keep him happy.

Even though I want Toben out of the cage, it still has been a nice week for me. I haven't been hungry, dirty, or beaten in over five days. If Toben could have been out here, then the week would have been wonderful. He promises me that he will do everything in his power to stay out and I just hope he stays quiet. I miss hugging him. Our food supply is low and we each only have one set of clothing left. According to the calendar, tomorrow will be a week since Acclimation Day and Toben says that he doubts Logan will come early in the day because he probably has to work.

I clean my room and make my bed. I want everything to look perfect for him. Then maybe he will see that we are trying to be good and he will be nice again.

My stomach hurts so badly that I can't eat and I even throw up. Toben tells me to calm down, that it's just my nerves, but I don't see him eating anything either. I finally do something I should have done a long time ago: I dance.

I turn up the radio and twirl around my room. I imagine I'm a fairy princess flying around the forest. Everyone looks at my incredible wings as I fly by them. Toben is captured by the dark fairy king and only my magical dance can free him…

"LOTUS!"

His booming voice jerks me from my imaginary existence and when my eyes fly open, his are burning into me. Fury consumes his face and I want to hide under my bed. I glance at Toben and his fingers are white from holding the cage too tight.

"Do not look at him. Look at me." My attention snaps back to him. "If you cannot hear me speaking to you, then the music is too loud. Do not do that again, Lotus."

"Yes, Logan."

He's wearing his suit again today. Slipping off his jacket, he walks to my radio to turn off the music.

"Kneel on the floor with your hands on your thighs." My knees hit the cold concrete and my gaze finds the black bag. He circles back around to face me as he firmly orders, "Do not move."

I nod and he glares. Oh, yeah, I have to speak. "Yes, Logan."

He picks up some grocery bags and takes them to the fridge before he removes clothing from the black duffel. He goes into the bathroom and we don't speak, even though our eyes tell each other to be brave. As long as we're both alive and he's out of the cage when Logan leaves, we will count ourselves successful.

When Logan emerges, he's wearing a blue T-shirt, jeans, and sneakers. He jogs back upstairs without acknowledging us. I knit my eyebrows in question at Toben, while he just shrugs.

We sit there in the silence until there is a loud bang at the top of the stairs. Once they are far enough down, I can see that Kyle and Logan are bringing down a washing machine on a metal carrier with wheels. After they bring it into my room, they set it down and go back upstairs repeating the process with the dryer.

When the machines are next to each other, Logan lights a cigarette and brushes past me to the cage. As he unlocks it, he tells Toben to take a shower. Toben seems to have a hard time and it takes him a while to stand up straight. He staggers to the bathroom, while I have to remain where I am.

This position is getting uncomfortable.

While Toben is in the bathroom, Logan and Kyle go back upstairs. Within moments, I hear the scraping of the cover being removed from the well. I expect them to come from the window, so it startles me when I hear them coming back down the stairs. Toben takes longer in the shower then he did last time, still, he finishes quickly. He's towel drying his hair when he comes out and I can tell he feels better.

"Get on your knees with your hands behind your head," Logan orders from across the room. "When I tell you to kneel, these are the positions I want."

"Yes, Logan," we say, together.

Toben kneels right next to me, lacing his fingers behind

his head, as we quietly wait for our instructions. The clanking of the washer and occasional murmuring between Logan and Kyle is the only sound until he finally addresses us. "You may both get up and sit in the window to get some sun."

We climb inside the window as they set up the machines. The warmth feels good on my skin and the fresh air seems to clean my head. The cuts have been healing well, though my flower is still horribly red and still hurts. It's even started to itch. I try not to scratch it though because he said to leave it alone.

"Do you feel better now that you are out?" I whisper.

He nods and grumbles, "We'll see how long that lasts."

I close my eyes as I enjoy the smell of outside, until Logan's voice makes my eyes open.

"Alright, that's enough, back inside." Once we are back through the window, he turns to us, and when he speaks, it's directed at me. "Kneel in front of your bed." I obey. Kyle is gone and the room has a heavy pressure as Logan steps to his bag.

"Come here," he barks at Toben. Once he is by his side, Logan gestures to the bag. "Pick one."

"W-what?" Toben's disturbed expression makes my palms sweat.

Logan towers over him, leaning forward to get closer to his face. "Pick a tool to use while I play with her." He speaks each word slowly and clearly. My blood goes cold and I feel like I might be sick. "Do not make me ask you again."

I can see Toben's whole body shaking from where I kneel, as he crouches down to look through the bag. Finally, he pulls out something long. It looks like a wooden stick, then I see it is actually multiple flat wooden sticks bound together by thick, brown twine. I think I hear a slight chuckle when Logan praises, "The five-core. An excellent choice, Plaything." He stalks over to me and his fingers grab his zipper to undo his pants. I shut my eyes tight. "Do not fucking dare close your eyes! Look at me."

I don't want to! I don't want this to happen and I don't want to see. No! No! NO! I want to scream, I just know it will make everything worse.

"NOW!"

I slowly open my eyes and he grabs my head. I'm instantly choking when the tears fall full force. As much as I try to pull my head away, he just pushes down harder and makes horrible noises. The hot burn of sick claws up my throat and spews out all over him.

"Fuck!" He yanks me away from him and throws me to the floor by my hair. "Disgusting cunt!" He storms off to my bathroom as I choke and gasp.

Toben is by me in a second. He runs his hand across my spine as he whispers, "Are you okay?"

My body trembles as I nod to him. My face is wet from crying and my throat burns from the vomit.

Logan has taken his shoes and socks off so I don't even hear him before he yells, "KNEEL!" We jump apart from each other and I frantically scramble to my knees. Logan jerks the tool that Toben has picked from his hand, and circles around behind us. "Take off your shirts, both of you." Without his shoes, I can't hear where he is and it adds to my fear. I can see Toben out of the side of my eye. I don't dare look at him straight on, though. It seems to be a long time before Logan speaks again.

"This is because of you, Lotus."

I hear a *swoosh* followed by a *th-th-th-th-thwack*. In the seconds after he hits him, there is nothing. It's perfectly quiet. Then his soul tearing howl rips through the silence, causing my head to involuntarily snap to him as he falls forward.

"Kneel!"

Slowly, Toben struggles back up and brings his hands

back behind his head. He barely gets into position when I
hear the *swoosh* and *thwack* sounds again. His cries hurt my
ears and my heart. I didn't throw up on purpose! I don't even
know how to stop it from happening again!

"Kneel!"

Poor Toben can barely lift himself with his shaky arms
before getting them behind his head, when Logan hits him
again. All I do is cry as he wails in agony. He's being hurt and
it's my fault. Toben falls forward again and Logan throws the
five-core on the ground next to him.

"Pick it up." Toben is so strong and brave when he pushes himself slowly to his feet. "Hit her." Toben's wet eyes go
wide and I see his jaw twitch, even though he stands behind
me without complaint. "Hit her hard, Plaything. Don't piss
me off."

I hear Toben inhale deeply, so I do the same and listen
for the swoosh sound. As soon as I hear it, my body gets
tight. I know I hear the *th-th-th-th-thwack* of it hitting me,
but Toben is a big ol' baby! This doesn't even hurt! As soon
as I have the thought, it's as if large vines of hot excruciating
torture climb up my back and wrap around my entire body. I
am screaming before I know that I am, and my body is lying
on the concrete floor.

"Kneel, Lotus."

I have to be strong like Toben and with weak arms I am
able to push myself back up.

"Again!"

Logan falls to his knees holding me up by my shoulders.
When I hear those haunting sounds of what is to come, I
squeeze my eyes shut. The explosion of extreme pain causes my screams to rip through my throat, as he rages, "Look
at me!" As he stands, he lets go of my shoulders and I fall
forward.

He doesn't make him hit me again, he just kicks my ribs

and tells me to get on my bed. I look up to Toben and his face is red and wet just like mine probably is. All I can do is crawl and once I reach the bed, climbing up is the hardest part.

Logan is back at his bag, quickly finding what he's searching for. I keep thinking I can't be anymore scared than I am, and then he does something else. He has a knife! We have done everything he's asked, and he's still going to kill me. I don't think I want to die yet.

Toben was right. It does happen again and we can't do a thing about it. He holds my wrists against my stomach while he cuts into my chest with the knife. He keeps asking Toben if he is watching, in between screaming at me to look at him. I want this to be over, and I keep looking at Toben, aching for the moment that we can sleep in each other's arms. Slice after slice he cuts me, the sweat causing them to sting and burn. I will never completely heal if he does this every week. I'm at least grateful that I don't have to feel his weight on top of me this time.

My soul falls to my toes when he orders Toben into his cage. The idea of another week with him in that box makes me sick. This hurts so bad and when I cry out in pain, Logan just smiles at me and says, "We need to work on your screaming. That will be next week's lesson: The art of shutting the fuck up."

He gets off of the bed and I sigh with relief because I think he's finally done, except he doesn't put his clothes on. Instead, he goes back to the bag. As soon as I lay eyes on the kit, I remember he had given it to me last time he did this. He heads to my table and begins opening it up.

"I understand that you are quite capable of cooking and administering heroin, is that right?"

"Yes, Logan," I whisper.

"Good." He turns to Toben. "You need to pay attention as well. Come out here and kneel." As Toben obeys, he goes to his bag and removes a spray bottle and a cloth. "Follow my instructions to the letter, every single time you inject, do you understand?"

"Yes, Logan," I answer.

"Yes, Logan," Toben echoes.

I'm both surprised and grateful for Toben's obedience. I thought for sure he would have slipped up by now.

"Very good. Now, wipe down whatever surface that you're using, with disinfectant, and then wash your hands." Following his own directions, he vanishes into the bathroom. Upon returning, he pulls out the spoon and looks at me. "Do you know why we bend the handle of the spoon?"

I nod and I'm so glad I know the answer. "Yes, Logan. It's so it doesn't spill."

He smirks at me and I don't understand him. He does horrible things even worse than Daddy, then he acts like he wants to be nice.

"That's right, Lotus." After he sprinkles the powder he opens a clear package and pulls out a syringe. "This is a new needle. Always use a new needle. Every single time, no exceptions. This is the most important rule. Do you understand?"

"Yes, Logan," we quickly answer.

I feel so bad for Toben, he looks like he's suffering terribly and his arms are trembling. It's not fair that I get to lie on the bed while he's down there like that.

"I want you to use bottled water only; I don't trust tap." He pours the water in the lid and continues preparing the fix. "When it's time to add the cotton and fill the syringe, make sure to not touch the needle to the spoon and make sure to get all the air out." He jerks his head toward Toben. "Get the tourniquet from the bag. When I tell you to, tie it around her arm." He tears open a packet and removes a sanitary wipe. "Always make sure that you clean the injection site. You have to be smart about it because there's the possibility of getting sick if you don't." It's wet and cold when he wipes the inside of my arm. "Alright, tie her off."

The tourniquet is tight and it pinches. When Logan taps my veins, my heart starts thrumming and my body suddenly feels so hot! I don't want to be like Mommy or Daddy. When he tells him to untie me and pushes down on the plunger, I look up at Toben before I fly away from him…

I can taste joy…
BURST….No more pain.
BURST….No more fear.
BURST…No more suffering.
Everything is just…empty…

Toben

How is this my life? He orders me to resume kneeling by her bed so I can see the terrible things he does to her drugged-up body. While he takes a break to smoke a cigarette, he makes me hit her with a whip. He says it's called a cat o' nine tails and he shows me how to use it. She reminds me of our rag dolls the way her limbs are hanging limp.

The air is sticky with the smell of sweat and when he finally finishes, he locks me back up so he can take a shower. Thinking about how her skin busted apart when I hit her, sends chills up my spine. I actually inflicted damage on her, she has a bloodied back because of my actions. Her scarlet, still, little body is lying on her sheets. We're going to have to wash them tonight.

Logan emerges from the bathroom, wearing his suit once again, and walks straight to my cage to let me out. Relief floods me. He isn't going to keep me in here this week.

"You did extremely well today, Toben." He hands me a little clear bag with bright colored chewy candies inside. "I would never have thought of having a boy, if your father wouldn't have offered you up as an option, but this is going to be fun."

I want to shove this bag down his throat and laugh as he chokes. I wish I could take that five core and rape him with it, see how he likes it.

"When she awakes, I want you to salt her wounds. She will cry and it will hurt. No matter, the salt will clean the cuts and help them heal." He raises his eyebrow at me. "I will know if you do not obey, do you understand?"

FUCK YOU!

"Yes, Logan."

He gives me a nod and hands me another bag of the candies. "Give these to Lotus when she becomes lucid. Although, my suggestion would be to wait until after you have salted her, then you can use it as a reward for her cooperation…if you so choose."

I hate the sound of his voice and the way he talks. I hate his hazel eyes and how they almost glow. I hate the way he acts so superior. I hate the way he smells.

Like cinnamon and cigarettes.

I've never felt so much loathing for a person, not even my dad, and I can't wait till I'm big enough to stop him. When that day comes, he will pay, and he will do it with his blood.

"Next time, we'll all go together, tonight though, I have an unavoidable engagement." He lays out everything I'll need to inject myself. "You can get yourself off now, or you can wait until Tavin wakes and she can give it to you."

I don't understand any of this. What's the point of giving us drugs?

It may be risky to ask, but I do it anyway. "Why the heroin, Logan?"

Holding out his hand, he gestures to the table. "Once you try it, my plaything, you will know."

He hoists the bag over his shoulder, ascends the stairs, and leaves us to our next week of confinement. At least I'm free of the cage.

I've heard at the D.A.R.E. rallies at school how bad heroin is. It's supposed to be the worst one out there, and yet, my dad doesn't look like the strung-out junkies they show you, and Logan definitely doesn't. I've never heard my dad talk about loving anything, besides my mother and heroin. He brings whores home and I know for a fact he's been fucking Tavin's mom. He just doesn't give a shit about any of them. Heroin though, that he cares about. He said it makes all his pain and suffering disappear into a cloud. I never asked Tavin what it was like. Now I wish I would have so I know what to expect. Still, having all my pain and suffering disappear into anything sounds pretty good to me. I don't want to ask her to do it for me, and she's already messed up, so we might as well be high together.

After spraying down the table and washing my hands, I prepare the rig like he showed us. I'm not sure how much to use, he didn't give me a lot though and I doubt he would run the risk of me overdosing, so I pour it all in the spoon. After a little mixing, a *flick* of the lighter, a tied tourniquet, and a full needle, I'm about to shoot up for the first time.

I sit down on Tavin's bed, next to her. Once the needle pierces my skin and enters my vein, I untie myself, take a deep breath and push down.

POW!

I'm gonna be sick...

WHOOSH!
Relief...
BOOM!
Beautiful...
I am free...

CHAPTER SIX
Katie

LAST NIGHT WAS THE MOST INTENSE, INCREDIBLE thing I have ever felt. I don't know if I've ever known peace like that. I was truly safe and indestructible. Tavin and I lay there, for I have no idea how long, and ran our fingers along each other's skin while smiling at each other. It felt so amazing. In those hours, we were genuinely happy:

"Mmmm, Toben, your fingers feel like butterfly wings."
Her skin is softer than clouds. "You are so beautiful."
"So are you. If I fell into your eyes I would never find the way out."
"I love you, Tavin."
"I love you, too."

This morning I feel fine, besides my back. I expected a headache, a hangover, or something. The worst is the pain from the five-core, and I have a week out of the cage to heal from that. I wonder if he plans to get us high every week. It would be great to have something to look forward to from his hellish visits.

I never salted her last night, so I know I have to today.

I finish my shower, and when I walk out of the bathroom, she's lying on her bed, tapping her foot to the Red Hot Chili Peppers.

I sit down next to her as I towel dry my hair. "Logan said I need to clean your cuts."

"I showered this morning, they're clean."

I shake my head. "No, we need to put salt on them. Come on, let's get it over with." Grabbing a bottle of water from the fridge, I take her hand and lead her into the bathroom. I give her a towel to cover up with and take off her shirt to get full access to her back. Mixing the salt and water to make a paste, I apply it to a small cut with my clean fingers.

Within seconds, her back bows. "Take it off! It hurts, Toben! Please!"

She tries to stretch her arms behind her to reach it. I need her to calm down. We have a lot of marks to go and it's going to take forever at this rate. "I'm sorry, I have to."

I reach for her and she pushes me away. "No!"

He said he will be able to tell if I don't salt her and it will be even worse if we disobey.

"Tavin! Stop! I don't want to do this either, but he said we have to."

"No, please, it burns! Don't make me."

Her violet eyes are shiny and wet as she pleads. I can't risk his wrath. I would much rather her be salted by me than be punished by him for disobeying. I don't want to get angry with her, it's just sometimes the only way to get things through her head.

"Goddamn it, Tavin. He will do way worse than this if you don't let me. Now, lie down on your stomach!" She narrows her eyes, while still doing what I tell her. She lies across the bathroom rug and looks up at me with tears. "Tuck your arms under your body so you don't try to touch it."

Sliding her arms beneath her, she takes a deep breath

as I continue with the next gash. I decide to start with the bigger and deeper ones to get them over with first. When the mixture soaks into the rips in her flesh, she howls out and tries to lift off the floor. I have to keep her down so I push my hand between her shoulder blades, keeping her against the linoleum, and pin her legs with my knee.

"He's not even here, Toben!"

As fast as I am able, I rub as much salt on as many cuts as I can before I just can't do it anymore. I finish most of them, though.

She pushes off the floor and lunges at me, hitting my arm with the hand not holding up the towel. It isn't hard, but she's never hit me before.

"Do I get to put that stuff on your cuts now?!"

I will absolutely let her if it makes her feel better. Lifting my shirt over my head, I turn around. "I don't want to do any of this, Tavin. I'm just trying to protect you."

I hear her sigh. "I know, Tobe, I'm just…" Confused, scared, hurt… I turn back around to look at her and she looks down at her feet. "I'm sorry I hit you."

Wrapping my arms around her, I hug her. "Believe me, I get it, you don't ever have to apologize to me."

I give her the candies and we eat them in the window well, while we pretend we can feel the sun.

⌒

Logan's next visit is just as horrifying as the others. He makes good on his promise to teach her to be quiet. He uses something he calls a scold's bridle. It's a metal helmet that encases her entire head. It has a flat bar attached with metal spikes, that fits into her mouth. As long as she doesn't move her tongue, she's okay, until he beats and rapes her, then her screams cause the spikes to pierce it.

She can't talk for days and she doesn't need to, for me to

know that she's pissed. I slipped up and called him a 'dement-
ed chomo' which got me back inside the cage. I made her even
madder when I laughed after reading the note she wrote me.

What's a cho mow?

I told her it meant child molester, but she didn't know
what a molester was. I just assured her that Logan was one.

He had been saying the most disgusting, terrible things
to her and I couldn't listen to it anymore. I'm surprised that
he still let me get high with them, first. I didn't get any candy,
though. That night, the nightmares started. She screamed my
name, but I couldn't do a damn thing about it besides try to
wake her by calling for her.

We settle into a routine of sorts and even though I try
not to, I often think about Christopher and where he thinks I
went. I wish I could have at least said goodbye. I miss school
sometimes and I definitely miss him, but most of the time
I just try to stay out of the cage. As long as I'm able to sleep
next to Tavin, she doesn't have bad dreams.

Every visit he makes her wear the scold's bridle for at
least a small period of time, though her screams and wails
are definitely decreasing with each visit.

While I still have to salt her wounds, I only do the large
ones. She doesn't fight him much anymore. We just try to get
through till the end of the playdate.

Once a week, candy and heroin bring color and joy to
our dark, twisted, melancholy lives. I hate and despise Logan,
but when he arrives, he brings with him an escape. An escape
where Tavin and I can be...*free*.

Six months later—September, 2002

Tavin

His arms are around my waist and his shallow breathing is one of my favorite sounds. He looks so much happier when he's sleeping, kind of like when he's high. I run my fingers through his hair, and I can't believe how long it's gotten. According to our calendar, we've been Logan's toys for six months. The needle temporarily hides the fear and it feels like we're a family in those moments, existing together in another world. He doesn't ever play with me after he shoots up. Everything is perfect as soon as it hits our veins.

I'm able to slip out of bed without waking Toben, to go to the bathroom. When I look in the mirror, I stick out my tongue and it's lined with little holes. Even though he barely makes me wear the mask anymore, all it takes is one time to make the holes. I'm able to stay quiet most of the time, sometimes though, the pain is too much and I just can't contain my screams.

He never hits my face. He says that and between my legs are the only things about me that aren't completely repulsive, so he wants to keep them nice. The lotus is almost completely healed now and is light pink. Cuts, bruises, gashes, and welts are all over my body.

Disgusting, dirty body.

Toben opens the bathroom door and rubs his eyes. When he looks up, we make eye contact in the mirror and smile at each other. He brushes his teeth and takes a shower while I eat breakfast. He has me read the letter from his mom. I don't tell him that I'm not even reading it anymore, I memorized it.

We dance together. He was hesitant at first, but now he always dances with me. We listen to each other's music and

I am starting to see why he likes the screaming. Sometimes I want to scream, too.

A few months ago, he wrote me a lullaby and now, as his voice gives life to the melody, his eyes droop as he sings himself to sleep. I lie there with him for a long time. I'm not tired, so I get up to sit in the window well and try to hear the birds or the cars. When I'm alone like this, I think about Logan. He scares and confuses me and I hate the way he makes me feel. I am cleaner than I have ever been in my entire life, and I still can't scrub away the grimy feeling. I take a lot of showers as hot as I can stand them, and it's still there.

I didn't know I was so ugly before. Daddy always said that I was stupid and ugly, but he was always mean. If Logan says it though, it must be true.

Ugly, repulsive cunt.

It seems so horrible when it's happening and I hate him. Then I think about not having to feel hungry or scared when he's not here. At least I have Toben, though. Logan can be so nice, but then he'll say things that I don't always understand, and what I do understand makes my stomach hurt.

"Tavin! Oh my God, what are you doing?!"

I jump at Toben's surprise appearance as he materializes by the window. I follow his gaze down to my fingers. They are all bloody and scraped up. Had I done that?

"I-I didn't mean to."

He wraps one of his hands around mine. "Come on. Let's go clean it." Helping me out of the window, he takes me to the bathroom. The water stings. It's also familiar and kind of feels good. When he's done, he pats it dry.

"There, how is that?"

I nod and smile as he kisses each finger.

He says that I know how to read pretty well, so I now need to know math.

I hate math! Reading is much more fun and easy. I know

how to count and I can add okay I guess, but division is hard. Toben always plays make believe with me if I try though, so I work hard to understand.

He always wants to talk about things and I really don't. I'm there, I know what happens. I don't need to talk about it. I can tell it makes him feel better though, so I let him.

"I don't know, Tav, I just don't think this is the first time he's done something like this. That stuff he always says about you being his 'favorite toy' or when he told me that he never would have considered me because I'm a boy."

For some reason, that makes me think of what Kyle had said.

"Kyle told me on Acclimation Day, if I was his he would have de-fleshed my fingers. Do you think he has playthings too?"

Scrunching his eyebrows, he asks, "Why didn't you tell me that?"

"I don't know, I never thought about it." I swing my feet off and spring from our bed. "Get up, I want to draw."

He does what I ask, still, I can tell his mind is working something around. He says the same thing he's said a gazillion times before. "We have to get out of here."

I respond the same way I have a gazillion times before. "Where would we go? Even if we are able to find food, a place to sleep, and no bad people get us, what about the police? What if they found us?"

I honestly don't know if I would rather be cold, hungry, and dirty or have Logan do the things he does. At least with Logan, it's only once a week and if I obey I get treats. I like the heroin and I'm happy that it doesn't make me like Mommy or Daddy. They must have just been mean on their own whether they were using or not, because it sure does make me feel happy.

"Yeah, yeah, I know, I just don't think I can handle many

more times of watching him say and do those things to you... Does it still hurt?"

I nod even though I don't want to talk about this! He must pick up on that, because after I move our bed out of the way, he lies back down and writes in his lyric book.

After a while, he rolls over so his arm and head are hanging off the bed. He's looking at me upside down and his hair almost touches the floor.

"Wanna listen to Rob Zombie?"

Some of his music I'm not too sure about, but I like Rob Zombie.

"Yeah!"

He pulls out his iPod, and he knows what song I want to hear without me saying it. I sing along with all the words.

"Blood on her skin
Dripping with sin.
Do it again
Living dead girl."

We listen to music while I draw on my wall and he sits next to me on the floor, watching. We both hear the noise and look at each other. It takes us a second to register what it is, but when we do, it's at the same time. Toben's eyes grow wide as he turns off the iPod and throws it in the drawer. I hurry to move our bed in front of the drawing and we scramble over each other to get into our kneeling positions.

Logan was just here two days ago, what is he doing back already? I'm supposed to get a whole week!

"Hello, my playthings."

"Hello, Logan."

He doesn't have the black bag with him today. In fact, he isn't carrying anything and he's wearing his suit. That's a very good sign. After three large steps, he stands in front of me. Cupping my jaw and running his thumb over my lips he says, "I'm not here to play with you today, Lotus." My chest falls as I slowly exhale and Logan turns to Toben. "Get up, you're coming with me."

He's taking him away?! Why? Where are they going?

Toben obeys and gives me a scared smile as he follows Logan up the stairs. My stomach falls as hot tears pour down my face.

I don't want to be alone...

Toben

What the hell? He's taking me out of the basement? I don't like leaving Tavin alone. I don't want to be away from her. He opens the basement door and I follow him out of the room that has been my confinement for half of a year. As soon as I cross the threshold, he shuts and locks the door. I turn my head to see Tavin's mother passed out on the couch.

Tavin's mom, Lacie...she's a strung-out whore if there ever was one, and the worst excuse for a mother I have ever seen. If I wouldn't have killed my own mom, she never would've let this happen to us. Fathers are usually dicks, but mothers, that's where kids are supposed to get their love.

I hate her mother. She's allowing her own daughter, the one she carried inside of her, to get beaten and raped right beneath her feet. She's a worthless slut. She doesn't deserve Tavin as a daughter.

If she likes getting fucked so much, maybe you should do it with Logan's knife.

The thought is quick and black and I hate that I have it at all.

We walk right out the front door and for the first time

in six months, I'm breathing fresh air as the breeze sweeps across my skin. I hate myself for turning my head to look at my house. I wonder if my dad has ever once even thought about me since I was sold.

"He's gone." Logan comes up beside me and looks toward my house as well. "Took the money and I'm sure never looked back." He gestures to the Benz. "Come now, get in."

My dad bailed out on me. I'm not surprised, so I don't know why I still feel a twinge of betrayal, that he left.

Logan allows me to ride shotgun and my stomach's in knots because I don't know what we're doing, but I do know when it comes to Logan, it's rarely good. He climbs in, his long legs filling up the driver's seat as he starts the car.

It's not until we're on the freeway that he finally speaks.

"I'm going to tell you a little bit about myself." Pushing back his shoulders and rolling his neck, he continues, "I met Kyle in the sixth grade, walking home from school. I always took the long way, through the woods, and one day, I came across a boy crouched down on the ground. I thought nothing of it until I got closer and saw him cutting the wings off of a crow. I had never actually done anything like that. While of course I had daydreamed of it, I'd never acted upon it. I knelt down beside him and he looked up at me, smiling as he handed me the knife with blood covered fingers. Even then he sensed our likeness-that we were the same."

He lights a cigarette and a minute later, he keeps talking. "In the beginning, it was innocent enough, mostly just the mutilation and murder of animals, getting into fights, watching violent porn... until we were seniors in high school. That's when everything changed." Blowing out his drag, smoke fills the car. "Kyle had a ten-year-old sister named Clarissa. He couldn't stand her, in fact, he was repulsed by her. He truly hated her. There was this one night, she wanted to go with us to a party. It was absurd; she was a child. Why would she think she could go to a senior party?" He shakes his head while looking into the rearview mirror. "Kyle had told her no, repeatedly. He even slammed her into the wall to get his point across, and the stupid, little bitch still wouldn't listen. She ended up stowing away in the back of my car, but the red ribbon in her hair made her stand out at the party. Once he spotted her, Kyle snapped. He let his fury take control as he dragged her outside. I thought he was going to throw her in the car, when instead, he pulled her all the way to the tree line. By the time I caught up to them, he had already bloodied her face." He clicks his tongue. "I do wish he hadn't done that, I would have liked to keep it pretty. I just stood watching, simply enjoying the show until his true intentions became clear. I've never been so Goddamn hard in my entire life. I held her down for him and he held her for me. All the while, my eyes kept drifting to that red ribbon. I've always felt it was a sign or symbol of the blood we were destined to spill. Our friendship shifted that night. Together, we destroyed her into a corpse."

Horrified. Repulsed. Disgusted. Terrified. All of the above. I'm sweating, and the way Logan is adjusting himself while he's telling me this is going to make me get sick all over his expensive upholstery. He exhales the smoke from his cigarette before he continues his twisted tale...

"That was my awakening. We wanted-no...*needed*. We needed to do it again. Thus, began the macabre string of dead little girls that were, for all intents and purposes, the embodiment of Clarissa. When I founded Rissa, it was named in her honor. A few years later, while at a company Christmas party of all places, my eyes were drawn to an innocent little angel with curly, blonde hair and blue eyes. She was a stunning creature and I was still so young, I did a poor job of concealing my...fascination. I was confronted shortly after by a man asking if I liked what I saw. I couldn't believe he outright offered her to me, easy as that. I later found out, he was her uncle and was left with the unwanted burden of being her guardian. We came to an agreed upon price and Kyle and I had our first playdate. Little Meagan West, with her framed picture of a Lotus flower above her bed. It stuck in my head so I began calling her 'Lotus'. She was the first one that we didn't kill right away, in fact, we kept her alive for four years. She is the reason I reward you with candy, though the first time was unplanned. I happened to have some cinnamon gummies in my pocket and I gave her one. She was so grateful for such a small gesture. To Kyle's dismay, I brought her a treat every time." He sighs, and if I didn't know better, I'd almost say he looks sad. "She died the night before I married my wife, and six months later I founded the Lotus Candy Company for her. She was our experiment and we found we have very different ways of doing things. After her, we found our own girls and quickly learned that desperation and greed is the magic formula when it comes to purchasing human toys. It's much safer as well, no missing person reports. And as far as legal documentation goes, they are all enrolled at River Forge Academy." He turns to smirk at me. "So are you." The *click, click, click* of his blinker is going to drive me fucking insane. "Within a couple years of obtaining Meagan, we were introduced to the world of heroin and it didn't take long to learn that when adding drug addicts to the equation, it became almost too easy. I keep them until they expire, dispose of them, then purchase another."

He's amused as hell with himself while he acts as if he is telling me the story of Peter fucking Rabbit. He's flat out admitting to me that he's going to kill Tavin, regardless. I don't know why he's telling me all this, but it makes me even more anxious to see where he's taking me.

I wish I was back in the basement.

He startles me when he speaks because I had hoped his

story was over. "It was by a stroke of luck that I found you and Tavin. Earlier this year, I was visiting the Wentworth plant and was in the bathroom when I overheard Jarod and Brian speaking of you two. Then they mentioned heroin, and I knew it was fate. Once I met her, it was sealed. I propositioned Brian for her and Jarod practically dropped to his knees begging me to take you. You didn't cost much and I'm confident you will be more than worth the investment. The idea of having an apprentice excites me. God knows my son is too big of a fucking faggot." He looks at me and tilts his head to the side. "You're more like how I imagined my son would be."

That's not a compliment, you sick freak!

"I'm a very busy man, so I can only comfortably keep two Lotus' at a time. I took you and Tavin on a little earlier than anticipated because I couldn't wait. She's fascinating, isn't she?"

He eyes me, actually expecting me to respond. "Yes, Logan."

Quirking his brow, he clearly loves making me squirm. "The last six months have been busy for me, though the time has come to decrease it back to two." His head turns toward me as his haunting smile spreads across his face.

"You're about to meet Katie Grace."

He's going to kill a girl tonight and his reasons for bringing me make my blood feel like it could shatter from being frozen.

We pull up to a small, one level, yellow house. It has white trim and a stone pathway that makes it kind of look like a cottage. There's even a picket fence.

"Come along."

As Logan gets the bag from the back seat, I get out of the car and follow him up the path. We climb onto the porch, and before he slides the key into the lock, he frowns at me.

"The rules have not changed, my plaything. Do exactly as I say or Tavin will end up like Katie, sooner rather than later."

"Yes, Logan."

I have to fight to keep back the tears. He's going to kill Tavin when he's done with her. The only thing I can do is delay the inevitable. How long will it be until he considers her 'expired'?

I swear on my pathetic life that he will have to kill me before I will let him do that. The only reason I have stayed compliant is to keep her breathing. Once that's off the table, so is all of my cooperation.

We enter a dark living room and go toward the back, into the kitchen. Nobody appears to be living here. There's furniture, just not any pictures or dishes. I don't see a phone or any electronics, either. Next to the kitchen table is a large rug, and as he pulls it away, I see a cellar door. After unlocking it, he lifts it by the latch and begins his descent down the steps. Shoving my hands into my pockets, I follow him deeper into his distorted reality.

The cellar is a large room consisting of a cot, fridge, toilet, microwave, TV, DVD player, washer, dryer, radio, rack of clothes, and drain with a shower head. Oh, and of course the red headed teenager kneeling before us.

"Good evening, Lotus."

"Good evening, Logan." She doesn't even look at me.

I think she's high school age. She refuses to take her gaze off Logan, and even though her face is hollow and empty, her eyes are on fire.

Logan's hand lands on my shoulder. "This is Toben. He is going to play with us today."

Her eyes flip to me and fill with horror, taking on an instant shine.

"Logan he's…so young."

He walks away from me to comb his fingers through her hair. "Don't worry, he won't be playing in that sense." Moving to stand behind her, he lets his hand trail across her neck. "Do you know what today is, Lotus?"

"Yes, Logan. It's our five-year anniversary."

"That's right."

She has on a spaghetti strap sundress that he rips before leaning forward so I can't see his face. I jump from her scream and when he lifts his head, there's blood covering his mouth and face. He makes a show of swallowing and grins at me with red teeth.

I don't know why I can't hold it down this particular time. Maybe it's my fear from what he just told me, or maybe cannibalism is where my stomach draws the line. Either way, I lose everything I had eaten earlier, with Tavin.

I don't even get it all out before his fist lands against my jaw.

"You fucking, faggot pussy! Hold your shit together." Katie is crying quietly when I hear the unzipping of the bag. "It's about to get a lot worse than that."

From that point on, things get blurry. I don't know if my eyes aren't registering to my brain what's happening or if I just shut down from time to time, because everything is in shards. I remember the sounds of bones cracking, the sizzle of burning flesh, her horrific wails…and all I see is blood. I know I participated in beating her, I simply can't remember actually doing it.

When I begin to gain my focus, I am staring at the first dead body I've ever seen. He really did it. He actually killed her. She is barely recognizable as a person. I want to weep for her, but the sobs are caught in my throat.

My hands.

My hands are dripping, actually dripping with her blood. Something cracks inside me as a howl tears from within and my body shakes with fear and fury. Up to this point, in the back of my mind, I still thought that we might get free of him some day. Now I know the truth. We will never be normal after this and we will never be free.

Logan is standing beneath the stream of water in the shower, ignoring me and my cries. I pass the dead girl to go to the bag and pull out the first sharp thing I see. It's round with little razors coming off of it. Turning, I charge straight for the shower with my eyes set on my sadistic target.

I pull back my arm for momentum, and bring the weapon down to slice at whatever piece of his body I can. He senses me at the exact moment before the blade comes in contact with his side, minimizing the damage I could have inflicted.

He knocks me to the ground and is on top of me instantly, his wet body is dripping water onto my face. While his voice is firm and hard, it's surprisingly not angry.

"I just lost a Lotus and I can tell that she's your first dead body, so I am feeling generous. I want you to be my protégé, Toben. I know this is still difficult for you, but if you will just *give in*, you will see this is all quite fun." He pushes off of me. "Now, clean yourself up, we need to head back."

Slipping the clean T-shirt he brought me, over my head, I watch him stuff the clothes I had been wearing into a garbage bag along with his and Katie's. He picks up the black tool bag, gives her corpse a last glance, and releases a slow breath.

"Come now."

We're just going to leave her here to rot? I quietly cry for her soul as I follow him out. I feel different than I did before I came into this cellar. Someday, that will be Tavin. I don't have any idea how to stop it, I just know I have to. I can't let that happen to her.

It's nearly three hours back to Shadoebox City. The trip back is mostly silent. Pink Floyd plays quietly through the speakers, and I want the needle so bad right now. I don't want to feel this, this…fear. Intense terror. I want to feel peaceful and happy again.

"Logan?" He raises a brow in question and lowers the music, so I continue, "I know this isn't mine and Tavin's day, but…can I get a fix when we get back to the basement?"

Nodding, he exhales his cigarette smoke. "Under the circumstances, I'll allow it this time. None for Lotus, though."

I choke out the vilest of sentences, "Thank you, Logan."

"Toben!"

Tavin leans over me, yelling. Why is she so upset? I sit up and realize I'm back in the basement lying on our bed.

"Relax, Tav…just come lie with me." She's cute when she's mad, so I smile.

Her skin is alive against mine when she sighs, "You're high."

Beautiful girl…my beautiful shadow girl…she's so incredible…everything is incredible… "Hmmm."

She snuggles up close to me and I think our skin fuses together, as I hear her crying.

"I was so scared that you wouldn't come back. I can't do this alone, Toben, I need you."

"I need you, too."

I kiss her tears and they taste like rain. Her skin smells like almonds. How could I not have seen that beauty is everywhere?

It's in her tears.

It was in Katie's blood.

It's in this sickness growing inside me.

CHAPTER SEVEN
Break

One month later—October, 2002

Tavin

I KEEP THINKING HE HAS TO BE ALMOST DONE. I'M SO tired that if it wasn't for my excitement to celebrate Toben's birthday, I would probably fall asleep. He turned eleven yesterday and we had our own party last night, but we didn't have cake.

Logan has cake.

This is our first playdate in over two weeks. Logan has been out of town and even though it was a really nice break, he's making up for it now. It makes me so mad that he forces me to be quiet when he hurts me. He doesn't want to hear any sounds other than breathing, while he can make all the gross noises he wants. It makes me sick!

And you make him sick, so you're even.

Toben is kneeling on the floor and even though I wish I could look at him, I can't. I have to watch Logan when we play.

Always.

Since the first time he left with Logan last month, something is different with him. It isn't a change in his personality or anything. Sometimes he just checks out. I've had to snap my fingers at him on more than one occasion, to get him to hear me. He says all they do is run errands, I just think he isn't telling me something.

I could cry with joy when Logan finishes and cleans up. Well, I could always cry with joy, but today I bounce with anticipation as I kneel, no matter how much my throat hurts from his hands squeezing my neck, and my body drums with a throbbing soreness.

It isn't until he's in the shower that I dare speak. "Do you think the cake's chocolate or vanilla?"

Toben snorts and releases his hands from behind his head. "I wish it was dope flavored."

He's so silly that I giggle. "There's no such thing as heroin cake."

Stretching his arms, he laughs with me. "Well, there should be."

By the time Logan comes out of the shower, we're both correctly kneeling.

"Alright, my playthings, you can get up."

Hurrying as fast as my sore body will allow, I go to Logan, who is digging in a bag. He lifts a big square box and when he looks at me, his face is soft and his eyes twinkle. Sometimes when he acts like this, I like him.

He raises the box with a grin. "Is this what you've been so excited about, Lotus?"

I hear Toben's foot steps behind me, as I smile back.

"Yes, Logan."

With raised eyebrows, he looks to Toben while still speaking to me. "Well, it's Toben's birthday cake, so it's up to him if he wants to share."

"What do you mean? Of course he does."

I look back at Toben and he has his chin in his hand like he's actually having to think about it!

"Hmmmm, should Tavin get cake?"

I can't believe it!

He starts laughing and waves his hand for Logan to give me the box. I pretend to frown at him as I carry it to the table. Ignoring the sting of the fabric rubbing my cuts, I open it and look inside. There's a cake with white frosting that says, 'Happy 11th Birthday, Toben' in blue letters. Getting a fork and knife, I cut a big ol' piece. It's chocolate! YUM! The piece is half gone before I make it to the bed.

While we eat our cake, Logan gives Toben his birthday presents. Our radio broke a couple weekends ago, so I'm excited that he gets a stereo and a CD.

Logan tells him, "The employee at Sam Goody suggested the band to one of my assistants, when she told him what genre you preferred."

"Slayer?" Toben scrunches his eyebrows as he looks at the case.

Logan shrugs. "Apparently."

He still gives us candy even though we already had cake! Today is cinnamon gummies and Logan says they're his favorite.

"Okay, my playthings, I've stayed much too late already. Lie on the bed and I'll inject you before I leave."

Toben and I are more than capable of doing ourselves up, but I think Logan likes to do it. We face each other and smile. We like to pretend that when we get high, we're actually dead for a few hours and our souls are free to be together without torment.

Logan fades into the shadows as we float away to ecstasy...

My eyes flutter open and I awake to Toben smiling. He seems to do that a little less lately.

"Do you know what today is?"

Stretching my whole body as far as I can, causes me to groan with gratification. Of course I know what today is.

"I met you a year ago."

He rolls onto his back and his hand drapes across his eyes. "I can't believe it."

I cross my arms over his chest before I rest my head on my hands. "Do you wish that you never met me?"

He jerks his hand from his face and his head snaps in my direction. "Why would you ask me that? Of course not." He leans toward me as his hand moves to rub over my hair. "You're the only person on this earth that I love."

"You're the only person that I love, too. I thought I loved Mommy, and now I don't even miss her anymore, so maybe I never did." Tracing my finger along the scar his daddy gave him, I explain why I asked. "It's just…if you didn't know me, then Logan would never have bought you. You would still be going to school, having friends, and sitting on the beach."

His face twists up. "Jesus. Just the idea of you going through this with that rapist fuck all alone makes me want to cut open my chest and rip out my heart. Even if I'd known this was going to happen, it wouldn't have changed a thing."

He makes my body warm. It's not like when you're hot, it's more like my heart is cozy. His fingers twirl my hair and I lift my head toward him, placing a kiss to his lips. He smiles his ornery grin and his cheeks pink. Pushing myself off the bed, I skip to the fridge. We saved the last two pieces of his birthday cake for today and I'm so excited to eat it.

"Do you want to eat the cake for breakfast?"

"Uh, yeah…duh." He laughs to himself when he sits up against the wall.

I return with two forks and two deliciously full plates. Sitting down next to him, I give him his. "Do you think I will ever get a birthday cake?"

His shoulders slump. "Oh jeez, Tav... I..." He shakes his head. "You would have had to have had a birthday since we met, you really don't have any idea when it is?"

I tap my chin. "Once Mommy told me she had to go outside when it was cold to get me food when I was born... I always wondered when she stopped feeding me."

"It was cold? That's all you know?"

I try hard to remember. "Uhhh...oh yeah, she said that she hated seeing all the lights."

He scrunches his nose. "The lights? Like Christmas lights?" I don't know, so I just shrug. Standing up, he goes to the calendar and lifts two pages. "Let's see...What number do you like?"

He always says such interesting things. I've never thought of having a favorite number. I have a favorite color though. It's purple! After thinking about it for a minute, I decide on one.

"I think I like eight." I don't tell him it's because his birthday is on the eighth, even though I think he knows.

He grins. "The eighth it is, then. Tavin Winters... Hey! Your last name is Winters and you were born in the winter. That's neat." He leans down to get a pen from the night stand and draws on the calendar. "Your birthday is now December eighth. Do you think that you'll be turning eleven or twelve?"

I really don't know because Mommy and Daddy would go back and forth, I just know I want to be the same age as Toben.

"Eleven."

I skip to the calendar to see what he's written.

Tavin's 11th Birthday.

Bubbles in my tummy and flips in my heart are going to make it so hard to wait that long! I've never celebrated a birthday before!

I try not to focus on my birthday because today is about

us, not just me. I think that I might cry when Toben hands me a small box wrapped in sparkly, blue paper. I almost don't want to open it because it's so lovely with the big, pink bow. He hid it under the stairs without me even knowing. He's so sneaky.

He throws his arms in the air. "Happy Friendiversary!"

"How did you do this?" Tears make my voice sound weird. "I didn't get you anything." How selfish of me! I should have drawn him a picture or something.

He puts his arms around me. "Oh, come on, don't get sad, and I cheated anyway. I had help from Logan." He smiles when I look up at him. "Besides, all I need is you." He gestures to the pretty package. "Open it."

I rip open the paper to find a wooden box with a black metal latch. When I lift the latch, my breath snags because I am looking at the most beautiful doll in the world. Her hair is brown and is in ringlets tied off with pink bows. Her pink dress has a ton of ruffles and her skin is made of porcelain. Her blue eyes are looking right at me and she's so small that she can fit in the palm of my hand. I've never had anything like this before and I love her so much!

"Toben, she's beautiful! Thank you!" I wrap my arms around him tight while he picks me up and twirls me around.

I love when he does that.

Five months later—March, 2003

Toben

I stare at the blood still under my fingernails, from our play-date with Morgan, Logan's remaining Lotus, and look out the window of the plane. One thing that I've learned while doing this, is that Logan favors Tavin immensely. He still gives Morgan everything he gives us and he doesn't touch her face, he just isn't affectionate with her the way he is with Tav. You wouldn't necessarily think that would be a good thing, but in this case, it definitely is.

Morgan is fourteen and still hasn't mastered keeping quiet, like Tavin has. She screamed so loud I thought for sure my eardrums would break, while I ran the sander across her shoulders.

There was so much blood.

He doesn't make Tavin bleed as bad as Morgan either. I hate it when she begs, I can't do anything for her and even if I could, my only priority is Tavin. I still can't believe I screamed at her.

"Shut the fuck up, Morgan!"

Logan thought that was funny, apparently, because I won't ever forget the way he looked, standing there laughing while he smoked a cigarette, while his hand was still wet with her blood.

I hate his smug smirk. "Gets annoying as hell, doesn't it?"

"Yes, Logan."

I hate myself for actually meaning it.

Even though we have to fly to get to Morgan, we're only on his plane for a total of three hours, there and back. I had never been on a plane before being on Logan's jets and the one we are on today is the most elaborate, by far. This thing is ridiculous. It's bigger than any house I have ever seen. There are multiple bedrooms, bathrooms, a conference room, a kitchen, a freaking theatre room, and that's just what I've seen so far. Tavin would lose it if she saw this.

Logan told me that Tavin isn't to know about the other girls, and to be honest, I don't know if I would tell her anyway. I don't want her to know what I do to Morgan. I thank whatever power is out there, that he doesn't make me do anything sexual to her, but I still mutilate her, and tear her apart, body and soul.

"Come now, sit with me, Plaything." He pulls a drag off his cigarette and I obey as I sit across from him in one of the comfiest chairs in the galaxy. I adjust my beanie and cross my arms as he carries on. "I'm quite pleased with your progress, you have proved to be more entertaining than I could have foreseen."

Pulling another Marlboro from his pack, he holds it out for me and nods in response to my hitched brow. I shrug and take it along with the lighter. I've only smoked once in my life. Christopher gave it to me and I just remember a lot of coughing. For the millionth time, I wonder how he is. We would be in middle school now.

Flick, light, inhale.

Even while I'm coughing, it isn't as bad as I remember.

"In the spirit of our one year tomorrow, I'm going to allow you a single question. You can ask anything without repercussion." Yeah, I don't trust this. I stay silent, so he asks, "Is there nothing that you'd like to know?"

Oh, there is a shit ton I would like to know. It all falls out in a mess as I blurt my word-vomit.

"Why do you do this? You're filthy rich and can have any woman you want. Why destroy, kill, and rape children? That's right asshole, I said 'rape' not fucking play. How do you not see that you're a morbid, disturbed, sick freak?"

His nails are probably digging holes into the perfect upholstery. "That's enough."

It isn't near enough, it will never be enough.

My voice raises as I yell, "How can you look at Tavin, at her gorgeous eyes, and do the things you do to her? Say the things you say? She's a little girl! How can you feel nothing?"

He flies out of his chair, and burning hazel is all I see. I crouch down, trying to get deeper into the chair.

"IT'S THE ONLY TIME I FEEL SOMETHING!"

His voice vibrates off the walls and into me. His composure has slipped and it's terrifying. He looks as though he's about to rip my throat out, when he moves back to his seat. He rolls his neck and takes a drag.

He's back in control now with his voice returning to its slow pace. "Their innocence is a drug. Their perfect, soft little bodies breaking beneath my grasp is better than any heroin. While the needle numbs the numbness, my Lotus'..." Closing his eyes for a moment, a groan rolls from his mouth. "They are little souls in the palm of my hand. I am their God-their maker. Their immaculate blood is the only way to sate the hunger. It's *only* through them that I feel alive."

"Why are you like this? What made you this way?"

There are times I feel myself becoming comfortable, and then I get a reminder like this one and the terror envelops me again.

"I've been a living corpse since the day they ripped me from my mother's cunt."

Inhale. Exhale. Huh, I'm not coughing anymore.

"I do not love my children and I do not love my wife, they simply decorate the façade. Nothing made me like this, Plaything. It is simply who I am." Relaxing his body, he blows out his last drag and puts out the Marlboro. "Sharing this with Kyle is the closest thing to a friendship that I will ever have, and teaching you is the closest thing to feeling like a father, that I will ever experience."

Am I supposed to feel bad for him? Yeah well, fuck you, Logan. I finish my cigarette as we fly in silence and I can't wait to get back to Tav. She's the only thing that keeps me sane. That keeps me...Toben. I already know I earned another night in the cage, and she'll be pissed about it, but he'll let me out tomorrow.

It's our anniversary, after all.

Four months later—July, 2003

"...Eighteen, nineteen, twenty! Ready or not, here I come!"

Tavin's voice has been sounding a little strained lately. I'm in her closet and she has to find me within three tries or I win. While we're too old for hide and seek, our entertainment options are somewhat limited and a person can only watch so much TV.

The light shines over me and I see the silhouette of her hands on her hips.

"The closet? Are you even trying?"

I crawl out. "There are five places to hide in this basement, so give me a break."

She huffs. "What do you want to do now?"

"How about smoke more of that weed Logan left us?"

Clapping her hands together, she says, "Okay!"

She really likes pot, it lets her relax and she smiles more.

As we pass the joint back and forth, I sing her our lullaby and she leans in close. I like her close.

I look at the clock.

"Fuck."

"What?"

"Logan will be here any minute to run errands." I tell that lie so often it's automatic. I feel cold as her warmth leaves with her, when she gets off the bed.

"I hate errands," she grumbles, and her head does its little jerk, while heading to the fridge.

Right on cue, we hear the basement door unlock and we both sprint to kneeling.

He quietly strolls up to Tavin and runs his fingertips along her body and kisses her head.

"Come now, Plaything."

I wink at Tavin and I follow him up the stairs.

⌇

I've been smoking quite a bit lately. I like it, and if it bothers Tavin, she hasn't said anything. The taste of tobacco coats my tongue as I look out over all the little buildings on the ground, and the jet engine lulls me into my thoughts.

I know I'm changing when it comes to Morgan. I don't want to hurt her, it just doesn't bother me as much as it used to. She drives me mad. She's been with Logan since before me and Tavin, and she still doesn't do what is expected of her.

"Please, Toben! Please, I know you don't want this! Please, stop!" Her screams are like a drill in my spine.

"Fucking Christ, Morgan! I swear to God, if you don't. Shut. The. Fuck. Up. I will cut your tongue out myself!"

Logan throws his head back and laughs. "Oh, Plaything, you are exquisite, but no. No, you won't."

Logan's voice snaps me back to the jet.

"I have a surprise for you, come here."

Sitting next to him, I see a tray with three powdered white lines. I've seen Scarface, I know what cocaine is. He sticks a rolled up hundred in a nostril, and with a harsh inhale, one of the lines disappears. The second line is gone in the same fashion. He sniffs and rubs his nose before handing me the hundred.

Leaning down, I inhale deeply as a jolt runs through my body like lightning.

"Whoa!"

He laughs and smiles at me. This is completely different from the weed or the heroin. I can do anything I set my mind to. I want to have fun, I want to blare the radio and dance with Tavin until we can't stand anymore. I grin back at Logan. I still hate the prick, I just feel so damn good.

Time flies forward and we're back home quickly. When we arrive at the house, the living room is empty. Usually at least one of her parents is out here strung out.

On the way down the stairs, I notice Tavin isn't kneeling. Shit! Hopefully, she's in the bathroom. My eyes land on the heap in the bed and I try to stomp louder to wake her up.

"Lotus, kneel!"

Logan screams and I keep expecting her to fly out of the bed, yet she still doesn't move. This isn't good. He'll make her pay for this, and me as well.

"KNEEL!"

A small shift in the blankets lets me know she has heard him, so something's wrong. My heart starts to pound so loud I can feel it in my wrist. I turn to warn Logan, and he's already storming to her bed, ripping off the blanket. He is in my way so that's all I can see.

His voice takes on an almost compassionate tone. Not something often heard from him. "Oh, Lotus… What happened?"

Making my way around him, I see what is affecting his demeanor. She's beaten to a bloody pulp. Logan's question had to have been rhetorical, because it's obvious who did this.

"Daddy." Her voice is barely understandable.

Her father has never hurt her this bad, at least not since I've known her. Depending on how you look at it, not even Logan has abused her to this degree. While he will cut, burn, rape and beat her, she's always able to move after, even if it is strained at times.

Then there's her face. Logan has never once hit her face, and my beautiful Tavin is completely unrecognizable. He leans over her, tenderly running his hand along her head, and places his mouth next to her ear. He whispers, and I still hear him clear as day.

"He will suffer, Lotus."

When he turns, his hard face has glowing eyes, a tense jaw, and straining features. I get a thrill at the fantasy of what he will do to Brian. I go to Tavin, lightly kiss her temple, and whisper, "I'll be right back." I stand behind a fuming Logan, drop to my knees, and lace my fingers behind my head. Submission is always the way to go if you want something from Logan James. When he spins around, he almost trips over me when I blurt, "Please, let me help. Whatever you do, I want to help."

He exhales through his nostrils. "I have a lot to consider, and I will take your request into account. Nevertheless, nothing can be resolved this evening." Rolling his neck, he says, "She needs a fix."

I hear him pounding up the stairs while I crawl into bed with her. Barely touching her face and hair with my fingertips, I'm able to really see her. Her nose is cut, her eyes are swollen shut, her lip is busted, her neck is red, and I can't even imagine what the bruises will look like in the morning. What the hell was he thinking? Does he just think Logan won't mind? I can't wait to finally hear him beg for death.

She's not able to open her eyes to look at me and the poor thing isn't even able to cry, so all she can manage are the saddest little whimpers I've ever heard.

"I'm so sorry that I wasn't here." I haven't cried in a while. I officially am now, though. "You'll be alright, Tav. I'll take care of you." I have the fear that Logan won't want her anymore because of her face. What if he decides to kill her before she expires? I can't think like that right now. "Just hang on, in just a couple minutes you will be free of all this. You're going to sleep on a rainbow while the fairies dance around and sprinkle you with their dust." She moans and tries to move. "Shhh, relax." I wish Logan would hurry.

He finally returns and has her fixed up right quick. Her poor body is finally getting much needed relief.

"Is she going to be okay?"

His nod is what I need, to exhale. "She will heal. Our playdate is cancelled for tomorrow and we probably won't play for quite a few weeks." That surprises me. I know he's mad about her face, I just never thought he would let it interfere with his activities. As if hearing my silent question, he adds, "These wounds are not from me. I'm not the one who broke her, this time. If I continue to hurt her, then I won't know which marks are mine for weeks. They should all be fucking mine." He irately shakes his head. "I want beauty among my destruction, and he completely fucked up her face. I have no idea how long that will take to heal."

He starts putting away the works and I sit up. Watching him cook the smack makes me want it terribly.

"Logan? Can I have some?"

He continues without pause. "No, Plaything, you need to keep an eye on her. Besides, your limit is twice a week and you've already had that."

"What are you going to do to him?"

While pocketing the little bag, he releases an irritated breath. "I don't know, Toben. I'm not going to kill him, though nothing would pleasure me more at the moment."

"Why not?!" I yell at him. He'll kill innocent girls, but not someone deserving of his wrath.

His eyes flash and that's never good.

"Kneel."

I do, and he glides to the corner of the room where he keeps a couple tools for occasions such as this. He chooses the flagrum. He modified it from its original version and actually made it less terrifying. Initially, it had little shards of glass and bone sticking out of pieces of lead at the end of each strap. Since he doesn't want to rip our backs completely off, he replaced them with little cast iron balls no bigger than a dime. While it won't cut me, it will bruise the shit out of me and it hurts like hell.

"Do not ever raise your voice to me again, do you understand?"

"Yes, Logan."

I can see his shiny black shoes coming toward me and as soon as they disappear from my sight, I hear the inevitable *whoosh*. The hard thud rolls over me and melts into steady, powerful anguish. While I may not be as quiet as Tavin, that doesn't mean I scream and cry like Morgan, either. I let out more of a growl than a yell and right myself, preparing for the next blow. He hits me two more times and it's becoming increasingly more difficult to get back up.

"Kneel." Once I am in position, he barks. "Get up." With a groan, I push myself to my feet. "I don't want an investigation anywhere near this house, but he knew the consequences if he ever came near her again. I won't kill him, however, I will cause him great pain." He returns the flagrum to the corner. "Don't let her move around too much and try to keep her comfortable. Remember to call me if anything worrisome happens."

"Yes, Logan."

Once he's gone, I lie down next to her. It's oddly a relief to know my heart can still break.

CHAPTER EIGHT
life

Tavin

"I KNOW, TAV, BUT YOU STILL NEED WATER. I PROMISE it'll make you feel better," Toben tells me.

It's almost been a week since Dadd-Brian came down here. He isn't my daddy and Lacie isn't my mommy, so I need to stop calling them that. I don't have a mommy and daddy anymore. I have Toben and Logan. Last week when he showed up for our playdate, he didn't do a single thing to me. He didn't even make me kneel! He just looked me over and we all got high together. It was wonderful. He even gave me a treat. It wasn't candy because it would be hard for me to eat. It was cherry cola and it was so delicious.

My throat is dry and it burns when I drink the water. I know Toben is right though, so I allow the cool liquid to trickle down. I'm able to move around, even though my whole body hurts no matter what I do. Logan says that just because my face is ugly now, it doesn't mean it will stay this way forever. If it means he won't touch me anymore, then I hope it does stay forever.

"There, now next time won't be so bad." I test his theory and take another drink. He's right. I didn't know I was so thirsty. He lifts my chin, inspecting my face just as he does every day. "Oh yeah, you're definitely healing up well." My expression must have told him everything because his shoulders sag. "You don't want it to get better."

"If my face stays ugly then he won't … *fuck* me."

Twisting his features, he barks at me, "Tavin! Don't talk like that!"

"Why not? You and Logan do!"

He rubs the back of his neck and shakes his head. "Jeez, I know, but coming from you it's just…weird."

I frown at him. It makes me mad that he thinks I'm such a little kid. For all we know, I could be older than him!

"I'm not a baby."

"I know you're not a baby. I'm sorry, you're right, you can talk any way you want."

Good, that's all I wanted him to say. I have to pee so I push myself off the bed. I'm still weak and my arms shake with my struggle.

"Hey, what are you doing?"

"I have to potty."

He gets up and helps me like he has every time I have had to go to the bathroom, since this happened. The first day was the worst because he had to carry me and hold me on the toilet so I wouldn't fall. His hand is on my waist to guide me, even though I don't think I need it. When we get inside, he begins to lift my dress and I stop him.

"I can do it myself now."

He nods and lets me do everything, while he still stands right next to me. After I wash my hands, he opens the bathroom door and I see Logan is sitting on our bed.

He's holding a stack of clothes as he rises and glides toward us, his gaze is on Toben. "Help her into her kneel position and then assume your own."

Logan heads toward the bathroom and before he closes

the door, Toben responds, "Yes, Logan."

Toben lowers me to the floor and is barely in position when the bathroom door opens again. Logan is dressed in his play clothes?! It's not even my day! He crouches down in front of me, pats my hair, and kisses my forehead before picking me up and carrying me up the stairs.

"Come now, Plaything."

Toben hurries behind us and I smile at him over Logan's shoulder. I haven't been upstairs in almost a year and a half, so I hope he's going to take me outside! Whenever he lets us sit in the window well, the hot sun feels amazing. I love summer, even if Toben hates it.

When Logan opens the basement door, I turn my head around to see my m-Lacie on the couch. It's strange, I haven't thought much about her, and now that I see her, I want her to have missed me. She doesn't though, she doesn't even smile at me as Logan carries me toward her.

"Get off the couch, cum dump, and go get Brian."

She sucks in her cheeks as she obeys him, and he lies me down. Moments later, I hear Brian screaming at her before he stomps down the stairs into the living room. She's following him and Logan points as he yells at her. "Lacie, get the fuck out of here or you'll become an unwilling participant." She doesn't argue as she vanishes back down the hall.

He towers over Brian as his arm gestures toward me. "Do you have an explanation for this?"

Snarling his lip, Brian rolls his shoulders back. "This is my house and that's my kid, so if I want to beat her to death, that's my prerogative."

He's never called me his kid before. I have always hated him, but my heart flips.

The vein in Logan's neck pops out as he reaches out and wraps his hand around Brian's throat, forcing him to his knees. "Did you think the five hundred thousand dollars I paid you was because I felt generous? SHE IS MY MOTHERFUCKING PROPERTY! My instructions were crystal clear. You not only played with my toy without my consent, you broke her, and now I won't be able to play with her for weeks." He releases his grip and while Brian gasps and chokes, he punches him in the face. Logan stands and turns his head enough that I can see his profile while he lights his cigarette.

"Toben?"

"Yes, Logan?"

Logan stalks around Brian, who's spitting blood on the floor. "Pick a tool and have fun."

"Yes, Logan!"

Toben's being more than compliant, he's...*excited*.

Bouncing to the black bag in the corner, Toben digs through it and settles on a pair of pliers. Marching up to Logan, he cranes his neck and looks up at him.

"I remember reading in a Steven King novel, once, about a woman getting her fingernails pulled out. I've always been curious about it. Can I try it?"

How can he be so enthusiastic about this? Even though I know he hates Brian, I never really thought he would be able to do any of those things he talked about.

Toben's body vibrates in anticipation as Logan nods and says, "Only do a couple of them, though."

Brian begs and apologizes for hurting me, as Toben backhands him across the face with the pliers. He sits down on his stomach and his hair touches Brian's face as he leans over him and grins.

"I have dreamt about this."

I've never seen Toben this way before. The tool is momentarily forgotten on Brian's chest while he grips his hair and jerks his head toward me. When Toben looks up at me, I am stilled by the deep shade of darkness in his eyes as they burn into mine.

"This is for her."

Brian's screams and pleas are a steady constant for the next hour until he finally passes out. When this began, it scared me to see Toben acting this way. He laughs at Brian's cries and Logan smiles in approval. As it continues though, Toben yells at him all the things he knows he did to me. I remember how horrible Brian was, he never once was kind. I remember all the beatings, the hate, the fear, and Mr. Tickles. My poor Mr. Tickles. I decide Brian deserves everything he's getting. They're doing this for me. I love Toben so much, I'm going to cover his face in kisses and give him big hugs when Logan leaves.

As they finish, Logan cleans his tools as Toben walks over to me, smeared with blood. Crouching down in front of the couch, he smiles and takes my hand.

"I guarantee he'll never come near you again."

He leans forward and kisses me, right in front of Logan. We kiss sometimes when we are alone, never in front of him, though. I'm surprised he doesn't say anything. In fact, he smiles at us.

As Logan puts away the last of his tools, he closes his bag and hollers, "Lacie, get your gaping cunt out here!"

She's back in the living room so quickly, I bet she never even went upstairs.

"Oh my God!" She runs over to Brian and drops to her knees to lift his head into her lap. "Is he going to be okay?"

"He'll live. As long as he keeps his mouth shut and stays away from Lotus." He grabs Brian's feet. "Remind him when he wakes, just because I don't want to be investigated, doesn't mean I fear it. I am untouchable and it would be in his best interest to not forget it. Now, where do you want him so I can clean his rank blood off of the floor?"

She glares at him and says, "In our bedroom."

They all three carry him into the hallway and up the stairs. For some reason, I have the feeling that this will be the last time I'll ever see the people who used to be my parents.

When Logan and Toben return to the living room, the sight of them covered in blood is so beautiful that I wish I could take a picture. I would save it with the one of me and Toben, on The Walk.

I look around my living room as they clean up the floor, I don't know if I will see it again, either. I don't like to think about Logan's threats to kill me. I like to not believe him. I imagine that maybe he's started to love me, but then I remind myself that he could never love someone so filthy and gross.

You are a very disgusting girl.

A jolt of pain takes me out of my thoughts. I'm being lifted into the air by Logan, as he carries me back to the basement. He takes me into the bathroom after snapping, "Kneel" at Toben.

Taking off my clothes, he puts me in the shower as he turns on the water and undresses himself. He doesn't touch me in the bad way, he just washes our bodies free of the blood and grime.

Once we are both clean, he wraps me in a warm towel and dries me off before he puts lotion on me.

He whispers, "It rubs the lotion on its skin or else it gets the hose again," before chuckling to himself.

"That's pretty. Is it a poem?"

He lets out a real laugh this time. "No, it's from one of my favorite films."

What the heck is a film? "Oh."

"What's your favorite film, Lotus?"

I shrug my shoulders. Now he will think I am so stupid.

You are stupid. A stupid, nasty, little bitch, and he already knows it.

"I don't know."

Silently, he stands and puts his clothes on. Nice ones this time. I let out a slow breath as he gently slides a dress over my head and I keep my hands on his shoulders for balance as he pulls my panties up my legs. Even though I can walk fine, he still picks me up and puts me to bed.

Kissing my forehead, he whispers, "Heal quickly, Lotus."

Not if I can help it.

As soon as the basement door is closed and locked, Toben climbs in bed, kissing me and holding me tight. He presses his forehead to mine.

"Do you feel better after your shower?"

"Yes." Tracing my finger across his jaw, I whisper, "It rubs the lotion on its skin or else it gets the hose again."

He pulls back with a smirk on his face and snorts. "Where did you hear that?"

"Logan said it to me. Isn't it pretty?"

His smile falls, replaced by disgust. "Yeah, pretty fucking creepy. Of course he would quote *Silence of the Lambs*, Buffalo Bill is probably his idol."

Sometimes he says a bunch of words, and I know what they mean on their own, just not together, so I stay quiet.

He falls asleep pretty quickly, the steady softness of his breathing is such an amazing sound.

I watch him dream and he looks like he did when we first met. He looks so much older while he's awake.

Something's changed with him. I've tried not to notice it for a while, and it doesn't make a difference anyway. I will always love my Toben, my only friend.

No matter what.

Nine months later—April, 2004

Toben

Fuck. FUCK! I'm not ready for this again!

Anniversaries. I hate motherfucking anniversaries!

I can't stand Morgan, I swear she's nothing more than snot and tears, but that doesn't mean I want her to die.

He's going to expect more from me this time. I've almost become comfortable with cutting, whipping, and beating her. This though, this is gonna get brutal. She'll be in pieces before this is through.

This is way too soon after the nightmare with Kyle.

Every time they get a new girl, the other one will participate in the initiation process. Logan keeps his girls from ages ten to fifteen. The 'sweet spot' he calls it. 'Revolting' I call it. Kyle on the other hand…well, his never last that long. He keeps his girls for as long as they live. He doesn't clean, feed, or clothe them. He doesn't want their respect or obedience, he just wants their blood. He also doesn't use any stupid words or give them drugs. I don't know why Logan brought me along to that particular one, and I couldn't have been more relieved when Kyle told him he didn't want me involved. It didn't matter that Logan was pissed, because it was Kyle's girl, so it was Kyle's rules.

I had no idea how he found them at the rate they must be dying on him, and I later found out he would go months at a time without a single girl because he couldn't keep up with himself. They cut off and skinned so many body parts, it kind of runs together. Logan has told me of their fascination with medieval torture, in high school, and it was apparent in the sinister bloodbath. I humiliated Logan when I got sick halfway through, earning me a few nights in the cage and an angry as hell Tavin. She wouldn't have been mad if I told her the real reason though. Not that it's an option.

Morgan's blonde hair is tinged with her blood and she's so far beyond crying or pleading. Both of her arms are broken, the part of her leg that's no longer attached is lying on the floor and she's covered in large gashes. If I'm honest with myself, I have become used to our playdates to the point they have taken on a normalcy.

This is not a normal playdate.

She knew something was up right away when we walked in empty handed. She was expecting her weekly food supply and anniversary gifts. As much as she grates my nerves, seeing the terror dawning on her face when her mind clicked together what was happening, was absolutely gut wrenching.

I don't get sick this time and my mind has no problem accounting every little detail of what happens. This is yet another event that will haunt me until the day I walk with the reaper. The upbeat, happy music seeping from her radio is a morbid backdrop to her demise.

I keep thinking that Logan will finally finish her off, she's barely hanging on anyway. Then he hands me a big knife and breathes out, "It's time, Plaything."

Maybe I jumped the gun on the getting sick thing because now it feels like I might.

"Logan I-I can't."

Even in the dim light I can see the rage in his eyes. "Did you just tell me no? I want you to remember this moment when I am slicing apart Tavin's soft ivory flesh. In her agony I will make sure she knows it's because of you." Rolling his neck, he adds, "There are some new things I've been wanting to do to her anyway."

FUCK!

This is it. I'm going to kill an innocent girl to protect another. Even though I've become somewhat numb to my playdates with Morgan, my feelings toward mine and Tavin's haven't really changed. It makes my heart physically ache to watch what he does to her and even though she takes the pain in stride, it's the sexual part that takes an emotional toll on her. She doesn't like to talk about it, and when she does, I can see it fractures her a little more every time.

She's become my world, my universe. She's so much more than a friend, I feel that we're connected in some ethereal way, that we're the same. She's my purpose, my joy, the only thing beautiful left in my so-called existence. She is love.

She is *my* love.

I take the knife from Logan. I'm about to rip a person's soul from their body for the first time in my twelve years on this earth, and it's all for the girl with violet eyes.

Slow and steady steps clash with the high speed beating in my chest. Morgan can't even hold herself in her kneel position any longer, so she's lying on her back as I straddle her stomach. I'm shaking and sweating so terribly that I'm worried I will drop the knife. I don't want to do this. I'm such a pussy, letting the tears fall as I raise the knife above my head.

The last thing I see in her eyes is horror.

"I'm sorry."

I say it as if it means something. It doesn't mean a damn thing because that's when I bring the blade down as hard as I can into her chest.

I thought it would be difficult, yet the opposite happens as the steel slides into her with ease. She coughs up blood, sputtering it on my face.

The life slides out of her body the way a song fades out at the end.

I might as well have completely submerged myself in her blood. Even my hair is dripping with it. It's actually quite stunning-the blood. It shines with the small amount of light in the room.

Like the crashing waves at the beach, the weight of what I just did knocks all of the air from my lungs.

I killed her. One less soul is on this earth and it's because of me.

Morgan Bishop was a blonde, fifteen-year-old girl who was left to a mother with a heroin and gambling problem. Logan once told me that he bought her at a huge discount because she wasn't even a virgin. Her mother had already rented her out by then. I always thought my situation with my dad was about as bad as it could get, until I met Tavin. Then I met Logan.

I hear his words echoing in my mind.

It can always get worse.

For a split second, I wonder if I did her a favor by finally taking her away from her nightmarish life. That's copping out and I know it. My whole body shakes; I feel cold and hollow. I look into her empty blue eyes and see her body for what it is now. A shell. An empty case. Morgan isn't here anymore. She'll never be again and it was me that took her away.

A large hand is on my back and his slow voice praises, "You did well, Plaything."

I want to scream. I want more than anything to pull this knife across my throat, but I could never leave Tavin alone with him.

We clean the tools, dispose of our clothes, shower and leave. I wait until we are back on the plane to ask him a question that's been bugging me.

"Logan?" He licks the paper to roll a joint and nods at me. "Why do we just leave their bodies? I've seen enough TV to know that's evidence."

He doesn't seem irritated by my question at all. He seems pleased by it in fact. "I have a man I pay very well to dispose of them safely and discreetly." Apparently, cleaning up his corpses is not considered part of the fun, to this particular psychopath.

I'm in a bit of a haze. I feel different-not better and not necessarily worse, just different. We arrive back at the house quickly, and before I know it, we're climbing up the creaky front steps.

I'm right behind Logan as we walk into the living room. Lacie's sprawled across the La-Z-Boy with her legs open for everyone to see her nasty snatch.

"Thank Christ gonorrhea isn't an airborne virus," Logan snaps at her before turning to me. "I need to speak with Brian. Go to Lotus and I'll be there in a moment."

"Yes, Logan." As I watch him disappear into the hall, I turn toward the basement. I glare at Lacie and realize this is the first time I've ever been alone with her.

"How do you live with yourself? Did you get like this over time or have you always been a selfish, diseased cunt?"

She sneers. "Get your little pecker downstairs like you were told."

"You really feel nothing for her? You're her mother for God's sake! Do you know what he does to her?" By the look on her face she knows exactly what happens downstairs. "You really are a soulless whore, aren't you?"

"You know nothing, you little shit. That bitch ruined my life and my body, and was she once grateful? No. I should have never had her in the first place." I hate this woman with white hot rage. My ears feel like they are on fire when all I hear is the *whooshing* in my ears. I don't respond as I go into the kitchen, get a knife, and quietly stand behind her.

Fuck this bitch.

Clutching a fistful of her hair, I jerk her head back, dig the blade into her neck, and whisper, "This is for my Love."

It's like slicing through Jell-O. Her skin separates and

blood blossoms from the wound. She gurgles and I glance at her eyes. She's still in there. Why won't she die? I bring the knife into her stomach three more times until finally, she dwindles away into nothing.

Lacie Winters is dead. Good.

I killed Tavin's mom… Oh *shit*.

Shit. Shit, shit, SHIT! I am so fucked! What was I thinking?! I just killed for the first time a couple of hours ago and now I've gone and done it again?

Oh my God. I think I'm a serial killer.

How many people do you have to murder to be considered a serial killer? Clutching at my throat, I drop to the floor, gasping for air.

I can't breathe.

"Oh, fuck." Logan says. I can't see him since I'm behind the chair, so he must have heard me because within an instant he's at eye level, crouching down in front of me. "Relax, Toben. Slow down. Don't focus on getting oxygen, just on the action of inhaling."

After a moment, my heart rate lowers allowing me to speak. I'm going to get a major beating for this. I just have to make sure Tav doesn't get punished. She'll never forgive me for this.

"Logan, I'm sorry, I don't know what happened, it was like I was on auto pilot! Please Logan, forgive me."

"You won't be punished, just calm down. I don't want Lotus to know about this until I figure it out."

I nod and he doesn't even mention my lack of verbal response when he pulls out his phone.

"I have a situation… I need an extra set of street clothes for Toben and myself… Yes, now make it quick."

He hangs up, standing to go into the kitchen, and returns with a black trash bag.

"Take off the clothes." I obey him and once I am

completely nude, I hand him my bloody shirt and jeans. "Go upstairs and shower so Lotus doesn't see you like this."

Two people. I have killed two people. One deserved it, and one didn't. I wonder if they cancel each other out.

I watch as the blood that was just inside her mother washes down the drain. Tavin can't ever know. I don't know what we're going to tell her. Whatever it is, it can't be the truth.

CHAPTER NINE
Nikki

Tavin

I HATE WHEN TOBEN LEAVES TO RUN ERRANDS. I HAVE TO be alone with myself. I look at my reflection and see what Logan sees.

My body is revolting. It's nothing but scars decorated in fresh wounds. The burn on top of my forearm is the ugliest mark so far, so I'm hoping it won't be that bad once it completely heals. I wasn't doing things the way he liked, so he held the knife over the flame and pressed it against my arm. It sounded like water on a stove and the smell made my stomach queasy. The pain though…burning pain is the worst, I think. Even when he removed the knife, the pain didn't go away at all and I screamed louder than I have in a long, long time.

Blowing my bangs out of my eyes, I reach down to put my clothes on, and notice my fingers are bleeding again. How do I keep doing that without even realizing it?

I decide to try to read one of the books Logan brought us, so I swing open the bathroom door and my face smacks into his stomach. Placing a hand to my back, he guides me into my room. I don't see Toben…where is he? I fall to my knees to kneel, just as he yanks at my arm.

"We don't have time, Lotus. Choose a toy that you want to bring. We're leaving for a couple of days."

We are leaving? I haven't left the house in over two years! Wait…does 'we' mean just me and him?

"Where's Toben?"

He hurries to my closet. "I said we don't have time! I will remember your insubordination and you'll endure twice the punishment if you don't pick a fucking toy!" I've never seen him like this, he's usually calm or angry. Right now, he seems worried.

I pick up my doll. She's one of the most important things I own. Logan pulls clothes from the closet for me *and* Toben. I let out a big breath knowing Toben will be wherever we're going.

Throwing the clothes into a paper bag, he snatches my hand and drags me up the stairs. He's walking too fast for me to keep up so I keep tripping, and he doesn't care, he just keeps pulling me.

The basement door swings open and I see Lacie sitting on the recliner. She must be on the nod. There's so much red everywhere.

Wait…it's blood…she's covered in blood!

"Mommy!" I jerk my hand away from Logan to try to help her. In an instant, I can't breathe as a large hand squeezes my neck.

He shakes me and I look up into his angry eyes. His voice is slow and steady when he reminds me, "She's not your Goddamn mommy." He releases my neck and I gulp down as much air as I can, coughing in the process. "We need to go."

He picks me up and when I wrap my arm around his neck, I rest my chin on his shoulder. As he carries me out of my house, I let my tears wet my face and watch her empty body until he closes the front door behind us.

He shoves me into the back seat of a car and I smash into Toben. The loud slam of the door makes me jump. I've never ridden in a car before and I can't even focus on it because all I can think about is what she looked like. I don't know why I'm so sad. She didn't love me and I've hardly even seen her in two years.

Toben holds my hand and as he looks at me, I can tell he is high on something. "Hello, Love."

I still smile even though all I want to do is cry. "Love?"

"You are my Love." He states it as the truest of facts.

He's blurry through the moisture in my eyes. "She's dead."

It's like someone erased all of his feelings. "I know."

Logan gets in and we are silent as the car makes a noise and music starts playing.

The car feels funny, but I think it's neat. Toben's thumb rubs over mine as we hold hands and look out our own windows.

Logan's slow voice fills the small space.

"We're leaving town. Brian killed Lacie and I don't want to be anywhere near this city in case he's stupid enough to mention my name."

Brian killed her? I've never even seen him hit her. Yes, he yelled at her all the time, I just don't think I've ever seen him hurt her. Why would he kill her?

"You two can't be there for obvious reasons."

It feels like we are in the car for a long time when we drive inside of a building. We keep going in circles until we're at the very top. We all climb out of the car and my eyes are working overtime. I can see the whole city from here! There are so many huge buildings and I feel like I'm standing in the sky. Logan pulls me by my hand and I grab Toben's. He takes us to the metal doors at the edge of the roof that lead to a room smaller than my bathroom. All off a sudden, the room moves! My stomach drops right along with it and I'm so glad it only lasts for a few seconds. Once we get to the bottom, he hurries all of us into a black car.

Within a few short moments, we're getting out of the car and standing in the biggest parking lot I have ever seen. There are no cars parked though, just planes, and they are huge!

"Come along, Playthings!" Logan screams over the engine as we climb onto the plane.

I've never seen one up close much less been in one! I wonder if Lacie had ever been on a plane...if she hadn't, then she never will now.

We climb up the stairs and once we are inside, it's so much more than I could ever have imagined.

Everything is colored in silver and cream. It seems to go on forever.

Toben grins. "It's like the Tardis isn't it? Bigger on the inside."

I don't know what a Tardis is, but Logan must know because he laughs. He's clearly more himself now that we're on the plane. "You two should go get some food, once we take off I want to play."

The tears sting my eyes as I try to hold them back. "But...today isn't our day."

He squeezes my jaw and his fingers dig into my skin. "I don't give a fuck. I will play with you whenever I see fit! Now go get some food."

Eating with Toben gives me my last moments of peace for the next four hours. Logan is relentless and I'm so exhausted I can barely kneel. He doesn't care, he just keeps going and going. He doesn't cut me or do anything that will make me bleed because he doesn't want to stain his plane.

Since he isn't doing a lot of physical damage, he tells Toben that he doesn't need him and he can go watch a movie in the theater.

Toben's face tells me that he doesn't want to leave me alone with him, but what choice do we have? It's not fair! The only movie that I have ever seen is the Wizard of Oz and that is because Logan gave it to me for my birthday. Toben and I have watched it a zillion times since then.

After what feels like years, he finally finishes and lights a cigarette, giving it to me to take a drag. Yuck! This is just as bad as I remember. I don't want to make him mad though, so I smoke it every time he gives it to me. He makes me stay with him in the bed and eventually, he falls asleep.

I want to see the plane. I've never been on one and I doubt I ever will again. As quietly and carefully as I can, I lift his arm from my stomach. I slide out of the bed like a snake, snatch my doll off the table, and pick up my dress from the floor, as I crawl to the door. Daring a glance at him, I stand and look over my shoulder. His chest rises and falls in a steady rhythm and I release my breath.

The door is quiet, earning my gratitude. As soon as I'm out of the room, I throw my dress over my head and look for Toben.

Windows are everywhere and I feel my hand cover my mouth as I gasp at the view. It's getting dark out, and the sky is the most beautiful it's ever looked. Purple and blues are everywhere. I can see forever.

"Awesome, isn't it?"

The grin that appears only for Toben makes its way across my face as I turn to him, "There's so much out there." His eyes take on a shine as he forces a smile and I know why. "You don't think I'll ever see any of it, do you?"

He adjusts his hat before shoving his hands in his pockets. "I don't know, Tav."

We explore as he shows me all of the rooms. The theater room has three rows of big, plushy, cream chairs and the biggest TV in the world. We watch a movie about a fish and I try not to cry when his mommy dies. Even though his parents love him, it still makes me think of mine.

"LOTUS!"

We both jump and look at each other. Toben's eyes go wide before whispering, "Did you do something?"

We fall from the chairs into our kneeling positions. "I wasn't supposed to leave."

"Fuck." Toben shakes his head.

Just then, Logan's frame takes up the doorway. His shoulders heave in sync with his flaring nostrils. My eyes shift to his hand where he's holding the cat o' nine tails. As long as he doesn't get too carried away, I won't be a bloody mess.

He's very angry, though.

In two steps, he's in front of me and his fingers are lightly combing my hair. His voice is calm, and usually, that's worse.

"What did I tell you, Lotus?"

"That you wanted me to stay with you while we were on the plane."

His fingers trail to the nape of my neck and grabs a fist full of hair, using it to jerk my head back so I have to look up at him. "Then what the fuck are you doing in here?"

He isn't fair. He was sleeping. Why did I need to be in there? He makes me so angry sometimes!

I narrow my eyes at him. "I just wanted to see the plane! You've kept me locked up for years. This is the first thing I've got to see other than my own house, in a long time!" His jaw clenches. Well, I'm mad too! "Today isn't even my day, and you fucked me anyway! I hate it and it's gross, so the least you could do is let me see your Goddamn plane!" I hear a loud slap and my cheek instantly stings hot.

He hit my face. He's never hit my face.

"That will be the last time you speak to me that way." He circles around behind us. "Toben, take off your shirt."

Toben's going to get punished, not me. "No! I'm sorry, Logan!"

He laughs, "You both know how this works, yet every time you plead." All humor falls from his face. "Say one more fucking word and he will get it tenfold."

Why did I do that? Looking at Toben, I try to quietly communicate how sorry I am. He gives me a crooked smile and winks right before the whip crashes into him.

Over and over Logan hits him while yelling at me that I'm the cause of his torment. Toben is much stronger and can handle pretty high levels of pain. Neither one of us has passed out in months.

Finally, when Toben is spent and my face is wet, he stops. His chest lifts with each of his heavy breaths. "I was going to give you the next few days to relax." He scoffs, "Not after that stunt." Marching over to the movie seats, he rips up my doll and throws her against the wall.

No!

More tears burn. Not my doll!

He storms to the door. "We'll be landing soon, so get the rest you can. We have a fun forty-eight hours ahead of us."

As soon as he disappears from my view, I break position and lie on the floor next to Toben.

"I'm sorry, I'm so sorry. I don't know why I do such stupid things. I just got so mad."

"Don't apologize, I'm proud of you." Even though he tries to sound strong, I can hear the pain in his voice. "I gladly took that beating and I'm sorry about your doll."

I am too. It's funny how much I cared about her, she was only a toy. Just like me.

Logan didn't lie. The next two days are agonizing. I'm so excited to get back to the basement and back to only once a week playdates.

We step through my front door and my chest throbs at the sight of the missing chair. They're both gone. Logan says Brian is locked away and will be for a long, long time.

He's still mad about what I did on the plane because he locks Toben in the cage.

And it's all your fault.

Toben

She's been getting harder and harder on herself as time goes on. I see the way she looks at herself in the mirror, the way she flinches every time Logan puts her down. I tell her she is pretty and smart, all the time, but she's becoming less responsive to it. Her fingers are almost always scratched up and bloody and she's had her nightmares almost every night this week because I've been locked up. She's been blaming herself for it this whole time.

She just crossed the line though, and now I'm pissed.

"I swear to God, Tavin. I better not ever hear that shit again."

"It's true though. I make him do those things by disobeying. Why can't I just be a good plaything? You're in there dirty and sore because I'm an idiot and opened my mouth."

Logan told me he thinks she has a neurological disorder that makes her head do the jerking thing. He calls it a 'tic' and right now it's happening pretty badly.

She's been giving me major attitude this week and I don't

know where it's coming from. I know she feels bad, and then she will bite my head off. We rarely get upset with each other so this has been a long week. I try not to piss her off even more, when she gets upset. I do my best to stay calm and she will usually relax pretty quickly. Although, her last few comments have crossed a line. Where did this come from? She's never felt that she 'asked for this' before. I'm seething and I can feel my teeth grinding.

Harshly, I breathe through my nostrils trying to regain my cool. "You are not any of the things he says you are and none of this is your fault. I can't change the way you feel, but it hurts me to hear you say that stuff. So just know, if you keep talking like that, you're not just affecting yourself."

She looks to the floor. "Okay."

I wish I could hug her, yet I have to settle for holding her hand. "Tav-"

The telltale sound of the door unlocking sends her flying across the floor to her knees. Today isn't our day and Morgan's dead…so why is he here?

"Hello, my playthings."

"Hello, Logan."

Greeting her first, he runs his finger across her jaw and down her neck before kissing her head. Walking to the cage, he unlocks and opens it for me. He tells her good bye and I wink at her.

I wish I could tattoo that smile on my eyes so I could see it forever.

Once we are upstairs, he hands me a stack of clothes and tells me to go shower. I obey and the water feels so good after being cramped in the cage. I finish quickly, so I don't agitate him by making him wait, and meet him back downstairs. When we get into his new, black Bentley, Kyle is in the front seat. Now I know why they're here. Logan has another Lotus and today is her initiation.

We stop driving after about forty-five minutes and pull up to a two-story, tan house with dark brown trim. The neighborhood is nicer than ours and the house is well kept. I follow behind Kyle as we enter the nearly bare home and go up a set of stairs. I don't think anyone lives here, either. There's barely any furniture and the house feels too still.

We turn left at the top and Logan unlocks the first door on the right.

The room is empty and plain. The walls are white and the floor is wood. The bed is simple with a white blanket. A wooden nightstand and a small fridge complete the room.

Logan drops the infamous black duffel on the floor.

"Do you think making me look for you is wise, Nicole?"

A little voice squeaks from under the bed. "Nikki." She crawls out and stands. Throwing her shoulders back, she lifts her chin. "My name is Nikki. Are you the guy who thinks he's my Master?"

"Master implies that you are a slave. Slave implies you are a person. You're no longer a person. You are a plaything. My plaything."

Her long, strawberry-blonde hair is up in a ponytail and she's wearing nothing besides a slip. She's already marked up.

"I'll tell you what I told the last guy: screw you!"

I can't believe her audacity. Logan squeezes her neck and throws her to the floor, slamming her on her knees.

"I have no patience for defiance, little Lotus. Now, take off the slip."

"Just wait till my father finds me, you sicko! He's gonna kill you!"

Wait…what?

Logan laughs as he turns to me and nods. "Hold her down."

I go to obey, and when she looks at me, my steps falter. She slits her eyes.

"Who are you?"

"A toy, just like you."

She scoffs. "Speak for yourself."

She'll see soon enough. She has no idea who she is dealing with. I hold her arms and for a moment, I flashback to mine and Tav's initiation. Logan crouches down to her level and she spits in his face.

Oh, fuck. This girl has a death wish.

He punches her in the gut causing her body to heave forward and she lets out a pained groan. He pushes himself up with force as he dashes to the bag and yanks out his stethoscope. He only used it the one time on Tavin. It must be part of his initiation ritual.

Placing it to her heart, his creepy as fuck smile appears.

"You put on a brave front, little Lotus, though the sputtering of your heart sings a different song."

Her eyes go wide and she tries with all of her might to pull away from me as Logan undoes his pants. I thought I was getting used to this after seeing it a hundred times with Tav and Morgan, and still, this is so intense. Up until this moment, she believed her father was going to barge through that door. When Logan takes everything away and she realizes it isn't going to happen, in that moment, I could feel her faith shatter.

I forgot how it sounded when someone's innocence gets ripped away. It's the worst sound in the world. I try with all my might to hold back the tears for this girl. She's fighting with everything she has and I just keep hoping that they will shoot her up soon to temporarily stop her torture.

I forgot how he used to always scream at Tavin to look at him. She just does it now and so did Morgan. Nikki keeps squeezing her eyes shut, refusing to give him anything he asks for. I'm worried he's going to kill her, her rebellion is the gas to his flaming fury. I hate the way he speaks.

"Look how pretty your body is. Look!"

The things he says are so vile, I try to tune it out. Finally, he tells Kyle to get the stuff.

"Get ready to fly, Nikki," I whisper in her ear.

Her eyes rip open and burn her hate into me. I'm grateful that Logan has finally climbed off of her to smoke a cigarette. I need her to know that I don't want this. As quietly as I can, I say, "I'm sorry. I'm doing this to save my best friend. A girl just like you."

Her eyes are so sad, the feisty girl from a couple of hours ago is gone. Before she has a chance to respond, Kyle starts tying her off. She's so scared, she thinks she knows what's about to happen, but she'll see...this is the good part.

The remainder of the evening is much more tolerable. She isn't in pain or conscious, so when Logan brands and takes the piece of skin from the top of her wrist, all she does is mumble.

He picks up her bloody body and places her on the bed. He'll change the sheets tomorrow. Kissing her head, he tells her, "Welcome to your new life, Lotus." He reaches into his pocket and places a sucker next to her head, just like he did with Tavin.

Logan picks up the bag and hoists it over his shoulder as he and Kyle stroll out her door. We have her blood all over us and I know that there's no way he's letting us touch a foot in his car like this, so why are we just leaving? I'm pretty sure one of the doors in her room leads to a bathroom.

I stand next to Kyle in the hall while Logan locks her door. He digs a towel and some clothes out of the bag. "There's a bathroom down the hall, hurry and get cleaned up." He shoves the clean garments into my hands.

"Isn't there a bathroom in her room?"

He lets out a frustrated sigh. "That's not how it's done, now go fucking shower."

Logan is back in his suit when I meet him downstairs. There's something about Nikki that I like and that isn't a good thing. It makes me curious about her situation, so I ask while Kyle is still in the shower.

"Logan?"

He exhales a drag. "Yes?"

"What's her story?"

Seemingly contemplating his response, he says, "I bought her from a dealer. I do that occasionally when I have difficulty finding my own. She was a decent price and the age that I prefer. Her father thinks she's dead so there is nobody looking for her."

"Whose house is this then?"

"Mine."

I don't know why this seems so much worse. With Tavin, Morgan, and I, we were all fucked from day one, but Nikki has a parent that gives a shit. She has a loving home. I almost forgot those existed.

~

When I get back to Tavin, I turn up what has officially become our song. *Miss You* by Blink 182 floods the basement as I hold her hand and dance with her across our room. I hold her tight as I smell her hair.

She's worth it all. All the fucked up shit I've done and all the fucked up shit I'm destined to do.

CHAPTER TEN
Disgusting

One year and five months later—September, 2005

Tavin

KEEP MY REACTION TO A SMALL GROAN AS THE DROPS OF boiling water splash against my skin. I barely have to try to stay quiet with the sprinkler, it's much less agonizing than most of the other tools. It's the whip I know Toben will be slicing across my stomach at any second, that will test me.

Whoosh! Crack!

That begs for more of a scream. I swear Toben is getting rougher and hitting harder. He sure didn't let up with these ropes. Logan rarely has me tied up and when he does, it's to a chair. It's so uncomfortable and the familiar anxiety of just wanting this to be over settles in my gut.

"Again!"

Another full force smack with the whip. Oddly, I am beginning to anticipate the pain. I don't exactly like it, I just don't necessarily reject it either. It definitely still hurts, and somehow makes me feel more vibrant too. Like I'm worth something for the few moments the sting is on my skin.

Logan drops the sprinkler to the floor and his mouth is all over me. This is so gross. I just try to imagine that Toben and I are somewhere else. Anywhere else. I dream of the sand between my toes and holding hands as we make our way down The Walk. How I always felt like I could fly when we would swing on the swings at the park. I think of the way I lick my lips after we kiss and it always tastes like his special flavor. He smokes when they go on their errands so sometimes there's a little of that. I don't mind it, I just wish it didn't make me think of Logan.

He's got to be almost done so I allow myself to get excited. I hope he brought rock candy today, I love rock candy. It's my favorite. He still only lets me have smack once a week, even though I know for a fact Toben has come home high more than once from their errand trips. At least he gives us pot. On a couple of special occasions, he has brought cocaine, and wowza, now that's fun!

Logan finishes inside me as he moans out what a whore I am. His sweaty body slides off of mine and when the cool air hits my wet skin I sigh, enjoying the relief.

Without a word, he takes a stack of clothes into the bathroom. As soon as the door closes, Toben is next to me. He wipes away the wet hair that's stuck to my face as he presses his lips against mine. His kisses have gotten a little harder and a little longer lately.

He picks my dress up off the floor and hands it to me before he gets me a towel. We kneel on the floor, and hold hands until the bathroom door opens, then we snap apart and get them where they're supposed to be.

Logan barely looks at us, he seems sidetracked. "I'm in a hurry, I can't stay." He puts a black case and a balloon on my nightstand. He kisses my forehead and gruffly says, "Good night, Playthings," before heading toward the stairs.

What about the candy?!

"Good night, Logan." It sounds a bit odd to hear only Toben's voice, we have always said it together.

Did I do something wrong? Is he mad at me? Even when he punishes me, he gives me a treat so I know I still please him. Is he bored with me? Why does that scare me? I don't know why I'm feeling this way. I hate when he touches me, I just like the way he is sometimes and I want him to like me back. I want him to love me. My eyes start burning and I can't stop myself from crying.

He's glaring at me because of my lack of response, but his face completely changes when he sees my tears.

"Lotus?"

I feel shattered, broken, worthless, useless.

"What did I do?! I'm sorry, Logan, please don't hate me!"

He's irritated when he snaps, "What are you talking about? I'm just in a hurry and this isn't helping the situation."

"You…you didn't give me any candy."

A smile fills up his whole face as a laugh pours from his throat. "Oh, Tavin, at times you can be so enchanting."

He rarely uses my name, so it assures me somehow. He reaches into the duffel and pulls out two clear baggies filled with rainbow colored jellybeans.

"I simply forgot, I've had a busy day." He hands us each our bag as he kisses my head again. "Now, I must go. Good night, my playthings."

"Good night, Logan," we tell him.

As soon as the door locks, we are up on our feet. I dig into the jellybeans and Toben goes to wash his hands. He comes out of the bathroom like a secret because I jump when he slides his arms around my waist.

"You ready to go?"

I turn my head to the side and look up toward him as he places a kiss to my lips. "Yes."

We jump on the bed and when the works are ready, we press the needle into our veins. We untie ourselves and at the count of three we push bliss into our blood.

It's been hours, and the high has made its way back down, as we stare into each other's gaze. "Are you still high?" he mutters.

"Not really."

"Do you want a joint?"

That sounds incredible!

"Yeah!"

The *click* of the lighter and the pungent leafy aroma already calms my nerves, as he pulls me next to him. His fingers trail along my neck as I puff on the joint.

"God, you're pretty."

He tells me that all the time. He just thinks I am because…well I don't know why. It still makes me feel good and I smile before I pass the joint to him and let my lips tenderly touch his. He leans in deeper and turns his body against mine. The joint is still smoking in the hand that now caresses my hair. His body shifts to put the weed in the ashtray making his frame hover over mine. He becomes more aggressive with his mouth and I feel the weight of his body against me. We've never kissed like this before. It's kind of nice, though. He lifts up and looks at me with a crooked smile before his lips go to my neck. This is definitely different.

We kiss like that for a while, until I feel his hand on my thigh. I don't know what to do, this is a new situation. He keeps moving his hand until it's up my skirt. As soon as I feel his fingers, I freeze. I don't want this, I just don't want to hurt him. He's starting to get determined and is so into it, he has no idea I want to scream for him to stop.

Such a dirty girl.

"Oh, Love, you're so-Tav? Are you okay?"

I can't stop the moisture from filling my eyes. Why would he touch me there?! He knows I hate it!

"Why would you do that?"

He flies backward off of the bed before he paces across the floor. "Shit!" He rips off his beanie. "Fuck!"

My stomach drops to my toes. He's mad at me. He's all I have, I need him. I can't let him hate me. I don't like to be touched like that. It makes me feel filthy, sad, and scared. I just can't lose him.

As hard as I try, I can't make the tears completely stop, but they decrease as I pull off my dress.

"I'm sorry! You can fuck me, just please don't stop being my friend."

"Oh, God. No, Love. I'm not mad at you!" He bounds up to me and wraps his arms around me. "Do not ever, ever think that."

I feel the fabric of my dress as he helps me put it back on and kisses my nose. "I only want what you truly want to give me." He sits and pulls me on his lap. "You need to understand, I'm almost fourteen and I sleep in the same bed with a beautiful girl that I love. It's getting more difficult to…keep things under control."

I don't know what to do. I'll never want to have sex and least of all with him! Why would I want something so terrible and disgusting between us? Why would he? He's acting like it's a good thing!

"Is that what you want? To do all those dirty things to me?"

I feel like my world is falling apart, this is going to ruin the only genuine joy in my life.

He shakes his head. "It's not supposed to be dirty. He made it that way for you and it isn't fair. I don't want to do anything *to* you Tavin, I only want it *with* you and if it never happens then that's okay too." He kisses me again and it helps me breathe. "This changes absolutely nothing, I promise." I press my forehead against his and he squeezes me tight. His fingers are playing with my hair when he tells me, "We are so much more than just best friends, we're bound together by something greater, I can feel it. Our situation is one that we're going to have to figure out as we go. We have to stick together because I don't think it's going to get any easier."

What he really means is: It can always get worse.

Nine months later—June, 2006

Toben

I feel like a freak. If I'm honest with myself, I am scared that I'm becoming just like Logan. No normal person has to work this hard to not get aroused by watching someone you love get beaten and raped.

Right now, he has a belt around her thigh that has a bunch of short needles poking out. When he tightens it, the needles puncture her flesh. It's absolutely sickening, yet I'm having to fight an erection.

It's not the actual act that turns me on, it's what she looks like during it. I have to shut my eyes and remember how much she's suffering and it hits me like the cold shower I need. Her body has been developing and with our close quarters, I'm going a bit stir crazy. I don't get a lot of alone time and it must be starting to affect my brain because I think I see her push into him. She would never do that, though. She always pulls away.

The next couple of minutes don't make sense. I know she hates sex, but right now it doesn't seem like it. When she cries out, it's not in pain. My face feels hot, the idea of her liking it turns my stomach to the point I actually might puke.

"Lotus? Did you just...?" Logan breaks into wicked laughter. "Oh, my little whore." He yanks her head back and her face is completely mortified. "This whole time you wanted it? You put on quite the show."

He's ruthless with her, forcing more and more from her. Every time I look at her face, my heart cracks a little more. I can almost feel the hate she's feeling toward herself. I don't exactly understand how all this works, I just know I can't always control my body.

Matters become worse when he discovers that pain is a necessary factor. He screams at her how sick she is.

That's rich, coming from him.

He finally finishes and as he goes into the bathroom, she doesn't move or look at me. She just keeps staring at the ceiling. I sit next to her and hold her hand.

"Hey, are you okay?" She still won't look at me or respond, so I hold her chin and turn her head. "Talk to me."

The tears fall from her eyes and when they do meet mine, they're desolate. "I didn't want him to stop."

As soon as she says the words, she falls apart. I haven't seen her cry hard like this in...I don't know how long. I pull her into my lap and kiss her shoulder. I don't know what to say to her, so I just hold her and let her cry. We don't have much time, he'll be out soon and I don't want him to see her like this.

"Come on, Love, I need you to calm down until he leaves." Her whole body shakes, and when I look down, she's pulling off the skin from below her fingernails. "Oh, Goddamn it." I hate that she hurts herself, she's suffered enough at the hands of others, me included. I sigh as I hug her tight. "I know you're thinking bad thoughts, Tavin. Please don't, it hurts me to see you like this."

"I didn't want him to stop." She whispers those words

again, with a darkness that's chilling with the rasp in her voice.

"Come on, we need to kneel." I hold her hand until Logan opens the bathroom door.

The fact that he's pretty proud of himself is apparent. Considering his preference is in torturing children, I'm sure this is somewhat of a rare occurrence.

In fact, when I think about Morgan, she never once seemed turned on or aroused and neither has Nikki. I don't know what changed and even if I did, I don't know if I would understand it. I never got to take sex education in school and my father never got around to 'the talk'. Besides porn magazines, everything I know, I've learned from Logan.

He stands in front of her and brushes his fingers across her face. "I would do just about anything to cancel my engagement and spend the night here with you. Now that I know what you can do, I will not ever finish a playdate without making you come at least once."

She inhales and he laughs as he adjusts himself. When he lifts the duffel, he takes out two long sheets of paper lined in colorful candy buttons, and hands them to us. "Do you want me to fix you up now or are you wanting to go with Toben?"

As much as I want to go with her, she seems like she needs it ASAP. Still, when her almost inaudible voice scrapes out, "I'll wait, Logan." I feel relief.

He glares down at her before he places everything we need on the nightstand.

"Good night, my playthings."

"Good night, Logan."

He stares down at Tavin once more before he leaves up the stairs. I raise myself off the floor as soon as I hear the *click*. Tears are streaming down her face when I kneel in front of her and pull her against my chest.

"Do you want to take a shower with me? We'll clean off this blood, I'll wash your hair, and then we can make all of this better, okay?"

"Okay." It's barely a whisper.

I place our candy on the nightstand and hold her hand as I lead her into the bathroom. Starting the shower, I tell her, "Come on, the warm water will help."

I take her hand and pull her into the shower. I wash her hair and hug her tight while the red swirls down the drain.

"Can you turn the heat up?" She asks.

I nod as the water runs down my face. "Just tell me when." I keep turning the knob until it's too intense for me to stand. "Shit, that's hot!"

"This is fine."

She speaks only as loud as she needs to be heard and her body is tense. I turn her so the water can spray her back.

I can't believe I am going to tell her this.

"I've gotten myself off before, and there's a certain point that I wouldn't be able to stop it if I wanted to. Maybe it's the same for girls. I don't think you could help it."

Maybe that wasn't the right thing to say. I'm sure she's crying even if it is difficult to tell with the water. She rarely shuts me out and I loathe it. She can tell me anything and she knows it, so why the hell doesn't she?

I kiss her shoulder and up her neck. "Come on, Love. Let's escape this place."

She nods. "Get everything ready, I'll be out in a minute. I just want to turn the water up a little more." I press my lips to her temple and climb out. As I go to shut the curtain, her eyes shine up at me through wet bangs.

"I love you more than anything, Toben."

I smile and gaze into her, needing her to feel my sincerity.

"I love you more than anything, too."

After I'm dry, I throw on my beanie and some sweat

pants before getting it all laid out and ready to cook. I hate how much I adore the Slayer album Logan got me. It's still my favorite and I swear it was written with me in mind. I've listened to a couple of songs already and I'm beyond ready to get high.

What's taking her so long?

I walk back to the bathroom and swing open the door. She's out of the shower, leaning over the vanity. Coming up behind her, I see it in the mirror before I actually see it in person.

Her left arm is sliced open from wrist to elbow.

"WHAT THE FUCK, TAV?!"

I know I'm screaming at her, but I'm not mad-I'm horrified. The razor Logan bought her because he 'hates hair', is in pieces on the counter. She's removed the blades, using them to cut a deep diagonal line all the way across the inside of her forearm.

There's no way she's leaving me in this shit-life alone.

I grab the blade, cutting as deep as I can, I slice up my arm diagonally. Just like she did. Wrist to elbow on my left forearm.

"What are you doing?!" She cries at me.

I take her hand and lace my fingers with hers, pressing our wounds together to mix our blood.

"When you cry, I cry, if you die, I die, when you bleed, I bleed. You think you're just going to check out? Well, I'm fucking coming with you." I squeeze her hand. "There, now our blood is inside each other. We're the same. Alone, we're just half people, but together…together we're whole."

Even with her tears falling, her glow is starting to shine again. I wrap my arms around her as we bleed all over the bathroom floor and wait to die.

It doesn't take long to see death isn't coming. We're

losing blood and our arms are sliced up terribly, but we're not dying.

Well, shit. I'm going to have to call Logan and he will not be pleased by this. It seems odd that he would care when he'll probably end up having our bodies dumped in the ocean somewhere. Still, I think I know him pretty well and he has nine months left with us. He'll be enraged that we tried to take that away from him. We are his to kill, and his alone.

I nudge her awake and help her up. "Let's go lie in the bed and I'll call Logan."

She spins around on me and her head tics. "No!"

"Tavin, these are really deep, we need stitches."

She obviously wants to keep arguing, I just think she's too tired because she climbs in bed and pulls the cover over herself.

We've never used the cell before and my hands are shaking as I press the call button. A number lights up across the screen and when it connects, I realize I haven't heard the sound in over four years. It seems to go on forever and I swear my heart pounds a little harder with each ring.

"This better be an emergency," Logan snaps.

"We cut our wrists and I think we need stitches." I'm proud of how I keep up the persona of not being scared shitless.

He doesn't respond for so long that I pull the phone away to make sure we're still connected. When he does speak, it is in the slow manner that at times is far scarier than when he screams.

"That was not an intelligent move, Plaything. I'm on my way."

When he disconnects I groan, "Yeah, he's pissed."

Tavin

Vile, nasty, little slut. You have always wanted it.

Toben climbs into bed with me as we wait for Logan. As he looks into my eyes, I realize I'm not only a gross freak, I'm selfish, too. I can't even kill myself right, and even if I would have succeeded, he would have either been left here alone or died with me. How could I have done that to him? I want to believe with me gone, Logan would just let him go, but what if he wouldn't have?

I'm a whore just like Lacie, as if it were always inevitable. I'm *his* whore. When he made my body burst, it felt like a muted heroin rush, and in that moment, I wanted him to continue in his horrid perversions. What kind of sick person would like that? As soon as it was over, I felt grimier and dirtier than ever before. Considering who I am, that is definitely saying something. He told me that he would make it happen again, over and over. I don't want to live that way. Even though I'm constantly feeling conflicted about Logan, I've always hated our playtime. I don't understand what changed, how I could ever think it felt good.

What if he is right? What if I have always wanted it? If that's true, then I am as sick as he is. I can't escape this through death, because I would be killing Toben as well. All I want to do is cut it all out so there isn't anything for him to play with.

All I know is I don't want to feel like this anymore.

"Shoot me up."

Toben sighs as he rubs his thumb over my cheek and kisses me, lingering on my lips. "Logan's already furious, if he gets here and we're high it will be worse."

He's right. We're going to get it because he has to come back and he already told us he has plans tonight. I want to scream and pull out my hair. I want to shred my skin so that it's in little pieces all over the floor.

I want to die.

"We can smoke some weed, though."

I nod at him, even though I need something much stronger than just a joint. He rolls and lights it in two minutes flat. He pulls me on to his lap as our bloodied hands pass it back and forth. My fingers leave bloody fingerprints on the paper from when I cut myself taking apart my razor. I'm starting to get dizzy and queasy so I lean into his chest, the only safe place.

The basement door unlocks and we get to our knees as quickly as we can. Toben still has the joint in his mouth and keeps puffing on it even with his hands behind his head. While there are two sets of shoes coming down the stairs, I only look at Logan. He walks up to me, crouches, and grabs my wrist to turn my arm over. He looks at the gash and his nostrils flare before he throws my arm back to my thigh. Storming over to Toben, he rips the joint out of his mouth to put it in his own. I shift my line of vision to the other man in the room. He looks to be about Logan's age though he's much shorter and wider. The eyes behind his glasses are looking everywhere other than me, as he approaches.

"Get up," Logan barks.

I glance at him to make sure it was me he was talking to and he's glaring at me like he is going to kill me. I hope he does.

I follow the man to the table by the fridge and sit in the chair. He puts on gloves and takes out the same thing Logan used on me the first night. It didn't hurt, it was just cold and I don't like it. He puts the ends in his ears before he runs his hand down the long chord connected to the round metal piece. He reaches for me and I don't want him to touch me. I pull away, making him huff.

"Lotus! Sit still and let the doctor work."

I hate how my body obeys him before my mind even thinks about it. I stay still as the man presses the metal against my chest. He holds up my arm.

"What did you use?" He still doesn't look at me as he asks his question, and his voice is neither kind nor cruel.

"A blade from my razor."

The Doctor turns to Logan. "Has she had her tetanus shot?"

Logan gives him the same look he gives me when I do something stupid. "What the hell do you think?"

The Doctor nods. "I'll give her one, and I'm going to need to stitch this up."

"Just make it fast." Logan lights a cigarette before he hits Toben across the back of the head. "I cannot believe you let this happen."

It stings when the Doctor pours liquid onto the cut and cleans up the blood. I think the stinging feels nice. When he puts the little needle into my skin and pulls the string through, it makes my body hum with the sharpness and I let out a sigh. His eyes flip up to mine for just a moment before he quickly returns to sewing.

When it's apparent he is finished, Logan snaps his fingers and points to the floor. "Kneel." He narrows his eyes at Toben and jerks his head toward the direction of the Doctor. "Go." When Toben sits at the table, Logan takes a drag and with the smoke still in his mouth he says, "This one is more up to date."

Once the Doctor starts sewing his arm, Toben smirks. "So, you're 'the Doctor' huh?" He cocks his head to the side. "Wouldn't this be easier with your sonic screwdriver?"

"Toben! Enough with the fucking *Doctor Who* jokes," Logan snaps as he takes a drag from his cigarette.

Toben slumps back in the chair until the Doctor finishes, then he quietly gets up to resume his kneel position.

As the Doctor packs up his things, he pulls out an orange bottle and hands it to Logan. "These Percocet should help with their discomfort."

Logan pockets them. "Use your head. Why would I want them to have pain meds?" His golden eyes burn a hole into me when he growls, "They deserve every ounce of pain they get and I want to be sure they feel it."

Reaching into his wallet, he hands the Doctor a stack of cash. The Doctor turns and with pounding feet up the stairs, he's on his way.

Now it is just us…with a furious Logan.

"Tell. Me. What. Happened." His wrath is about to burst from the seams. His control is stretched to capacity.

Toben speaks before I can. "She hates herself because of what you do to her. She doesn't want to suffer anymore, feel the way you make her feel. You've messed her up so bad she wants to die. She couldn't remember which way she was supposed to cut so she went diagonal." He's speaking calmly and with respect, but Logan is seething. "I did it because I live only for her. If she goes, so do I."

I adore Toben and the way he talks.

My eyes shift to Logan and he is mid stride toward me. He reaches down to pull at my arm, yanking me to my feet.

He shakes me as he screams, "You are my fucking property! It's not up to you whether you live or die, it's up to me! You do not get to destroy yourself. That is my Goddamn privilege because I. Paid. For. You." I think he might rip my arm off when he yanks me to the bed and throws me down. "You don't get to feel anything unless I want you to feel it. You are nothing, you are less than nothing, yet I give you purpose. I am your Maker!"

I can hear him undoing his pants and the tears well up.

I know Toben doesn't believe in God, but I don't know what I believe, so I pray.

No more, please God, just no more. I can't take it.

"How do you repay my kindness? You try to fucking steal from me!" God doesn't hear my prayer. "You will suffer for it, Lotus."

And suffer I do.

Now he knows it isn't the pain that will destroy me, it's the pleasure. I try to fight it every time and every time I fail as I become dirtier and more like Lacie. He says repulsive things about my taste and smell. When he cuts me, I want him to force the knife inside of me. He never does though.

I try with all my might to imagine being somewhere else, anywhere else. I can't get my mind to leave this basement. I want to do it again. I want to mutilate every vessel and vein making my blood fill this room so I will drown in it. I wouldn't fail this time.

I won't though because I can't bear the thought of Toben dead. One day he will be able to get free and have his normal life back. Maybe he can go live with one of his old friends. It makes me smile to think of him laughing and having fun at school, doing whatever he did before I ruined his life. I will repay him for his love and friendship by living every day, finding peace in him and the happy things. I will seek out comfort in his smile, his smell, the way he constantly wears his beanie, and calls me 'Love'. I will sink into the deliciousness of the candy and the numbness from the needle. I will even enjoy Logan's kindness and the times it feels like we are a family. I will exist in between the nightmares, accept what I am and move on.

I am Tavin.

I am Lotus.

I am broken.

I am dirty.

I am a plaything.

I am his whore.

But I am not alone. Toben is my saving grace. He is the boy whose name sounds like mine. He's how I will survive.

Logan takes everything I can give tonight, yet he continues. I just can't keep my eyes open anymore.

I smell him and I feel his chest rising and falling. How did I end up in bed with Toben? I lift my head and am instantly aware of the ache throughout my body. He's asleep and I watch him as I run my fingers across his stomach and chest. He has his beanie on, so I slip it off and as if he can sense it missing, he begins to wake up.

"Hey, Love," he rasps.

"What happened?" I prop myself up on my elbows, and he pulls me on top of him so that I'm straddling him. He runs his hands along the outside of my thighs, before reaching up to pull my mouth against his.

"You passed out. Not that it stopped Logan. He said he wasn't done and that we would both pay for this later." He moves his lips across my neck to my shoulder. "When it was apparent you weren't going to wake up for a while, he finished, put you to bed, showered, and left."

His lips move back to my mouth as he rolls us over to place me on my back. I know what happens when Logan is ready to have sex and right now, it's happening to Toben. He isn't doing anything besides kissing me, I just hate that he wants to. He pulls my leg around his waist and presses himself against me. I have to ask him to stop. He groans against my lips.

"Let's get high, Love." I could cry with relief. He isn't making me stop him, he's stopping on his own. "Get it ready, I'll be right back."

I have his hit ready and I have just mixed the water into the spoon for mine when he comes out of the bathroom. He kisses my head and cleans his arm. When my hit is ready, we sit cross legged on the bed and face each other. We slide the needles in, untie our arms, kiss, and push in our freedom.

Finally, I am a beautiful nothing...

CHAPTER ELEVEN
Birthday

Four months later—October, 2006

Toben

EVER SINCE MY BIRTHDAY, A COUPLE DAYS AGO, MY entire body has been tight from living in a state of constant fear and anxiety. I've known it was coming for years, but turning fifteen made it sink in. I can't let it happen. I can't let him kill her. There has to be a solution. I have to come up with something. He favors her and there's got to be a way I can use that fact to save her.

I put all these thoughts in a box as I climb the stairs behind Logan. He slides the key into the lock and swings open the door to Nikki's room.

I hate that I get excited to see her. Even though it's not anything like what I feel for Tavin, I do like her. She's strong and she can keep almost as quiet as Tav. Whenever I get the chance, I try to comfort her. I'm sure it means nothing though, when I turn around and make her bleed. Regardless, she doesn't look at me like she does Logan and that does mean something to me.

I look to the floor in front of her bed and she's on her knees with her hair all over the place. God, she's so thin.

She's already earned so many beatings from Logan seeing that her food is hardly touched.

"Good evening, Lotus."

"Good evening, Logan."

"Good evening, Nikki."

"Good evening, *Toben*."

She says my name with spite. We've had our moments, though. I try to make her smile when Logan isn't looking and she tries to fight it.

He puts his bag on the floor and kneels in front of her. "I have a surprise for you today." His head turns to the side to address me too. "It's yours as well, for your birthday." Oh shit. This can't be good. "Lie on the bed, Lotus." Her eyes flicker to me, but I know as much as she does. "Take off your clothes." He faces me and nods. "You too."

What?!

"Can I ask why?"

He sighs. "Why do you think, Toben? Its time. You don't have to hurt her if you don't want to, this time. Regardless, you will not be a virgin when you leave this house."

No. No. No. I've been terrified of this. I thought I was in the clear.

"You want me to rape her? I don't think I can physically do that, Logan."

He laughs. "You've never been touched by someone have you? Trust me, you'll be able to."

Of course I haven't been touched, you fuck! You bought me when I was ten!

"I don't want to do this, Logan. She's only thirteen."

He forces me back against the closed door, slamming his hand against the wall as he grinds his teeth.

"You have two choices. You can get over there and fuck her like I told you to, or when we get back, you'll do it to Tavin. Either way, it will happen tonight."

My skin heats up a thousand degrees. Even though I definitely don't want to do this, the alternative isn't an option.

I nod my compliance and he pushes off from the wall. The pounding of my heart beats in my skull as I drag my feet to the bed. I've never kissed a girl other than Tavin. I only want to do this stuff with her and only if she wants to. I feel like I'm about to betray her.

Nikki's eyes are filled with tears. I have no idea what I'm doing, but I want to try to make this less horrifying than it has to be. I climb onto the bed and lie on top of her. Leaning down, I kiss her tears, softly trailing down her neck.

Damn it! Logan's right, my body is reacting to hers. I make all my kisses and touches tender, until she reacts by kissing me back. It's like a switch goes off and suddenly, I don't want to be gentle.

Things are going to be different between us now. I honestly don't know how Nikki feels about what just happened. It didn't last long, and there were times she didn't seem miserable. Then she would cry and beg me to stop, screaming that I was hurting her. I hated how that made me feel. Even though I tried to stop, Logan made sure I saw it through to completion.

As I watch Logan with her, I think I might kind of understand what Tavin may have been feeling when she tried to kill herself a couple months ago. At first, I didn't want to do that with Nikki, and then I did. Now I hate myself for doing it. It takes a while before the truth of what I've done sinks all the way in.

I am a rapist.

I am a murderer.

I am just like him.

The reality seems to rush through my body in a surge of

violence, and I explode. Grabbing the first tool I can, I lunge and bring it down on her, hitting over and over. Blow after blow. I let go of my mind and let the rage take control…

"TOBEN THAT'S ENOUGH!" His voice brings everything back into focus in an instant. "KNEEL!"

My knees hit the floor and when I look up at Logan, I'm taken aback by the expression in his eyes. It isn't the anger I am prepared for…it's pride.

I'm his little fucked up protégé.

He almost smiles. "You've earned the right to give her the treats this time. Now, go get cleaned up."

Rising to go to her bathroom, I look at her bloodied body. It wasn't Logan that did that to her.

It was me.

I try not to feel sorry for myself, if I can help it. These girls are suffering so much more than I am, and it's me causing it half the time. I just never wanted my first time to be with anyone other than Tavin. I sure as hell never wanted it with a non-willing participant. Nikki will hate me for forever, and I deserve it. The only silver lining is keeping Tavin out of it. If I had lost it on her like I just did Nikki…I don't even want to think about it.

After my shower, I reach into the duffel and pull out the candy and the kit. Today he brought her sour gummy worms. Tavin loves these. Then again, Tavin loves all candy-she's a little piggy. Logan passes me to go to the bathroom.

His showers are the only time Nikki and I get to be alone. Today though, I am dreading the privacy.

I can tell she's awake by her whimpers. My throat is dry and I try to swallow as I stalk around her bed. I kneel on the floor and rest my head over my laced fingers on the edge of her mattress as I look at what I've done. Her face is the only place untouched other than random blood spatter. He'd kill me if I ever marked her there.

I destroyed her with the whip; little gashes are everywhere. I used my bare fists on her as well and although I can't see the evidence now, it'll be there the next time I see her.

As my eyes tether to her blue ones, she whispers, "You're worse than him."

My tears well up as I whisper, "Nikki, I don't know what happened, I just snapped. I hate that he makes me do this."

She shakes her head, with a wet face. "No. You like it and just pretend not to. He's at least honest with who he is, he's real. You? You make people love you before you tear them apart."

I shouldn't get angry with her, yet I am. She has no idea what she's talking about. I throw the candy on the bed.

"I'm sorry that you think you love me, but I love someone too, and she is why I do this. I will rape you and beat you every day for the rest of my life if it will save her. I never asked for your love. I don't want it."

Even if the part about not wanting it isn't completely true, the last thing I want to do is string her along. This isn't high school. It's Hell.

I can see my words crush her, turn her to dust. It's like I've had a knife in my chest for years and when shit like this happens, it turns again. My heart must be a twisted, mangled mess by now. Grabbing her arm, I clean her and prepare the fix.

As her eyes become vacant, I let out a sigh and rub her hair in between my fingers. "Enjoy the peace, Nikki."

I have everything packed up and ready to go when Logan finishes in the bathroom. He pats my shoulder as we pass through the door. "You've made me feel a new emotion, Plaything." When I look at him he grins. "Pride...for someone other than myself."

That makes me feel even shittier. Not only because I

made a child rapist proud of me, but also because part of me feels pleased that I made him happy. I hate to admit that he has been more of a father than my own, and there are times I enjoy being with him as much as I loathe it.

We do a line of coke in the car before I go home to Tavin. He even gives me some to share, as a reward for my performance.

As soon as I see her, the guilt hits me in the face. I don't know why, it's not like I had a choice in the matter. I still feel like a lying asshole.

She's standing by the fridge in a little blue dress, looking gorgeous while she smiles at me. I'm across the basement in four large strides when I hold her face and kiss her. Picking her up, I wrap her legs around my waist, carry her to the ta-ble, and sit her down, all while never leaving her lips. I know this can't go far, I just need her, any little bit that she's willing to give me. I squeeze her thighs as I open her legs further, allowing me to get closer. I need to be closer. Her lips taste so sweet and she smells so good that all I want to do is lift up this dress and become a part of her.

Goddamn it.

I have to stop. I'll get off in my pants if I don't, and that would be humiliating. I also think it would probably freak her out. I pull my lips from her mouth and press my fore-head against hers. My voice is lower than normal when I murmur, "Hey, Love."

She giggles, "Hey, back."

I hold her hand and press my healed wound against hers. "I have a surprise for you."

After cutting the lines and rolling up the hundred Logan gave me, we're on our way to a fun night. We dance to our song, finding happiness, purpose, and love in one another. All the terrible things he's done to us and the sick things he's made me do, are almost worth these moments with her.

Later, when she draws on her wall, I sit on the floor next to her, writing in my lyric book, that is quickly becoming filled with words meant for her, as we listen to Slayer. Her art has always had a fanciful and erratic feel, lately though, it's taken on an eerie nature, even if it is kind of hard to tell. She doesn't want Logan to see it, so she'll only draw in the little space that can be hidden by our bed and it all kind of melts together.

My mind keeps going back to the proverbial clock counting down to our demise.

Five months.

Five months is what we have left to live if I don't come up with some kind of solution. I look at the other half of me, the person who makes me more than a husk, my reason for not sinking one of Logan's knives into my half dead heart, and I know no matter what the sacrifice-I can't let her die.

Two months later—December, 2006

Tavin

The ropes dig into my skin and I try to move my wrists so I can feel the burn. I steal a glance at Toben and he's watching Logan. Part of me hates that he watches this and I despise that it turns him on.

I wish I could give away four of my five senses. Then I wouldn't have to hear these horrible sounds and smell the stench of sweat, sex, and cigarettes. I wouldn't have to watch what he does to me and wouldn't have to feel any of the things he makes me feel, and maybe I wouldn't detest myself for when it feels good.

I swear he hears my thoughts because he looks up at me and asks, "Do you like this, Lotus?"

No! I don't like it! It makes me feel slimy and sick!

"Y-yes, Logan."

He goes completely still, and when my gaze locks into gold, I see the storm that tells me I just did something bad.

He stands, picks the knife up from the floor, and cuts the rope, nicking my wrists and ankles in the process. Placing a hand over each of my wrists on the arms of the chair he leans forward. We're so close that our noses are almost touching.

His cinnamon scent burns my nostrils as he growls, "Do you not think I fucking know when you're lying?" He yanks me out of the chair and picks me up. I hate that he still picks me up, I'm freaking fifteen now! He slams me on the bed so hard that my head bounces forward. He wraps his belt around my neck before he punches me in the rib and I stifle a groan. "Tell me what you are, Lotus."

"Your whore."

"That's right." When he pulls tight on the belt, it isn't long until I see black spots everywhere…

I awake, but he still isn't finished. After what must be an eternity, he finally abandons all tools and with a disgusting moan, he rolls off me. Leaning across the bed to get his cigarettes out of his pants pocket, he lights one. Toben is kneeling on the floor and I peek at him before Logan pulls me on to his sweaty chest. He strokes my hair with his free hand and tells Toben to get enough ready for all three of us.

We sit on the bed together and Logan gets me fixed up first. Right before the liquid pleasure is pushed into my bloodstream, I flick my eyes toward Toben and he winks at me.

I think I smile…

We're still all in the bed and Logan still has his arms around me. According to the clock, we've been in this same position for over three hours. The heroin is still lingering and Logan allows me to run my fingers across his arm and stomach while he trails his across my thigh. I look up at him and in this moment, I want him to love me, I want him to tell me that I am smart and pretty. Toben is lying across the foot of the bed propped up on his elbow looking at us. I want to know. I will only ask for me, though, Toben might not want me to ask for him.

"Logan?" He turns his head to look at me in question. I'm suddenly nervous. Still, I want to hear what he says so I take a big breath and whisper, "Do you love me?"

He smiles softly and rubs his thumb over my jaw and across my lips. He kisses me and holds my chin so I have to look into his eyes.

He does love me! He's going to say it!

"No, Lotus. You are my plaything, and that is all."

I'm grateful the heroin is still in my system because I might cry, otherwise. He pushes me off of him to go into the bathroom and Toben hands me my dress while he kisses me.

"Fuck him, we don't need or want his love."

Tonight is black licorice and Toben doesn't like it, so he gives me his. I chew on it as I rest my head in his lap and he sings me our lullaby. There's something he's hiding from me, I think. I hope it isn't anything I've done.

All of a sudden, he asks, "What do you think happens when we die?"

Even though it's something I've thought a lot about, how am I really supposed to know?

"Maybe we live forever and we go somewhere magical after we leave here. Someplace where everyone is nice and you can have all the candy you want. Maybe we go to a whole world made of candy!"

He laughs. "I think you are confusing Heaven with Willy Wonka's Chocolate Factory." I don't know what that is, but any kind of factory that makes chocolate sounds like a place I want to be. He looks at the ceiling. "I think I'm going to Hell."

Well, if he's going to Hell then so am I.

"I thought we were already in Hell?" I tease him. He sure says it enough.

He kisses me with a smile. "Smartass."

I get up to straddle him and kiss the scar his dad gave him. Lacing our fingers, I rest my lips on his.

"I don't care if its Heaven, Hell, or a chocolate factory, as long as I'm with you."

"When you bleed, I bleed, Love."

Two months later—February, 2007

Toben

Two weeks. That's what remains of our lives. In two weeks we will have been Logan's toys for five years. I wake up nauseous every single day. Every time I look at her, I want to scream. I hate myself because every time we make out, or she touches me, or looks at me, the desire to throw her down is almost overwhelming. How can I think that way when I know how much she hates it? Maybe it's because I don't want to die without having been with her. She's the only one I ever wanted.

If I were a normal boy I wouldn't even know what half the things were that I want to do to her.

I'm not a normal boy.

I need to stop thinking about Tavin when I'm with Nikki, though. It's not fair to her. She's in love with me. She wants me to save her, to take her away from here like some Goddamn hero. She even says as much while I'm cleaning all the tools.

"We could run, right now, before he gets out. My dad taught me how to drive once, and we could stop and get your friend."

I shake my head. "Do you really think that if I could just take off with her that I would be standing here with you? I would be long gone, sweetheart."

She shuts her eyes and tears fall. "How can you be with me and not care about me?"

It isn't true. She's lying and doesn't even know it. I do care for her. A lot.

"Because I have very little heart left and it belongs to her."

"Why don't you then? Just take her and go?" I hate that she feels for me at all.

"Because I have a fourth-grade education. Because she's been starved enough in her life. Because I don't know if I can protect her or keep her clean. Because I have no way to take care of her, and to be completely honest, I'm scared of what else is out there."

"We can steal food, and there are ways to make enough money for a room. Plenty of men would pay for what he makes me do, anyway."

That last line hits my brain like lightening and after months and months of trying to come up with a way to save us, I finally have an idea.

I can't stop the laugh as I grasp her face and kiss her. "You're a fucking genius, Nikki." I have no idea if it will work.

At least I have a plan. I turn to her and her face is filled with hope, making me feel like a major dick. "Oh shit, Nik. I didn't mean-it helps me with another problem I'm having. I can't take you away, I'm sorry."

More tears rim her eyes and she rolls over, turning her back to me just as Logan emerges from the bathroom.

"Alright, Plaything, get cleaned up."

I stare at Nikki once more before getting my clean clothes and obeying him.

The warm water of the shower feels amazing. Though nothing is guaranteed, at least I have a solution, and if I know him like I think I do, it will appeal to him. It's far from ideal, but anything is better than being killed. Right?

After my shower, Logan already has Nikki high, with a bag of candy on her nightstand. I hover over her for a moment before pressing a kiss to her head. If I am honest with myself, I know she means so much to me, and I do feel bad for being a jerk, there's just nothing I have left to give her.

Driving back, my palms are sweaty and I can't stop my leg from bouncing. Logan keeps glancing at my movement, growing more irritated by the second. If I don't hurry and spit it out, I imagine he will stab me just to get me to sit still.

"What is it?!" He screams at me.

"I-it's almost our anniversary."

He's silent for so long I think he isn't going to respond until he clears his throat. "Truthfully, I do feel a bit melancholy when it comes to the expiration of you two. I don't know if it's something about you as individuals or as a set, nevertheless, I have become quite attached." He shakes his head. "Such a shame."

"It doesn't have to be," I blurt out.

He sighs and lights a cigarette before handing me one. "Toben-"

I'm being ballsy, cutting him off, I just have to get it

out. "You're a businessman, right? Well I have a business proposition."

He quirks an eyebrow and smirks. "Do you now?" Even though he's trying to sound condescending, I have his attention.

"You have a lot of hot shot friends, right? I bet they would pay big bucks to have a go at Tavin. She's still considered young by most standards and could probably still pass for twelve or thirteen." I hope I'm going about this the right way. I know that pimping her out is terrible. I would just rather her be used up and abused than dead.

"Her tolerance for pain would add a certain novelty to her as a product..."

He's considering it! I just have to keep this going. "And you could make it exclusive, like by referral only or something."

He whips his head in my direction. "Plaything, that's... that's brilliant."

He's pleased with me and I have an extreme love/hate relationship with his approval. We sit in silence as we smoke our cigarettes. When he speaks again, his question floors me.

"You would be for sale as well, correct? You'd be surprised how many men would love to tear apart a little boy. Obviously, that was never my cup of tea."

He gives me an impish grin like what he just said was hilarious. I hadn't even considered things heading in this direction. I'm light headed, queasy, and sweating bullets. If it was just a simple matter of death or a dick in the ass, I would tell you to pass the cyanide. It isn't though. This is Tavin's life on the line.

I'm so ready to trade her body for her life, am I not willing to do the same?

Of fucking course I am.

"Yes, Logan, I would be for sale as well."

CHAPTER TWELVE
Clients

One month later—March, 2007

Tavin

"I WONDER WHAT HE'LL BRING US TODAY, I HOPE IT'S another movie. Maybe he'll let us do some coke before we play, if I ask sweetly. Oh, and I am not going to eat my cupcake right away this time, I'm gonna to save it for breakfast tomorrow." He doesn't respond so I look up at him from my drawing. "Toben! Are you even listening?"

He clearly isn't because he jumps. "I'm sorry, what, Love?"

He's been checking out for weeks, gone in a private world. Every time I ask him what's going on, he says he's tired.

"You left me again."

He climbs to the floor. "I would never leave you. I'm just tired, is all."

"Yeah, sure."

He moves my hair over my shoulder and kisses up my neck. I turn my head so my mouth is on his as he moves my body to face him. He lies back on the concrete floor, pulling me with him as his fingers entwine and tug at my hair. His hands make their way down my back. We can never do this for long before he has to stop, and I love him for never making me feel guilty about it. Even if I still do on my own.

His kisses become more aggressive as he presses my body harder against his. He groans into my mouth when I hear the *click* of the lock. Jumping off of him, I cover the wall, and slide into my kneel position. Toben isn't far behind.

I can't wait to see what Logan brings us!

"Happy Anniversary, Playthings."

"Happy Anniversary, Logan."

He goes straight to the table, placing two bags and the familiar box that has our cupcakes in it, on the table, before coming to stand in front of me. His hand trails softly from the top of my head, down my face to my neck. He suddenly grips tight and pulls me up by my throat before smashing his mouth to mine.

Something is different. I can't place it. Logan is off. I'm going to ask him anyway.

"Logan?"

"Yes, Lotus?"

"Since it's our anniversary, can we do a couple lines before we play?"

He sighs, even though he's already reaching into his pocket. "Here. Only two each." He hands me the baggie as he disappears into the bathroom to change. Toben hurries from his kneel position and follows me to the table where we cut and inhale two lines each. Lickety split.

I'm grateful for the lines because today is extra rough. I kind of wonder if Logan is mad at me.

He's been at it for a while, when I start coming down. That's the bad part. Toben's whip slashes across my back.

Nasty, dirty, sickening.

Logan's laughs, "My filthy little plaything. Do you like it when Toben hits you?"

He flips me to my back as I hold back my tears and answer him. "Yes, Logan."

Finally, his aggression quickens as he jabs my ribs with the hilt of the knife. He moans and groans out, "Take it all, Lotus," before falling on top of me.

After Logan smokes a cigarette, he goes to shower. As soon as he's gone, Toben kisses the cuts he just gave me and hands me my dress. My hair sticks to my face from sweat and blood as we lie on the bed for a few moments before having to crawl back to the floor.

Walking from the bathroom, Logan barks at Toben to take a shower, as he sits down on our bed.

"Come here, Lotus." I obey and sit on his lap. He runs his hand through my hair, down my arm, and over my thigh while he lets me trace my fingers over his tattoo. "You aren't a little girl anymore, Tavin…" He trails off as if his thoughts carry him away. Shaking his head, he kisses my forehead. "Where would you like to go?"

My fingers stop moving and my heart momentarily stops beating. Is he asking what I think he's asking?

"Do you mean…outside?"

"Yes, Lotus."

I can't help it, the excitement overwhelms me as I throw my arms around his neck. "Thank you, Logan!"

He smiles at me, while prying me off of him. "Alright, now go pick out a pretty dress."

I do. The prettiest one. It's so pale blue it's almost white, the lace sleeves stop right at my wrist and the lace trim continues across the neckline. It goes to my mid-thigh and there's also a different kind of lace trimming the hem. I pick out my white slip-on shoes to match.

Toben leaves the bathroom with wet hair, no shirt, and

jeans. I hope Logan makes him dress nice too, then we will look like a fancy family.

I rush through my shower and hurry drying off. I wish I would have made sure I was completely dry because the lace is itchy on my wet skin.

When I swing open the bathroom door, a smile stretches across my face by itself. Toben is wearing light colored pants and a lightweight, black sweater that fits him perfectly. His hair is shorter than usual because Logan made him cut it a few weeks ago, and he looks so handsome.

He really is beautiful.

Holding out his hand to me, he squeezes it as we follow Logan up the stairs. I feel kind of sick because I'm so excited. The last time I left the basement was when Lacie died. I feel like I'm walking into a dream when the front door opens and sunlight fills my house. I take the steps two at a time and I just know I am going to burst. It's so much prettier out here than I remembered. Toben and I jump into the backseat.

When Logan climbs inside the car he asks, "Where are we going, my playthings?"

I want to go to the beach. I ache to feel the wet sand squishing between my toes and to watch the water come alive. I should probably ask to go somewhere I've never been since I don't know when I'll get to be out of the basement again. What if I don't like what I pick? I know I will like the beach.

Toben looks at me with a grin. "Wherever you want, Love."

"The beach!"

⟜

We take off our shoes and Toben rolls up his pants as we run hand in hand to the shoreline. The waves crash in my ears and the birds squawk above us. The wind blows the hair from my water misted face and I smell all the incredible smells that I've missed horribly.

It's been five years since we've been here and it's even more incredible than I remember.

Logan doesn't come to the shoreline with us. Instead, he sits on a bench near The Walk. I glance up at him every once and awhile because for some reason, I'm scared that he's going to leave us here alone. What if someone bad gets us? He's always there when I look, though, and this time, he's talking to a man in a black suit.

When he crooks his finger for us to go to him, Toben stands completely still, so I yank his arm to get him to hurry up. What's wrong with him? We are at the beach for goodness sake.

As we approach, the man stares at Toben making him freeze again. I turn to look up at him, and he's as pale as my dress.

"Hey, Tobe, are you okay?" I think he might pass out or throw up. "Are you sick?" The man sucks in through his teeth and when I look down at his pants, he has an erection!

Toben doesn't move a muscle until Logan addresses him. "Toben, this is Mr. English. He will be your playmate for the evening."

Yanking Toben's hand from mine, Logan pulls him close and growls something about arrangements, in his ear, as he shoves a cell phone into his hand.

Toben's face is smeared in fear and I yearn to hold him. What's going on? That man is going to play with him?! I didn't even know that was a possibility. I can't let this happen to him! I reach for him as the man jerks him toward the parking lot and Logan holds my arm.

"Sit down," he demands.

"Why did you give him to that man?!" Is he going to stay with him?! The tears come flooding out. "Is he coming back?"

"Sit. Down. Now."

I lower to the bench, wishing I could hit him for doing this. "Why?"

He sighs and lights his cigarette. "You are nearly adults. You need to learn that things like food, clothes, and shelter don't get handed to you; you must earn them." His eyes squint from the sun. "Toben is earning them." My mouth feels dry, I still don't understand. He faces me and I notice he's gotten more wrinkles. "Do you know what Lacie did for a living?"

Swallowing, I force the sound from my throat. "Yes, Logan."

"Say it."

"She was a prostitute."

"That's correct. She opened her legs for anyone with three hundred dollars and would swallow a dick for a hundred." He rolls his neck and clicks his tongue. "Fucking repulsive." Reaching out to touch me, he changes his mind and takes a drag instead. "You will only play with who I tell you to. You will not cry. You will do whatever they ask and then tell me what that entails, after each playdate."

He stands, pulls at my hand to lift me off the bench, and leads me back to the car. I'm so confused! Logan wants me to be with other men? I thought I was *his* Lotus. *His* plaything. *His* whore.

He pulls onto the freeway and I want to jump from the car. How often is he going to make us do this? No, no. NO! I DON'T WANT ANYONE ELSE TO TOUCH ME! The skin under my nails is bleeding and I don't care. I wish I could pull all of my skin off.

I'm scared!

I should have been enjoying the silence because more horrible things spew from his mouth.

"I know you like cock, Lotus, so at least drop the act in front of the Clients, okay? They are paying a lot of money for your little cunt, so just do what I've taught you and you'll be fine."

I'm hot and sweaty, my eyes burn, and my throat's sore when we pull up to a ginormous building. He hands me a cell phone and it looks completely different from our emergency one.

"Call me when you finish and I'll pick you up. In the future, you'll get a cab." He's gonna make me ride in a car by myself? "We'll work up to that. Now, go inside, don't speak to anyone, and take the elevator to the nineteenth level. Knock softly three times and wait for Mr. Sørensen." I open the car door and I almost fall because my legs are so weak. "Address him by name and when you get into the room, take off your clothes, kneel and await his instructions." He clears his throat. "Lotus?" My eyes match his. "Do not humiliate me."

"Yes, Logan."

I shut the door and go inside the big building. I find the elevator like the one we were on the day Mommy died. I don't like these. My stomach already hurts and this thing makes me feel worse. I wonder if the man and woman standing in here with me are staring at me, I'm just too scared to look up and see. My hands are shaking so bad that I stick them beneath my arms.

After the fifteenth floor, I'm alone. Once I see the one-nine light up and hear the *ding*, I wonder if I stick my head in the doors if it will smash my head to mush. As soon as the doors open, my eyes lock on to the red door in front of me. Everything else falls away, besides that door.

Nothing exists but that door.

I just pray Mr. Sørensen is a brutal killer and leaves little bits of me for Logan to find. Then I take it back because of Toben.

I hold my fist in front of the door for what feels like an eternity, before I finally bring it down and knock.

Three times.

The door quickly swings open, and a man that looks about Logan's age stands in front of me. He's tall and lean like Logan, but his hair is light and his narrowed eyes are green, not gold.

"Jesus, he wasn't kidding." He rakes his fingers through his hair. "Come on in."

His voice sounds funny. I like it. I've never heard anyone talk that way before. When I follow his guiding hand, my stomach twists and tightens. He touches my back and I look up to him. His eyebrows are scrunched. I think I'm making him angry.

"You're shaking like crazy. Are you alright?"

He puts his hands on either side of my face and I'm able to swallow while I drop my gaze to the floor. "Yes, Mr. Sørensen."

"Look at me when you speak to me." My eyes snap up and his face softens. "Call me Bjørn."

"Yes, Bjørn."

He smiles as he removes his hands, trailing his fingers down my neck and across my collar bone. "What's your name?"

"Tavin."

He inhales a breath. "He said you were young...how old are you?"

"Fifteen."

His nostrils flare as he moves his fingers to my lips. "Fuck. I don't know if I can."

I remember I'm supposed to take my clothes off, so I

pull my dress over my head and drop to my knees. He releases a harsh breath and chuckles.

"Well, shit."

It isn't that horrible, really, as far as playdates go. He made me do gross things too, but he was gentle about it. He didn't hurt me, either. He just tied me up and spanked me. He's nice to me and doesn't call me nasty names.

As I lie on my stomach, he traces all my scars and cuts with his fingers. "I wish more than anything I could stay here all night with you." He kisses me as he touches between my legs. "I want to schedule another playdate, would you like that?"

I don't know what to do. If I say no then maybe he won't schedule one and Logan will just give up and we can go back to normal. He would be so mad at me though. He told me they have to think I like it.

"Yes, Bjørn."

His cell phone rings, making him release an irritated sigh before answering. "What is it, Alexander?" He continues touching me as he frowns at the phone. "And I am well aware. I'm finishing a few things at the office and then I'll head over."

Hanging up the phone, he presses a kiss against my forehead before he removes his hand and gets out of bed.

Giving me a stick of rock candy, he says, "You were more than satisfactory."

He puts on his clothes as I eat my candy. When he's finished, I get up and pull on my dress. I need to call Logan and I don't know if I am supposed to in front of him, so I ask, "May I leave?"

Stepping over to me, he cups my chin and kisses me. "It

was nice to meet you, Tavin."

"It was nice to meet you, Bjørn."

Toben

This must be how Tavin feels. All I want is to stop breathing. I've never hated myself like this. I'm a queer now. Not that I care who anyone else wants to fuck, I just never wanted to be with men. A dude made me come. That's how I know I'm gay. My body hurts unlike anything I have ever experienced, and again, I wonder if her body felt like this.

I keep reminding myself this isn't her fault. Even though this was my idea, I did it for her. I did it to keep her alive and I will have to keep doing it.

Fuck!

I want to dig into my flesh and rip out all my veins. I can't handle feeling this. I need to get high. Logan's car pulls up next to Mr. English's Rolls-Royce. His greasy fingers lace into my hair as he yanks my head toward him and shoves a lollipop in my mouth.

"There, in case you weren't done sucking," he laughs and unlocks the car. "See you next time."

I scan the console for something sharp to stab in his throat, as I pull the candy out of my mouth. "Yes, Mr. English."

I get out and try not to slam the shit out of the door. The cool evening air hitting my face stirs up my emotions like the sand beneath my feet. I simultaneously get the overwhelming urge to scream, punch something, and cry all at the same time. The sucker falls from my hand to the dirt.

I climb into Logan's car and I have to sit carefully because

I'm pretty positive Mr. English tore me.

"How did it go?"

I snap my head in his direction. "How the fuck do you think it went?"

His hand squeezes my throat instantly. I can't breathe and I welcome the lack of oxygen.

"Talk to me like that again and I will terminate our arrangement."

He releases me and I involuntarily gasp. He doesn't speak to me again until he drives onto the freeway.

"Did he wear a condom?"

The tears won't stop threatening to fall and I hate hearing them in my voice. "Yes, Logan."

"And he made sure you were lubricated, correct?"

"No, Logan."

"What?!" His voice thunders through the car. "He didn't prepare you at all?"

My humiliation is threatening to choke me as I shake my head and whisper, "I think I'm torn."

"Motherfucker!" His hands slams against the steering wheel. "I had them sign a Goddamn contract for a reason!"

I don't know why he's so mad and I don't care. I just want to be alone and I live with the last person I want to see right now.

How am I supposed to face her? I did this for her! I know it's not fair. She didn't ask me to do it and I would never trade her life to undo this… I just don't want to see her right now.

I've been so lost in my self-loathing that I haven't considered that Tavin was probably terrified when she figured out what was happening. At least I was informed. I'm sure she had just as bad of a night and will need me. I just don't think I can be there for her. Not tonight. That's selfish as hell, too, because this was all my idea.

"I did try to prevent that from happening. I don't want your genitalia scarred." He hands me a cigarette. "It lowers product quality." Fucking prick. "You won't be seeing him again, Plaything, and he will pay for that stunt. Consider it a promise."

Well at least that's something.

My stomach's in knots when we arrive home, and all I want to do is lock myself in the window well or the bathroom and shoot so much dope I don't even know who I am anymore.

We walk inside and I'm taken off guard to see Tavin sitting on the couch in the living room. She drops to her knees and Logan touches her face.

"You may stand, Lotus."

Running over to me, she doesn't look the least bit upset. "Toben, are you okay?"

She holds out her arms to wrap them around me. I do not want to be touched right now, least of all by her.

"Not now, Tav. Just-I need to be alone." I turn my back to her and face Logan. "May I have my fix?"

He stares at me for a moment and I almost think the bastard is going to deny me on the night I need it more than ever. He hands me the case, and instead of the balloon we usually get, he gives me a clear little bag with just enough to do the trick. He knows I would have loaded it full. I snatch it with just as much force as I dare and brush past Tavin, to go downstairs.

"Toben!"

I cannot deal with her right now! I spin around and her eyes are wet. "I said I need to be alone!" I scream at her.

"Please, don't shut me out. Talk to me!"

That's it! She just pushes too far. She won't let the hell up. I grip her arms and squeeze her.

"I JUST TOOK A FUCKING DICK, OKAY?" I roar it at her before I let go and she almost falls back. "I'm a faggot, just like my dad always said!"

She still isn't deterred. "Please let me help you! It's happened to me too!" She reaches out for me and I pull back.

"Yeah, but you're a girl!"

Stopping in her tracks, her head tics. "So, because I'm a girl that makes everything that's been done to me okay?" She's never looked at me with fury, like she is right now. "Fuck you," she whispers before she spins around and storms to the kitchen.

"Tavin! I didn't mean it like that!"

I follow after her and I'm interjected by Logan's hand on my arm.

"Leave her be and come with me." Leading me back across the room, he opens a door leading to a staircase I've never seen before. "Maybe with your new freedom you two may want to have separate bedrooms."

That makes me both sad and relieved. There are times I need my own space-tonight is the perfect example, but I love waking up next to her. I don't know if that will ever happen again after what I just said to her. When we get to the landing, I see there's a bathroom to my left with a bedroom and a closet next to that. I follow him into the bedroom that has a bed, radio, computer, and TV.

"Sit." I carefully lower to the bed and he sits next to me. He hands me a cigarette after lighting his own. "What happened tonight does not make you gay."

The fury over what I can't undo, the regret of what I said to Tavin, and the disgust I feel being in my own body causes me to finally burst. He's the closest thing to a father that I have. I fall against him and weep.

"He made me come, Logan!"

Lifting me off of him, he taps my chin. "Look at me,

Plaything." He's almost kind in this moment. "Enough stim-
ulation is what made you come, not the source. You know
my tastes, yet my wife can bring me to completion while I
find her revolting." His wife is still a woman, though. I don't
know what to think or feel. I want to believe him. He shakes
his head before taking another drag. "Trust me, Toben,
you're not gay. I see how you look at Lotus. I watch how you
are with Nikki." He does make sense. When I think of the
things that happened with Mr. English, I want to throw up.
When I think about the things I've done and want to do with
Tavin, that's when I feel turned on. "Now take down your
pants and let me see."

I don't know how much more embarrassment I can take
tonight. "What?!"

Just like that, he's back to himself. "If I have to ask you
again, not only will I beat you bloody, we'll go downstairs
and do the same to Lotus. I need to see the damage."

I stick the cigarette in my mouth and drop the drugs on
the bed. "Fuck," I mumble under my breath as I pull down
my pants.

"Bend over the bed." More tears fall as he searches me
over. At least he's quick about it.

"You have a small tear, though I don't believe it will scar."

After I pull my pants up, I wipe the tears off my face.
"How often do I have to do this?"

He rolls his neck. "You'll not exceed five playdates a
week." Reaching into his pocket, he pulls out a stack of cash.
"Here, use this for whatever you want. I will continue paying your bills and I'll bring you food for the next few weeks
to allow you two time to get used to the independence and
responsibility."

I flip through the money and my jaw drops. "This is
three thousand dollars!"

"You may spend it on anything besides drugs. Buying

off the street is dangerous. You might get poor quality or robbed completely. You would also be risking getting arrested. Should that ever happen, do not be foolish enough to mention my name."

"Yes, Logan."

"You're getting complete freedom. Just know this, Plaything: If you run, I'll find you. I have more resources than you can fathom. There is nowhere you can go that I can't reach you." He sniffs and looks at his watch. "While there's much I need to go over with you, it's getting late and I still need to talk to Lotus. Would you like me to fix you up before I go?"

"Yes, Logan." I ease my way onto the bed and lean back. While he prepares my reprieve, all I can think about is what I said to Tav. I just don't want to feel.

"Good night, Plaything."

"Good night, Logan."

I close my eyes and wait.

There is nothing more to fear…

CHAPTER THIRTEEN
Products

Tavin

E'VE NEVER HAD A FIGHT LIKE THIS BEFORE and he's never talked to me that way. Ever. How could he say that? He's been here through everything, seen what Logan has done to me. It happens to him once and it's worse for him because he's a boy? What does that have to do with anything? He's never hurt my feelings like this before.

I miss him. I haven't spent a night away from him in five years, to the day. Even when he got put in the cage, he was here with me.

I was so excited for today and it ended up being horrible. I can't even think about all the men I will have to have sex with, without having to run to the bathroom to throw up. I don't want to be like Lacie.

I'm not high anymore and I wish I was because I'm so sad. I can't stop crying. I'm fifteen and I still act like a baby. I miss Toben and I feel guilty for what I said to him, but he was being a jerk. Does he think it didn't humiliate me in the beginning for him to watch all that stuff? Sure, it doesn't bother me anymore, and in fact, I want him there, it's just, I know what he's going through. He had that look, he wanted to climb out of his body just like I do. It makes my chest hurt when I think about what that man could have done to him. I don't know though because he isn't here. He doesn't want to be around me.

My eyes are getting heavy so I turn off the light and climb under my covers. I think I fall asleep when a noise startles me. I lie perfectly still and don't dare move. I wish I would have slept the other way because then I'd be facing the sound. Suddenly, warm arms wrap around me as I feel the bed dip and Toben's scent brings more tears.

"I'm a douche bag prick, and I'm deeply sorry, Love." His soft lips press against my neck. "Please know I didn't mean it. Today just…fucked me up."

I roll over to face him and bring my lips down on his. "When you bleed, I bleed. Remember?"

He lets out a teary laugh as he presses his forehead against mine and holds my hand. Even in the dark I know our scars are together. "I know, Tav. I just-I feel so fucking gross." His voice cracks as he breaks down. He's never cried like this. His body shakes the bed as he weeps and all I can do is hold him. I can't erase what happened and I can't make him not feel it. Only heroin can do that. His words stab my soul when he chokes, "Do you feel differently about me?"

How could he even think that? Even though I can't give him what he wants, I'll give him what I can. As I sit up, I pull off my dress and push him onto his back when he tries to sit up. Straddling him, I lean down and kiss his neck.

"Did you feel differently about me after the first time?"

He's breathless when he answers, "No."

"Then why would I?" I bring his hands to my chest. I wish I wanted to have sex with him. I wish I could, I just can't have something so dirty between us. It would ruin everything.

His breathing picks up and his temperament switches to a domineering one. "Stop me before I go too far, Love. I fucking mean it." Flipping me to my back, he kisses me hard as he keeps his hands on my chest. I touch his back and feel his lotus beneath my fingers. This is getting more aggressive than I want, but he's had a hard night so I'm giving him everything that I'm able. "Logan's right, I'm definitely not gay." There's a smile in that groan and I can tell this is helping.

He presses himself against me and after a deep breath I think I'm okay, it's just getting intense and I don't know how much more I can do. The sick fear is creeping around me like it does every time I have sex.

Then he does it, he crosses the line. He's violent with his fingers and it makes me freeze. I can't speak. My voice is caught when all I want is to shove him away and scream for him to stop. Finally, I am able to push a soft, "Stop," from my lips. He doesn't. Instead, he gets rougher. I'm sweating and when my heart almost pounds through my body, my throat opens up and the scream finally escapes.

"Stop, Toben!"

He jumps back instantly. "I said before, Tavin!"

More stupid tears! Why do I keep crying and why can't I stop them? "I'm sorry, I tried! It was like I couldn't move." Why can't I just give it to him? "Am I a bad friend because I don't want you to touch my-"

"Do not finish that fucking sentence." Even when his voice is stern, he doesn't sound mad. He lies back down next to me and pulls me next to him. "I thought you understood. We don't have to do anything, and you'll still be my Love. You're the other half of my soul, Tav. Nothing will ever change that. I love you."

"I love you, too." He kisses my head and shifts around in the bed. I hear the *click* of the lighter and it lights up his face and the end of a cigarette.

"Can you believe we can just leave whenever we want?" His arm wraps around my shoulder as he pulls me close. "Tomorrow will be our first day of freedom and we have enough money to do whatever we please."

I'm scared of the police and all of the bad people. I'm just more excited to leave the house. I guess if anyone hurt us, Logan would make them pay for it. I want to go somewhere new, now that I know we aren't locked down here anymore.

"Where should we go?"

The end of his cigarette lights up in the darkness as he pulls on it.

"Would it be lame to say I want to go to the mall? We could buy our own clothes and more music. We could go ice skating or play mini golf. Who knows how much it has changed since the last time I was there."

The mall sounds like a lot of fun and the excitement starts to creep up my belly. "Yeah! Let's go to that place!"

I can feel his body vibrate with his laugh. "Well then, the mall it is."

⌒

I wake up, take a shower, and get ready while Toben still sleeps. I can't be patient anymore, I want to eat my cupcake and go to the mall. I'm not waiting all day, on his sleepy butt. I jump on our bed.

"Wake up! Let's go to the mall!"

"Ah, damn it, Tav!" He grumbles before he pulls the pillow over his head. "It isn't even open yet, come back to bed."

Is he nuts? There's no way I'm going back to sleep when I'm so excited. The clock reads seven forty-two.

"When does it open?"

"Ugh!" He throws his arms down as he sits up and glares at me. He's barely even trying to make it believable. "Fine. You win." He throws his legs off the side of the bed and lights a cigarette. He sure is smoking a lot. "Let me shower and we can go get breakfast." His face lights up in remembrance. "Oh my God, Tavin, we can get pancakes! You'll love the shit out of some pancakes, I promise you that."

"But I saved my cupcake for breakfast."

"Trust me, you want pancakes."

"Well…I guess it does have the word 'cake' in it."

He laughs as he takes a drag. "Yeah."

Pancakes are AMAZING. I also have strawberry milk and I think it may be the best drink ever made. Toben says the mall is open by the time we finish at the food place, so we take a cab.

We're dropped off in front of a humongous building and pass underneath a huge archway to get to a set of wooden doors. As soon as we walk through, my voice gets stolen and I think I'm imagining this. My eyes climb up and up until they finally find the ceiling and I can see the sky. It must be glass or else everyone would get soaked when it rains.

There are people everywhere, and I almost want to cover my ears because it's so loud. Toben says there are stores on every level and I count four levels above us. There's no way we're going to be able to see everything today.

It isn't scary at all. Nobody is being mean to us and we don't see any police.

"Where do you want to go first?" I have no idea. There are so many choices! He must sense that I'm overwhelmed because he says, "Let's get a smoothie."

I drink my 'smoothie' as Toben had called it, while I flip through clothes and wait on him to try on jeans.

"The girl's section is over there, you know."

It's a boy's voice and it's not Toben's. I turn slowly, and the mouth that the voice is from is smiling at me. He's taller than I am and probably shorter than Tobe. He looks about our age and is wearing a bright orange T-shirt and faded jeans. His eyes are thoughtful blue and his brown hair is short.

He seems nice so I smile back at him. "I know, but I'm waiting for my friend."

Tilting his head to the side, his face hardens. "You look familiar, have we met?"

I shrug. "I don't think so."

His features relax as he stuffs his hands in his pockets. "Huh, that's weird. Well, anyway, hi. My name's Christopher."

"Hi. I'm Tavin."

He smiles at me again before I hear Toben's bossy voice. "Tavin, come here."

I turn to see what has him so upset when Christopher gasps, "Toben?!" Toben turns white instantly. "Holy crap, dude, are you back from boarding school?"

What the heck is boarding school? Toben looks about to bolt, he's freaking out. I think Christopher is an old friend from when he went to school.

"Uh…hey…yeah, I'm back in town for a while."

He keeps shifting his weight and his eyes keep flickering to the exit. What's he talking about?

"God, man, are you not allowed to text or email? You just up and vanished," Christopher says.

Toben adjusts his beanie and a sad, nervous laugh jumps from his lips. "Oh, yeah well, the headmaster's an epic douche bag."

He doesn't want this boy to know that he's been with me this whole time.

"If you're going to be in town awhile, you should hit me up and we'll party." Christopher takes out a pen and writes on Toben's hand. "I need to be back before third period, but it's good to see you." He turns to me and smiles. "Later, Tavin." I smile and nod to him before he leaves the store.

Toben lets out a huge breath and leans over the clothes rack.

"Are you okay? Why did you lie to him?"

His composure is slowly coming back. "We can't tell people about our lives, Tav. Nobody can know." I remember Logan telling me that last night, I just never thought of a lie to tell.

Christopher is our only hiccup in an otherwise perfect day. After we finish buying clothes, we get ice cream and play mini golf.

I sift through rows of CDs and I don't know any artists besides what Toben tells me, so I look at titles and covers. Then I see it. I can almost hear it calling to me. It has a girl in a black dress and she's removed her face. If I could remove my face nobody would ever touch me again. I pick it up and look at it closer to see she has chains around her neck that come up into a crown behind her head like a wicked princess. *House of Secrets* is written on the front.

I guess I live in a house of secrets, too. I can't ever tell anyone what happens there, not that I know anyone to tell, anyway.

Written next to it is 'Otep'. I wonder if that's the girl's name. "I want this one." I hand the CD to Toben.

"You know this is metal right?"

"So?"

He shrugs. "Fine by me, I've never heard it before."

As we leave the music store, I see a place that sells cameras. I've been out of film for the camera Logan got me for my birthday last year, so I drag Toben inside. They say they don't sell the kind we need, but that we could probably order it online.

When we leave the camera store, I ask Toben, "Where's

online? Is it in the mall?"

He laughs and laces his fingers between mine. "It's not a place, Love. I'll show you when we get home. We can get more film, we'll just have to ask Logan because I don't have a credit card."

I don't understand how you can get something from somewhere that isn't a place, but he says he'll explain it later, so I forget about it. We play games at the arcade and we get a pretzel, before deciding to leave.

After we drop off the stuff we bought at home, I talk Toben into going to the park. He says we're too old, so I have to beg a little. I've missed swinging on the swings and they are just as fun as I remember. Afterwards, we go to the beach and lie in the sun as I sit between his legs with his arms around me.

Everything is perfect until we hear a high pitched musical ping coming from my pocket. We look at each other, both scared of what will happen when I answer it. The screen reads Logan's name and after I push the button, I'm able to find enough of my voice to scratch out, "H-hello?"

"Hello, Lotus. You have a playdate in a few hours." My heart sinks. "If you're not home, get there and clean up. He will arrive at five p.m."

I don't want to cry, I'm just scared. What are the chances he will be as nice as Bjørn?

"Yes, Logan."

Toben

Apparently, Tavin's first client wasn't that bad. Her second one is, though. The last I saw, he was hitting her with his belt and God knows what all he's saying to her. I did hear him say something about her 'decorating his cock'. He doesn't want me around and that's fine with me, because watching her with Logan is bad enough. I have no desire to see her get destroyed by yet another man.

As I turn to leave, right before I shut the door, her eyes lock with mine. I wink to tell her to be brave. She's gotten accustomed to Logan and she knows him. She doesn't know these new men or what they will do.

She keeps the tears away until he leaves, and I'm proud of her for it. As soon as he's out the door, I take her into my arms as I let her cry it out all over me. Once she composes herself, which is fairly quickly, she picks up her phone to call Logan to tell him about her playdate. I know he says he wants to know what happens to make sure that they follow the rules, but I think he gets off on her humiliation. He's probably jerking off while she explains it.

Apparently, everything the Client did is within his boundaries so if he ever wants to reschedule, he'll be able to. After hanging up, she lies down on the couch and I lie down behind her, holding her hand and smelling her hair.

"Lacie got fucked on this couch and now I have too." Her voice is cold and I hadn't noticed how raspy it has become, until now. Even though the words are ugly, they almost sound pretty.

"Come on, Love, don't do this to yourself. You're nothing like Lacie. That heartless whore was born trash. You weren't, you're pure."

"I'm not pure anymore."

I sit up so I can see her eyes. "Yes, you are. You're never hateful or malicious even when it's surrounded you your whole life. I have never heard you demean anyone besides yourself. You have a caring and gentle nature and whatever these men do to you doesn't change that."

I know she doesn't believe me, even as she nods. "I just hope Logan hurries."

"He's coming over?"

A little smile peeks out. "Yeah, he's bringing us some dope." She's been holding caramels in her hand and she hands me one before popping the rest in her mouth. "Thank God."

While I won't be thanking God, it's definitely good to hear. He never lets us have it two days in a row.

He doesn't make us wait long for his arrival, but doesn't just hand over the drugs either. The bastard actually makes her play first. As if she hasn't been through enough today.

It breaks my heart because recently, she's become almost neutral when it comes to sex with Logan. I know she still despises it and it takes away little pieces of her, but if someone were to ever walk in on them, she would appear to be a willing participant. Whenever they finish, she acts completely normal, and on most days, if I hadn't seen it myself I wouldn't be able to tell it had happened.

Right now, though, she's clearly uncomfortable and I don't think it's because of the doubled-up playdates. We're in her parents' room. She never talks much about her past with them. Then again, I don't talk about my past either, really. I can't help wondering what all she saw, heard, and endured in the years before I met her. I still don't see how she survived it.

Her eyes dart around the room and she won't stop fidgeting. We're kneeling in front of her parents' bed as Logan returns from his shower. Her head tics as he runs his fingers through her hair,

"Alright, Lotus, you can get up." He nods at me. "You too, Plaything." We stand as he nods toward the door. "Come now. I want to speak with you before we go."

We follow him back downstairs and I have to suppress a groan. I'm beyond ready for the needle.

My thoughts shift back to Christopher like they have a hundred times since seeing him in Macy's. I want to hang out with him, see how much he's changed. It would be nice to forget this life for a while. I love Tav, she's my world, but she's also a constant reminder of our tortured existence. He would be a breath of normal air. Then I remember I've been locked in a basement for five years. I have no clue what the popular movies are or the newest iPod or whatever, is out now. I would have to avoid him for months at a time to keep up the pretense of boarding school and I have no clue how Logan would react if I asked to text him.

"Sit." We hold hands and obey. "I know the Clients are a new dynamic in our relationship. I'm feeling my way around just as you are." He pulls out a cigarette and lights it before throwing the pack to me. "There are rules that need to be followed for everyone's safety." He waits until I light mine. "Rule number one: they must wear a condom. Every time." His head snaps toward me. "Toben, if you will be inside them, you must wear one also."

Whoa, whoa, whoa what?! I'm going to have to fuck them back?! The thought had honestly never occurred to me. Somehow that's so much worse. I need dope. Right now. I don't want to feel this fear, this disgust, this hate. I need the nothing.

"There are absolutely no exceptions. It's the most important rule and must not be broken under any circumstances. If a Client ever forces himself into either of you without one on, you must inform me immediately. He rolls his neck and begins to pace. "Rule number two: they are only allowed to mark your backs, from the bottom of your necks to the top of your thighs. While I understand accidents happen, marking your face or genitalia at all is unacceptable. If any evidence remains from it, I need to know."

The sun is setting causing the rays to highlight the smoke in the room. For whatever reason, the sight allows me to relax a bit. Just let him get through his stupid ass rules so we can escape this place.

"Rule number three: no outside sex. If it's not me, each other, or a Client, you may not fuck them."

I think we're both made uncomfortable by that statement. He knows we haven't done anything, yet he would obviously be cool with it if we did. I've always kind of wondered about that. He doesn't mention Nikki for obvious reasons, and she's clearly part of the okay-to-fuck list. He flicks his cigarette and the ash falls to the floor.

"Rule number four: they must lubricate you before they enter. You will know if you aren't correctly primed. Rule number five: they can hurt your backside in any way they see fit, however they're not permitted to break bones or remove large pieces of flesh or body parts, and they cannot beat you to excess. You must be able to move around fairly easy afterward. Rule number six: they may not defecate, urinate, vomit, or bleed on you." Gross. Why would anyone want to do that? "In case I haven't made it clear enough, if any of these rules are broken, the first thing you do is call me. Do you understand?"

"Yes, Logan."

"A playdate is a five-hour session and is spent at your playmate's discretion. There are also one-hour playdates available at a prorated cost, which will be a large part of your business." He gets down on one knee in front of Tav with his hands on her thighs. "When I find a prospective client, one of my selling points is your silence. You will be playing in offices all over the city and doing so quietly is essential." He lets out a frustrated sigh because Tavin has let a mess of tears pour out of her eyes. "What is it, Lotus?"

"I just…I thought I was your Lotus, your plaything. Why do you want all of these other men to be with me?"

"You are still my plaything, both of you are, I'm just letting my friends play with you, too, is all." He holds the cigarette to her lips and she takes a drag. "One last thing. You two do not come cheap. It's forty thousand dollars for a complete playdate, so you must do your best to please and pleasure them. I know neither of you are particularly fond of this, though the Clients mustn't know that. Apparently Tavin was quite exemplary, however, I forgot to ask Mr. English and by the time I remembered, he was unable to speak correctly."

I feel two very different things. The easily overpowering emotion is fear. I not only have to let these men do whatever they want, I have to act like I like it? Pretend to be willing? That's asking a lot. Although, the thought of Logan beating Mr. English so bad he couldn't speak, does make me want to smile.

Logan stands and smashes the butt into the ashtray. "Most Clients will address you by your names, however, if they request your titles, simply tell them 'Sweet Girl' and 'Sweet Boy'. If they ask to see your logo, then show them the brand."

He's really dedicated to us being 'products' isn't he?

"Once a month, the doctor will come take your blood and I will be bringing you to the dentist next week." He straightens his suit sleeve. "I'm trusting you two and I'm not fond of regret."

"Yes, Logan."

Oh, hallelujah, he just pulled out his kit. "Alright, Lotus, are you ready?"

He barely gets the question out before she answers, "Yes, Logan." She scoots back to lean up against the arm rest and he kneels down to fix her up. I lick my lips in anticipation as

I watch her drift away.

He stands, while making no move to prepare more.

"We will have ours in a moment. There are some more things I want to discuss." Aw, come on, you dick! "Nikki has started bleeding, so we won't be playing with her until I get her on a birth control regimen. Tavin still hasn't gotten her period?"

"Ewe! God, I don't know."

He smirks at me. "Believe me, you would know." Reaching into his pocket, he pulls out a fresh pack. He's chain smoking so something's eating at him. "It has become increasingly more difficult to take on more girls. Since I have decided to leave Tavin alive, as well as take on this new business endeavor, I've decided not to get another Lotus until Nikki expires."

I've had so much on my mind, I didn't think about it being time for another girl. His words still relieve me and my stomach loosens a notch.

I nod. "Yes, Logan."

He places a hand on my shoulder, right over the lotus, "Alright, let's go get high." Thank fuck. As he opens the needle package, I lie next to a far-away Tavin, and he says, "When she starts her period, I need to know immediately. I can't have her getting pregnant. She'll bleed for days and I'm sure it will freak her out, so don't worry about not being aware of it."

"Yes, Logan."

My mind keeps flipping to Christopher. Seeing him today made me feel like a ghost. The boy I was when I knew him, is dead. I didn't know how much I missed him until I saw him. I take in a deep breath.

"Um…Logan?"

He doesn't look at me as he adds the water into the spoon. "Hmmm?"

"I saw an old friend from school today…I want to hang out with him."

He completely stills. I think I crossed a line until his eyes flick up to meet mine and understanding shines in them.

"I sometimes forget that you had a life before you became mine." He furrows his brow and huffs. "While I trust that you'll keep your mouth shut, in case you ever feel like opening up to him, remember doing so would put him in the ground. I won't hesitate to break some little shit's neck. Spin whatever story you want, as long as you do not breathe a word about me or anything that's happened since you came here." For good measure, he reaches up and grabs my throat, cutting off my oxygen. "I'm untouchable. Do not become disillusioned, otherwise. Trust me, Plaything, if a word is spoken to anyone, you will find out what real pain is and so will she." He releases my neck as I gasp in the air.

I croak out, "Yes, Logan."

When the needle punctures my skin, I sigh in relief.

Finally.

CHAPTER FOURTEEN
Monster

Three years and one month later—April, 2010

Tavin

CHRISTOPHER'S SO WASTED BY THE TIME WE SHOW up to his house. His mom gushes over how Toben has grown into a 'man' and it's painfully obvious that he's eating it up. I glare at him as we go downstairs and he laughs. Jerk.

"Relax, Tav, I just like the attention."

Another unconscious jab. He wouldn't ever make me feel bad about it on purpose, but he says stuff like that all the time, lately. He likes the attention that I'm not giving him—that's what he really means. It isn't fair though, because I'm trying. I let him lick my nipples and rub against me when we make out. I even let him touch his hand over my panties. He's even come from it a few times, I just can't go past that yet and I get scared that I won't ever be able to.

He's gorgeous. I've always known it and it's even more true now that I've seen so many other men. He's also my closest friend, my deepest love, and my only family. The idea of him inside me literally makes me weep and I don't understand why.

"Toben! Oh, hey, Tavin!" Christopher's big grin makes me laugh. "You guys want shots?"

I really like Christopher. He's my only other friend and he really cares about Toben. He truly is such a good friend to him and they clearly have a strong connection. No one can make Toben laugh like he does, not even me.

Christopher always tells me he is in love with me. I know he's just playing around, except the other night, he kissed me and it didn't seem like a joke then.

I nod and Toben smiles. "Sure."

Christopher hands me a shot glass. "What do you want to listen to?"

Last week, I saw he had my favorite Nirvana album downloaded. "Can we listen to *Nevermind*?"

"No! For the love of all that is holy, no." Toben shakes his head. "I hate grunge and I've already been forced to hear the shit out of that CD." Christopher's finger hovers over his keyboard as Toben points a finger in his face. "Don't you fuckin' do it." He loves to egg Toben on, so he clicks the button to play *Smells Like Teen Spirit*. He laughs his drunk butt off as Toben tries with all his might to give him a straight-faced glare.

I love how he is around Christopher, it's as if he is floatier. He definitely smiles a lot more. He finally told him that he dropped out of boarding school and is back to stay. Thank goodness, because now he won't be so dang paranoid every time we go somewhere. I down the first shot and it burns the whole way. Jeez this stuff is disgusting. Christopher hands me his soda to chase it and Toben gets a kick out of my reaction. Pulling me into his lap, he takes his shot. He pulls it off better than I do.

I take two more and Toben takes three. He kisses down my neck while he moves my hair off my shoulder. As he holds my hand, our matching 'When you bleed, I bleed' tattoos almost touch. We got them after our eighteenth birthdays. They're right beneath our scars. His is in my handwriting and mine is in his. When Logan saw them, he beat the crap out of us both. It was the worst beating we've had since being let out of the basement, and they're worth every second of it.

Bright orange glows as I light the bowl and I watch the smoke fill the glass. I lift it before I suck in all of the smoke and hold my breath as it burns my throat. After I pass the bong to Tobe, I can't hold it anymore. I cough harshly as I start feeling the brain vibrations.

Christopher does an impression of some famous person, except he's completely smashed so I'm pretty sure he's doing a terrible job.

"Do I make you horny, baby, yeah, do I?"

Toben finds it amusing though, and it's his laugh that makes me smile. My phone goes off and the caller ID says its Logan. He must be back in town. Dang. Oh well, it had been a nice few weeks while it lasted.

"Hi, Logan."

"Hello, Lotus. It sounds like you're having fun."

"We're at Christopher's."

"Well, I want to play. I'll be there in twenty minutes and I want you both kneeling when I arrive."

"Yes, Logan."

I hang up and Toben groans, "Sorry dude, we gotta bounce. Are you coming to the club with us tomorrow?"

"Yeah I-argh-" He bangs his knee against his dresser. "Just text me."

We use the walk home to get sobered up as much as possible, before Logan gets to our house.

I can't take anymore. He's been pounding into me for more than two hours now. Lately, he's been getting quicker. If I suck hard enough or fuck fast enough, he will come within thirty minutes, but today, nothing is working.

He finally gives my pussy a break to slide into my mouth. I swallow him as deep as I can as he pumps himself in and out.

"God, I did a good job with you." I flick the head with my tongue before taking him all in again. He groans as he pulls my mouth off of him and shoves me down on the bed to push himself back into me. I want to cry from how sore I am as I press my body hard against his.

He slices his knife across my thigh while his other hand rubs over my clit. No, not again. I can't do it anymore. He's drained me, I don't have anything left.

"Come on my dick, Lotus."

"I'm trying." He bites hard onto my nipple. "I'm too sore."

"Oh, you don't know sore, my little slut." Rolling over, he pulls me on top of him. I use all my force to slam my body down, biting my lip to keep quiet.

Sickening.

"Toben, hit her," Logan orders. Toben has been waiting for that. His whip seems to be connected to the pulse between my legs as the dirty sensation builds. It's going to happen again. "Beg for it, Lotus."

"Please, Logan." I hate myself when I can't stop a soft moan from escaping as the tightness falls over the edge and my body bursts into a thousand pieces.

Little, fucked up freak.

He slaps my breast. "I miss these not being here." Finally, his pace picks up and he curses me. "Fuck you! Dirty bitch!" Oh, thank goodness, he's almost done. The repulsive, hot pulsing pushes his come inside, and I'm grateful he's finally done. As soon as it's all out of him and into me, he shoves me off and leaves the bedroom to take a shower.

Toben's next to me in an instant, just like always, holding my skirt and tee. I get dressed and wrap my arms around his neck, kissing him. His tongue rubs against mine and his erection presses against my stomach. I let him rub himself against me. He doesn't usually do it for long. We kneel in front of our bed as we lace our fingers and wait for Logan.

When he emerges, he digs through his bag and throws us each some taffy.

"You two went through your dope supply way too fast this week. If you can't use responsibly, then I'll go back to controlling each dose." He storms to Toben and smacks him across the back of the head. "And I heard how out of it you were for your playdate yesterday with Mr. Andale. Do not ever pull that shit again."

"Yes, Logan."

His movements seem so fluid at times. He glides to the bag and removes a small wooden box. "We're going to do something different tonight." He's on me in an instant. "Get up."

I keep thinking I will grow more. I haven't gotten any taller in a few years. The top of my head barely reaches his chest. Toben is much taller than I am, too. It sucks. I still feel like a little kid and everyone still treats me like one. Especially *him*. His hand runs through my hair before he grasps my chin and pushes my head back.

"Open your mouth and stick out your tongue." He sticks a finger into the box and when he pulls it out, there's a small, square, white piece of paper stuck to it. "Leave it alone and don't swallow it until it's dissolved."

"Yes, Logan."

He puts the paper on my tongue. When he gives one to Toben, he nods toward my bathroom.

"Now go take a shower together, it will probably hit you while you're in there." We can't speak with the paper on our tongues, so Toben just holds my hand and pulls me into the bathroom. When he shuts the door and turns to switch on the faucet, I pull my tee back over my head and pull my skirt back down. He looks down at me and presses his forehead against mine while pushing my body against the door. Our fingers lace together, and when our scars align I can almost hear his voice:

When you bleed, I bleed.

He releases our hands to remove his shirt and his messy hair falls into his face. I run my hands over his hard chest as he removes the rest of his clothes. He's been working out a lot recently. He already had a lot of natural tone, but now he's much more defined.

Dang. He looks good. I rarely see him completely naked these days. It's getting more difficult for him to restrain himself and being skin to skin always makes matters worse. His cock is begging to be touched and I know it's horrible for me not to, it just still feels like a line I can't cross with him. His hand softly trails from my pubic bone up my stomach to my breast as his thumb strokes the hard pebble.

The paper has finally dissolved. "Tob-" He kisses me with restrained aggression. He's always so worked up after we play with Logan. His hands reach around to my ass when he lifts me up and wraps my legs around his waist. I can feel his tip pressing against my ass and I'm pretty sure he can feel my wetness against his stomach, as he carries me to the shower. He puts me down and puts his mouth on my nipple, sucking softly.

"Toben, we have to actually shower. Logan's waiting for us."

Moaning against my breast, he licks a few more times before he grumbles and reaches for the shampoo.

"Turn around, Love."

He washes my hair as I scrub my face. I open my eyes and I swear I see something move in the shower.

"What was that?"

"What was what?"

It's so fast and it's just a dark spot when it moves behind me. "There!"

"I don't know what the fuck you're talking about."

He puts the conditioner in my hair and his face lights up with amusement.

"Whoa!" He waves his hand around and little lines are following it like sparklers on Fourth of July. "Holy crap!"

I swipe my hand in front of my face and the lines are following mine as well. The shower curtain and the shower walls are pulsing like a heartbeat. Toben washes his hair while his eyes dart around. I think he sees the dark spots now. As we finish up, I hear the bathroom door open. Toben turns off the shower just as Logan opens the curtain and it seems to go on forever, like it won't ever stop opening.

"Are you feeling it yet?"

I know there's a big grin on my face, I can't help it. "Yes, Logan."

"Hell yes, Logan."

Logan tries to glare at Toben and ends up laughing instead. "Get dressed." When he looks at me he shakes his head. "Not you."

I truthfully don't care. It doesn't make me uncomfortable to be naked anymore. To be honest, I only put pants or a skirt on half the time, and that's if I'm leaving the house. They just seem too heavy, all those clothes. When he opens the bathroom door, the room flies past me like I'm in space. There's a whole new world on the other side of that door.

Whoa. This stuff is crazy. Logan guides me with a hand between my shoulder blades. He has laid pillows and blankets out on the floor in a makeshift bed. It reminds me of the ones I've made next to Toben's cage so many times.

"Pick out some music, Lotus."

That's surprising. He hates our music.

"Anything?"

He nods and I test him by putting in one of my favorite Otep CDs. I know he won't listen to the lyrics or care, and still, I secretly hope they will make their way inside his head to show him what he has done to me. The first time I heard her, the music made me feel like she was just like me.

The blankets are moving like water, they just aren't wet when I lie down. The boards on the ceiling are curvy and wobbly. I hope they don't fall in on us. Toben throws on jeans and a beanie when he lies next to me on our floor bed. Logan's hands are roaming down my body and I barely even notice. Toben begins licking my nipple, and though normally I would hate for him to do it in front of Logan, right now I don't mind. His mouth comes over mine as his hands squeeze at my breast. In the distance, I feel my legs open, it just doesn't seem real for a long time. I'm finally able to stop kissing and look down. I know it's my body as I watch Logan's tongue lap at me, I just feel disconnected. Toben is kissing my neck and sucking on my tits when his hand moves in between my legs with Logan's mouth. They do this for I don't know how long. Again, I would normally be upset, but I'm just not. I watch as the corners of the room sag like they are made of putty.

At some point, they take their mouths off of me and just lie on either side of me. All three of us are enamored by the movement in the room as if it had come alive. I can smell the music and taste their touch. I know I am smoking a cigarette, and when I see it snaking in between my fingers it surprises me and I laugh. It is a bit maniacal, and still, Logan and Toben join in. Everything is moving and bright.

We lie on top of each other chain smoking cigarettes and joints while watching the radio melt off the table, as Otep oozes into the oxygen.

> *Crooked spoons on every wall*
> *Genocide lines the wall*
> *Ten-gauge needles and a prayer*
> *Smearing sin everywhere*

This is how I want to remember us, just having fun and getting high as a family. Laughing so much that we're almost happy.

This is what I want to keep.

Toben

I'm not seeing anything anymore so I must be completely sober. That was freaking bad ass.

Acid. I'm definitely going to do that again.

Jesus, what time is it? Ugh, six a.m. I flop back down on the blankets and see Tavin's nude body next to me. I can't stop myself from touching her soft skin as her eyes flicker over to me.

"Good morning, Love."

"Good morning." Her smile is worth waking up for and when she stretches like a crazy person it brings joy to my mangled soul, every time. I kiss her as I trace her curves with my fingers. I slip my tongue into her mouth when I hear the bathroom door open. He's still here?

"Toben, I need you today. Hurry up and take a shower." I risk giving her one more kiss before I rush to obey. When I finish, I throw on some clothes and a beanie before kissing her goodbye and following Logan to the car. Lighting a cigarette, I quickly realize we're heading to Nikki's.

"We need to have a talk." Oh fuck, that doesn't sound good. "I've had another Lotus for a year."

I knew it was coming. Nikki passed her expiration date last year and he still has her. I was just hoping that maybe he was done. He has said himself he's getting older. I feel a few different emotions right now. I feel confusion because this isn't the way he does things, and honestly a little hurt because he didn't tell me. Mostly though, I feel relief I didn't have to take part in another initiation. I never realized exactly how young we were until I saw what ten-year-olds actually looked like, now.

"I'm not going to ask for your participation with her, which is why I have kept Nikki this long…" He looks as if he's having a hard time getting the words out, "…I wanted to spend time with you."

His confession is a hard one to swallow. He's made it abundantly clear that we're nothing more than objects for him to use as he sees fit, so what the fuck is he trying to say now? My mouth is dry. I don't know how to respond and the realization that we're on our way to kill her, hits me in the gut. I avoid thinking about this because the emotions are more than I allow myself to feel. I lost my virginity to her. She's the only girl I have ever had sex with. I would never tell her this, but I do care for her. Quite a bit actually. It started off as obedience, to keep Tavin alive, and now…I love what I do to her. I don't want her gone and I never thought it would affect me like this. I think I might hyperventilate.

"Do you want to keep her?"

My head yanks around toward him. Is he serious?

"What do you mean?"

"I mean, do you want her to be your Lotus? Do you want to continue playing with her by yourself?" As soon as he says it I know I do want that. Very fucking much. The idea of having complete control to do whatever I want to her causes a tightness in my jeans. I can't control my smile as the excitement consumes me.

"Yes, Logan."

He smiles with pride and we both take a drag.

When we arrive at Nikki's, my skin is thrumming and Logan hands me a gray bag just like his black one. "These are your tools. I suggest keeping them here so Tavin doesn't see them."

I can't wait to tear it open.

"Yes, Logan."

"Well, go on, I'll wait here until you're done."

"Thank you, Logan."

Damn it, I mean it.

He smiles. "I've told you, you're the closest thing to a son that I will ever have."

I turn with my bag in hand and head up the stairs. She's mine. All mine and I can do whatever I want to her. When I open the door, she's already in her kneel position and my cock twitches at the sight. I drop the bag and close the door.

Her head lifts and when she sees me, she glances around. "Where's Logan?"

I stalk up to her, running my hand along her jaw.

"You're no longer his. You are my Lotus, now."

Her shoulders slump as she starts to stand. "Oh, thank God."

She thinks things are going to be easier with me? She's in for a rude awakening. I grab her by her throat and slam her back to her knees. "You misunderstand. You're mine. I own you, Nikki."

She has the audacity to scoff at me. "Fuck you."

"Well, you have that part right."

She cries harder than she has in a few years, but she

needs to understand our new dynamic. It's exhilarating. I come so fast the first time that I take her again. When I'm finished, I hold her bloody body against mine and kiss the top of her head.

"Are you still doing this for her?" She whispers.

Her tears are falling, and I can't stop myself from touching them.

"No, Nikki. I'm doing this because it's fucking fun."

She gives me a look that makes me feel like what I am, what he made me: a monster.

I lift her off the bed. "Come on, let's go take a shower."

While I wash our bodies, she kisses my chest and stomach. If she needs the tenderness after the violence, I'll give it to her. Once she is in her clean clothes, I search inside the duffle and sure enough, there's a clear baggie of sour tarts and a works kit. I set the tarts on her bed before I prepare her for injection.

"If you would just give in to me, this could be quite pleasurable. I made you come, didn't I?"

She barely gives me a nod.

I clutch her chin, pinching and forcing her to look at me. "Acknowledge me with words, Lotus."

Her glare is venomous.

"Yes, Toben."

Tavin's body is pressed against mine and we move together so naturally it's not even a thought anymore. The lights are pulsing in cohesion with the music as Christopher dances in front of her. He won't get too close, though. Not after I lost it when he told me he kissed her. Punching him may have been an overreaction, but we're constantly hanging all over each other, it doesn't take a genius to see she's off fucking limits. I didn't let Tav off the hook either. I went off. She didn't tell me because she knew I'd be pissed and that just pissed me off even more. So hopefully, I made myself clear to both of them.

I know Logan says to not buy drugs, he can be stingy as hell, though. Besides, it's just a little extra coke. It'll be gone before we leave tonight. I hold out the carved ivory stash necklace Logan gave me.

"You want some, Love?"

I have to scream over the music and she still can barely hear me. She leans back against me and nods. I spoon out a hit for each nostril, giving her the bump that loosens her all the way up. Hurrying to get a couple hits in, I hand the necklace to Christopher before she wraps her arms around me and gives in to her high.

I've wondered if she would let me inside her if I try while she's coked out or at least let me taste her pussy. She allows herself to fully relax when she's high and she might not stress out about it so much. She would hate me for it though, and I would hate myself. I want her completely aware and willing when I am finally with her. She rocks her pelvis toward me and I'm not even sure she's aware she's doing it. God, I'm hard. I try to adjust myself and I just make it worse.

"I'm going to run to the bathroom, so dance with Christopher. Nothing dirty." She flinches when I say 'dirty' and it's too loud to explain, so I just yell, "That's not what I meant."

She nods and I make my way to the bathroom with every intention of jerking off in the stall, when I bump into a red head in the hallway.

I actually poke a random girl with my boner.

"Shit. Sorry. I was just…gonna take care of that."

Now I just admitted to the same random girl that I am going to beat off in the bathroom like a creep. She looks me up and down before she presses her body against me and rubs my cock through my jeans. She's probably close to ten years older than me and hot as hell, while I'm high and horny.

"Why don't you let me 'take care of that'?"

Seriously? I must have nodded because she drags me into the women's bathroom and shoves me into a stall. Next thing I know, she's on her knees with my dick in her hand. Her tongue swirls over the head before her mouth takes half of it and starts sucking. Oh yeah, this feels awesome. I fist her hair to hold her head in place as I shove myself deeper down her throat. I can't stop myself from pounding her face.

"Eat my cock, you filthy whore."

She's gagging and all I care about is coming. She tries to pull herself off of me, but I'm about to finish, so she isn't going anywhere. The final pulse pushes my orgasm down her throat. I make sure every drop is out before I release her.

"What the fuck, psycho?!" Her tears meet my come at her chin.

"You're willing to suck a complete stranger off and now your feelings are hurt because I treat you like the cum-dump you are?" I pull up my pants. "Whatever. You suck good dick, so...thanks."

I step past her to wash my hands. That was exactly what I needed, I feel much better now. When I get back, Christopher and Tavin are dancing closer than I'd like, although, I just came in some skank's mouth, so I'll let it slide.

I come up behind her, wrap my hand around her throat and push her head back to press my mouth against hers.

CHAPTER FIFTEEN
Call

Five months later—September, 2010

Tavin

I HATE NEW CLIENTS. I NEVER KNOW WHAT TO EXPECT. The type of clientele is a little different since we turned eighteen and this one in particular has me a little on edge. I've never been to a Client's home before. Playdates are mostly in hotels and offices or sometimes they prefer my house for discretionary purposes, but never in their own home. The cab has to get let through a gate before he can drop me in front of a huge, stone castle looking place. There's a big knocker and there's also a doorbell. Crap. I was never told which one to use. I stand there, contemplating which would be the safer option, when the door opens.

Another suit. I look up to see the head on the suit and it's a pretty one. He's probably in his late thirties to early forties with tan skin, thick dark hair, and a short dark beard. He's tall and huge with wide shoulders. His eyes are chocolate brown and his face is completely unreadable.

"Is knocking a foreign concept for you?"

Suit? Check. Rich? Check. Condescending jerk? Check, check.

"No, Mr. Saxon."

He glowers down at me. "Well, come inside."

This place is kind of ridiculous to be honest. The décor reminds me of old times when there were still Kings and Queens. Does this guy think he's royalty or something?

I follow him past the huge staircase to a little alcove.

"Have you ever seen a playroom?"

Oh, good Lord this is going to suck.

"No, Mr. Saxon."

He spins around on me, pinning me against the wall in the narrow passageway. "While I appreciate your respect, you will address me as Master. Is that understood?"

Wow. Really? Not 'your highness'? I have to refrain from rolling my eyes.

"Yes, Master."

He releases me and leads me down a set of twisted stairs to a wooden door. When I step into the room, I'm inside an actual torture chamber. I wonder if Logan has seen this. There are tools everywhere and the larger equipment pieces include a giant wooden X and a wooden horse with a big, black pad across it. There isn't a bed, just a large lounge in the center of the room. What really gets my attention, are the chains hanging from the ceiling.

"Dispose of your clothes and kneel." I slip off my skirt and tee before I bend over to untie my boots. Suddenly, my panties get ripped from my body.

Great. Now what am I going to wear home?

"Next time wear clothes easier to remove."

"Yes, Master."

He slips off his jacket and undoes his tie as I roll down my thigh highs. Throwing my bra onto the pile, I drop to my knees and place my hands on my thighs. He relieves his shirt of its straining, to reveal a well-kept body. Lifting a rope off the wall, he wastes no time tying my wrists behind my waist.

He keeps his hand in contact with my skin constantly, as he circles around and crouches down in front of me.

"Your back is a little more marked than I would have preferred," his hand traces over the lotus, "this though... this I like." He pushes my legs apart, trailing his finger along my slit and slides it inside. I know I clench around him. My body naturally reacts, further confirming my filth. "Very nice." He's almost smiling, but I have a feeling this guy doesn't do that. "You're already dripping for me. There aren't any scars here and you have quite the vice grip." He takes out his finger.

After standing, he unzips his pants, and there it is. Another cock. A big cock. I take it in my mouth as deep as I can. I relax my throat and allow it to slide down, as I use all my force. He startles me as a growl rips from his gut, as he grabs a fist full of my hair.

"Fucking Christ." His thrusts are deep, and still I don't gag. I don't make any noise other than the unavoidable wet sounds. It isn't long before I feel the hot streams as he rumbles out a groan. He pulls out of my mouth and brushes the hair away from my face and lifts my chin. "Oh, I'm going to like you." He walks to a small dresser before he opens one of the drawers. "Have you ever tried suspension before?"

"No, Master."

He places multiple packages on a metal tray just before adding four big ol' hooks on a cart and wheeling it over.

"Stand."

I obey, even though I'm a little wobbly at first without the use of my hands. I feel something cold and wet wiping across my back, causing some of the newer cuts to bubble with a delicious sting.

"While it might seem scary, it can also be extremely soothing if you let yourself relax."

He slips on gloves and rips open a package that has a

large needle in it. He lightly pinches a piece of skin right by my shoulder blade and I feel the stick of the needle as it punctures through. My pussy clenches and I release a small moan. He repeats the process three more times, going across both shoulders.

Once he's done piercing my back, he lifts up one of the hooks and slides it through the fresh holes. As soon as all four hooks are in, he leads me to the chains and picks up a stool. He tells me to stand on it while he connects the hooks to the chains, attached to the ceiling. Walking away, he takes off his pants and finishes undressing. While I hate to admit it, at least the view is nice. He strides back to me and I'm almost eye level with him. I like that. Flattening his tongue against my sternum, he licks my lotus before he wraps his massive arms around the top of my thighs to lift me up.

He kicks away the stool beneath me and my heart starts racing. What if my skin rips? Taking a deep breath, I pull myself together. So what if it does? It's not like I haven't fantasized about that very thing.

He looks into my eyes and knits his eyebrows together before kissing me. That's kind of rare actually, for a Client to kiss on the mouth.

"I've been aware of you and your services for a couple of years, I'm just not into the kiddie thing." He pulls back to look at me. "You're not what I expected, though I have the feeling you'll be well worth the wait." His lips move next to my ear as he whispers, "Are you ready?"

"Yes, Master."

Slowly, he releases me and backs away as the tightness pulls on my shoulders. It's not painful at all, really. He was right, it is kind of nice. I look at him and his raised eyebrow. He is pretty cute. I smile at him and his dick jumps.

"What do you think?"

"It feels like I'm in water, but I'm not wet."

"Are you sure about that? I can smell you from here."

Oh God.

He steps to the wall and pulls on a chain. I feel the tug in my back as he lifts me higher, and it hurts wonderfully. Once I am at his desired height, he fastens the chain back to the anchor. As soon as he reaches me, he throws my right leg over his shoulder, my pussy level with his mouth. He spreads me apart and slides a couple fingers in and out of me, watching my face the whole time. His tongue suddenly darts out and wet warmth is repeatedly flicking along my clit.

"When you come, call for me."

"Yes, Master."

Dang it. I'm breathless and as he continues to suck and finger me, I'm about ready to explode. His mouth devours me as he pulls my body down, causing the hooks to shoot pain down my back. That's all it takes. I feel myself contracting while my pelvis thrusts against him. "Oh God." His eyes narrow at me while his tongue is still working overtime. "You're making me come, Master."

He moans against me, not stopping even after my orgasm is complete. The sensitivity is excruciating. Still, he continues until he gives me another. Only then does he release me from the chains. He pulls the hooks from my back and spins me around. "I know for a fact that we're both clean, so I'm going to feel everything inside your tight little body before I fill it with my come."

Hot panic raises my body temperature instantly.

"No! It's against the rules! He says no."

My head's shaking. Logan will be furious and I don't want to know what he'd do. This is rule number one.

He glares down at me before he storms to a nearby table and yanks out a condom. When he returns, he grips my arm and throws me to the floor. I hear him putting on the condom two seconds before slamming into me.

"Do not ever fucking tell me 'no' again."

"Yes, Master."

My knees rub against the concrete as he rams me so hard my body keeps scooting forward. He's vicious with each plunge and I can't stop a few soft grunts from escaping.

There's amusement in his tone when he asks, "What's your name?"

Seriously? He wants to know my name mid thrust? He's bigger than most, strong, and I think I'm getting whiplash every time he hammers into me, so I have a hard time finding my voice.

"T-Tavin."

"Why aren't you coming, Tavin?"

"I n-need pain."

He completely halts, and it takes me half a second to realize it, so I rock back on him before I stop myself. I feel his hard chest against my back as his lips brush against my ear. He bites my lobe sending chills to ripple all the way through me.

"Is that so?" Maybe I was wrong. I think I can hear his smile as he pulls out of me. "Rest your head on the floor and spread your legs." The concrete floor is cold against my cheek when his fingers run along my folds and pinch my clit. "Beautiful."

He unties my wrists from behind my back and reties them above me, all while my head is still on the floor. I can't see and I can't hear him walking, but I do hear some kind of movement across the room.

All of a sudden, a small *whoosh* sounds and I feel splitting pain across my butt. I'm almost positive he's hitting me with a cane, and from the feel of it, he broke skin. The harsh tearing sensation trickles through my body pulling a soft whimper from my lips. He does it three more times, one right above the previous. I am stretched and instantly full as he pounds back into me. His abdomen slams against the fresh wound and the waiting pressure releases.

He quickly flips me to my back and my head hits the floor before he pierces into me again.

"Your cunt is squeezing the life out of my dick."

Throwing me around like a rag doll, he takes me in every position imaginable. It takes a long time, but he finally finishes and with both of our bodies breathing hard, he unties me.

He hovers over me. "That was the best sex I've had in a while." Leaning down, he kisses me hard on the lips. Again.

While I dress, he hands me a bag of colorful square hard candies, and I pop one in my mouth.

"Next time wear a dress and easily removable footwear."

"Yes, Master."

Toben

"He did not."

Clients are douche bags, but making her call him 'Master' is Grade A.

She rolls her eyes. "Yes, he did." She plays with the string on my shirt as we lie next to each other on the beach. "The suspension was pretty fun though, I wanted to swing. I bet it would feel like flying, even more than at the park."

She can be a little freak sometimes. I would never tell her that though because she would take it the wrong way and I promised her eight years ago I wouldn't call her that name again. I guess I'm in no position to be calling anyone a 'freak' these days, anyway.

"I'll take your word for it."

We smoked a joint before we took a cab here and still haven't decided what to do with the first free day we've had together in a while. Both of us have had our five playdates for the week so we're free for the night.

"Christopher wants to go to the club tonight. What do you want to do?"

She shrugs as she rolls over and lays her head on my chest. "As long as I am wasted and with you, I'm good."

I kiss the top of her head. "Preaching to the choir, Love."

Then like a screeching record, her cell phone rings. There are only two people that call her besides me, and Christopher would call my phone first. Her eyes flip up to meet mine.

"I'm going to ignore it."

Is she high right now? "What the hell, Tavin? Answer the phone."

"No! We've both had our playdates this week. There's no reason he needs us. I'll just call him later and tell him I lost my phone."

I know I'm not hearing this. Where is this defiance coming from?

"You seriously think he isn't going to call m-"

Right on cue, my phone starts going off.

She grabs my hand. "Don't answer it. We deserve a night off. What is he really going to do to us?"

"Oh, I don't know, Tavin…slit our throats?"

"Because we didn't answer our phones for a few hours? Please. He'll beat us and play with me until I'm numb. That's it."

I don't feel good about this. I guess it is just a few hours. We can tell him since we're finished with Clients for the week, we weren't expecting his call and had our phones down. Maybe she's right, it's not that big of a deal.

After a couple of hours, we decide to take a cab home and smoke a joint to calm our nerves, before calling Logan. That plan flies right out the window when we see his new Mercedes parked out front.

Oh, yeah. We're fucked.

Her tic is acting up. "Maybe we should go in through the basement."

I don't know if that'll make any difference, but I go for it when the front door swings open. His voice is low, slow, and quiet. Not good. Not good at all.

"Get. The. Fuck. Inside."

We hurry to obey and when he slams the door behind us, the walls vibrate.

"Our phones were turned down," Tavin pipes up.

I just shake my head. The girl blinks her eyes like she's having a damn seizure every time she lies. Logan back hands her hard.

Oh no, this is bad.

"Get downstairs, now."

We nearly trip over each other trying to get down there. I feel like we're fourteen again. His fury hasn't reached this point in a while. Damn it, Tavin! Why didn't we just answer the fucking phone? We kneel as soon as we're in front of our bed and glance at each other. She's regretting her rebellion now, and so am I.

When Logan comes down behind us, he storms over to her, yanking her up by her hair.

"You have obviously become much too comfortable in our relationship. Take off your dress and get on the bed."

She rips away her clothes, jumping on the bed in a flash. He snatches the spiked belt he made for her and buckles it around her thigh, just tight enough for the needles to barely puncture her skin. His fingers wrap around the knife on the table and I think I might have a heart attack. I can tell by his demeanor that this is about to get very ugly.

"Toben. Take off your shirt and come here." Throwing my shirt against the wall, I hurry next to him. "Spread your legs," he barks at Tavin. She immediately obeys. Turning to me, he orders, "Put your dick in her mouth."

It takes a second delay before I understand.

"No!" Tavin screams as she sits up.

At the same moment, I start my pleading. "No, no, no, Logan. Please! We're sorry! Do not make me do this!"

This can't be happening, not after we've made it this long.

"THIS IS NOT A MOTHERFUCKING DEMOCRACY!" His voice resounds through my veins and the entire basement. He leans into my face. "I have no problem plunging this knife into her right now! She's more than served her purpose." He backs off and rolls his neck. "Now, go do what I told you to."

FUCK!

I want her, I always have, but not like this. I never wanted this. She's horrified. As the tears stream down her face, I lean down to kiss them.

"This is not a Goddamn date. Do not make me tell you again."

My disgust with myself only grows when I undo my pants and find myself hard as hell. While I may have had a million fantasies about her mouth around my cock, she was never scared and crying in any of them. I pull myself out and beg her with my eyes to just go along with it. To make it easier on both of us. She either doesn't understand or refuses to give in. Logan is about to march over here and choke her with it himself. I press the tip against her lips and she backs away.

"Come on, Tav, just do it okay?" I beg.

"No, Toben, please! Not you." She cries in a whisper, her

eyes full of fear.

She's looking at ME with fear. What the hell am I supposed to do? Logan's fists clench. I want to cry as I take hold of her hair and shove myself in between her lips. She still tries to pull off of me. I can't believe I'm doing this to her. She won't look at me and I just want to keep eye contact with her to try to apologize in silent conversation.

"Suck it, Lotus!" He screams at her.

After a couple seconds, she submits and her mouth is fucking heaven. I can feel her tongue massaging along the base of my cock as she takes me deeper with each suction. I move her hair from her face. God, this is such a beautiful sight. So much more beautiful than I pictured. Her tears have wet her eyelashes making them look even longer, while her little pink lips slide up and down my shaft. I thrust into her mouth as my release already starts to build.

"Fuck yes, Love. Oh my God. Suck my cock with that perfect, fucking mouth."

"Don't you dare come in her mouth." Then I need to stop right now. I take myself out and the look on her face obliterates my heart. "Her turn. And don't stop until she comes," Logan barks.

I want to see her eyes and she still won't look at me. I spread her legs back apart as I get on the bed and situate in between them. I hate this. I have wanted to eat her out for years, to hear her cry out my name when I make her come. That's clearly not going to happen. I spread her apart and go for it. I probably will never get this chance again, I'm at least going to give it my all. I stick two fingers inside of her and holy Goddamn she's soaking wet. How can she be so turned on if she doesn't want me? Want this?

Did I really just think that? I know better than anyone that you can get aroused as hell and truly not want it to happen. I kiss her. I can't kiss her mouth, so I stick my tongue inside and she tastes so much better than I could have dreamed. I slide my fingers back in, fucking her with them as her pelvis starts to move. I flick her clit with my tongue and she reaches her hands in my hair spurring me on even more. I can't help it. I've played this over and over in my head so many times.

"Come for me, Tav." I pull on the belt strap, tightening it and causing the needles to dig deeper. As she bucks her hips, her pussy squeezes the shit out of my fingers and warm, sweet juices flow onto my tongue, but I want more. I keep eating her, licking it all up. "Fuck, you taste so good." When I look at her, she's shattered. She looks completely broken.

"Fuck her." Logan lights a cigarette as he jerks off. I get up to my knees, pulling her down the bed and still, she won't look at me. As if he can read my mind, he yells, "Look at him, Lotus." She does, and I wish more than anything that she didn't. She hates me and it burns through the violet.

Fighting tears of my own, I align myself along her folds before finally sliding inside of her for the first time.

I whisper, "I am so sorry, Love."

A few rogue tears fall down her cheeks as I ram into her tight, little pussy. Dear God, how can something so fucking terrible feel so fucking good? Her tits are bouncing from my thrusts as I lean down to take one in my mouth. I move to kiss her logo before making my way up her neck. She smells so amazing. She's milking the shit out of me as I tug on the belt and it isn't long before her cunt is contracting with another orgasm. I lean back to pound out my climax.

"She's tight as fuck, I'm gonna come."

"Do not pull out. Come inside of her."

"I love you," I gasp as my semen fills her body.

As soon as I'm empty, I'm regretting saying pretty much every single thing I said. I pull out of her and she chokes out the cry she's been containing as she rolls on her side, holding her face in her hands. I reach to touch her back and she re-coils away from me.

"No."

I pull my hand back as if it's burnt. Oh my God, what the fuck just happened? Terror that this is going to destroy us, overtakes me. What if we can't come back from this? I can't lose her. I need her. She's the other half of my soul. Logan appears next to me and he pulls her to him by her ankle. He pushes her legs open, and you can see my come dripping out of her. He slides two fingers in, pushing it deeper.

"Did Toben's cock feel good?" She cries harder so he grabs her hair to make her look at him. "Answer me!"

"Yes, Logan!" She screams through tears.

He bends over and eats her out before he kisses her. "There, now you know what he tastes like." More tears fall when he slams his erection into her. "You're about to have two different men's come inside of you. I don't even think Lacie was that repulsive."

That motherfucker. He knows exactly what to say to crush her from the inside out. All he's ever wanted is to break her. This isn't about me at all, it's about her.

I can't form a conscious thought about what life will be like after this. Who will I become? She's the part of me that is pure, without her I am just like him. How will this work if she never speaks to me again? Neither of us has anywhere else to go. To be perfectly honest, I don't know if I would want to leave even if I did. Yeah, the Clients suck, but the heroin takes that feeling away. Everything else I like. Tavin, the money, the drugs, having Nikki…hell, I even like hang-ing out with Logan half the time.

I always wonder who she would be if Logan never exist-ed. There've been countless times that I wished it would have just been me, even though it really wouldn't have worked out the same now, would it?

"Get your whip," Logan snaps, bringing my attention to him. The belt around her thigh is as tight as it will go with her leg over his shoulder, as he batters into her. He rolls onto his back, bringing her on top of him, slamming her down as she thrusts her hips down onto him.

"Show me how much you want it, Lotus." She quietly whimpers as she grinds her body against his. "Hit her!"

I will never admit this to her, but I've grown to love hitting her. It's the sting from my whip that brings her to her quickest climax. While I would love to claim the credit, in her eyes it would be the blame. Her back arches in the most beautiful way when she gets hit. Her body curves in such an erotic position and her moans are sexy as fuck. She's my Tavin, my Love, my best friend in the whole world, and I know I've lost her. She'll never be with me after this. I think I can hear my heart break, and I know I can feel it. As I watch her, I can physically see the shift. I don't know what exactly it is, but something is changing.

Flip goes my switch.

I hit her hard. All my anger, frustration and fear travels to my whip. Over and over; harder and harder. I've done everything I thought was best for her! Every decision was for her! Every horrible act was for her! It's all been for her and she still hates me. All I want is to protect her!

"TOBEN!" I am breathing hard and sweating like crazy. Tavin's back is shredded and Logan is glaring at me. "I said enough!" She falls against his chest. "She has a weekend Client and now she has to show up like this. That's unprofessional and not how I do things."

How do I just check out like that?

"I'm sorry, Logan."

He ignores me as he looks at Tavin's back and shakes his head before he pushes her up. "Go shower and wash our come out of your filthy snatch. Mr. Saxon has paid for you this weekend." She almost falls off the bed as she stumbles. Rushing past me, she gets her clothes and hurries to the bathroom.

"She will never forgive me for that."

I say it out loud because I can't accept it while it's only a thought in my mind.

"Are you under the impression that I give a fuck?"

He doesn't make any Goddamn sense. I thought I was 'the closest thing he'll ever have to a son'?

"No, Logan."

"You both need a reminder of how things work. Besides, she was never going to give it to you. Consider it a gift."

It's been a while since I've had the desire to slice open his throat. Now, though, it's back with a vengeance. He smokes his cigarette as he lies on our bed. I wonder if I will ever wake up next to her again. He packs her a bag for the weekend and when she emerges, he hands it to her.

"Take a cab to Mr. Saxon's. Just think of it as a two-day playdate."

"Yes, Logan."

"Will you ignore my calls again, Lotus?"

"No, Logan." There's a deep sadness in her voice that is killing me. He kisses her head and disappears into the bathroom. She turns and sprints up the stairs immediately.

"Tavin! Wait!" I run after her and catch up to her in the living room.

I reach for her arm and she yanks it out of my hand, spinning around. "Did you enjoy yourself?! Was it everything you imagined?" She cries with tears pouring down her face.

She has to stop looking at me like that. "Come on, Love, you were there, you know I didn't have a choice."

She shakes her head. "All those things you said." Her furious eyes lift up and burn into me. "How long?"

"How long what?"

"How long have you been fucking other girls? You knew what you were doing, Toben. You don't learn how to eat pussy by getting dick in your ass."

I don't even know how to respond to that. She spins around to the kitchen and I know she's going for the coke stash. She cuts three lines and they are gone in a blink. She sniffs and wipes her nose as she tries to push past me. She has to stop. This isn't my fault. I squeeze her arms and push her against the fridge. Pictures of our years together are scattered around her head.

"Do not let him do this. Not now, not after all this time."

"Let me go!" She tries to pull herself free.

"I need you, Love."

"Are you going to let me go? Or are you planning on raping me again, first?"

When her last sentence sinks in, the only emotion I feel is rage. I release her with force causing her head to slam against the fridge. I have to get away from her right now.

I slam my hand against the refrigerator by her head. "I didn't have a motherfucking choice!"

Storming back downstairs, I wait for Logan to finish so I can shower, get lit, go to the club, and ruin the first hot bitch to open her legs.

Whoever she is, she's in for a world of hurt.

CHAPTER SIXTEEN
Cadence

Tavin

H E'S RIGHT, I WAS THERE. I SAW THE WAY HE LOOKED at me, he wanted to rip me apart. I heard the ecstasy in his voice when he moaned out all of those things. I've felt guilty for years because I didn't want to have sex and I knew he needed it. Even though I tried to give him what I could, I knew it would eventually not be enough. Apparently, it hasn't been enough for a while.

He's been lying to me for how long? Three lines is definitely not going to be enough. I do two more before I throw on my flip flops and new sunglasses. My blue T-shirt dress is short and easy to take off as ordered.

Mr. Saxon, or excuse me, I mean Master, wants to play with me again already? For a whole dang weekend? Since when is that even an option? I guess the whole five-play-dates-a-week thing is out the window.

In the back of my mind, I think I might be being unfair. It was my choice to ignore Logan's call after all. It would never have happened if I wouldn't have tested him, I just really didn't think it would be that big of a deal. I only needed a break. These Clients take a lot from me and I get tired of hearing what a whore, cunt, or bitch I am. I already know. I hear it from Logan, too, it's just normal with him.

I know that what I said to Toben was harsh and I don't doubt that he didn't want it to happen that way. Even if it felt good, he should have still hated it. He was more turned on than ever before and I've never seen his eyes that dark. What's worse is that he was good at it. He got me off quicker than Logan does and I wasn't lying when I said he felt good. So why do I feel so gross? It was Toben, the only person in the world that I love and I'm scared that when I look at him all I will hear is his words bouncing around in my head.

Fuck, Love. Oh my God, yes! Suck my cock with that perfect fucking mouth.

I hate that he's been inside me. I hate that he made me come so effortlessly and I hate that we can't take it back. I hate that this changes things. He's the only one I've ever wanted and I did want to want to have sex with him, but it's DIRTY. Now our pure, perfect relationship is tainted and will never be the same again. Still, the idea of not having him near, makes me physically ill, even now.

I need to stop this…and do more coke. We will deal with this when I get back Sunday. I put white powder into a vile so I can have some bumps on the way and to sneak, over the weekend. God knows I'll need it.

The cab drops me off and I crane my neck looking at Master's castle. I would have freaked out if I would have seen this place when I was little. It would be better with a mote. I shove the vile in my dress pocket. He mentioned knocking last time so I opt for that and wipe my nose.

When the door opens, there's no suit, just a bluish-gray T-shirt that's working way too hard, and white linen pants. I glance up at him and quickly look away. Eye contact, while I'm high, makes me uncomfortable.

"Hello, Tavin." Was his voice that deep last time?

"Hello, Master."

"You need to speak up when you address me."

I yell, "Yes, Master."

His nostrils flare and he steps so close that our bodies are touching, "I understand that you're a teenager, but give me attitude again and we're going to have a very big problem."

Sheesh.

"Yes, Master."

I follow him inside and he hands my bag to a woman in a blue dress. We go the same way as last time and once we are in his playroom, I quickly undress and kneel. He lightly trails his fingertips along my jawline and up my face.

"Your choice of clothing today pleases me."

Duh, that's what you asked for.

I smile on the inside because that would be so funny to see his reaction if I actually said that to him.

He circles behind me. "I want y-". When he stops talking, the entire room is still with a tense thickness. It moves again when he yanks me to my feet by my arm. "Your back is completely destroyed! How am I supposed to suspend you when you're in shreds?" He paces in front of me and shoves a hand through his thick hair.

"Would you like to reschedule, Master?"

"No," he snaps. "Never mind, I'm putting you up anyway." On his way to the wall, he picks up my dress and I know I'm screwed when I hear the *tink* of the vile hitting the concrete floor.

I close my eyes and crack them back open to see him bend over to pick it up. Once he realizes what it is, I can almost see the steam coming out of his ears. His head snaps in my direction and I jerk my head forward. I must have blinked because he's instantly in front of me.

While he's gripping my neck, all the pressure is coming

from his fingers holding my jaw so I have to look him in the eye.

"You show up high? Are you serious?!"

He throws the vile and it explodes against the wall.

Dang it.

He grabs my arm to turn it over and look at my track marks. "Don't think I didn't notice this shit last time. If you were mine, this would not happen." He throws my arm back down. "Completely unacceptable. I'm calling Mr. James."

No!

He turns to leave and I jump up to follow him, grasping his hand.

"No, please, Master, don't call him!" He glares down at my hand on his and I pull it away.

The same hand I just held grips my shoulder as he digs in his fingers. "I told you to never tell me no again."

I lower my voice to a whisper, pleading. "Please, if you don't tell him, I won't tell if you decide to come inside of me." I can't believe I just offered that. I guess I'm already a whore, at least this is kind of my own payback to Logan.

His eyebrows stay knit together while his face softens and he releases my arm. "How long until you're completely sober?"

I shrug. "It depends. I'm reeeeally high."

He growls. Actually growls. Like a dog.

"I'm not fucking amused."

"A few hours," I rush out. I can't risk pissing him off more and him calling Logan.

"I want you completely lucid, so it looks like you have some time to think about how disrespectful this is."

"Yes, Master."

He seizes me by my forearm and drags me to the big wooden X attached to the wall. He picks me up and slams me against it as he fastens the straps around each ankle and wrist. He gives me this disappointed look like I'm supposed to feel bad or something, and then he just storms out.

That's it? Um…okay?

This guy has no idea who he's dealing with if he thinks tying me up is going to do anything. I am Logan James' plaything for goodness sake. It's gonna take a lot more than this if he actually wants me to suffer. I wonder how mad he will get if I tell him as much.

How long have I been up here? My nose itches and I'm thirsty. It's had to have been at least an hour…

I know it's been more than two hours now. I have to pee like crazy and my arms are killing me. My legs are starting to ache and I can barely move. He's got to be coming back soon…

This is starting to get extremely uncomfortable and I am pretty sure the coke is long gone…How long has it been?

OKAY, I GET IT! This officially sucks. I think my arms might break off and my entire body throbs. My bladder is about to burst and I'm definitely not high anymore and it looks like I won't be for a couple of days. Where is he?

When the door opens, I almost cry with relief. The woman in the blue dress enters.

"Hello, Tavin, my name is Misty. I'm Mr. Saxon's assistant. He would like to know if you have any food allergies."

I shake my head, the only part of me that I can still move. "No…Can you please help me down?"

She smiles at me like you would a small child that doesn't understand something. "Now, I'm sure you know I can't do that. You must have made him pretty mad for him to punish you like this. He usually likes to be more…involved."

I sigh. "It was worth a shot."

She's quite pretty. She looks about his age, tall, with blonde highlighted hair, and tan skin.

"Does he play with you too?"

She looks a little detested and scoffs, "He wishes." She winks and laughs. "I'd play with you though." I think she's kidding, though the thought of playing with a girl has never occurred to me. "Just stick it out a bit longer, okay?"

I don't know how to address her, she isn't a Client, so I simply nod. She shuts the door and I am alone once again. Without the distraction of the drugs or Master, my thoughts go to Toben and what happened. I still can't believe it. I keep hoping this is a dream. That I will wake up and none of this ever happened.

I don't even know what to feel about it anymore. I know I'm angry. I'm angry he lied about the other girls, I'm angry that he enjoyed it so dang much, and I'm angry that Logan took this from us. I'm also sad because I know this changes things. I'm sad because it's like one of the threads holding us together has snapped and can never be repaired.

Then I realize that there are still thousands of threads. We are two parts of one whole. Half people. I can't survive without him. I won't. I just don't know how to fix this.

What if we can't?

"Tavin." My eyes fly open. I'm crying. They aren't supposed to see me cry. I can't wipe my tears so I stare at him with a wet face. "It's not that bad is it?" He doesn't seem angry with me anymore as he reaches out his thumb and wipes away a tear. He puts it to his mouth before he unties me.

"No, Master." My legs have stopped working at some point so when he unfastens them, I fall flat on my face.

"Shit." He lifts me up. "I may have had you up there a little too long." I would give him a dirty look if he wasn't the only reason I'm standing. He helps me walk around the room. "Are you sober?"

"Unfortunately so, Master."

He gives me a warning glance and narrows his eyes. "If you ever come here intoxicated again, I will have you begging me to put you up on that cross for five hours. Do you understand?"

Five hours?! That jerk!

"Yes, Master."

I can feel my legs again and they tingle like someone is poking me with a billion little needles all at once.

"Come on, pet, it's time for dinner." He leads me out the door.

"Plaything."

"What?" His head is cocked to the side. He isn't mad, just confused.

I would never normally correct a Client, they can call me whatever they want. I mean heck, he can too, but I'm here for the whole weekend and he seems kinder than most, so it's worth the try.

"I'm a toy-a plaything. Not a pet."

"You prefer to be called 'plaything'?" He still isn't mad, he just looks curious.

I shrug. "It's what I am."

I can't decide if the way he looks at me creeps me out or not when he nods. "Alright."

Wow really?

"Thank you, Master."

He guides me through the house that has the same ancient style as the foyer. We go up a huge staircase and it isn't until I see a man in a suit holding a bunch of papers, that I worry about still being naked. He doesn't look at me, so he must be used to this. Master takes me into a room guarded by large, dark wooden, double doors.

When we enter, the first thing I notice is the bed and it makes me recognize my exhaustion. It looks so comfortable. It's a huge four poster with a white canopy. There's a writing desk and two large armoires. Two ginormous windows are on the back wall and a few ornate lounge furniture pieces are scattered around the room.

I look up at him. I don't know how much longer I can hold it. It's starting to hurt. "Master?"

"Yes, Plaything?"

"Can I use your bathroom?"

He nods and walks past me to open a door and turn on a light. I follow him inside and when I stand in front of the toilet, he crosses his arms.

"Are you going to watch me, Master?"

I shouldn't mouth off to him, but I really have to go and he's making it take longer.

He nods his head toward the toilet. "Yes."

My face is burning hot and my eyes widen as I sit down. As bad as I need to pee I can't with him watching. I've met plenty of men with fetishes, but none ever watched me use the bathroom. After a few painful and embarrassing moments, he smirks at me and leaves. I glare at the empty doorway, though I'm finally able to relieve myself.

I wash up and walk back into the bedroom where he's standing next to the bed. Looking closer, I notice a long cream-colored gown laying across the comforter. He picks up the dress as I walk to him.

"Lift your arms."

That's asking a lot considering they have been lifted for the last *five hours*. I obey and I'm disappointed in myself when they start shaking. Sliding the silky fabric down my body, he keeps his hands on my hips as he leans down to kiss me. He removes his shirt before turning and taking off his pants, disappearing behind a door. Emerging quickly, he's in a suit and it's different somehow. It's nicer, not like what they wear in offices. He looks so handsome.

He sticks out his elbow and his expression is cute. I wonder if that's supposed to be a smile. He's still standing there with his elbow out like he's expecting me to do something. I mirror him, hoping that's what he's implying. Sighing, he takes my hand and places it inside his arm. God he's weird. We walk like that all the way downstairs.

This guy is too much. His dining room is enormous with high ceilings and one of the walls is completely made of little colorful diamond windows making it look like it's glowing. The medieval theme continues with this ridiculous table. It's so freaking long. He holds out the chair and gestures for me to sit. This feels bizarre, this isn't how things are done. I've never been fed by a Client, besides the candy, and I've certainly never been given a dress by anyone other than Logan. I'm sure it's not really mine, still, it's unusual.

I didn't think he was actually going to sit at the opposite end of the table, and yet, he does. We're going to have to yell if we are going to have a conversation. Which is seemingly the point, since we don't say a word the entire meal. I don't mention that it's complete crap that he has a glass of wine and a glass of something harder with his dinner when I don't get a single drip of alcohol with mine.

Since we don't speak through dinner, I have no idea what crawled up his butt between then and now. All of a sudden, he shoots up so fast that the chair skids out behind him. Storming to the end of the table, he yanks me out of the chair.

He drags me back into the playroom before he finally speaks.

"Take off the dress and kneel."

I quickly obey as I watch him get all the hooks and cleaning supplies put on a tray. Grabbing the rope from the wall, he barrels towards me. He is much rougher than last time when he ties my wrist behind my back.

"Get up," he grates out.

I'm evidently not doing so fast enough because he jerks me up the rest of the way by my arm. He flings my hair over my shoulder before putting on gloves and cleaning my back. The wonderful stinging sensation makes me push my thighs together. I hear him lift a hook from the tray and mumble, "Christ." Once all the hooks are in, he takes me by the arm and leads me to the chains. After he has me suspended, he rips off his jacket and shirt, fastening the chain to the wall.

"I should have already been inside you today," he shoves off his shoes and pulls off his socks, "and because of your poor choices, that hasn't happened." His pants and underwear are pushed to the floor. He doesn't even make sure that I'm wet before he wraps my thigh around his waist and slams into me. "You're gonna make up for that."

Okay. I loathe sex. The sounds, the smell, even the way if feels. It's disgusting, perverted, and vile. While I will never admit it aloud, this physically feels good, even if inside I still feel like a repulsive gash. The hooks pull with each thrust causing a steady flow of orgasms. His hands are squeezing my ass while he bites my neck and shoulder. He hasn't slowed in his tempo at all, if anything, he's going harder and faster.

No, please, not again. Another one is building, I just don't think I have anything left.

"Please, Master, I can't come anymore."

"You should have thought about that before you shoved all that powder up your nose."

As he pulls out, he walks to the chain to lower me to the floor, pushing me to my knees once he returns.

"I can't stop thinking about your mouth." Brushing my hair back, he presses the soft tip against my lips so I lick lightly, which makes it twitch and him groan. "Suck my dick,

Tavin." I swallow as much of him as I can, suctioning with vigor. "Ah, Fuck." He pumps into my mouth a few times before removing himself and unhooking the chains. He doesn't take out the hooks when he throws me to the floor on my back and buries his head in-between my legs.

The pain from my arms still being tied and my hooked back rubbing against the floor mixed with his tongue brings tears to my eyes.

"I'm coming again, Master."

He moans into my wetness before climbing on top of me and rams himself inside me. "Your pussy feels so amazing." His tongue laps at my nipple as he opens my legs wider. "I will never wear a condom with you again." He stops to stand and pick me up. He shoves me down on him as he carries me to the wooden horse, inside me the whole time. I am flung back around as he places me face down, straddling the horse when he pummels me deep and hard. He shows no mercy. When his tempo increases, I know he's about to finish.

"Every drop. Take every drop, little plaything."

I can feel it shooting inside of me and it seems to just keep coming out. His body gets finally slack as he slowly pulls himself out with a groan. I sigh when he removes the hooks and close my eyes. I could go to sleep right here. Lifting me off the wooden horse, he puts me on my shaky legs and moves the sweat-stuck hair from my face.

"You just redeemed yourself."

I don't get to put the dress back on, but that's okay though because I'm too sweaty anyway. He pulls on his pants before guiding me back to the same bedroom as earlier. We take a shower before he puts me to bed and as soon as my head hits the pillow, I fall asleep in his arms.

Toben

I can't go to Nikki's to get my tools because I am too furious to trust myself with her, so I'll just have to get creative. I'm not going to shoot up-not tonight. I've never done meth though, and Christopher gave me some yesterday. He said it won't take much, so I load it up in the Pyrex he gave me, rotating it over the flame of my lighter. Once it's ready, I take a big, slow hit.

Oh yeah. Oh, hell yeah. Oh, fucking hell yeah. I can definitely work with this.

I randomly find a hand rake along with a few knives and a cheese grater in the kitchen, after I cut the chords off the blinds. Logan always leaves the belt he made for Tavin here, so I retrieve it before I carry it all up to my room. I pour a couple of shots of vodka, load up my stash necklace with some coke, and call a cab.

I still can't believe she actually used the word rape. What was I supposed to do? Just let him stab her? She isn't wrong that I enjoyed myself, though. She felt incredible. Shit. Maybe she's right. I should have pushed the knife into myself before doing that to her. She's gone. I know it. She will hate me for the rest of her life. Part of me fears she won't come back after her long playdate and I'll never see her again. It's horrible that I'm relieved at the fact that Logan would find her even if she did leave.

Why the hell is he letting this freak have her for so long? This is going to be the longest weekend of my life.

I take a bump in the cab and light a cigarette.

"You can't smoke in here."

I reach into my back pocket, pull three hundred dollars from my wallet, and hold it over the front seat.

"Will this make you shut the hell up about it?"

He snatches the money and keeps his mouth closed until he drops me off. I told Christopher that Tavin and I were busy tonight because the last thing I need is him asking his questions.

The club is packed, giving me quite a selection. I don't even know what I'm looking for until I see her. She's dripping with innocence and just waiting to be destroyed. She is uncomfortable in her skin, if the way she holds herself is any indication. There are a few other girls with her and she seems to be the odd one out, not quite fitting in. She's small with dark hair and I realize that she resembles Tavin.

That's just a coincidence, though…Yeah.

A hit up each nostril gives me the rush I crave, as I step up toward her table. All four of them look at me and I charm every single one. Now I bet they all have wet, little panties. I turn my focus on my fun for the night.

"Do you want to dance?"

She blushes and looks to one of her friends for approval.

"Go, Cade. You need to loosen up."

I hold my hand out to help her from the booth, and while I lead her to the dance floor, I lace my fingers with hers.

Pulling her around so her back is in front of me, I squeeze her little hips and press her ass against my pelvis. She's stiff as hell. I place my mouth next to her ear so she can hear me over the music.

"You need to listen to your friend and loosen up."

She gives me a weak smile and turns her head to respond. "I've never done anything like this."

I laugh. "Anything like what? Dance?"

"I've never been to a bar. My dad would kill me if he knew."

Oh, this chick is so fucked. Literally and metaphorically. I spin her around and place her arms around my neck, slowly trailing my fingers down them, creating goosebumps beneath my touch. She looks up at me with such a sweet expression, I almost feel bad for what I am going to do to her.

"Just relax, you're in good hands."

We've been at this a while and I think she's finally loosening up. It's hot and the music fuels the energy under my skin. Her ass is pushing against me as she starts to move her body with mine.

"There you go. Just like that." I make my move. I kiss her neck and bring my right hand closer to her pelvis. "My name is Toben."

With a coy smile, she watches me through long eyelashes. "I'm Cadence."

This is going to be easier than I thought.

Placing my hand on her neck, I tilt her head back to kiss her and she's more than receptive. I move my hand down to her inner thigh, slowly lifting her skirt. I feel her rock her body toward my hand. I stop to give myself a bump and by her expression, I think I might have just screwed myself.

"Is that drugs?!" She doesn't pull her body from mine though, so that's a good sign.

"I'm shy...it helps my confidence."

Wow that was bad. There's no way she is buying that load.

Her face softens. "I understand that."

Holy shit.

I can see her wheels turning. Oh my God, she totally wants some.

"Do you want to try it?"

"What will it do?"

"It just makes everything better." I dip the little spoon in and hold it under her nose. "One big inhale, that's it."

She does it.

This shit is done, she's mine.

I get her nice and coked out, which makes getting her to agree to come home with me nearly effortless.

"Eighty-three twenty-six South Morningstar Avenue," I tell the cabbie.

We start kissing and I can't believe how her legs just fall open for me. I pull her panties to the side, running my finger along her slick folds.

"God, you're all wet."

She moans and pushes her pussy onto my hand, wanting more.

Oh, she'll get more.

We get to my house and I take her straight upstairs. I can't risk her seeing something of Tavin's. When we're in my room, I lock the door. She can't be running out before I'm done. I kiss her hard and press my body against hers while I walk her to my bed. I slam her down and push open her legs. Ripping her panties down, I shove my tongue into her pussy while I rub her clit with my thumb.

"Oh my God." She's already panting. I move my tongue to her clit, replacing my thumb. I haven't been down here long when she tenses up and tries to pull away. Wrapping my arms around her thighs, I keep her against my mouth.

"Wait." She gasps, "I think I'm going to pee."

She isn't going to pee. Pummeling her with my fingers, I keep sucking and licking while she keeps bucking. "Toben, stop! Something is wrong!"

The sound she makes is hot as fuck and I smile. I'm tasting her first orgasm. When she completely stops pulsing, I remove my mouth.

"You've have never had an orgasm before?"

Her chest is heaving while she shakes her head. Wow. No wonder she's so uptight.

Nice time is over now, though. It's time to play.

"Get naked."

Her eyes flick to mine as she takes off her skirt and I get the chords. When her shirt and bra are on the floor, I order, "Get on your knees and spread your legs."

Now she looks a little worried and she most definitely should. I use the chords to tie her wrists. I don't need Logan seeing scratch marks. She starts freaking out and rolls to her side while trying to crawl away.

"Get back on your knees."

"What are you doing?!"

Questions. At least Nikki knows when to shut up. "Telling you to get back on your fucking knees!"

The waterworks start. "I don't understand! Why are you doing this?!"

I clutch her hair and drag her back up to the correct position.

"Because I had an epic day from hell, now open your mouth." She actually does it and I unzip my jeans. "Have you ever sucked a dick?"

She shakes her head. Nonverbal responses are so insulting. I crouch down in front of her and squeeze her jaw. "When I ask you a question, you need to answer and address me by name." I stand back up and stroke myself. "Now let's try this again. Have. You. Ever. Sucked. Dick?"

"No, Toben."

Much Better.

"Good."

I push into her mouth and she gags. Gross. I'm not going to get her to stop doing that in one night, so I'll just have to endure it. When I'm satisfied with her mouth, I pull out and go for a tool. While I wish I had my whip, I'm curious about what this cheese grater will do to her perfect porcelain skin. I bet Tavin's skin would look just like hers without the scars. I grab one of the knives as well.

"Get on the bed and open your legs."

"Toben I-"

"I didn't tell you to talk, I told you to get on the bed. I don't like repeating myself, Cadence."

She gets up, and sprints for the door.

Not happening.

I'm on her in half a second, pressing her chest against the door by pushing mine against her back, and I wipe her hair off her face.

"Tag. You're it."

I lift her by the waist and carry her to the bed while she cries, "Please, please don't do this!"

Those words give me pause. How many times have we pleaded with Logan not to do something? This afternoon was one of those times. Did he ever relent?

Hell no.

I slam her on the bed, momentarily lying down the cheese grater and the knife to lift her wrists above her head and tie them to my headboard. I'm losing my mind and so fucking alive at the same time. There are only three things that make me feel anything anymore. Tavin, drugs, and playing.

Right now, it's time for play.

I spread her legs open and run my hand over her cunt that's still slick with her earlier orgasm. I get the head wet with her juices before slamming into her and she screams.

Good God she's tight.

I cover her mouth because I am not listening to that all night. When I look down to watch myself pull out of her, my dick is covered in blood. I'd be lying if I said I wasn't wondering if she was a virgin, but what nineteen-year-old doesn't have sex?

"You didn't mention that."

When I release her mouth, she gasps before crying, "I

thought you wouldn't like me."

Honestly, knowing would have just guaranteed this further. I don't stop battering her and as soon as she starts crying I cover her mouth back up. Picking up the cheese grater, I flip her over so that she is on her knees, lift her ass and shove back into her bloody pussy. I know this is going to make her scream so I shove her head down into the pillow before swiping the grater over her shoulder. While the pillow muffles her, the bitch has some pipes on her.

Well, that's disappointing.

I hoped it would cut little slivers of skin, and all it does is takes out one big chunk. Tossing it to the side, I pick up the knife and slice perfect little lines into her back. I get the idea to sign her like an artist would a painting. Right over her right shoulder blade, where the lotus is on me, I carve a *T* about the size of a fist. She bucks to try to get me off of her, and really, it just feels even better. As soon as I pull out and lift off of her, she begins screaming full volume, again.

Goddamn it! I snatch her underwear off the floor and shove them into her mouth.

"Seriously, Cadence, you need to shut the fuck up."

I pick up the belt and hit her with it, causing the little needles to rip her supple tissue. I hook it onto her leg and receive more muffled screams as I shove back into her. I completely understand why Logan uses the scold's bridle on his Lotuses. I sure as hell wish I had one right now.

She's so damn tight. Pumping her this hard is going to get me off and I'm not quite ready. I pull her up by her hair and sit back on my legs, lifting her onto me. At least she isn't screaming anymore, though the snot from her crying is pretty damn gross. Reaching around, I rub her clit.

"I'm almost done, I just want you to come first."

Eventually, she cries harder as she contracts, getting me drenched. When I'm sure she's done, I push her face back down into the pillow. The hand rake is my final tool, and I think I might take it to Nikki's. Thinking of her house gives me an idea.

I can keep Cadence.

Logan gets two Lotuses at a time, why can't I? I would love to watch Nikki eat her pussy while I'm fucking her. This little escapade has served its purpose well. I haven't thought about what happened with Tavin this whole time.

Damn it, I am now, though. It still pisses me off that she said I raped her. I did not rape her. I was forced-there's a difference. This, what I'm doing to Cadence, this is mother-fucking rape. I would never do this to Tavin. This is what I am without her. I don't even know when I started liking this shit. The ten-year-old version of myself would be appalled, I'm sure, but I am what I am and I truly love this. For once, I'm the one with the control.

The way Nikki basically begs me to let her suck my cock, all because she wants to please me, is seriously so erotic it's ridiculous. Little Cadence here will get there eventually. The idea of breaking her makes my blood hum in my veins. She's finally stopped making noise, thank God, and I've done quite a number on her with this rake. With her back all torn up, I can almost imagine her as Tavin.

Beauty among my destruction.

While I know she's not her, it might feel good to get out things I will never actually say to her.

"I did everything for you. Fucking everything! I have killed for you, I have raped for you, and I have gotten raped for you! Still, you don't trust me. The idea of having me inside you is repulsive to you. Do you know how that makes me feel? All I ever wanted was you, and what was it all for? What did it get me? A fucked up life, that's what. Now you hate me and I don't even know if you are coming back." My semen begins to flow into Cadence as I rest my head on her neck and whisper, "I love you so much it hurts."

That actually was very cathartic, I feel much better now.

"There, that wasn't so bad was it?" I pull out of her and she just lies there. I grab her arm to roll her over and as soon as I do, all of my organs drop to my feet. I think I am going to puke.

I did it again.

I killed her.

Shit, shit, shit, shit, shit! I did not mean to do that! I must have held her down for too long. I don't know what the fuck to do and I'm spun as hell, so I light a cigarette and call Logan.

"Hello, Plaything."

"Hello, Logan… I killed a girl."

With a heavy sigh he orders, "Stay put and give me a couple of hours."

He takes an hour and a half and shows up with some random sketchy guy in a brown coat. The man goes upstairs after I tell them where she is and Logan hits me across the back of my head.

"What were you thinking? This is what Nikki's for."

"I know…I was just pissed at Tav and I didn't want to take it out on her, so I picked a random girl at the bar. I never wanted to kill her, I actually wanted to keep her in one of the other rooms at Nikki's."

He sighs and pinches the bridge of his nose. "Toben, you cannot just pick a 'random girl at the bar'. She probably has a family that will report her missing. What if someone saw her leave with you or a camera caught you on tape? If it was just so easy as to pick a girl off the street, I wouldn't shell out the money I do for my Lotuses." He clutches my hair and makes me look at him. "I know you probably want more variety besides Nikki, so I am willing to allow it, though you cannot do this again. If you're going to continue to fuck bar trash, then you cannot hurt them, and you better wear a Goddamn condom. If you get a disease you're worthless to me."

"Yes, Logan."

"Good, now give me your clothes and go shower."

As I hand him my bloody clothes with my bloody hands, I shake my head. I cannot believe I did this again.

CHAPTER SEVENTEEN
Alexander

Tavin

So cozy. Today is my last day at Master's and I admit that I'll miss this bed. It's even more comfortable than the beds at the hotels. I stretch from my fingers to my toes.

"I'll miss your morning stretching shows this week." He bites my ear as his hand goes in between my legs, sliding in a finger. "You woke up wet for me again, today."

Being the whore that I am, I open my legs wider for him as his mouth makes its way to join his fingers. He's done this a few times, he gets into oral and then gets frustrated because he can't make me come without some kind of pain.

He moans into my pussy, "Damn it." Taking a knife off the tray we had cheese and wine on last night, he goes into the bathroom to clean it. On his way back to me, he says, "I don't know if I like this. We need to find another way."

I hide my smirk as he goes back down on me because he must not dislike it too much, he's about to do it again.

As soon as he accomplishes his goal, he shoves in so hard that my head slams against the headboard. "I can't believe I have to wait a whole week to feel this cunt again."

"A week?"

He wants me to come back next weekend? For the whole thing? I'll never get any time with Toben and that is just so much sex. He doesn't slow his pace as he bites my neck.

"I've already paid for next weekend."

Awe, seriously? I won't ever get a break or day off if he keeps doing this.

"Is that a problem?" He scowls at me so my face must be showing my lack of enthusiasm.

"No, Master."

He pulls out momentarily to flip me on my stomach and grabs the ruler off the nightstand. Master has a student/ teacher fetish.

Last night he made me act out a scene. It was the most ridiculous thing I've ever done, and I wasn't able to get through it without laughing, which in turn pissed him off so bad he pulled me downstairs and caned me bloody. If I'm honest with myself, it was kind of fun. Besides, I learned that Europe isn't a country like I always thought. It has a ton of countries inside of it! It doesn't seem believable that the world is so big. I think he is holding back just enough to keep from breaking the ruler, as he hits me.

"That's the second time you lied to me since last night, so I will ask you once more. Is that a problem?"

I don't know what to do. I'll make him mad if I talk about other Clients, but he'll know if I lie anyway. I guess if he gets mad, then at least I might get suspended again.

"It's just...he'll keep making me see my five clients a week and if I'm with you all weekend...it's a lot and I'll never get to spend time with Toben."

My head hits the headboard again. "Who the hell is Toben?"

"He's my best friend. He's Sweet Boy."

That must be an acceptable answer because his voice

drops when he grumbles, "I'm not canceling next weekend, however, we will work something out for the future. You have my word."

That surprises me. Why does he care how I feel about it? He's the one paying.

"Thank you, Master."

I like the sounds he makes when he comes. It's not gross sounding, it's more of an animal sound. It's cute.

He traces his fingers over my back and kisses in between the cuts. I don't understand why he would ever pay for me or anyone for that matter. He could have any girl he wants. Maybe I'll ask him sometime.

"Time for breakfast."

He takes me back to his playroom for one more playdate, and afterwards, as I get dressed, he gives me a bag of sour hard candies.

If you ask me, I should have gotten at least two bags of candy for a whole dang weekend.

We don't speak as he walks me to the door and helps me into my cab. He nods at me through the window as the driver pulls out of his drive and asks me my address.

Now that I'm on my way home, I'm starting to freak out. Master was actually a nice distraction from the shambles my life is in. I have no idea what to say to Tobe. I'm aware Logan threatened him with my life, but he's done that a ton of times and I don't know if he will ever really go through with it. I wish so badly that Toben would have held out a little longer and tested that theory. Regardless, what's done is done and no number of what-ifs will change it.

I've gone back and forth, over and over in my head, and even though I'm still confused, it's time to face the music. I pay the driver and climb up my steps. The door is unlocked as usual so I slowly open it while my stomach twists.

Toben is on the couch sleeping in nothing besides jeans and his notorious beanie. As soon as I see him, tears fill my eyes. We've been through everything together. I can't be without him, I would wither away. We live together, bleed together, and we'll die together.

Things will be different now though, they have to be. I know that I can never willingly have sex with him, not now, and that scares me. Will he be too angry or hurt to continue being my friend? I don't know what he'll feel, I just know I want his arms around me. I want to smell him and touch his face. In this moment, I want my Tobe. I crawl onto the couch next to him and pull his arm around my waist while I hold his hand. Tears fall more from the relief of his touch than from sorrow.

"Tavin?" He moves to sit up and when I raise my eyes to his, he's staring down at me, bordering on tears.

I can't contain myself, I cry into his chest. "I'm sorry. So, so sorry."

He squeezes me tight. "Jesus Love, you're killing me. Please don't apologize."

"I need you too, Toben," it pours out of me along with the tears, "but I will never be able to be with you like that. I love you, more than anything, I just can't give you want you want."

Toben rarely cries. Right now, though, he's choking on his sobs. "All I want is you."

It's tempting to believe him. To think that we could make it work. I just know that isn't fair to ask of him. It's not enough, as much as he wants it to be.

"You've already been with other girls, so that's obviously not true."

His eyes become fearful as he hovers over me. "No, Tavin, please, I'm so sorry. I will never touch another girl again, I swear."

"How is that fair to you?" I shake my head. I've made up my mind. "I just want to go back. Back to before things got so sexual between us. I just want to be with you again."

"I don't know how to not touch you, not kiss you."

It's so natural for us to physically show our affection. It's been that way forever. Even now, as we hold each other we become whole. The idea of not having those things with him brings a cloud of dread down on me and I feel nauseous.

"I want to still do that stuff. I need it. I need you. We just can't be together in the romantic sense. It won't work, Tobe."

His fingertips lightly touch my face and he allows his tears to fall. "So what changes?"

"I don't think we should make out. If we don't really let it start, we won't have to worry about things getting confusing. Everything else should pretty much be the same. When you get a girlfriend, then we'll reevaluate."

He laughs. It's the most comforting sound and it eases my soul. "That's not going to happen. I have no desire to be in a relationship with anyone other than you."

I sigh, even though I can't stop my smirk. It makes me feel good that he says that. For a minute, I consider being with him and just letting him get the sex elsewhere. That would hurt too much though. It already breaks my heart to think about.

"Okay, I guess we'll see. I just want to be your best friend, the other half of you." I hold his hand so our promise and our scars are joined together. "When you bleed, I bleed, and that will never change."

He kisses me, testing my promise, and I kiss him back. He pulls me against him and holds me tight to him.

We lie like that for a long time until he leans over to reach under the coffee table. When I see what he's getting, my heart leaps. I've just been through two days of drug free, constant sex, so as soon as I imagine the needle going into my skin, I actually moan with anticipation.

"Let's get high, Love."

Four Years Later—October 2014

Toben

"I wish he would have let me have the day off too," Tavin grumbles as she throws on her sunglasses.

I put down the birthday gifts she got me and wrap my arms around her. "I know, Love. We'll celebrate tonight okay?"

"Fine. I love you." Kissing me, she whispers, "Happy birthday." Just before she closes the door she adds, "Wait for me so we can pick out your cake together."

"Sure thing," I chuckle at her.

Sitting on the couch, I put on the new beanie she got me and cut some lines. Once I'm thoroughly coked out, I go outside and wait for the cab to pick me up.

Logan let me have the day off for my birthday, and since Tavin has a playdate until this evening, I'll be celebrating with Nikki. I have the driver stop at the bakery so I can pick up a cake before taking me to her house.

Nikki's waiting for me on her knees like the perfect plaything she is. "Hello, Plaything."

Her smile is small and sweet. "Hello, Toben…Happy birthday."

"Thank you, Lotus."

I place the cake on the dresser and as I stand in front of her, she reaches up to undo my pants. She loves sucking my cock and when she's compliant like this, it makes me want to give her the tenderness she craves.

Her light, strawberry hair has gotten so long, and as I run my fingers through it, she pulls down my boxers and leisurely licks the tip. Trailing her tongue up my length, she continues until she reaches the base. The way she looks up at me makes me so fucking hard while simultaneously making me have guilt because of how she feels about me.

I enjoy letting her suck me as I slowly slide between her lips. With both of my hands, I brush her hair away from her face and hold her head to pull her up, kissing her once she's standing.

"Put your hands behind your back and bend over the bed," I murmur against her lips.

She nods and when she obeys, her tiny nightie slides up, exposing her little panties. She really is so beautiful. I remove my jeans and boxers before kneeling next to her. More of her lightly freckled skin is exposed as I pull her pretty underwear to her knees, and off her legs. Her hips lift in invitation, and I run my fingers over her wet entrance.

"Do you want me inside you before we play?"

"Yes," she responds immediately. Looking over her shoulder, her hair falls in her face. "I want to look at you."

Sometimes, she gives me this feeling. I can't explain it and I don't want to. So, I abolish it. Holding onto her clasped hands, I pull her arms back to lift her up. When she cries out in pain, I release her and spin her to face me like she asked.

"Just don't get confused, Nik."

Tears fall as she nods. "Yes, Toben."

I let out a small breath as I kiss her neck and pick her up to lay her on the bed. Continuing my kisses to her shoulder, I pull down the strap of her night dress and expose her breast. I trail my tongue around her nipple as she arches her back, urging me to suck. Her hands trail down my back to my ass, pushing our bodies closer. She's so slick that it's easier than usual to slide right into her. Her moans are soft next to my ear, and she feels so good that I can't stop myself from pumping her faster.

The sound of the door opening behind me causes me to jump off of her and Nikki to gasp. I whip around to see a smiling Logan in the doorway.

"Oh good, you're here." He strolls into the room as my heart rate slows. "I brought you a birthday present."

I take in a breath as he looks at Nikki. "Thank you, Logan."

He reaches out and holds his hand above her pussy, looking at me with an arched brow. "May I?"

I want to lunge at him and almost do when Nikki looks at me in horror. It's been awhile since she's seen him.

"I'd prefer you didn't, Logan."

He smirks with a nod as he walks back to the door. "Come now, Plaything."

I grab my jeans and kiss Nikki. "I'll be right back."

Rushing to follow him, I button my jeans as I meet him on the stairs. When we turn into the hall on the main floor, my pulse quickens.

No way. He didn't.

He takes a key from the top of the doorframe and smiles. "What is the one thing you've continuously asked me for, Toben?"

He fucking did.

There's no stopping the grin from spreading. "Another Lotus."

Unlocking the door, he swings it open to show me a girl, blindfolded and bound, on her knees on the floor. "Meet your new plaything. Her name is Tiffany."

She's shaking as I kneel down in front of her and remove her blindfold. Her wet eyes are brown and rimmed in red.

Her hair is dark and decently long. I like long hair. When she focuses and makes eye contact with me, I smile.

"Thank you, Logan. She's perfect."

"Happy birthday, Plaything. While I'm sure you prefer to choose her clothing, I did put some things in the closet to get her through the next few days."

I stand to face him. I can't believe he finally did this. I need to know if she's truly all mine. "Is she…a virgin?"

He grins with pride. "It's been confirmed that yes, her hymen is in place." Patting my back, he says, "I'll leave you to your initiation."

I let out a big breath because I wasn't completely sure how he was expecting this to go. I don't want him near her ever again. I loathe how many times he's had Nikki.

"Thank you, Logan."

As soon as he shuts the door, I turn to my gift. Tonight is about to get a lot more interesting.

"Hello." Her eyes narrow as I crouch down. "My name is Toben, and you are my new plaything."

"Why am I here?" She cries.

"To play with me, of course."

My tools are all upstairs. I hadn't wanted to have her initiation in front of Nikki, but she's going to need to understand this new dynamic quickly and Nikki is not going to like this.

She's still bound, so I tie the blindfold back on and pull on her arm to get her to stand. I lead her up the stairs and unlock Nikki's door to find her in her position once again.

She looks up to me and as soon as she smiles, it fades away. I drag Tiffany to the bed and throw her on the mattress before I remove her blindfold.

"Do you like the gift Logan got me?" I ask Nikki.

Her tears are coming down in a steady flow when she whispers, "Who is she?"

"She's our new playmate. You'll be seeing a lot of her."

Her head shakes as if she refuses to hear the words. "But, I'm your plaything."

"And now, she is too." While I try hard not to admit it to myself, I do hate when Nikki's heart breaks. It's just necessary, and we both have to get used to it.

Her eyes beg me not to do this, so I turn to a whimpering Tiffany. "Do you understand what you are now? What your role is?"

She shakes her head and I don't understand how none of these girls know to answer questions with words. I grab her throat and her eyes bulge in fear. "Use words to respond from now on or you won't have a tongue to speak with."

It's an empty threat. I won't ever mutilate her that way, she doesn't know that though.

Beauty among my destruction.

She nods quickly and says, "Yes, Toby."

I don't know why that pisses me off so much. She isn't intentionally misspeaking, but it makes me feel like she isn't scared of me enough to remember my name. I'm going to change that and make sure she pays better fucking attention.

I backhand her so hard she falls back on the bed. "My name is Tob*en*. Don't make that mistake again."

Her cries are loud and since I still don't normally have a use for one, I never asked Logan for a scold's bridle. "Yes, Toben."

Nearly touching my nose to hers, I unbind her wrists. "You are being really loud. I don't like loud. If I end up having to gag you, this will be a lot worse than it needs to be." I tie her to the bedframe and pull down her green panties before turning to a silently crying Nikki. I spread Tiffany's legs and slide my fingers into her dry pussy. She squirms and fights, but I keep my eyes on Nikki. "What would you like to see me do first? Lick her pussy or fuck her mouth?"

Nikki shakes her head and cries, "Don't make me watch this, Toben. Please."

"Keep talking to me like that and that's all you'll be doing."

She bites her lip and sniffles. "Make her suck your dick, Toben."

Tiffany shakes her head as I get up to my knees and undo my jeans. I move closer to her face and lift her head so she can reach my cock. She tries to move away, but I still force myself into her mouth.

"Suck me, Lotus. Trust me, you want to go along with this." Finally, she complies and I turn to Nikki, "Her hot little mouth feels amazing, but not as good as yours. Would you like to come share?"

Nikki stands up and answers through cries. "Yes, Toben."

Walking around the bed, she climbs on and kneels next to Tiffany. She takes my erection out of her mouth and slides it into her own. "That's right, Plaything. Show her how good little sluts take cock." As Nikki passes me between both of their lips, I finger them both. "Have either of you ever licked pussy?"

"No, Toben," they both respond.

"Nikki, I want you to sit on her face." I rub my finger over Nikki's clit as I look to Tiffany. "Lick her here. If you make her come, I won't hurt you this time besides giving you my mark. Understand?"

She sniffs. "Yes, Toben."

Continuing to finger Tiffany, I watch as Nikki puts her pussy over Tiffany's mouth. As soon as her tongue darts out and flicks over her bud, Nikki grinds against her. I keep my eyes on them as I situate between Tiffany's legs and spread apart her lips. I lightly trace my tongue between her folds before making my way to her clit. It doesn't take long for her body to beg me to continue.

Once she's wet enough, I get on my knees and line the tip with her hole and shove inside, taking her purity with a single thrust. She screams into Nikki's pussy and it makes me fuck her harder. Blood drips onto the sheets as her body shakes.

"Scream like that again and this is going to get a lot worse."

She cries as I spread her body with mine, but her tongue starts moving again. This is so fucking hot. They are both mine and they both have to do anything I want. As Nikki bucks against her tongue, my orgasm explodes into Tiffany.

"Fuck, Playthings, we are going to have a lot of fun together. I lean forward and taste some of Nikki's orgasm before I get up and pull on my pants. "Nikki, clean her up, while I get ready to sign her."

"Yes, Toben." She climbs off the bed for a towel. "No, Plaything. With your mouth."

Her horrified expression makes me chuckle as I go to my bag of tools, retrieving a blade and the blowtorch.

"Alright, Nikki, untie her and show her how to wait in position." Tiffany is still sobbing as she's untied and follows Nikki's actions. I turn on the torch and heat up the blade just enough for a clean cut. "After today, you will not doubt who you belong to. Nikki, show her your marking." Nikki obeys turning to show her the healed *T* on her back. "You are now my art, my possession, and today I'm signing you."

She looks to Nikki for help and her face falls at the expression of neutrality she sees. I kneel behind her and dig the blade into her skin, carving two quick lines, one horizontal and one vertical, making a *T*.

She gasps in pain, though she doesn't scream. She should be grateful that I'm not Logan. His marking hurt a hell of a lot worse than this. The blood drips from the fresh cuts and I stand to get a cloth from the bathroom.

When I walk back out, Tiffany is still sobbing and Nikki snaps, "Would you dry it up, bitch? You have no idea how good you have it." She scoffs, "Actually, keep it up and maybe he'll kill you sooner rather than later."

I grin at her possessiveness as I walk back into the room and dab the cloth over Tiffany's cuts. Once they are passible as clean, I grab the rope and pull her up by her hair.

I smile at Nikki. "I'm going to get Tiffany situated, then we'll have cake and get high together, okay, Plaything?"

"Yes, Toben."

Yanking Tiffany down the hall, I pull her down the stairs. As soon as we're in her room, I drag her to the bed and tie her to the headboard. "If you happen to get free before I return, just know, the windows are bolted shut and made of ballistic glass, so there's no way out." I dig in my pocket and pull out one of the chewy fruit candies and place it in her mouth. "I have a gift for you since you did so well."

Taking the works kit out of my pocket, I prepare the rig. She whimpers when she sees the needle, but once it's in her veins, she's gone in the realm of dreams.

"Welcome home, Plaything."

Six months later—April, 2015

Tavin

He's doped up already? He did it less than twelve hours ago and it's not even noon yet. Logan is going to start figuring out that he's been buying it elsewhere. Not that I don't smoke, snort, and shoot half the stuff he gets, still, I try to keep the heroin to at least every other day.

Last year, we developed a bad habit and Logan cancelled

ot at all happy about it. At least it's not nearly as bad as last time.

"Toben, hey, wake up."

"Hey, Love." He slurs the words as he rolls off the couch.

I hold his face in my hands and look into his eyes. Yeah, he'll be out of it for a while. I kiss him.

"I gotta go. I have a Client. I love you."

"Uh huh. I love…"

I sigh as I take off his beanie and pull the blanket off the couch to cover him up. The pink lollipop on the coffee table catches my attention. He left it there after his playdate last night. Well, it's mine now. He knows how this works.

<hr />

Another office, another suit, another cock, another day. The cab drops me off at the address for Mr. Davis.

The structure is a decent size compared to the surrounding buildings, but what really stands out, is the giant vulture on the front. Even though it seems a bit flashy to me, it's definitely different. It almost looks like they smooshed two separate buildings together.

The main entrance is a blue glass cylinder, while to the left it becomes more square and blocky with setback windows making it appear to be inside of a box.

I walk through the glass front doors and the way it looks inside is just as showy as the outside. I've never seen an office quite like this. A quiet *boom* sound forces me to look over my shoulder. A huge screen that takes up the entire wall, like the ones in theaters, is playing movie trailers.

First, it shows a cartoon, then switches to an action blow 'em up. Glass framed film posters are strategically placed in between dolls, T-shirts, and all sorts of other random objects covered in movie paraphernalia. There are also a ton of pictures of pretty girls dressed up in costumes. This place is definitely unusual. Every single chair looks so comfortable and the yellow-brick-road yellow and gray color scheme is exciting and inviting. Behind the large, curved desk to the left of the entrance is the same vulture from the front of the building.

Vulture Theaters

It's written in large black letters trimmed in the same bright yellow.

I'm never supposed to talk to the receptionists or the secretaries. My instructions are simply to go to the intended office and knock three times. On occasion, they will stop me, usually though, if I don't give them a reason to notice me, they won't.

There are two sets of elevators toward the back. To get to Mr. Davis' office, I'm to take the one on the left to the top floor. Once the doors open, I step inside with two men and a woman. I'm thankful there's a railing lining the elevator and I clutch it as the car jolts, taking us up to our floors. The other passengers leave at their desired destinations and when the *ding* sounds for mine, the doors open and I panic.

I was told Mr. Davis' office would be to the right of the elevator, but there are *three* of them to the right.

I can't ask the receptionist, so I pick the one closest to the elevator and pray it's the right one. When I lift my hand to the door, I hear a muffled banging sound. I knock three times and wait. The noise stops abruptly and after what feels like forever, the handle turns. I suddenly realize that having candy might make it look like I just came from another play-date. Well, that's not good. I take a deep breath and when I look up, I have to look up more.

For about three seconds, my body shuts down. I can't speak, I can't breathe, and I definitely can't take my eyes off the man standing in the doorway.

I don't know what's going on.

His hair is messy and the most gorgeous blond I have ever seen. While it's nowhere near as long as Toben's, it's still long enough for him to run his fingers through it…which he's doing right now. His skin is light and golden, like the sun hugged him. His broad shoulders are beautifully on display in a dress shirt that's partially unbuttoned, showing me not near enough. He has a five o'clock shadow on his strong jaw and his lips are…oh my.

The door is open just enough for him to stand in the space, as he looks me up and down with burning eyes that are the color of the castle in Emerald City.

Please, please let this be the right office.

Whoa…I did not seriously just think that. I shift my eyes away from his daunting gaze to see his name plate and my stomach takes a nosedive. Why in the world did they make the nameplates so freaking small?

Alexander Sørensen

Not Mr. Davis. Oh no.

"Shit."

"Can I help you?"

His playful voice is lined with a smile and when I look back at him, it's gorgeous. My heart is thumping and my stomach is fluttering. I feel so excited and I don't know what for. I need to go.

"Oh no, uh…I'm sorry."

I spin around and I know my face is bright red. Hurrying

to the next office, I only stop long enough to read the name.

Silas Hamilton

I want to turn around to see if he's still there. Just give myself one more look, but I chicken out. Sadly, I toss the small remainder of Toben's lollipop in the garbage next to the last door. It's the one I'm looking for.

Eric Davis

I knock three times and when I do, I hear the blond oxygen thief's door shut, and I can exhale properly again.

The door in front of me opens, and while Mr. Davis is tall, he's nothing like the angel I just saw. He has jet black hair that matches his cold eyes, and the way he's standing in the doorframe makes me think he's going to strangle me to death.

"Do you know what time it is?"

I dig for my phone in my jeans. "Not exactly."

"It's 11:06. Our playdate was at eleven. Not a good start." He moves so I can pass. I waste no time getting undressed and on my knees. He's already pissed and I don't want to make it worse. "Well that's better. Stand up." I do and he runs his hands across my stomach before his fingers feel my wetness. "At least you show up ready." He wipes his fingers across my cheek before he marches to his desk. "Bend over here." Lying my stomach across the cool wood, I spread my legs so he can get a better look.

Whoosh

Sheesh. He doesn't waste any time does he? I think that was a belt.

"I can see your cunt tighten. They told me you got off on this, that you were a sick little freak." He wraps his belt around my neck and bites my shoulder before straightening my arms. His fingers touch my track marks.

"A bit cliché isn't it? To be a junkie and a whore?"

Is that an actual question? "Um…yes, Mr. Davis?"

He laughs, though it isn't meant to be kind. "Let's see if you're worth the seven grand I'm paying for you."

Our prices went down after we turned eighteen. Apparently, being underage is worth more.

I hear the telltale sound of a condom wrapper seconds before he rams into me. I hold onto the edge of his desk and push right back, clenching around him.

"You know how to take a dick don't you?"

"Yes, Mr. Davis."

He tightens the belt, completely cutting off all oxygen. I can feel myself drifting when he quickly removes it and I gasp in the air as quietly as I can. Grabbing my arm, he spins me to face him as he pulls off the condom.

"Get on your knees and swallow my cock." He's an average size so I have no problem taking him all the way down. The harder I suck, the faster they come. He slams into my mouth violently, pushing my head down to get deeper. "That's right, suck it, cunt." I feel him pulsing and I take every ounce he has to give me. I haven't even been in here thirty minutes yet.

There's no way he's done playing.

Oh, he's not done. I've never been burned by a lighter before. That one's new. Logan's burnt me with implements before, just never a straight open flame.

I'm sitting on the desk as he shoves himself into me. His pace picks up and he reaches into the pocket of his partially still-on trousers and removes a cherry bubblegum pop. He rips off the package and shoves it in my mouth as he pulls out of me and takes off the condom again. He strokes his hand up and down his length, jerking off as he watches me eat the candy. Suddenly, he rips it from my mouth, puts it next to the head of his dick and comes all over it.

Awwww dang it. Seriously? The jerk just ruined my sucker.

He hands it back to me, making me put it in my own mouth. "Don't be fucking late next time."

"Yes, Mr. Davis."

"Do you have any appointments next Friday? I have an unpleasant event that evening and I would like you to be available to relieve my frustrations afterward."

"I don't know. He doesn't usually tell me until a day or two before."

"Alright, fine." He puts his suit jacket on. "Now get your gash out of my office."

He's a charming one. As I leave, I linger a little too long in front of the first office, and let my fingertips run over the engraved letters.

Alexander.

Two weeks later—May, 2015

The alarm beeps and Toben groans, "Damn it, Tav, turn that shit off."

I lay a big ol' kiss on him and shoot out of bed. "Oh, hush, grumpy. It's not my fault you drank so much last night. I have a playdate."

As I go to the bathroom to get my toothbrush, I hear the *click* of his lighter. "That party was epic though, you have to admit," he calls.

I grin. "Yeah."

He isn't lying. Christopher came through on the coke in a big way, and I have no idea who most of the people who were over here were, last night. Logan doesn't care if we throw parties as long as the cops don't get called. I still can't believe people actually call the police.

We don't blare the music too loud and our neighbors

mind their own business. Besides, I'm pretty sure Toben is sleeping with Courtney next door.

When I finish brushing my teeth, I go back into my room to pick out my clothes and get undressed. Toben snorts a line and holds out the bill, so I take a couple too.

"I need to get in the shower."

"Hold on Love, I'll join you."

He washes my hair and I wash his. Once I'm dried off, I hurry to get ready. Today is my playdate with Mr. Davis and I have been excited ever since Logan told me about it. I know it's stupid, I just want to see him again, not Mr. Davis obviously, but *Alexander*. I like his name…and his face. I'm queasy and not exactly in a bad way. I don't know why. I've seen handsome men before. Master is truly beautiful, and so is Toben, but he was just…wow.

I don't know what seeing him is going to do, anyway. Give me something to dream about, I guess. I'm a little embarrassed that I'm having these thoughts. I'm acting like those girls at the bar that get all giggly over a cute guy.

Oh, cute doesn't even begin to cover it.

Maybe Mr. Davis will refer him?

What?! I need to stop. Why would I want another Client? I do not need that, uh uh, no way.

"Why are you in such a hurry for a Client?" Toben asks as I throw on my sunglasses.

"I was late last time, I can't be this time."

It isn't a lie, even though he narrows his eyes before kissing me.

I trudge way too slowly by the first office before going to Mr. Davis' and knocking three times.

"Good to see you know how to tell time."

Good to see you're still a prick.

"Yes, Mr. Davis."

He lets me in and slips off his jacket. I get naked while he pulls out his erection.

"It's not gonna suck itself, bitch."

Very clever. I've only heard that six thousand times. I drop to my knees and take him into my mouth. For some reason, I get scared that Alexander might walk in and see this. While he might already know what I am, I don't think the Clients are supposed to discuss this with just anyone. I know Toben and I aren't supposed to.

He pulls me up and shoves me so I'm laying over his desk before he grinds himself into me. "Fuck, you're such a disgusting slut. Look at how much your pussy begs for my cock." His fist jabs into my ribs and I swallow down my groan.

I know it's entirely possible that I won't see Alexander at all. I still don't know what I would do even if I did. I just want to look at that face one more time. See that smile. He kind of reminds me of the prince doll I wanted as a kid with his pale blond hair. His eyes though, they were the brightest green I've ever seen.

Suddenly, my head bangs against the desk so hard my ears are ringing.

"Am I boring you, whore?"

"No, Mr. Davis."

He licks his hand to get my ass wet before he pulls out and shoves himself in. "You like this? Tell me."

"I like your cock in my ass, Mr. Davis."

"Yeah, you do, skank." He grunts as he comes and lays his chest against my back.

Pushing me to the floor, he pulls up his slacks. I grab my stockings and as I stand to roll them on, he tosses my bra at me before grabbing my chin.

"Stupid bitch! Look what you made me do!" He throws

my face away from him. "I'm not supposed to mark your face and now your head is bleeding!" I get dressed as he throws his door open. In a low voice he orders, "Get out."

I shove my hands in my dress pockets and step into the lobby. Where's my candy?

"I won't tell Logan," I whisper.

Gripping the door frame, he glares down at me. "You better not, you junkie, and I won't tell him how poor your performance was." He pulls another cherry bubblegum pop out of his pants pocket. "I expect you to be more Goddamn attentive next time."

I yank it from his hand. "Yes, Mr. Davis." He doesn't respond other than slamming the door in my face.

Sighing, I toss the wrapper in the trash, pull down my sunglasses, and slip the candy in my mouth, as I turn toward the elevator.

My stomach implodes as I realize Alexander is standing right outside his office. All I have to do is lift my head to see him. My face heats up and my heart quite literally skips, yet I'm able to make myself keep moving.

I feel panicked. This is what I wanted, so why can't I just raise my head and look?

As soon as I'm in the elevator, I let out a harsh breath. Why couldn't I just look? Just as I'm about to reach for the button, I swear to God, he slides into the elevator with me.

Holy crap.

I lift my sucker to my mouth, mostly out of habit, but for some reason I feel self-conscious about him seeing me with it. My eyes are probably the size of silver dollars so I'm thankful for my sunglasses. As he stands next to me, his scent fills the elevator. He smells the way he looks. It reminds me of summer. It's how the sun smells, I bet.

His deep warm voice tickles my stomach giving me an intense urge to laugh. "Hi."

Speak! "Oh…uh, hi." I need to get out of here. I don't know what's going on. This is way too overwhelming.

"I'm on my way to grab a coffee. Would you like to join me?"

Did he just ask me out?

I do laugh then, he has no idea what he's talking to. The thought is so absurd.

"Oh no, no, no, you don't want that."

Oh, God, can you imagine? If he only knew that I just had his co-worker in every single one of my orifices.

He lets out the sexiest little chuckle. "How could you possibly know that?" I think he has an accent, it's just so subtle I can't place it.

I'm tempted to just say it: because I am someone else's toy. Because I'm a filthy whore and a drug addict. I'm sure that would change his tune, but I don't want him to know. I have no idea why I care so much, I just know I would give anything right now to be anything else, to have any other life.

I sniff from the stupid coke and hold out my hand to emphasize my point. "Just trust me."

There. Now he'll stop torturing me.

I'm sure my eyes go wide again when he releases a deep rumbling laugh that fills the entire elevator, warming me all the way to my toes.

"Well now I'm intrigued."

What?!

He turns to face me, and he's so freaking tall. He isn't as wide as Master, but I can tell by the way he wears that suit, he looks good under there.

Jeez! Why am I thinking this way? I see way too many naked men to spend my time thinking about them. He has such a lightness about him, yet his eyes are burning with lust and somehow, I don't hate it.

"Go out with me tonight. At least let me decide for myself."

Wow he's relentless. My stomach is going spastic and I wish he would stop. This isn't fair. I want to go with him to see who this person is. It's impossible though... Isn't it? What if I did go? Just one date. One night. I could pretend to be a normal girl on a normal date with an anything other than a normal guy. It would be harmless. It's not like we'd have sex or anything. It would be a nice break from my life. Christopher does it all the time. He'll go out with a girl once and never see her again.

I can't keep myself from smiling.

"Are you alright? You're bleeding."

Oh crap. I forgot Mr. Davis cut my head. Next thing I know, he's touching me. My head is warm from where his finger is. Even his touch is like the sun. It startles me, so I jump away from him. Reaching up to wipe, I see he's right, there is blood. At least it's close to my hairline.

"Are you okay?"

He looks genuinely worried. It's cute though, because he's concerned over a little cut that I can't even feel. Imagine what he would do if he saw under my shirt.

Answer him!

"Oh yeah, I'm fine, um...thanks though."

God is this elevator ever going to stop? I need to get away from him so I can breathe properly.

Finally, the *ding* signals our stop as he says, "Do you know where The Necco Room is? Say...ten o'clock tonight?"

Oh, come on!

You know what? Why shouldn't I? I've never been on a real date before. Granted, I never have wanted to, but still...I want to now. I can't believe I'm doing this.

I sigh and repeat the information so he knows I have it. "The Necco Room, ten o'clock."

The doors open and I have to keep myself from sprinting from the elevator as he calls after me.

"Wait! What's your name?"

The tickle in my stomach from his enthusiasm makes me grin. "I'm Tavin, Tavin Winters."

That was dumb. Why would he want to know my last name? I turn to see that smile that makes me-oh my God. Am I...am I turned on?! How is that even possible? He's holding the doors open, and with his arm spread like that, he really does look like an angel.

"It's nice to meet you, Tavin. My name is Alexander. I look forward to tonight..." his face flashes with an ornery expression, "and wear the knee highs."

That pulls a little laugh from my mouth. I pop my candy back in and head outside toward the fresh air.

I'll do what he asks because if I am anything, it's an obedient plaything.

Toben

I haven't been sober for a playdate in over a year, so I must be getting better at hiding it. Mr. Stride is in his mid-forties and a lot more physically fit than most Clients. Not that it really matters, but not hitting your head on belly fat while sucking dick is always a good thing.

He sits in his chair taking calls while I lick and take him in my mouth, when he suddenly, yanks me up by my hair and starts jerking me off. It's so different to have such large, rough hands stroking me after Nikki's small, soft hands were doing the same just a few hours ago. When he hangs up and wraps his mouth around me, I can feel his beard scraping me as his head bobs up and down. I thrust into his mouth and fist his gray hair.

"Fuck, oh God yes, suck my cock, Mr. Stride." Damn, he really knows how to do this. I thrust into his mouth as he slides a finger into my ass and fucks me with it. "Oh, shit," I moan. Fuck. "I'm coming…please, drink my come."

He moans around me, the vibrations sending me over the edge as he draws out every last bit. When he flips me over on his desk, he pierces his tongue into my ass before putting on a condom. He pounds me against the desk as he hits me with a flogger.

"Does my cock feel good in your little ass, Sweet Boy?"

"Yes, Mr. Stride."

I can't believe how used to this I've become. It's just another day. When he is finished, he gives me strawberry licorice and tells me I am a good boy and he will see me again soon.

When I get home and through the front door, I see Tavin sitting on Logan's face.

"Hi, Toben."

"Hey, Love."

Logan runs a knife across her ass and when I kiss her hello, she moans against my lips. He pulls her away from me and flips her to her back, shoving her up the couch.

I head into the kitchen to do a few lines of coke, and within a few minutes, he tells her he's coming. As I go back out into the living room, they're getting dressed and Logan orders us to kneel.

"I brought you some more needles and money in case I'm not able to come back before I leave town next week. It should be enough to last until I get back. If you need anything while I'm gone, just call Kyle. My plane departs Thursday morning and I'll be gone for a month." He runs his fingers through Tavin's hair. "I left all this information and your client schedules in your rooms. Toben, you have a weekend playdate coming up."

That's complete bullshit. Whatever. When I had my last weekend playdate, the guy let me get so high I didn't even know I was getting fucked.

Finally, Logan leaves and I get the kit out while Tavin cuddles up next to me.

"Hey, Love. How was your day?"

"Weird."

I kiss her temple and clean off the table. "Yeah? What was so weird about it?"

"A guy asked me out. Like on a real date."

I freeze. "Oh yeah?"

There's no way I'm letting her see me react to this.

"Yeah, we're meeting at some place called the 'Necco Room'. Now I have to figure out where it is."

Whoa, whoa. What the hell now? She's actually going? Nope. Not gonna happen.

"You can't actually go, Tav."

She seriously looks broken up about it. "Why not?"

"Why do you think? Nothing can come of it, so why waste either of your time?"

"Because, I want one night to feel like a normal twenty-three-year-old girl, like the ones at the bar. Because I like him and I want to see how it feels. I know nothing can come of it, Tobe. As soon as he found out what I am, he'd be gone. A guy like him would never talk to me if he knew."

I don't like this at all. I hate the way she looks right now while she's talking about it. Her cheeks are flushed and she keeps running her hand down her thigh.

"Logan will never allow it, Tav. He isn't paying for your time."

"The girls that you go out with don't pay."

I try to hide them from her, I do, it's just tough when I never know exactly when she'll be home. She's ran into a few of them here and there and she doesn't seem to be bothered by it much anymore. I hate it.

"That's different-"

"If you say it's because you're a boy, I'll punch you in the throat." She's so cute when she gets pissy.

"No, it's because Logan doesn't care what I do as much as he does you."

"So, you're going to tell him?"

Well, shit. She's clearly made her mind up. It's not like they can keep seeing each other and I know she won't fuck him, so I just need to relax. Let her get it out of her system and see that it's not all she imagines it to be. I just worry about her. What if this guy hurts her?

"Of course not, it's just not safe, Love. There's no contract keeping him from doing bad things to you."

She laughs like is such a stupid notion. "I don't think he's dangerous and I know what dangerous looks like."

Yeah, she thinks she does, but it's staring her in the face right now and she's completely oblivious. "I can't stop you, just know I don't like it. I think it's a dumb and risky idea."

"You're right. You can't stop me. I'm going."

Now I definitely need to bang up. I huff and she huffs back at me before she smirks and kisses me.

"It's just for fun, Tobe."

I cook the mixture, anxious for it to be in my veins.

"Yeah, well, so is this."

By the time we're sober, she says she has to get ready for her 'date'. I can't decide if I'm going to follow her, go to Nikki's, find a random, or just get so high I don't know where I am. Honestly, I never thought I would have to deal with this.

She's never shown the slightest bit of interest in anyone, besides maybe Master, and he's still a Client. Who knows what this guy's agenda is?

While she curls her hair, I smoke a cigarette on our bed.

"Where did you meet this guy, anyway?"

She smiles a smile that until today, I had only seen her give to me.

"I have playdates with a colleague of his." She smirks because she knows exactly how fucked up this is. She's being absurd.

I laugh, "Wow, Tav, seriously? You want one 'normal' night and you choose to do it with a suit? How is that any different from a Client?"

It better be because there won't be any sex involved. Oh my God, she just giggled.

"Oh, trust me. He's different."

That's what the fuck I'm afraid of.

I realize how thin she's become as she tries on her clothes. Maybe we should try to lay off the smack a little. My nerves are slightly calmed by her outfit choice, until I understand her reasons. She's wearing a sweater in the middle of May and not because she wants to make sure he doesn't get the wrong idea, it's because she doesn't want him to see her track marks and scars. She cares enough that she doesn't want him to judge her and that's too Goddamn much.

I think I'm going to puke. She's *excited*. She likes this asshole. Looks like I'm going to Nikki and Tiffany's tonight after all.

I'm beyond furious right now and Logan says no more dead bodies. If I kill either of them then I can replace them, but fuck! I don't want to. I love my little Nikki and I've only had Tiffany a few months.

I'll just have to keep my cool with some bar trash. Yeah, I can do that.

Tavin looks beautiful and seeing her walk out the door makes my heart drop to the floor.

CHAPTER EIGHTEEN
Carousel

Tavin

WHILE TOBEN'S CLEARLY NOT EXCITED FOR this idea, he has no room whatsoever to be pissed. I am twenty-three freaking years old and have never been on an actual date. I probably will never be able to again and definitely never with someone like Alexander. Besides, Master has been talking nonstop about wanting to buy me from Logan. Honestly, the thought doesn't really scare me other than not being able to see Toben. I mean, I would only have to be with Master, no more Clients and no more Logan. Although, he would basically keep me locked away in that castle just ready and waiting to be played with.

Things with Master are kind of weird. I do like him, he's my favorite Client by far, and even though the sex feels good, it's still sick. Not to mention, I will never do another drug again if that happens. At least I have some freedom with Logan. I just know if it does come to pass, I won't ever get an opportunity like this again.

I walk in through the door of the Necco Room and snort at the man in the suit holding open the door. This place is all fancy pants. I'm questioning what I'm wearing, but it's too late now. This is my third time trying to get the courage to do this and now I'm at least fifteen minutes late. He's probably not even here anymore. Oh God, I can't do this. I turn around and change my mind again. No, I have to do this. I need to do this. One night. That's all I need, a night that I can think about, when my life seems too dreary.

The night I was a normal girl.

I make my way through the tables when I see a full shot sitting on a table, all alone. Well now, that's just asking to lose your drink. I take it and feel the burn as it rolls down my throat. I scan the large room. I doubt that he stuck around this long. Then, I see him standing by the bar.

Breathe, breathe, breathe.

My throat is dry despite the drink I just had, so I swallow and put one foot in front of the other. Here goes… My stomach is doing that twirling thing from his smile, and before I know it, my feet have carried me to him.

I wave. "Hi."

Wow. I thought the suit looked good, but good Lord those jeans were made for him, and his shirt somehow makes his eyes even brighter green.

He's wearing an expression that I have seen many times, just never on a face like his. It makes me feel electric. I cross my ankles so I can press my legs together. He hasn't even touched me, how the heck is this happening? He looks me over. Probably wondering what's up with my outfit.

When he speaks, his voice makes me want to sigh. "Hi." He looks to the bar. "Do you want a drink?"

I definitely do.

"Yes, Alexander." His flawless eyebrows, which are a shade darker than his hair, shoot up.

Crap. He's not a Client.

"What do you want?"

What does he mean by that?!

"What?!"

His lips lift in the sexiest smirk. I'm amusing him. Lovely. "To drink?"

Oh, jeez. Of course. I need to act like I'm with Toben so I will sound more natural. "Oh yeah, um, whatever will fuck me up."

Oh God, that was horrible. I'm no good at dates.

He laughs again. I just hope he isn't laughing at me.

"Well, okay then."

This is nothing like the bars Toben and I go to. This is the kind of place Logan would go. Oh no… what if we see him?! Logan would be furious and I would be humiliated. I can't stop myself from scanning the tables for him.

Alexander nods that gorgeous head toward the seating area.

"Why don't you pick a seat and I'll bring over our drinks."

"Yes, Ale—uh…okay."

Dang it! I know my face is red again. Why am I getting like this? I do what he asks and pick a table off to the side so I can see the people in case I run into Logan or…oh God-a Client.

He meets me at the table and sits my drink down.

"Bourbon. One-thirty proof. Guaranteed to fuck you up." He smirks as he sits across from me.

I smile at him. "That's great…thank you."

He nods in response as he leans back. His arm muscles move as he lifts his drink. "Are those your natural eyes or are they contacts?"

I feel the urge to laugh. He wants to know about my eyes? That's not usually the body part men want to talk about.

Why do I keep thinking about sex? I have spent most of my life trying not to think about it.

You have always wanted it, you nauseating skank.

"They're natural."

I keep an eye out for anyone that I don't want to see, while I look at the décor. I think it's beautiful. It's a bit Victorian Gothic with a modern edge. Everyone here screams money.

I take a drink when he asks, "What do you do for a living?" and I almost choke on it.

I knew he would ask this stupid question.

Generic answer time: "Oh you know, a little of this, some of that."

His face flashes for the first time. It's small and quick, but clear. He's not happy with that response. Well, too bad, because that's all he's getting.

I know I should ask him about his job, I'm just not sure I would understand it, anyway. I wonder if he took me to this ritzy place to impress me. He'll be disappointed if he did.

"So, do you come to bars like this a lot?" I ask him.

He laughs again. I've never met anyone so happy. "Are you asking me if I come here often?" Isn't that what I said? He straightens himself and rolls his shoulders. "Yeah, a few times a week."

I glance down at his arm and am greeted with bright pops of color. How did I not notice the whole bottom half of it was tattooed? It's incredible and I don't even know what it is. I wonder if it means anything like Logan's. Thinking of him makes me check the bar again.

I need more blow. I'm way too paranoid. If I'm going to get through this, I need to relax. Scanning the bar again, I think I see a Client. Right as my heart is about to go into panic mode, he turns and I realize it isn't even him.

Whew.

"Tavin." Alexander's voice is commanding for the first time, forcing me to immediately look at him. "Do you want another?" He's pointing to my drink.

I finish what I have left. "Yes…" I don't see a bathroom

sign. "Um, where are the restrooms?"

He shows me, and once I'm inside, I can't get into the stall fast enough. Taking out my little bag of confidence, I sprinkle it along the toilet paper dispenser. I may be over doing it, but three lines later I know I can do this.

I wash my hands and when I look in the mirror, I tell myself, "You can do this. It's supposed to be fun." The girl next to me thinks I'm crazy from the expression on her face. I don't care though. I've made up my mind. I know what I have to do. He might tell me to leave or push me away, but I'm going to kiss him. Toben is the only boy I have ever kissed just because I wanted to. This is my choice. He's not a Client, and he's not Logan.

Tonight, I get to make my own decisions.

I have one more bump to make sure I don't chicken out. Walking back into the main room, I see him returning with our drinks and my stomach flips.

Here goes.

I head straight for him. He's so tall that there's no way I'll be able to reach him from the ground, so I march right up to the seat and climb on. His flawless face is priceless as he wonders what I'm doing. I grab him and kiss him with everything I have. His mouth responds immediately giving me the tingles again. Of course, he's an amazing kisser. My fingers are in his beautiful hair and his hands grip around my ribs. While the world around us is in chaos, we stay still. My heart pounds like a drum in my ears and my stomach is freaking out.

I don't want to, but still, I stop. I separate my lips from his and when his emerald eyes open I can feel the desire in them rippling beneath my flesh.

I did it! I'm floating and I don't want to lose this feeling so I hop off the seat and gulp down the entire drink he just got me. Too bad I'm way too coked out to be able to feel it.

I want to dance with him.

Stabbing my finger towards his full drink on the table, I tell him, "Why don't you finish that, and then we can dance." He doesn't waste any time throwing it back before he takes my hand and we make our way to the dance floor.

I love how bright he is. Not like smart, which I am sure he is, but actually bright. Toben once told me that some people believe in multiple Gods. The God of water, God of air… Well, he's how I imagine the Sun God would look.

Even though we can't talk much because the music is really loud, his smile is infectious and I can feel myself doing it as well. His big hands are on my hips. I don't think he dances very often because he seems a little out of his element. He keeps buying shots and smiling though, so I think he's having fun. I know I sure am. Maybe I'm not that bad at dates, after all.

The more we drink, the more natural his dancing becomes. He's aroused and I can feel his erection against my back. I'm confused and scared as to why that doesn't bother me. It oddly makes me feel special that he wants me.

His warm breath tickles my neck and I can feel his lips move against my ear when he asks, "Do you want to take a break?"

I don't care what we do, I just like being around him. "Whatever you want, Alexander." We walk back to the table and I look at the bathroom sign. I need another line. "Just let me run to the restroom really quick."

Once I'm in the stall I check my phone. There's a text from Toben.

Having fun?

I roll my eyes. He's so transparent. The messed-up thing is, he's probably with a girl right now.

Relax. Let me enjoy it. I'll see you tonight, now leave me alone. I love you.

I pull my vile and ID from my skirt pocket and cut a line on the toilet paper dispenser. I really should have asked to borrow Toben's stash necklace. My phone *pings* when he texts me back.

Be safe. I love you, too.

I inhale, deciding to do one more line before I go back out.

Now that's better.

As I walk back out to meet him, he sprawls his hand across the small of my back and gestures his head toward the doors.

"What do you say we hit another bar? There are a ton of them on this street."

I will go anywhere he asks me to and it's freaking me out. What is it about him? It's more than his beauty and his smile. Maybe it's his warmth and joy. He's happiness and sunshine when I'm from a world of pain and nightmares.

I smile at him. "Let's go."

If his intoxicating cheerfulness isn't enough to keep the grin on my face, him holding my hand as we search for another bar, is. He tells me a cute and funny story about his housekeeper and I laugh when I hear odd music. It's not the kind on the radio or at the club, it's closer to what the ice cream truck plays. I turn my head to see a wonderful display of colors, lights, and sounds.

A large red and yellow banner reads: **Carnival.**

I've seen a carnival once before. I didn't get to go though, and I couldn't really see it, I just remember watching kids running in excitement, screaming about rides and games. It was about two years after Logan let us out of the basement. I was on my way to see a Client, and when I dragged Toben back to go, it was gone. As if it never existed. I actually remember wondering if I dreamt it. It does seem magical in a way. It's late and it's still open, so maybe when I get home

I can talk Toben into bringing me. Even though he might moan about it being for kids, he always gives me what I want, eventually.

"What do you say we go check that out?"

I jerk my head towards Alexander and he's looking toward the carnival. Is he serious? I hope he's not teasing me. My stomach bubbles up in overwhelming excitement and I don't know if I can keep myself from squeaking in glee.

"Really?!"

I always worry about all the bad people, I never think about all the good people there must be. He takes my breath away with that smile.

"Of course."

We make our way across the street and he's walking way too slow for having such long legs, so I pull him to the counter. He gets our tickets before giving them to a man by the gate who lets us through. I'm surrounded by more flashing lights and noises.

There are game booths covered in toys. There are clowns and food carts. There are so many rides and the Ferris wheel stands above it all. The carousel seems to glow and has beautiful horses and chairs to sit on with golden poles coming out of them. It's one of the most beautiful things I have ever seen. A giant slide is next to a man trying to get people to play his game. There are so many vibrant people, and their energy bleeds into my skin.

"Where to?" He asks me with a smile.

I feel a little overwhelmed. I don't know how long we're going to stay so I want to pick the best stuff. I see a huge circular ride that spins and tilts, another one that jumps and shakes. I just know I want to ride the carousel.

I can't make a decision, I'm not used to making my own. "I—uh. Well, um…"

His big warm hand laces with mine and his enchanting

face smiles down at me.

"We'll get to all of it, I promise. How about we start with the tilt-a-whirl? That was always my favorite as a kid." The idea of him as a kid makes me smile for whatever reason and I'm excited to do anything that was his favorite.

The ride has a bunch of half-egg-shaped seats all connected to a round, metal platform. When we sit down, the man locks us inside together and I can't believe I am about to ride my first ride!

With him.

As it starts, the platform pulls us in a circle over little hills. Our cart is swinging back and forth until all of a sudden, it spins us around so fast, my stomach falls to my toes. I find myself trying to force the cart to make more spins, anticipating the rush it gives me. I can't stop laughing. I've never experienced anything like this.

He looks like he is having as much fun as I am when he asks, "Do you want to ride the slide?"

I nod. He doesn't say a single thing about my not responding with words, he just grabs my hand and doesn't let go as we get in line.

There are kids in front of us and one of them challenges the other to race, so when it's our turn, I tell him, "Race ya."

Arching an eyebrow, he smirks. "You're on."

He beats me by a mile three times in a row and he's actually getting cocky about it. Dear Lord, he wears cocky well. I don't think I'm heavy enough to go fast, so I look to the guy behind me. He's definitely smaller than Alexander, but added to me, I bet I would win.

I turn to him. "Will you ride with me?" Alexander snaps his head toward me. I don't think he's mad, just wondering why I didn't ask him. I grin at him. "I want to win."

There it is again. The smile that shows his perfect white teeth and makes the emerald in his eyes sparkle.

I step up to put my feet into the gunny sack and the man I asked gets in behind me. Suddenly, we fly over the first bump on the slide and just as I look to Alexander, we're passing him. Before I know it, we're gliding onto the mats two seconds before Alexander does.

Ha! It worked. I win this time.

He pretends to be upset when he says, "Cheater." Then his lip lifts into a smirk.

After the slide, he finally takes me to the carousel. I squeeze his hand. I can't believe how this feels. I'm so glad I did this. I never would have imagined it would be this freeing. The coke is wearing off and I don't care. This is unimaginable.

He leads us to a booth seat and it slowly goes in a circle allowing me to see the entire Carnival. I wish I had my camera, this would be an incredible picture and a perfect memory.

"It's been so long since I've been to one of these places," he says as his hand goes to my thigh.

I don't move a muscle. He's touching me! My skin buzzes beneath his palm. I don't know what a normal girl would do so I just pretend not to notice. God, this view is breathtaking and I want him to know that he's giving me something new.

"I've never been."

"Never?" He cinches his hand closer to my skirt and I wait for the filth to crawl over me. "So how do you know Eric?"

Eric? Oh…Mr. Davis…crap.

"Oh…um, he's just…an acquaintance." I feel hot. This stupid sweater is like a strait jacket. My stomach jerks when he squeezes my thigh.

He turns to me and removes his hand from my leg to tuck a piece of hair behind my ear.

"Do you like cotton candy?"

My breath is sucked from my body. He has no idea what he just said or what he just said it to, and still, it makes my body floaty.

I've done nothing more than kiss him and I know he would have still offered even if I hadn't. That's not what this is about. He's having a nice time with me and that's enough to reward me.

Not only is he offering me candy, but it's a kind I've never had before.

I grin at him. "*Cotton* candy? I've never tried it."

"Do you want to?"

"Very much."

He hands me a big pink fluffy ball on a stick. This isn't like any candy I've ever seen. I can't believe he got this for me. He tells me to try it, and when I do, it melts as soon as it hits my tongue, sending the most incredible flavor into my mouth. That thing's gone so fast Alexander doesn't even get a bite.

He makes excuses to touch me and I make them to get closer as we walk around the carnival. We ride swings that make you go so far out I wonder if the chains will break and I will fall to my bloody death. If that does happen, tonight, I would die happy.

I watch him knock down all the bottles in a game and win me a pink, stuffed dragon. He doesn't even know me and he's giving me gifts. My heart pounds because I think he's about to kiss me when the little girl next to us starts crying, catching his attention. She's upset that she didn't win the game and I feel bad for her. I don't want him to think I don't like it, she's just so sad that I want to give the dragon to her.

He's standing behind me and I feel his fingers brush my hair away from my ear. I hold my breath, forcing myself to slowly exhale when he whispers, "I swear I'll win you another one."

I want to kiss him again so badly right now, I'm just a wuss. I give the little girl the dragon and she's so cute when she says, "Thank you," to us. I think her mom smiles a little too long at Alexander, though.

He's making me laugh so much because as hard as he tries, he's never able to win another dragon. I have to pull him away because I want to ride more rides.

I get scared that we will fall out of the ship that's rocking so hard, we're almost upside down. He holds my hand the whole time and swears it won't happen. I've never ever had fun like this. Never could I have planned a more perfect night.

I look around for our next ride when I see a funny looking, almost animated building that has 'Wacky House' painted in wonky letters. I don't know exactly what it is, but with a name like that, it has to be neat.

I point it out to him as I'm already pulling him in that direction. "Let's go to the Wacky House!"

It's so nice to not worry about if I'm doing what I am supposed to. I can just be me. We enter through a crooked doorway and the floor slides down, causing my body to tumble over right into him. Big arms are around me and I laugh with embarrassment as he stands me up.

"You got it?" He laughs.

I nod with a smile. I like not having to speak every time.

Okay, now this is crazy. Everything from the furniture to the art is an illusion. He takes me down a hallway and there's a broken box with a diamond inside. The hole is just big enough to put my hand through and I almost do it. I don't know if I'm supposed to touch things, though. He nods in approval so I make a fist and slip it through the hole. A loud alarm goes off and I jump back. Why would he tell me it was okay? Then I realize that it's supposed to do that, it's a joke. I smile at him and taking a note from Toben, I wink at him in a silent thank you for how wonderful this has all been.

Suddenly, his hand wraps around my wrists and pulls me to a nearby door. He shoves me through and before I can figure out if I did something wrong, I'm in a room of mirrors. There's a zillion of us that go on forever. This would be nuts on acid.

"Whoa, this is trippy!"

My back slams against the mirrored wall, knocking the wind out of me, and his lips are on mine before I have time to register. He's kissing me! He has me pinned and he's almost forceful in his desire, yet somehow, I know that if I wanted him to stop he would.

I don't want him to.

I tug on his soft hair, loving the feel of his mouth on mine. His tongue is gentle while his kisses are hard. I can't believe I'm making out with him! I feel his fingertips on my thigh and they are moving higher up my leg.

The grime will envelop me soon. He's going to want to touch me and I can't let that happen. It's dirty. Except...not right now it's not. His fingers are barely touching my panties and I automatically lean into his caress. I actually crave it. What's wrong with me? He pulls my panties to the side and I can feel the cool breeze as his fingers barely touch me. I'm actually okay with this?

WHORE!

I still and barely whisper, "No," before the feeling vanishes as quickly as it arrived. It's never just stopped like that before. How did he do that?

He backs away as he runs his hands through the light strands. "Shit. I'm sorry-"

"No, don't stop...I...that wasn't a no..."

His hand drops and he scowls at me. "That most definitely was a fucking no."

I ruined it. Our night was perfect until I messed it up. It left. The feeling left and I'm confused about what that means. "I…I didn't mean it." I can barely make my voice work. I'm so mad at myself.

His arms cage me in and his shoulders flex as he leans forward to pierce his eyes into me. "I don't take pussy that isn't offered. If you want this to continue, you're going to have to make the next move."

I do want this to keep going. Partially because I'm curious if the feeling will stop again. Mostly though, it's because I like him a lot and his warm touch leaves me wanting for the first time in my life. I keep eye contact as I take his right hand from the wall and place it on my thigh before pulling my panties to the side. He doesn't move an inch as I hold his finger and brush it over my slit. His eyes light up and he smirks in the most devilish way as he slips his finger inside of me. I tighten around him as I watch his shoulder flex with the pumping of his arm. No clawing fear, or filth, just his incredible finger sliding in and out. I've been fingered countless times and it's never been like this. Not even with Master.

His forehead is pressed against mine just watching me. He eventually slips in another while his thumb softly presses against my clit. I swear if he cut or hit me I would come right now. I don't know if this is how normal girls are, so it might be bad to push my body onto his hand. I'm not even in control of myself anymore. I almost feel high even though I know the coke is nowhere in sight.

There's a noise in the room, it's just irrelevant while his hand is inside me.

He whispers, "Shit," before he takes out his fingers.

Before I can react to the loss, he holds my hand and pulls me to the end of the mirrored room and back outside.

Once we burst through the exit, he laughs while running his hand through his hair.

I want him so bad.

Surprising myself, I use all my strength to push him against the wall. Why do I have to be so short? I'm never going to be able to reach all the way up to his mouth. He sees my struggle and the sexy jerk smirks before he bends down and cups my face. Clearly, he likes to have the upper hand because he picks me up and turns us so that I'm the one against the wall. We kiss for a while and I keep getting frustrated that he isn't replacing his hand.

I'm so close to dropping to my knees and giving him what he wants. It's what all men want. The difference is, this time, I want to give it to him.

"Come home with me," he murmurs.

The words seem to reverberate through me. I know exactly what will happen if I go back with him. I nod my response because all my words have vanished. I don't want this night to end, I want to feel what it should be like. Toben always says it's not supposed to be bad, now I see what he might mean.

I can't believe that I'm doing this of my own free will. I won't get this opportunity again. As soon as the dirtiness shows up I can stop it, but what if for some reason it doesn't? I'll never know if I don't try. This is my one night to make my own choices, and tonight, I choose him.

CHAPTER NINETEEN
Mine

MY HEART GOES CRAZY AS WE CROSS THE STREET to the Necco Room. He talks to the valet and a couple moments later, a ridiculous yellow car pulls up in front of us. It takes a lot of self-control not to laugh. Is this seriously what he drives? Of course it is. Even though I've only been inside a few cars, they're always black or gray and none have had curves like this. This thing screams attention, just like its owner. I think it's cute he's so proud of it. He opens the door for me and I immediately recognize the song playing on the stereo. First the candy and now this? He slides in and turns down the music.

"You like Nirvana?" I ask him.

He looks at me in disbelief. "Oh yeah. You?"

"My best friend got so sick of this album."

I can almost hear Toben now:

Christ on a cracker, Love. If you play that fucking CD one more time, my ears are literally going to bleed.

My heart jumps when he laughs. "That's actually pretty funny, so did mine. He threatened breaking it on more than one occasion."

He pulls off from the curb and I smile at him in the dark. He has no idea what he's doing for me. This has been one of the most incredible nights of my life. The only other day that was this amazing was the first time I left my house with Toben. The intensity of what that statement means is huge. I want to thank him and I know how to do it.

I know how to do it well.

I reach across the console and press my hand to his jeans and his erection pushes against my palm instantly. For the first time in my life, making a man hard gives me a thrill. I do that to him. He desires me. I unhook his belt and the thought of him striking me with it makes me smash my thighs together to suppress the need. I quickly undo his pants as his breathing changes, causing my nipples to harden, and I know I am probably soaked. I reach inside of his boxer briefs and holy cow! He's even giving Master a run for his money. I pull his underwear down making it easier to stroke him. My hand doesn't reach the whole way around and I lightly squeeze before I gradually pick up speed. It's dark, but as we pass the lights, I can see him keep glancing down to watch my hand pump up and down. He starts to push himself in and out of my grasp as his small groans escape occasionally. I want to make him react. I want to hear what he sounds like when he comes. I lean down and I'm able to get a little over half of it in right away. I swallow and suck as I am able to get him to slide further down my throat.

"Jesus!" His hand softly rests on my head while he pushes himself deeper and grows even freaking bigger. I take it gladly. Every time he whispers a 'fuck' or a 'shit', it just makes me want to suck harder and make it feel better. When did sucking dick become fun? Eventually, his hand pushes my head down when he starts pounding the heck out of my mouth. "Okay, I'm gonna come."

I'm curious how he tastes. Every man has their own flavor, I guess. I can feel the pulsing that lets me know he's ready and as he pours himself into my mouth. I'm not disappointed when a low moan tells me of his satisfaction.

I hope that this isn't enough for him. I actually want to have sex with him. A lot. I want one guy on my list that's mine and I want it to be him. It can only be him. Once he's empty, I make sure he's wiped clean before I sit up. I brush a drop from my lip when I feel the cloud of guilt come over me. What am I thinking? I had his business associate inside me this morning! Never mind the fact that Logan came inside me this afternoon. Then I think about Toben. How am I going to willingly let a guy that I talked to for the first time today be with me, while I won't let my best friend, my love, my everything have me?

Toben can never ever know about this.

Filthy bitch!

I don't understand myself, and I'm starting to get that dirty feeling when his hand makes its way up my skirt, and somehow it all falls away. I grasp onto his strong forearm as his fingers are inside of me once again. The muscles in his arm move beneath my touch, as he fingers me. I want more. I want him deeper. Sliding my hand down to his wrist, I hold him there as I thrust onto his fingers. His thumb softly rubs small circles over my little bud and oh, what I would give for a knife right now. This feels insane and I wish I could come. I've wished I could come before, just not for this reason. I want to show him what he's doing to me and how he's making me feel. I close my eyes as I lose myself in the sensations when I hear a little *clank*. My eyes slowly open to see a gate letting us through, as we pull into a driveway.

The house is large. Not quite Master's castle large, though it's a completely different style. It's multileveled, square, and boxy with a lot of huge windows. We pull into a garage as he rips the keys out of the ignition. He gets to my side inhumanly fast as he pulls open my door and yanks me out. I can barely keep up as he jerks me through a door and into a short entryway. One minute, I'm in his kitchen while he completely misses the bowl he attempts to throw his keys into, and the next, I'm up against a wall with his mouth crashing against mine. I melt into him and can't believe the relief I feel when his fingers are back inside me.

He kisses my neck and braces his free hand against the wall. "Those raspy little moans of yours have me hard as fuck."

I inhale sharply while the heat intensifies at his words. His fingers slip out of my skirt and he holds my hand, tugging me across the living room and up a set of stairs. I see three different doors while we speed walk down a hallway before we eventually turn into one. The bedroom is open and simple like the living room. A black dresser is to my right and a big four poster bed is directly in front of me. There's a door to the right and a door to the left. I'm guessing a closet and a bathroom. The bed has a big, fluffy, white comforter and blue accent pillows. I let go of his hand as he turns on some music.

Okay, this is it. I'm doing this. I walk to the front of the bed and hurry to get my clothes off. I don't want him to have to wait and I don't want to change my mind. I just have to remember not to kneel. That might freak him out.

"Whoa, slow down. There's no need to rush."

I feel like I'm going to pass out when he towers over me. I can't do this. If I sprint really fast I'll be long gone before he figures out what happened.

His fingers fondle the strands of my hair and I almost blurt, 'I fucked Mr. Davis this morning'. Thankfully though, his soft lips start softly kissing mine. His aggression from downstairs is gone, replaced by gentleness. His arm wraps around me and lifts me up, pressing my body against his while his kiss deepens.

Maybe I can do this. I just need to chill.

His hand moves over my butt at a leisurely pace, and I feel his fingers on my thigh. For a moment, I worry that he will feel the welts from Master's cane, but he doesn't seem to notice. His hand finds its way up my skirt again and squeezes my bottom. Can he feel the scars and cuts? He squeezes and kisses me harder for a moment before placing me back on the floor. His eyes are blazing and his lip is lifted ever so slightly in a subtle smirk. I'm shocked his cock isn't out yet. He is taking his time which is not something that I am used to. This is supposed to be my area of expertise. I'm literally a professional at fucking and he has me so flustered, I don't know which way is up. Maybe he's waiting for me to take the initiative, another new experience for me. I reach for his jeans button, when his hand suddenly wraps around my wrist to stop me. When I look up at him, he is shaking his head.

"No. Be patient."

What's his deal? "Yes, Alexan-…okay." Dang it, I have been doing so well with that. I'm too nervous.

He knits his eyebrows together before he lifts my chin, kissing me sweetly as I sense his hand move to my back. I almost push away when he lifts the hem of my sweater because there's no way he's seeing my back or the lotus. I let out a breath when I realize he's just going for the zipper on my skirt. It's like he knows we're only going to be together once and wants to enjoy it. I know I'm enjoying it. My skirt falls to the floor and I get nervous about the needled belt and knife marks. I pray that he doesn't get turned off or ask me about them. Maybe he won't notice?

That hope is shattered when after he kisses my neck, he crouches down so his head is directly level with my panties. I hear him deeply inhale before he kisses me over the lace fabric. He softly moans and I use all of my will power to stop myself from pushing against him. Just a little kiss before he squeezes my hips and slips them off. He acts as though I'm the most beautiful thing in the whole world, and even though it isn't true, I like feeling like it.

"You have got the cutest little pussy I've ever seen." I bite my lip and I know I'm flushed when he places a light peck on my swollen pussy lips and looks up at me, eyes smoldering.

His eyes flick over to the belt marks and he slightly frowns for just a second, then his face quickly relaxes. I wouldn't have even noticed if I hadn't been waiting for it. He ignores the scars and moves on, which causes a warm, swollen feeling in my stomach. No callous words or disgusted looks, barely even a reaction at all. Standing back up, he continues to shower me with tender kisses. I've never been kissed so softly, leisurely, and gently. Even Toben has always been aggressive in his affection. I don't want this night to end and I want to feel this man inside me. I want to be a part of him, even if it is only for tonight.

I bend over to take my stocking off when he grips my wrist again.

"No. Keep them on."

He's dead serious. I bite back a grin at his leg wear fetish. It's cute. His hands squeeze around my waist as he lifts me up so I'm eye level with him. I lean forward and give him a soft peck on his nose which gets me that Godlike smile. Next thing I know, I'm flying through the air and I feel panic until I land on his pillowed bed.

I never knew sex stuff could be like this. This sure isn't anything like playing with Logan or the Clients. Not even Master. Laughing during this stuff is frowned upon, but that was fun and a giggle falls out anyway. He's on me instantly and the sweet, slow kisses are gone. His body weight on top of mine is almost too much, I can't believe I'm feeling this way. My body almost hurts, I want to be touched so badly. I want to see all of him and I know that isn't fair because he won't get to see all of me. His shirt is a button up, but there's no way I am wasting that much time. I find the hem and push it up, feeling the hardness of his body under my fingers. Once it is off of him and on the floor, he chuckles and pulls away from me.

Okay let me get this straight: he has a face that's been touched by God, he's one of the nicest people I've ever met, he smells incredible, he's an amazing kisser, he's fun, he likes Nirvana, he gave me candy *before* sex, and he has a killer body?

His hands go to my knees as his fingers lightly caress beneath the hem of my stockings before he pushes down, opening my legs for him. His head drops and I feel myself clench at his close proximity.

Nasty trash.

It's just a flash and once again, it disappears. Lips are kissing my thigh right where my knife scars are. I hope he doesn't notice them and I'm so grateful that nobody has done that to me for a few months. Master has come up with a few other options lately. I can't see his face well enough to know if he is seeing them. If he is, he isn't reacting to them. He moves to the other side repeating the action. His kisses are as warm as his touch, and I am dying here. He's taking his time, when all I want is his tongue on me. Slow, soft kisses everywhere other than where I need them. When his nose presses against my clit, I almost cry. When he finally puts his mouth where I want it, it's Heaven.

"You taste even better than I imagined," he mumbles between licks.

He's thought about me.

His speed and expert pressure is causing a build. I actually think he might do it, he's going to make me come without pain. Then it falls away. This is so sexy to watch. He looks like he's having a great time down there and don't get me wrong, this is…wow, it's just painful and not in the way I need. He brings me to the brink of orgasm three times, only to have them suddenly stop.

I want to scream at him to cut me, burn me, something! I want him to make me bleed, destroy my flesh, and mark my body. Oh, just thinking about it… He ceases his feasting and kisses me on my pubic bone before he begins to lift my sweater.

No!

This night will end abruptly if he sees. I'm sure normal guys would go flaccid at the sight of my mangled body. There are plenty of Clients who love to tell me how hideous it is.

I pin my arms down so he can't move it an inch more. "Leave it on."

While the expression on his face tells me that he isn't happy about it, he would be a lot less happy if he actually saw. His actions tell a different tale when his lips slam into mine before making their way to nipping at my jaw. Then he bites my ear. It's such a tease move and he has no idea. While it isn't enough pain to push me over, it's enough to intensify the ache. When he leans over to retrieve what I hope is a condom, I try to undo his pants again. He lets me continue, so I slide his jeans and underwear down, exposing what feels like a firm, marvelous backside. I wrap my hand partially around him, stroking steadily and he rocks into the motion for a moment before backing away from me and climbing off the bed. He kicks off his shoes and socks before removing the rest of his clothes.

When he stands up straight, I just know I'm gaping. Master is a sight, believe me, and Toben's six pack induces mouthwatering, so it's not like I have never seen a nice body before, but Alexander is perfectly proportioned in every way. Muscles that are large without being bulky, lines cut exactly where they need to be, and with his skin and hair, all he's missing is wings and a halo.

"God, you sure do have a body to go with that face, don't you?"

As soon as the stupid words leave my mouth, I could die. My only saving grace is his laugh paired with that up-to-no-good smirk he gives me while sliding on the condom. Even that is overwhelmingly hot to watch.

He crawls back to me on the bed, looking like he will eat me alive and God, I hope he does. He kisses my neck and when he's back on top of me, I can feel his cock pressing against me.

This is it. Time to freak out.

Shit. Shit. Shit. I can't do this! What am I thinking?! I'm choosing this?! No, this can't happen. What will I tell him? I look up at his face, his incredible face and I know he will hate me. Just as I'm about to tell him to stop, he slides himself into me. He groans at the same time I gasp at being stretched to the max. I reach for his hips to push him away, when he thrusts back into me and it feels so good I find myself pushing onto him. I'm not getting the dirty fear yet and I might hate myself along with him after this, but for now, I feel amazing. He knows how to fuck and he knows it. He lifts my leg, opening me further as he pushes in deeper.

"Jesus, that clenching thing you're doing feels insane."

His breathing hitches here and there and it's so erotic. The muscles in his shoulders and stomach flex every time he pumps, causing the agonizing build of release. When he bites my neck, I think I might scream at him to actually bite me.

As in: draw blood you bastard.

I can't believe I'm actually doing this and liking it. He pulls me on top of him and I ride him with all I have. He's given me so much and he will never know it, so I show my appreciation the only way I know how. He looks at me with fire and it would be so easy to believe this is real. I forget that he has no idea that I'm nothing. A plaything for men to do as they wish. If he only knew he was inside of such filth.

He squeezes my hips. "Damn, you're good at this." His voice is much gravellier than it was before and with the slight accent, it's the sexiest sound I've ever heard. If I were a normal girl I might be able to come from that alone.

I want to tell him that this is the first time I've ever willingly slept with someone and that it's amazing. He will always be the one I chose. The one I gave my body to because I wanted to. He will always and forever be mine.

"So are you."

He flips me onto my back again and holds both of my hands over my head while he pounds away. This is so unfair. What I would do for him to hit me with that belt he was wearing. It has a pretty heavy-duty buckle on it.

Other than the small sounds that escape, I stay quiet. No man wants to hear a girl howling while he's trying to come. I look up at his beautiful face and notice his jaw clenching.

Oh no, did I do something? Is he mad? He kind of looks mad. He pulls out of me and I ache for him to come back. When I lean up to ask what's wrong, his mouth is back on the little bundle of nerves. Oh great. Here we go again. He's well versed in how to use his tongue, and I don't know how much more of this I can handle. He's going at it and I wish more than anything that I was a normal girl so I could come like one.

He mumbles, "Shit," and is back inside me before I even know what's happening. His aggression is much more intense causing him to fuck harder and torment me further. Why is this so agonizing? I usually hate to come because of how I feel afterward, and right now, I would kill for release. Harder and more violent he becomes until his voice, low and angry growls out, "Tell me what I need to do to make you come."

Oh crap. He's one of those. Time to lie.

"Uh...I already did."

He glares at me. "That's bullshit. Tell me. Now." Slamming into me hard to emphasize the last word. Clearly, he's angry.

What the heck am I supposed to say? If I tell him the truth, he'll be disgusted and this amazing, incredible, perfect night would have been ruined. I don't know what to do, so I just make it up and hope to God it's a thing.

"I can't come when I've been drinking."

"Are you kidding me?"

Well if he wasn't mad before, he is now. I don't know what else to say besides apologize.

"I'm sorry, Alexander."

That's actually a loaded statement. I'm sorry that I'm not normal, I'm sorry that I dragged him into this, and I'm sorry that I'm not sorry that it was him.

An erogenous groan coupled with the way his body looks when he comes is quite a combination and I know I am squeezing around his climaxing cock. Now that he's done and angry, I am left unsure. I feel his finger pressing under my chin, pulling my gaze up to him.

"You have to give me another try."

I bite the inside of my mouth so I don't smile. He's a determined thing. Even though I want to consider it, I know he will just get more frustrated and I refuse to tell him about my needs. He isn't the type to be into that kind of thing. I like the way he looks at me and I know that would go away if I told him.

When he slides out of me, I'm immediately saddened at the fact that I will never feel him again. This is it. It's over. My night as a normal girl is finished.

After he gets up to throw the condom away, he comes back and stands next to the bed as he slides two fingers back in. Slowly, he pushes them into me and I know he isn't angry anymore. Maybe he never really was.

"I'm going to take a shower. You are welcome to join or you can go downstairs and have a glass of wine…" He seems to consider that, "actually no wine. Coffee. You can have coffee." That's sweet. He wants me to sober up so he can get me off. Oh, how I wish that was the issue. I need to get dressed so I can leave while he's in the shower. It seems mean, but how else am I going to get out of here without hurting his feelings? When I go to put on my clothes, he pulls out his own and holds them out for me. "These will be much more comfortable for the night."

He's expecting me to stay the night and for the trillionth time tonight, I wish I could be who he thinks I am. Whoever that is. He bends over to kiss me and I know this is goodbye. He will visit me in my dreams, he will be with me while I'm with the Clients, and he will exist in my memory. I almost want to cry when I think about having to go back to the Clients, so I focus on how I got more than I ever knew I wanted, with this date, with him. I kiss him back and try to tell him everything with this kiss. I try to make him feel what I feel with this kiss. I don't want to stop, I don't want this to be the end.

It is the end.

His fingers play with a piece of my hair, "I'll be right out."

He gives me that smile and I lock it away to save for an especially sad day. I give him the best happy face that I can before he leaves forever, behind the door on the right.

I let out a slow breath, throw my skirt and panties back on, and grab my boots. I hurry down the stairs, back across his living room and into the entryway before I exit the front door. Once I am at the end of the path, I turn to get one last look before I climb the fence. I find myself smiling as I stroll to the end of the street and call a cab. I'm still smiling the whole way back to my house and when I climb the steps, I have to forcibly wipe it from my face before I go inside.

Toben jumps from the couch as I walk in and I roll my eyes at him. "Seriously? You're waiting for me?"

His arms are wrapped around me as soon as he reaches me. "How was it?"

I can't make myself look at him. "It was fine."

He pulls back to stare at me. "Just fine? This was supposed to be your one night being normal and it was 'fine'? What did you guys do?"

Ugh! What's with the interrogation?

"Nothing."

I move away from him, and he clutches my arm with more force than I'm normally used to from him.

"Tavin."

"What?" I finally look him in the eyes and my heart cracks because I know he knows.

"You fucked him." It wasn't a question. He stumbles back as he whispers, "You fucked him?!"

"Toben I…I don't know what happened."

"Did he force you?"

Oh my God, he almost sounds hopeful. His heart is broken and I don't know what to say because I don't understand it.

"No." I don't want to end this night crying, but he's crushing me.

"What the fuck, Tav?!" He's never looked at me the way he is now. I hurt him. Badly.

I shake my head as the tears fall. "I'm so sorry, Toben. I don't know why I did it. He isn't you, he doesn't mean what you do to me. If I hated him afterward I could have lived with it. I can't live with it when it comes to you. I'm confused, the night just got away from me. Please, Toben. You can't hate me for this."

"Are you seeing him again?" I can't tell if he is going to break down or explode into a rage.

"No, Toben, I swear. This was it." I make my way back to him. I need his touch. I need to know we're okay. He lets me touch him and even kisses me back when I kiss him. "Please forgive me, Tobe. I'll never do it again. I love you. I love only you." I hold his hand so our scars and words can be together. "I know I hurt you. When you bleed, I bleed. I can feel your pain. I never wanted that, he just made me feel…"

"Normal." I nod through blurred vision. I shudder with relief when he hugs me. "I get it, Love." He runs his fingers in my hair as he kisses me again.

I look up to him searching his now glazed expression. "Are we okay?"

"Come on, don't be crazy. We've been through way too much for some random guy to come between us." He picks up his cell phone and puts it in his pocket. "Did he freak out about the pain thing?"

I don't want to talk about this with him. "I didn't tell him."

He snorts as he loads up his stash necklace. Is he going somewhere?

"So what… he didn't get you off?"

I don't like his smug expression, but I know he's hurting. "God! No, okay?"

"Well that's embarrassing," he chuckles.

Even though I don't like him making fun of Alexander, I would rather him do that then look at me like that, ever again. He stuffs his wallet in his pocket and takes a bump.

"Are you leaving?"

"Oh yeah, I told Christopher we would go to the bar, I just wanted to make sure you got home okay." He glances at the black case on the table. "You want me to fix you up before I go?"

That's weird. He isn't even going to ask me to come with him?

"Are you sure you're okay?"

He's sighs as he begins to get my fix ready. "Yeah, we just want to find some girls. Guy's night, ya know?"

No, I don't know. They have literally never had a 'guy's night' and he never talks about other girls with me. He's deflecting, and to be honest it has been a long day and I'm ready to get high, so I won't ask questions.

"When you wake up in the morning I will be next to you just like always, okay?"

I nod and lean back on the couch as he ties me off. The night flashes through my mind as I wait and I'm able to hide my smile from Toben. Alexander is more than I could have ever dreamed. He's the only one who didn't make me feel dirty, after. He's the only one I ever wanted inside of me. He's the only one that was my choice.

He gave me a night of magic and happiness. He will never know that he gave a girl, who is nothing more than a dirty broken toy, a night to feel…special.

I hate that Toben is hurting. He knows he's my best friend, though. My companion. My other half, and nothing will ever change that. Tonight made me happy and he always says that's all that matters to him.

He runs his hand across my cheek. "I love you, Tavin."

"I love you, too, Toben."

As my body drifts, he sings me our lullaby.

Pretty little Shadow girl, please don't cry.
I'll stay with you until I die.
In the dark we dance and stay.
While the monster steals our souls away.
Bloody little Shadow girl, my dearest friend.
It's you and me 'till the very end.

EPILOGUE

Toben

SHE FUCKED HIM? HOW IS THAT POSSIBLE? MY SKIN feels like it's going to rip apart and my veins are about to burst open. How could she let him touch her? He's a Goddamn stranger!

She won't even let me, the one who has done nothing besides love her and care for her, have that part of her. I would be lying if I said I didn't want to find out who this asshole is and send Logan after him. Make him regret the moment he ever laid eyes on her.

How dare he lay his disgusting suit hands on her. I want to vomit when I think about the things they did together. As I walk out the door, I call a cab. My original intent was to spend the night with Nikki and Tiffany, but tonight, I want to taste more than tears.

If Logan found out about this, he'd probably beat me within an inch of my last breath, but he won't find out about this one.

Suicide Slums is crawling with whores and working girls. Nobody will miss one less walking fuck hole standing on the corner.

Directing the cabby to the center of Shadoebox's shithole, I tell him to stop. I can't let him see where I'm going.

As I walk down the alley to the next street, I turn the corner to see four girls wearing outfits that barely serve a purpose and leave little to the imagination. One of the girls smokes a cigarette as the other three keep an eye out for their next John.

Stuffing my hands in my pocket, I walk up to them and I don't even get within speaking distance when I choose my playmate for the evening. The one closest to resembling Tavin, between the four of them. The one smoking the cigarette.

They turn up their noses at me as if they're anything more than sloppy holes to slide into. I nod to them in greeting.

"Hey."

"This isn't a charity, little boy blue. We's needs cash."

I ignore the one who speaks as I pull out a wad of bills and give them to the girl smoking. "I'm Toben. Do you wanna kick it tonight?"

She raises a brown eyebrow before a smile slowly stretches across her face. Crushing her butt under her stiletto, she holds out her hand for me to take. "Let's go, handsome."

Leading her down the alley, I give her the vial of coke.

"On the house."

Her hair is much shorter than Tavin's, though long enough to flip over her shoulder. "Score. Thanks."

I'm really just flying by the seat of my pants here. I don't want to take her to Nikki and Tiffany's and I can't take her home, so I grin when I see the bridge. "Come on."

She follows me down a hill and under the bridge. As soon as we reach the water, her hand rubs over my pants and she undoes my zipper before lowering to her knees. It has to hurt to kneel down here on bare skin, but she doesn't seem to care as she digs into my underwear and removes my already hard cock.

"How old are you?"

She giggles and sucks me a few times before responding. "Twenty-one."

Her tongue is slurping and she's doing this with way too much vigor. I shove her back against the bank and she spreads her legs like the repulsive whore she is. Pinning down her shoulders with my knees, I shove myself between her lips. I fuck her mouth and she takes it impressively, though she doesn't have much choice.

"Fucking eat it, you cock-sucking bitch."

Her body squirms beneath me as she chokes and pushes at my thighs. I pump a few times before pulling out and hearing her gasp.

"Please don't-"

I punch her in the jaw. Her face doesn't matter. She won't last past the next hour anyway.

"Please don't what? Fuck you like I paid you?"

She grabs her face and starts crying, so I wrap my hand around her throat as I dig into my pocket for a condom. She's a street whore. Who knows what disgusting diseases she's riddled with. I rip it with my teeth and slide it on with my free hand.

Pushing up her mini skirt, I tear her panties to give me access. "So, is it just me? You can fuck some random guy, but you won't let me near you?"

"What? What the hell are you talking about?!" She screams, so I hit her again.

I shove myself into her. "What did I have to do to be enough for you?" I squeeze the girl's throat as she claws at my hands. "I would do anything for you and you know that and I'm still not good enough!" Her body fights beneath me causing me to squeeze her neck tighter. "I'm gonna kill whoever this fucker is, do you hear me?! I'm going to cut off his cock so he can never put it inside you again." I ram into the body beneath me, feeling my balls get heavy and I tighten my hand. "What do I have to do? I'll do anything, Love... please just don't let me go..."

The deeper I fuck, the harder I clench my fingers into her skin as her thrashing eventually stills beneath me. "Fuck you! Fuck you! I love you. I love you!"

My orgasm explodes into the condom as I pump into the limp corpse wrapped around my cock. I know she's dead before I even remove my hand.

"I love you so much, Tav." I brush the hair from the dead girl's face. "Please, don't give up on me."

I take myself out of her and roll her body across the sand as I remove the condom and toss it in the water. Pulling my pants up, I take my money back and climb up the hill.

Two weeks later

Where the fuck is she?! It's been ten days since I've heard from her. Ten motherfucking days! Her cell phone was left on the table as well as her keys. My stomach knots up even tighter with every passing day regardless of how much blow I snort or smack I shoot.

I can't even remember the last thing I said to her because I was too fucked up. She wouldn't just disappear though, not without me.

The last I heard, she had a playdate downtown and that was only supposed to be for an hour. As much as I want to, I'm refraining from getting Logan or Kyle involved until I know what's going on. Of course, I'll get beaten for not telling him as soon as she went missing, but what other choice do I have? At least if I can find her before he gets back I can prepare myself for how bad this is.

Poor Tiffany and Nikki have had a rough couple of

weeks. Ever since Tavin's 'date' and even worse since she's gone missing, I've been on edge more than normal. They've gotten the brunt of my frustrations and fears and they both need a break or they won't be of any use, anyway.

I have to figure this out because I went too far with the hooker under the bridge and I can't do that again.

Snuffing out my Marlboro under my sneaker, I open the door to a shitty bar I haven't tried yet, walk up to the bartender, and toss my ID on the counter.

"Double shot of Jack." He grunts in acknowledgement as he pulls down a bottle and takes out a glass from beneath the bar.

I wrap my hand around a photo of Tavin at one of our parties this past winter and place it on the bar. Tapping the picture, I ask, "Have you seen this girl in the last few weeks?"

He narrows his eyes and puts down my drink before picking up the photograph. Pulling a pair of glasses over his face he gives it an honest once over.

"Sorry, kid," he snorts and shakes his head, "we don't get girls like this in here too often."

Nodding, I swallow my drink and take back Tavin's photo. I can't get too drunk because I have a playdate with Mr. Wallace. Too much whiskey can make it difficult to get hard with the Clients, sometimes. Seeing as he's the Mayor of Shadoebox and I've never played with him before, it would be in my best interest not to try my luck.

Taking a cab back to my place, I get ready for Mr. Wallace. Like many of my Clients, he wants to come to the house so he doesn't risk being seen in a hotel with a paid whore...and a male one at that.

I walk inside and go straight to the kitchen to dip into the coke stash. Her smile in the photo makes my heart ache as I hang it back on the fridge. It's getting more difficult to stop imagining her dead body chopped up in someone's trunk.

I ache to kiss her so I settle for kissing the picture instead. "You better be fucking okay."

Fuck, the teeth on these clamps are gonna rip my nipple right off. Mr. Wallace yanks on them causing blood to seep from the broken skin. I'm lying on my back on the couch while his tongue traces my balls. His hand strokes me fast and I pump my hips, thrusting up into his hot mouth, forcing me to moan.

"Does that feel good, my little Sweet Boy?"

"Oh, yes, Mr. Wallace."

He sucks hard and I grab his hair before he removes his mouth long enough to say, "Daddy." Just as I'm about to ask what the hell that's supposed to mean, his finger circles my asshole and he tugs on the clamps again. "I want my little boy to know how much I love sucking on his big boy cock." Goddamn it. I hate fetishes. Swallowing my grimace, I nod and earn another yank on the clamps. "Tell me how it feels."

He wraps his lips around me and swallows me all the way to the base. Playing the part, I give him what he's paying for.

"It feels so good. I like it when you lick my dick...Daddy."

That riles him up. He slurps me a few more time before sitting up and taking his erection out of his already undone trousers. "Now it's time to make Daddy feel good."

He stands next to the couch and presses the tip to my lips. I look up at him and lightly lick the hole. His cock jerks as he groans and caresses my head over my beanie. "Be a good boy. Do it just like I showed you."

Slowly opening my mouth, I take as much as I can. He fucks my face with vigor and I don't have the skills Tavin does when it comes to gagging. Apparently, not everyone hates it, because the more I gag, the harder he thrusts.

Saliva runs down my cheeks as he pulls out of my mouth and leans down to remove the clamps, licking the blood from my nipples. "Do you want to be a big boy?"

I nod. "Yes, Daddy."

"Bend over the couch and show me your little hole."

I do as he says and once he's licked me to the point that I'm ready, he rolls on the condom. The hardness of his length begs my hole to open up. With one thrust, he's all the way inside and I successfully cover the unexpected pain with a moan. He picks up his pace and reaches around to stroke me. He's starting to hit that spot and it causes my balls to tighten.

"Yes, Daddy," I moan.

I think I might actually get this over with fairly quickly as long as I just give him whatever he wants in this twisted fantasy. My fingers grab at the fabric of the couch as his thrusts intensify.

"Fucking hell!"

I jump while still on Mr. Wallace's dick because the voice that just yelled wasn't his. I jerk my head up to see some random guy leaving my living room…next to *her*.

My heart explodes in my chest with both relief and fury. She's safe, but who the fuck is she with and where the hell has she been?

"I'm so sorry!" She calls in almost a playful tone as she shuts the door behind them. Well, I'm glad she's in a fucking good mood.

There's no way I can wait till the end of this playdate to find out what the hell is going on. Mr. Wallace jumps away from me at the shock, and now he's pissed.

"Who was that?! This is supposed to be confidential!"

I touch his chest to calm him down. "It's still confidential. That was just Sweet Girl. You have nothing to worry about." His nostrils flare so it's probably stupid to continue. "If you wait for me upstairs in my bedroom, we can start our playdate all over again." He sniffs, but he's at least considering it. I swallow the vomit in my mouth before I say, "Please, Daddy?"

He huffs, though he nods and takes his things upstairs. Pulling up my pants, I barely get them buttoned before I swing open the door.

She's okay.

I need her in my arms right now more than I need to inhale the oxygen around me. I fight tears as I pull her inside and hold her tighter than I have in a long time. I breathe in her scent and feel her skin beneath my fingers. My respite from my fear transforms into anger because this whole time, she's been perfectly fine and just left me here to freak out.

And who is this asshole?

"Where the fuck have you been?! Do you have any idea how terrified I've been? Do you?"

She opens her mouth to speak when the unwelcome motherfucker cuts in. "Hey. Take it back a notch."

The rage I'm feeling for this fuck is going to cause me to slit his throat sooner rather than later, if I give him an ounce of acknowledgement.

"Who the fuck is this?"

Her face softens and is graced with the same look she had the other night after her date. Oh my God…is this him? Has she been with him this whole time?!

She touches my face and it's that touch that keeps me from painting this room in red. I feel like throwing up. This isn't happening.

Looking over her shoulder she tells him, "I need a minute. Will you go into the kitchen, please?"

I don't like the way she said that. What the hell is going on?

He obeys her like a bitch and as soon as he's out of the living room, I grab her arm. "What the fuck, Tav?"

"I don't have a lot of time to explain…"

"Then you better do it fucking fast." I can't explode on her, especially with the jolly blond giant in my kitchen, so I breathe in through my nose and cross my arms.

Her fingers pry my arms apart as she holds my hand and leads me to the couch. She sits on my lap and squeezes my face between her hands. "I am so sorry that I worried you. I didn't know what to do. Logan can't know about him and he can't know about Logan."

I pull out a cigarette and light it. I don't understand what's happening. I gnaw on my lip because I have to ask, "Why are you with him, Tavin?"

She shakes her head and her bangs flop around. "I didn't mean for any of this to happen. A couple weeks ago, I got really upset and put too much in the needle. He found me here and took me to his place. I tried to tell him I had to leave, but he wanted me to get over the withdrawals and it's not as if I can explain everything to him. He's trying to be nice and I have been having so much fun with him, Tobe. You wouldn't believe what it's been like with him, without the Clients, without Logan…"

"And without me."

Her eyes narrow as she kisses me. "You know that's not true. Please try to understand, I won't ever get a break like this again. I need a break Toben and I really like him."

"You mean you *needed* a break. You're home now, so your vacation is over. Now we have to come up with a story that won't get us killed."

She glances toward the kitchen and seems to be struggling to look me in the eye. "I want to stay until Logan gets back."

The ringing starts in my ears and in my head, I'm

screaming. She's choosing to be away from me to be with someone else and she's putting us both in danger.

"What?! Are you fucking insane?!"

She shushes me in our own damn house. She's obviously not telling this guy much and that fact comforts me. She wants to play make believe with this twat? Fine. I've never been able to deny her anything if I could help it, and I won't start now.

We won't ever fit into the world she wants so badly to be a part of, and it's better she learns that on her own. I just hope she comes to that conclusion real fucking quick because I hate being away from her.

Two Weeks Later

"Where is she?!" Logan doesn't even get the front door opened as he bellows, "Where the fuck is she?"

I'm stupid enough to waste time by taking another drag when he rips the cigarette from my mouth and presses the burning cherry against the back of my neck. I take a sharp inhale as I stand.

Lifting his leg, he brings his shoe down hard against my thigh, knocking me to the floor. "Kneel!"

I hit my back on the coffee table as I struggle to obey and answer him. "I don't know, Logan." As I bring my hands behind my head, he kicks me in between my shoulder blades.

"Stay up."

My heart pounds against my chest. I knew something was wrong when I arrived home to an empty house right after he told me to get my ass back here.

I don't know why I can't think of a legitimate lie to tell. I just don't know what happened. She told me she was coming home when Logan got back in town and now he's irate and she isn't answering her phone. I can't believe she let it go this far.

My ability to breathe is suddenly severed as something is wrapped around my throat. His warm breath brushes against my lips as he says, "There is nothing keeping me from tightening this belt until you're nothing but a bag of blood and bones."

My eyes begin to burn and I've always feared dying this way. Stab me or blow my brains out. I don't want to struggle for my last moments like I have my entire life. He squeezes and I know I deserve to feel the pain and fear up until my final thoughts. I deserve it for the girl under the bridge, for Cadence, for Morgan and even for Lacie.

Relief sweeter than any candy he ever gave me floods my body as he releases the belt around my neck.

"How could you let this happen? She was your Goddamn responsibility!" The buckle on the belt crashes into my spine and I bite my lip, faltering in my position. He paces in front of me and growls, "Give me a reason not to kill you, Toben."

I grit my teeth and I'm so grateful I was born a better liar than Tavin. "She hid this from me, too. I don't know where she is and I don't know where she's been these last few weeks." I look up at him and realize his face is cut. He walks closer and I see it's not just a cut. The whole right side of his face is red and swollen. What happened there? Props to whoever the hell was able to pull that one off. "She won't talk to me, Logan."

Kneeling in front of me, his hazel eyes blaze.

"Don't let me find out that this is anything less than true, Plaything."

"Yes, Logan."

"Goddamn it, Tiffany! Stop fucking crying or it's going to get a lot worse."

I rub my thumb over the *T* scar on her back as I walk around to kneel in front of her. She sniffles and glares at me, but she still attempts to dry it up. Dropping the whip I just hit her with, I reach between her legs to finger her and turn to look over my shoulder at Nikki.

"Are you going to play nice, now? No more biting her pussy or I won't fuck you for the next three months. You got it?"

"Yes, Toben," Nikki pouts.

I grin back at Tiffany, "That would mean a lot more playtime for you." Both girls whimper for their own reasons and I laugh. They're so cute. "Go lie on the bed, Plaything."

Tiffany obeys and I walk over to Nikki to untie her from the radiator heater. I lean in, gently kissing her. She knows I don't kiss Tiffany this way, and sometimes, I want her to know she's my favorite. "Now help me kiss her better, okay?"

She chews the inside of her cheek as she nods. "Yes, Toben."

Taking her hand, I lead her to the bed and spread Tiffany's legs. I grip a fist full of Nikki's hair and push her face into Tiffany's pussy. My fingers comb through her hair as I watch her little tongue lick at Tiffany's clit. I kiss down her jaw and touch my tongue next to hers to help her. Our fingers fuck Tiffany's hole as we make out and I roll on my back lifting her on top of me. She slides over my cock when I point to the edge of the bed. "Get my belt and choke her out while you ride my dick, Plaything."

She gives me a partial smile as she reaches for the belt. I climb up the bed and lie down before pulling Tiffany on top of me. Her back presses against my chest with each heavy breath as Nikki wraps the belt around her neck.

Nikki's pussy is so warm as she rides me and tightens

the belt. She moans and hesitates when I tell her to release it. "Put me inside her."

I can't see, but I can feel myself leaving Nikki's body and entering Tiffany's. After a few pumps, she takes me out again, and puts me back into her even though I never told her to. I don't scold her for it this time. I want to finish inside her anyway and I need to get home and make sure I haven't missed Tavin.

"Make her come, Nik. Then we'll go upstairs and you can ride my face."

That gets her ass into gear as she rubs Tiffany's clit and grinds her body against mine. Tiffany is quickly moaning and thrusting with her orgasm as my own bursts inside Nikki.

Leaving heroin and a treat on Tiffany's nightstand, I grab a bottle of water out of her fridge and kiss her head before locking her door.

Nikki and I hold hands as we walk up to her room. Once I keep my promise, we have sex in the shower and I leave her with her drugs and candy.

The cabby drops me off and even though I knew it wasn't likely, my heart falls because there is still no sign of Tavin. My leg is killing me from when Logan kicked me, so I fall back onto the couch and light a cigarette. As soon as I take the first drag, there's a knock on my front door. I swear to fuck, this better not be those cookie bitches again.

Opening the door, my eyebrows shoot up because there's a hot chick standing on my porch.

"Hi, my name is Sasha. I don't know if you remember me," she peeks over my shoulder, "but we need to talk."

As soon as she says it, I recall who she is. This is the prick's sister. "This better be about Tav-"

She stuns me into silence when her hands wrap around

my face, and I swear to Christ, she kisses me. I push her back and she whispers, "Come on, let's talk in my car."

I'm too scared to begin to imagine what this is about, so I follow her to her surprisingly average vehicle. As soon as I climb in, she starts the engine.

"Are we going somewhere?" I ask.

She's all twitchy as she looks over her shoulder and in her rearview mirror. "Is anyone following you?" She's whispering even though we're alone.

"What's your deal, tweeker?"

Pulling off the curb, she sighs, "Tavin is staying with me while we figure out this whole thing with Logan and I need to make sure we aren't being watched."

What the fuck, Tavin? When is she going to stop this? "What whole thing? As far as I know, nobody's watching, but that won't last long with this bullshit. What the hell is going on?"

"We're still figuring that out. At the moment, I'm just trying to keep her hidden from Logan. She's just so scared and needs to know you're okay."

I drop my head against the seat. Everything is falling apart and I have no idea how this could possibly not end in a nightmare. Still, she needs me and I will always be there when she needs me.

Two Weeks Later

I don't know why she thought it was worth it to risk coming here, though feeling her body against mine again is the only thing that really matters right now.

She's been cooped up hiding from Logan, and I get that she needed some breathing room, but she made the choices that put her in this situation. We're both having to sneak around because she has some half-cocked idea of being able to escape Logan. I honestly don't know what's gotten into her the last couple of months. The only silver lining is that shit finally hit the fan with 'Alexander'. I hate that she's hurting, but I knew he couldn't handle her and I just wish he would have come to that realization a hell of a lot sooner.

She's living with that bitch, but at least I'm welcome to stay there with her. Now that the douche is finally out of the picture, I'm hoping that I can eventually talk some sense into her and some mercy into Logan. Every time I see him, the more agitated and angry he is. I honestly don't know how we're going to come back from this. It's only a matter of time before he follows me to her.

Lifting the coke vile to her nose, she inhales the drugs that make her lean into me. As much as I know this is dangerous, I wouldn't trade this moment for anything. I've missed watching her dance.

I laugh at Christopher grinding against the girl on the dance floor. He's a terrible dancer and somehow always gets them to come home with him. Tavin's head hits my chest as her body slams against mine and she spins around toward the exit. Whoa…what's going on? I lift my eyes in fear that I will see Logan, but who I see is worse.

It's the fucking douche.

He holds his finger out to me and I consider biting it off when he says, "You stay here."

Turning to the woman he's with, he tells her to wait and he follows behind Tav. I almost tell him to 'fuck off' and stop him from going after her. As much as I hate admitting it, I know that Tavin cares a lot about him, for whatever reason, and I want her to have a minute with him. Especially since from the look on his face, he isn't going to be saying anything nice.

His date is shifting on her feet looking like she'd rather

be anywhere else. Maybe I should take her into the bathroom and fuck her like he's fucked me.

Christopher snaps at me, "You're just going to leave her out there with him? What the hell, dude?"

"What am I really supposed to do? Interfering with him won't do anything besides push her further away. Let him fuck it up on his own. When he knocks her down, I'll be there to catch her."

His lips press into a hard line and he nods. Just as I'm about to go out there and do what Christopher is suggesting, the door to the exit opens and he storms back inside. He throws his hand out at me as he walks by us.

"She's all yours."

That's fucking right, you prick.

Christopher follows me outside and while my heart breaks at her tears, I feel a twinge of relief that maybe he'll stay the hell out of her life forever, now.

I hate that she feels for anyone besides me. She's given him everything I've ever wanted from her, and he's throwing it away like the dumbass he is. I would never hurt her on purpose like he does, and I want to kill him for it. I wrap my arms around her and wish I could soak up all the pain he's making her feel.

***

This is when I miss her the most. When I'm all alone in this house we've shared together. I can't stay with her every night because then we'd definitely get caught, and I stayed with her last night after we left the club. She finally got high with me though, and I have missed it so much. Ever since she met that asshole, she's been having this guilt bullshit about using anything. I don't understand it. There's something that can take all of our suffering away, even for a few moments, and he doesn't want her to have it? And he has the audacity to act like he gives a fuck about her?

I want her to just walk through the door and I know she won't. All I have is a shred of hope that she'll give some real thought into what we talked about last night. I want her with me, and her plan to 'go wherever we want' is going to get us both killed. She thinks the Clients are bad, but that's the safest and most controlled environment we're ever going to be in. We know what's expected and it happens. The world out there? There is no safe. There is no control. It's unpredictable and without any real regulation.

Maybe I should just go stay the night with Nikki and Tiffany. At least it would help me keep my mind off her. Inhaling a line of coke, I adjust my beanie and straighten another one. A loud knock at the front door makes me drop the business card I'm using. Who the fuck is that? Logan wouldn't knock and I don't have a Client.

I swing open the front door and internally give the finger to whoever is playing this cosmic joke.

You've got to be fucking kidding me.

"She's not here and she's not meant for you, so 'fuck up someone else's life' as you so eloquently put it, and leave her alone. She's not meant for you."

There are so many things I want to do to this asshole, but I'll settle on slamming the door in his face. I reach for the handle when all of a sudden, I'm being squeezed tight.

Is this prick hugging me?

"What the f—"

"I've seen the tape."

He says it as if that makes it completely acceptable to go around hugging people. I don't even know what the hell he's talking about.

"Uh…what tape?"

"I just need to see."

In an instant, he's rushing past me as he goes to the

basement door, pulling it open to go downstairs. This motherfucker.

I sprint after him and find him standing in her room. "Hey! What the hell are you doing? We don't let people down here." He mumbles something about kids and my skin dries up and goes cold. His back is to me so I step in front of him to make him look at me. "Tell me about the mother-fucking tape."

"He recorded it."

Logan would have never left evidence like a recording. Besides, he gets his jollies off on interacting, not watching. "Who recorded what?"

"Right here where we're standing. This is where it happened isn't it? The day Logan came down here with that cage and destroyed your lives. I can't believe he made you hold her down."

Fuck.

Fuck, fuck, fuck. This isn't good.

He knows way too much and I can't believe he's still digging his nose in this shit. I don't want to, but I have to give him props for that. Most people would never be able to deal with this. Still, he's going to make things so much worse for us and himself. He barely has a sliver of the truth and it's still enough to get him killed. Which would be more than fine by me if I didn't know how much that would hurt Tavin.

What really bothers me is that I can see that this is important to him. *She's* important to him. Tavin and I never knew the tape existed and we were the ones being taped, so how the hell does he? It had to have been Brian who did it because Lacie was way too stupid to do something like that. I see the pain and worry on his face as he fondles Tavin's needled belt. He's actually hurting over this and surprisingly, I can feel myself soften a shade for the guy.

I know she's worth all the pain and suffering. The only

problem is, now he does too.

I still hope he gets hit by a bus.

He what?!

I don't fucking understand how this is possible. Two days ago, Logan told me he found that a P.I. was looking into him. When he confronted the guy, he learned that he had been hired by non-other than the douche bag himself. He found out where Tavin had been staying, and he was so angry that he killed the P.I. and forcefully shot up Sasha for good measure.

All that, and now he just gives her to *him*?!

"You sold her?!" This isn't happening. His glare and flaring nostrils tell me I need to tone down the attitude. "Why, Logan? How could you just let her go?"

I knew when Alexander begging for Tavin's forgiveness was inevitable, and of course, she gave it to him. Once I spoke with Tavin and she confirmed it, it broke my heart for the millionth time.

"Plaything, I need you to trust me. I don't do anything without reason and I don't allow myself to be double crossed without someone suffering for it. You should understand this by now."

"It's just…she's under the impression that she's free. Is that not true?"

Ignoring my question, he wipes down the table. "You are to continue on as Sweet Boy, as normal." He grabs my face and holds it tight. "Trust me."

No person on this earth has ever made that more difficult and natural than him.

"She wants me to make friends with the guy like we're in some kind of bromance."

"Then do it."

"He knows about a lot of it, Logan."

More casually than I would have expected, he nods. "I'm aware." Loading up the spoon, he asks, "Now, would you like to get high with me?"

I sigh and lean against the couch. "Yes, Logan."

Two and a half weeks later

Jesus. Mr. Western really did a number on my ass. God, it's been a while since I've been this sore. I toss the money at the cab driver and as I climb the steps to my front door, my phone rings. I don't recognize the number, but it's a Shadoebox area code.

"Hello?"

"Hey, Toben? My name's Silas." My heart starts to pick up pace because none of the reasons I can think of that he would be calling me are good. "I'm friends with-"

"The douche, yeah, what's up?"

He chuckles which helps me relax. "Well, Alex wants me to come pick you up and bring you to his place."

Scoffing under my breath, I mumble, "And I want him to take a bath with a hairdryer." I pull out my house key. "Yeah, that's not happening, guy."

"There's something going on with Tavin."

Just like that, my stomach twists at the fear that something happened to her while I'm not with her.

"That motherfucker swore to me countless times he would protect her! She had better be okay or things are gonna turn red real fucking fast."

"Whoa, chill, dude, as far as I know, she's fine. I honestly don't know what he wants you for."

"Goddamn it. Fine. Come get me at eighty-three twenty-six Morningstar Avenue."

I don't even have to guess it's him when he pulls up in his nice ass car. I take a drag off my cigarette as he jogs up to me sitting on my porch.

He points to the pack sitting on the top step. "Hey, can I get one of those?"

"Sure?" I hand him one. "Do you even smoke?"

"Sometimes. Sasha hates it and it's too hard to get the smell out of my suits, but I like one every once in a while."

I gesture to his car. "What kind of car is that?"

Laughing, he ashes his cigarette. "It's a Porsche Cayman, but don't get any ideas. I like the shape it's currently in."

I bite back a smile at that. I talked Tavin into letting me drive her boyfriend's car a little while ago. Let's just say, it didn't go as planned and he doesn't have that car anymore.

We finish our smokes and walk to his Porsche. I scoff at him when the first thing he does is look at himself in the mirror and style his hair. He's as big of a tool as Alexander is.

We drive in silence. Well, I wish it was fucking silence-what the hell is he listening to?

"I want that Ferrari then I swerve. I want that Bugatti just to hurt."

I know my eyes widen in horror because he's fucking singing. Or at least some variation of it.

"No, man. Just no."

He clears his throat and looks in the rearview mirror. "How are you doing?"

"What?" I deadpan.

"Look, I don't know all the details, but I know enough to know that you're kind of getting screwed in this."

Hmm. Maybe this guy isn't as bad as I originally thought. I look at him. "Yeah?"

"Yeah, I mean, you grew up in this crazy situation with her. You obviously care about each other a lot, but the way you look at her?" He shakes his head. "You look like you'd sooner skin yourself alive than see her in pain." He switches lanes and sighs. "I fell in love with Sasha Sørensen the very first time I saw her. Watching her in a serious relationship with someone else was the most painful thing I've ever felt." He turns to me and furrows his brows. "And I broke my leg once."

I can't believe an honest laugh boils over. "Yeah, sure. It's like that."

"All I'm saying is, you love her enough to go through a lifetime of pain just to see her happy. I think that's pretty fucking awesome."

I give him a smirk. He may not really get it, but he's trying in his own way. He is right about one thing, though. I would do anything to keep her happy.

We pull through the gate and into the driveway of Alexander's house before I follow Silas inside the front door. Alexander paces back and forth with a drink in one hand and his hair in the other.

What's up his ass? I laugh at myself. Maybe that's what he needs. A good fuck in the ass might loosen him up.

"Go upstairs and get Tavin. She's in her room."

"Uh…okay."

What the hell is going on? I never thought he'd let me over here again after the last time I saw him. I told him about the one and only time I fucked Tavin and needless to say, he was pissed. He may have killed me if she wouldn't have shown up when she did.

I climb the steps to her room and lightly tap as I open the door.

"Tav?" She's pacing around the room with Blind Mag on her heels.

She runs up to me and wraps her arms around my waist. "He's so mad at me. I messed up bad this time, Toben."

I pull back to look down at her. "What happened, Love?"

Shaking her head, she wipes the tears from her cheek. "I used what you gave me. He came home and found me."

I sigh because I hate that she has to feel so guilty about doing something that has always been basically encouraged. "Come on, he wants us downstairs."

As soon as we step into the kitchen, she cries an apology. "Alexander, I know I messed up. I'm so sorry. I—"

"Are you sober?"

"Yes," she responds.

I'm about to tell him to cut the suspense and just tell me what's going on when he nods his head toward the basement.

"Come on."

We follow him down the stairs and as soon as he opens the door to what I know is his theater, my stomach falls. He was adamant about her not seeing the tape, but I can't think of any other reason we would be in here.

"Both of you, sit."

I'm pretty sick of this asshole ordering me around. I don't move an inch. "What's going on?"

"You both have become numb to what Logan James is. You've clearly forgotten and it's past due time you remember."

This motherfucker. I haven't allowed myself to think about this video because I didn't think I'd ever have to see it. I didn't think she would either because this fucking prick can't keep his word.

He presses play and I'm about to tell him to turn this shit off or I'm going to, when I hear the voice that whispers to me in my dreams.

"Toben! Look what I made!"

My head snaps toward the screen and I see her. I never thought I would see her that way again, besides pictures and in my mind. Without my permission, my body lowers into the seat. Watching us together before everything was tainted causes tears to spring up into my eyes. Her laugh makes my heart throb in pain. I miss those days. I miss the times where we still thought we would grow up and chase our dreams away from here.

As I watch the last few moments of our innocence, I force back the urge to weep because I know what happens next. Just as Logan and Kyle enter the frame, I am transported back into my ten-year-old body. Fear wraps itself around my chest and I feel frozen in place.

Though I hear cries and screams from the Tavin that is next to me in the present, I can't stop wishing I could stop the fate of the Tavin from thirteen years ago.

My skin sweats as I watch this man who I've grown to look up to, to hate, to love, and to despise. The man who taught me everything and showed me more compassion than my father ever did. I watch him mutilate and destroy the most beautiful thing on this earth.

If it weren't for him, she would be sleeping in my arms every night instead of in this world that she doesn't belong. If it weren't for him, she wouldn't be in so much pain and hate herself so much.

If it weren't for him, she would still be fucking mine.

Somewhere along the way of drugs, and praise, and pain, and sex, I forgot that I want nothing more than his heart to stop beating. I swore it to myself so many times, I would dream of it. I've had more than enough opportunities over the years to do it, but I sold out for drugs and pussy.

How could I have forgotten? The more I watch, the hotter my rage burns in my veins. All the things I've done because I allowed him and myself to justify it. I hate that I have developed feelings for him and that even now, they exist. They don't matter though, because they are nothing compared to the desire to empty his body of its insides.

The screen goes black and her wails grow louder next to

me. I need to hold her. I won't ever be able to make up for all the pain I've caused her over the years, but I can end it.

Like I should have done years ago.

For the past two days, thoughts of killing Logan have consumed my mind. Telling Tavin about my plans felt like the obvious thing to do. Now I wish I would have thought it over a little more. She's too good. Too pure. Even after everything he's done to her, she still doesn't want him to hurt. I on the other hand, want nothing more.

She was about to freak out in the middle of the burger joint when I told her my plan, so I stupidly agreed to hear what her boyfriend has to say and pretend to listen to whatever hippie bullshit he wants to spout.

Looking out the window of the cab, she squeezes my hand as if she lets go, I'll vanish. Since watching the video, I can't shut my eyes without seeing what Logan did to her, so I force myself to imagine the things I will do to him until he's dead, and maybe even after. The things he taught me will come in handy. There's no such thing as a quick death for his victims, so he'll get the same. I'll happily take my time to make sure he feels every second. Of course, I'll have to incapacitate him first, which will require taking him by surprise. Not the easiest of tasks.

I've felt like Logan and I had developed a relationship over the years, but the truth is, we didn't develop anything besides an understanding. Watching him play as an adult has affected me in a way I wasn't prepared for. It's been years since I've seen Logan with one of his Lotus', and I forgot what it was like. It's even worse since it's Tavin.

It's not that I blocked it out, really, I just allowed it to get tucked away. Seeing that video brought it right to the fucking front of my mind and until he's gone, it will stay there.

The cabby drops us off at Alexander's weird ass house and I'm relieved when we walk into an empty kitchen. Blind Mag, the dog he got her, is sitting in the entryway and I pick her up. Even I have to admit, letting her keep this cute little pup was a pretty awesome thing to do.

Following Tavin around the house as she calls for Alexander, I pet Blind Mag. It isn't a thought I've had since I was about six and really realized that my father didn't love me like other parents, but I used to really want a dog. Even a tiny fluff ball like this one.

I follow her downstairs and avoid looking at the giant screen. Her face is down in a frown at the fact he's not here.

"Maybe he went out?"

Blind Mag licks my cheek as Tavin calls him, frowning when he doesn't answer. "Huh." She tucks her phone into her pocket. "That's weird." Her fingers lace between mine as she smiles at me. "Want some expensive alcohol?"

That's the best suggestion she's had all day. "Hell yeah."

I search through the bottles and pick a fancy looking vodka. Score. I unscrew the lid and pour it into the glasses, as she asks, "Do you have any weed?"

I'm not sure why that question stings so badly. I'm sure she was just asking offhandedly, but I feel like she's getting so far away from me.

"What do you think, Love?"

She shoves my shoulder and gives me a smirk. "Shut up."

I hand her the joint and finish making our drinks. Walking to the chairs, she sighs as she blows out her hit.

"This doesn't feel right. It's the first time Lex has left me alone since he came back, and now he isn't answering my call? It doesn't feel like something he'd do."

I want to be mad that she can't be away from him for more than a few hours without worrying where he is. The truth is though, she's not wrong. It feels a little off to me, too.

On the other hand, he could just be getting drunk with his friend.

Walking to the theater seats, I sit next to her and hand her the drink. "I'm sure he's just wasted. Stop over thinking and do the same."

She murmurs, "Maybe your right."

Clearly, she doesn't believe me and I'm not sure what to say. It's never been like this between us. Ever since Alexander came into the picture, things have been slowly changing.

I hate seeing her with him while at the same time, I adore seeing her so happy. Imagining his hands on her makes me want to die, but so did imagining her with the Clients.

It's impossible for me to not wonder if when I kill Logan, if she'll come back to me. If she'll see me as her savior and realize that we are meant to be together.

Slayer begins to play, and all three of us jump at the intrusion of sound. I look down at Blind Mag and her un-amused expression makes me laugh. I take my phone from my pocket expecting Christopher. I see Logan's name and the alcohol I just drank begins to make its way up my throat. There's no way this is good.

"It's Logan." She nods as her body tenses. I swipe the green button, letting out a breath before I hold the phone to my ear. "Hello, Logan."

"I told you to trust me, Plaything. I never planned to let him keep her. This is ending today. Now, bring Lotus home. She has someone to say goodbye to."

My heart is pounding. I can't let her know how scared I am because then she'll worry more than she already is. Logan never said what was going to happen to her. Of course, I want Alexander out of the picture, but losing him that way would destroy Tavin.

We hold hands until the cabbie drops us off and she runs into the house. I toss the driver some cash as I holler at her to wait. She doesn't slow as I chase after her. I'm right behind her as we sprint down the stairs.

"Lex!" The way she calls his name chokes me up. There's enough emotion in that one syllable to break my black heart.

Logan's hands already have blood on them so he's been warming up. He gives me a wild smile.

"Good evening, Playthings."

We both say what we are supposed to. "Good evening, Logan."

My eyes dart around the room for accessible weapons. I hadn't planned for this. I thought I had more time to figure out how I was going to do it. He tells us to say hello to Alexander, and I do, but her delay makes my pulse skip. She finally does what he asks and I let out a slow breath.

Logan's hand trails down her neck, and her idiot boyfriend is stupid enough to scream about it.

Ignoring him, Logan smiles at her. "This is our last playdate, little Lotus. We are going to have so much fun."

A chill climbs over my skin and I know he has no intention of letting her leave this basement alive. Whatever I'm going to do, I have to do it now.

Logan barks at me to pick a tool, so on shaky legs, I stand to obey. Walking to the bag, I remove my whip. I could wrap it around his throat. With Tavin's help, I bet we could bring him down. Then we could finally end this together.

He drags her in front of Alexander. He wants to make sure he sees what she is. Who she belongs to. Logan smiles as he walks over to me, retrieving the scold's bridle from the bag.

"You aren't playing nice and are being much too loud," he tells Alexander.

I can't say I'm disappointed. The scold's bridle will make

him shut up so I can think. I refuse to look at Tavin as he places the tool on his head. Her heartbreak for him is more than I can take.

He returns to Tavin and makes her suck him off, for Alexander to watch. After a few moments of his taunting, he barks at me, "Plaything, use your whip."

I've never enjoyed hurting her, but we haven't had a playdate together in a while and it's odd how it makes me feel close to her. Even after everything, I love the physical response she has to my whip.

It warms my frozen soul to see her still get turned on from the pain I give her. She holds back her moan as I hit her, until she can't keep her pleasure quiet.

"That's enough for now, Plaything. Run upstairs and get me the meat mallet from the kitchen."

I almost thank him. A minute out of this room is exactly what I need. I nod to him and say, "Yes, Logan."

I climb the stairs and as I look down, Tavin is looking up at me. I can almost see the little girl from years ago. I couldn't save her then, but I'm going to now. Winking at her, I make my way upstairs. I go into the kitchen and get the meat mallet that Logan requested. I squeeze the handle in my hands as I look at our fridge. The pictures of my youth with her don't tell our story on the surface. You have to look into our eyes to see the suffering that has been endured for years. As I look at the Tavin in a photograph, I silently promise her that we are almost free of him. That I will finish this tonight.

I lean against the wall to gather my breath and thoughts before making my way back downstairs.

Tavin is on the bed and Logan is standing in front of Alexander as I descend the steps. Logan throws a few punches into his gut and I actually kind of feel bad for the guy. I've never personally worn the scold's bridle, but I've seen it used enough to know it hurts like a bitch if it pierces the tongue.

Tavin pleads with Logan to stop, but she should know that's pointless. He tells me to use my whip on Alex and while I have definitely wanted to cause him pain in the past, I don't want her to blame me for any of his suffering.

Too bad I don't have a choice.

I bring my arm back because if I don't try to make this hurt, Logan will know. I hit him hard three times in a row. With the fourth strike, his pain becomes too much. The blood drips down the scold's bridle with his muffled scream as I hit him twice more. Logan speaks to her in the disgusting way he always has, and when he orders for me to bring him the meat mallet, I know that this is my chance. If I don't act now, I might not be able to later.

The time has finally come. After all these years.

He leaves Tavin on the bed and as he reaches for the mallet, I bring it down as hard as I can on his head.

It's enough to cause him to stumble, but not enough to stop him so I bring it down a few more times, letting it land where it may.

Eventually, I discard the mallet for my fists. Part of me aches that these will be the last moments I spend with him. He did give me some good memories. He gave me more than Jarod ever did, that's for sure. He also made me hurt my best friend for years and allowed so many men to use me however they wanted.

My fists come down harder as I remember the tape and the intense fear that has consumed me my whole life. I have to ignore that he made me feel useful and wanted because this was never for me or her. This was for him.

Suddenly, Tavin's fingers grasp onto my shirt as she pulls me away from him. She looks up at me and I see Alexander going for Logan.

Oh, hell no. He didn't spend years suffering at the hands

of this fuck. There's no way he gets the pleasure of ending him. I cut him off before he reaches Logan.

"No fucking way! He's ours. Don't touch him." He's no longer wearing the scold's bridle, so I can clearly see his 'fuck you' expression. Honestly, I can understand. I loathe the idea of anyone being in love with Tavin besides me, but the truth I don't want to face is that he is. I really can't blame him. She's so easy to fall in love with. He watched what Logan did to her and I can respect his rage. He won't have the honor of taking Logan's life, though there's no harm in allowing him to inflict some physical damage onto my maker.

"Don't you dare kill him. We deserve that." He gives me a stiff nod and all but gives me the knife in his hand. It's a silent promise that he won't take away what we've rightfully earned.

He's going to leave the killing to us and I must admit I'm surprised. I half expected him to suggest we call the fucking cops.

Logan stands, giving me a smile. "I must say, I didn't think you had it in you, Plaything. I'm proud of you."

He speaks as though defying him is what he's always wanted me to do…as if I haven't tried. What a Goddamn joke.

"Fuck you," I scoff.

Alexander goes for him in a fury as his fist crashes into Logan's jaw. While Logan jabs at him, Alexander clearly has more experience fighting because he catches his punch and uses the force to push him to the ground.

For a moment, I enjoy watching the simple act of raw fighting. There's something about a natural fight. Not the shit they do for sport with rules and refs, but an all-out brawl with blood and broken bones.

He isn't holding back or taking his time and if he doesn't stop soon, he's going to crush his skull.

"Okay, you had your turn. That's enough." Instead of stopping he just hits him harder. "Stop," I yell. The look on Alexander's face is surprising. He looks more heartbroken than angry. Continuing to ignore me, he straddles Logan as his fists rain down. I don't need this shit. Killing Logan will be hard enough without this douche bag fighting me. I storm over to him, grabbing his arm to pull him up. "Stop, damn it!"

Glaring at me, his nostrils flare. I have no problem beating the shit out of this motherfucker if that's what it takes to finally finish this. Logan stands and as I turn to look at him, he rushes past us and it isn't until I see Tavin grab at her arm that I realize he cut her.

That's the last time he will ever hurt her.

I use all my speed and strength to knock Logan to the floor. He gets in a few punches, but he's weaker than I have always imagined him. I wonder how much suffering I could have saved us if I would have done this sooner.

I head butt him and knee him in the stomach before I sit on his chest and hold down the wrist of the hand grasping the knife. Landing as many punches as I can with one hand, I don't know how long I can keep this up. He's putting up a decent fight and I worry that he's just biding his time, waiting for me to wear myself out.

For the first time, I'm grateful Alexander is around when he walks over and steps on Logan's arm. He shifts his weight until Logan releases his grip on the blade. I'm surprised at his support in this as he hands me the knife. If he wasn't in love with the same girl I am, he might not be so bad.

I turn my attention to Logan. Even with his face covered in blood, he wears a smug expression as if he still doesn't take me seriously.

"You're done. You've taken everything from me, from us. It's ending now."

He looks at me as if I'm lying to him. "Oh, come now, Plaything. That isn't true. I gave you your Lotuses, didn't I?"

As soon as he says those words, my body freezes and my heart drops into my gut. I can't believe he just said that. He never promised me he wouldn't tell her, but it was an unspoken agreement. She was never supposed to know this.

I back away from him like it will reverse his words. I don't want to look at Tavin, but I need to know how she's reacting to this. When I lift my eyes to hers she's horrified.

"What's he talking about?" My fist tightens around the hilt of the knife and I can't bring myself to speak. She's looking at me in a way she never has before. "You have your own girls?" She knows what being a Lotus entails and the torture that it indicates. Her features become overrun with anger and I can't stand her expression. "Why? How long have you done this?" She doesn't understand! It's not how she thinks. Yes, I've made mistakes, but he's the one who fucked me up. He's the one who turned me into this. For the first time since I killed Morgan, I wish I would have been honest with her about everything. Maybe I didn't give her enough credit and she would have realized I didn't have many choices. Now I don't know if it's too late for that. "Answer me, Toben!" She screams.

Her head jerks as I see Logan standing in my peripheral. I want him to stay down, I just don't want to take my eyes off her. I open my mouth to try to explain when Logan speaks first.

"You think he's innocent in all this. He's caused you more suffering than you realize, my little Lotus. There's so much you don't know. He helped me play with my Lotuses for years before obtaining his own."

Squeezing her eyes shut, she shakes her head as the tears fall. "You have another Lotus?"

Logan smiles one of the most honest smiles I've ever

seen from him as he takes out a cigarette. "Oh, I've had several."

She looks in so much pain and I regret all the lies I've told her and secrets I've kept. I wish more than anything I could go back and change things. I would do them so differently.

"There are more Sweet Girls? There's more like me?"

"Oh no, my Plaything," Logan says. "None have been like you. The others all kept their expiration date. Besides Nikki, of course."

"They're dead?" She flinches as she looks at me the same way she did the day we had sex. "You've killed people?"

She doesn't understand! I want to tell her this was all to save her and protect her, but I don't want her to feel like any of this is her fault. I'm still Toben when I'm with her, that has never changed. I reach out for her; I need to hold her. She backs away from me to stand next to *him*.

Black and red are all I see. After everything, she still trusts him more than me.

That's because of Logan.

I grip the knife and press it to his neck as I tackle him to the ground.

"You made me just like you!"

"I didn't make you who you are, Plaything," he spits, "I simply brought it out. You love what you do to your Lotuses. You know you do. It makes you feel alive."

He's right, but it was his fault! His words are true, but he's twisting them.

"No, no, NO! I never would have done those things if it wasn't for you!" I dip the knife into his lip and slice across his face. He is going to suffer the same fate he's put us through for over a decade. "It's my turn to play, Logan."

He has beaten, scarred, and tortured me and God knows how many girls. It's time he wears the mark of what he is, just as he's made us do. Not the Lotus though, he doesn't deserve that. No, he needs something as ugly as his soul is.

Cutting open his shirt with the knife, I stand and tell Alexander, "Don't let him get up."

I walk over to Logan's bag and am pleased that the torch is right on top. This is going to be fun. I grab it and as I make my way back to Logan, Tavin cries for me to stop. After all the terrible things he's done to her, to those she loves, and she still doesn't want him to suffer.

Well, sorry, Love. He's going to suffer immensely.

I fall to my knees and lean over to his ear. "This is the last time I ever kneel for you." He won't ever show it intentionally, but I know him well enough to know there's fear there. He always tries to act as if he's beyond human emotions. He's just as killable as the rest of us. "You're so fond of marking your toys, I think it's time you know how it feels."

I turn on the blowtorch and watch as his skin bubbles beneath the flame. He doesn't last long before he screams out in pain. My heart is racing and my stomach is flipping in excitement. The sounds of his agony are more satisfying than I thought they would be. He's not fighting me other than his body's natural reaction to the pain. I wonder if he knows this is the end. He always said when he died, he would do so gracefully.

Keeping him pinned down, I finish dragging the flame across his chest to tell the world what a sicko he really is. He's a predator and his prey were children.

I turn off the torch and his body goes still besides the rise and fall of his chest. His breathing is heavy, but he's done screaming.

I don't want to do this alone. Tavin deserves this vengeance just as much, if not more than I do. Setting the torch on the floor, I pick up the knife. Please let her still trust me and love me enough to do this with me.

As I turn to her, I hand her the blade. "This is it, Tav. He's used and abused us for over half our lives. He stole who we were supposed to be. It's time he suffers for it. He deserves to die."

She shakes her head as she reaches for the knife, though I can exhale better when she doesn't back away from me.

"I don't know if I can," she whispers.

I need her to do this with me. She has to understand that this is the only way. "He won't ever stop. If we want this to end, we have to end it."

Forcing back the tears when she takes my hand, I lead her to Logan as Alexander watches us. She's shaking as she sits on his stomach and I crouch down by his head.

"I've taken care of you, Tavin, kept you safe. You, Toben, and I are a family," Logan tells her.

I almost scoff. Some family. I see her soften at his words and it makes me so angry that he can still manipulate her feelings after all this time.

"You've never said we are a family, before," she cries.

Her tears pour down her face as she closes her eyes. I won't let him trick her or lie to her anymore. "He's trying to confuse you. He's a liar, Love. I need you to remember. Please, really remember what he's made you feel like." I rub my thumb over her temple so she knows I mean all the horrible thoughts he made her have. "Here."

The time has come to end his disgusting excuse for a life, once and for all. I look up at Alexander who is hard faced, staring at Tavin. I stand and hold out my hand to him.

"Give me your knife."

He does so automatically. He wants this just as much as I do and I'm happy for it because he isn't fighting us on this. I get back down behind Logan, causing the blade to indent into his throat.

"He's forced us to be with countless men, he's done unspeakable things to you, and he's made me do them to

others. I need you to do this with me, Tav. When you bleed,
I bleed, right?"

She closes her eyes again and when she opens them,
my heart leaps at the fury blazing within them. Her brows
scrunch together and her angry tears continue to fall as she
frowns at Logan.

"You never loved us. We were always just your toys."

Saying the words seems to release a hidden rage within
her and I involuntarily let out a harsh breath. I am so proud
of her. She's finally allowing herself to see him for what he
really is.

"Though that may be true, Lotus, I've had many toys,
and you two were always my favorites. If I could love, I
would have loved the both of you."

I look at her, fearing she'll believe the words she's always
wanted him to say. Instead her nostrils flare and her head
jerks just before she stabs the knife into Logan's chest.

His eyes widen as he coughs blood all over himself. He
won't ever hurt me, her, or anyone else ever again. I grip the
knife in my fist and press the blade into the soft skin, watching it split apart as I cut.

For half of a second, I almost feel regret. I have a flash
of sorrow that I won't ever hear him call me 'plaything' in
that borderline endearing way that he did, ever again. That
abruptly ends when Tavin screams at the top of her lungs
and plunges the knife back into his body six more times.
Finally, the blade falls from her fingers and clatters onto the
concrete.

"Good bye, Logan," she sobs.

After thirteen years of fearing this man, it's surreal for
him to be nothing more than a bloody sack of flesh. He always seemed so powerful. Now he's nothing.

For the first time since we arrived, Alexander speaks,
though he sounds weird with the holes in his tongue. "We

need to go, grab anything important. You need to clean up and change your clothes." My eyes shift up to Tavin, but she makes no move to do what he asks. I need her to look at me, I need to see what's changed between us. "I'm sorry, we have to get out of here," Alexander adds.

She gets up and when she kneels next to me and presses our heads together, I can't keep myself from crying. What happens now? We don't have Logan to force us together and I don't know if she'll forgive me for Nikki and Tiffany. My last hope is that she'll come home now that there isn't a threat. I'll try to explain everything and hope she truly understands that I will do anything for her.

We hold each other for a few silent beautiful moments. For the first time in our adult lives, we're free.

She chose him.

As soon as we got into Silas' car, Alexander made his anger over Nikki and Tiffany abundantly clear. I gave him the address to their house and Tavin chose to go with him.

Until that moment, I thought I might be able to convince her to forgive me, if she would have just stayed with me and talked about it. She didn't though, and she didn't even argue with him when he suggested calling the cops. That never would have happened six months ago.

As I watch her drive away, I realize in this moment, that she's truly in love with him. I guess I've always known it, I just refused to believe that I lived in a world where it could be true. How could she love anyone more than me? I could never come close to loving anyone like I love her. She smiles at him like she used to smile at me. When she's in his presence, her body glows like a shooting star. I had hoped when they had their falling out that they were finally over, but now I know.

She's really gone. I finally lost her.

They are going to see Nikki and Tiffany and as soon as she sees what I've done with her own eyes, she'll never look at me the way she used to, ever again.

For as long as I can remember, she's been my only purpose. She is quite literally the reason I breathe. I care for Nikki, but they are going to take her from me, too. They are going to lock me in a cage until I'm old and gray. By the time I get out, Tavin and I won't even recognize each other.

What was it all for? Why the fuck have I spent my entire life fighting to survive? Because at the end of the day, I had her. Now, even she has left me.

I have nothing.

I am nothing.

Silas pats me on the back and leads me inside his building. As we take the elevator to his penthouse, he asks, "You wanna drink some beer and order a pizza and watch the new *X-Men* movie?"

As if my life isn't falling apart around me. I scoff and shake my head, "Nah. Today took a lot out of me. Do you have somewhere I can lie down?"

He nods as the elevator doors open to a swanky living room. "Yeah, sure. Come on." I follow him toward the back of the penthouse to a hallway. Opening the door to a bedroom, he gestures inside.

The bed looks like it's on stilts and I can see all the lights across Shadoebox through the huge window. I toss my bag on the floor as he leans against the doorframe. "I can actually be a good listener if you're interested. I won't be biased, believe it or not."

I smile at him. I'm not used to this type of kindness from people. Maybe in another life, we could have been friends.

"Thanks…maybe later. For now, I just need some sleep."

Grabbing the doorknob, he backs out of the room.

"Alright man, holler if you need anything."

"Okay."

He closes the door and I dig my phone out of my bag before I walk to the window. It really is an awesome view. Choosing Christopher's name in my contacts, I call him.

"Hey, man what's up? I thought you had some big thing to talk to me about?"

The tears burn at the thought of never seeing him again. He was never anything, but an incredible best friend. "Hey, ah, nah. That doesn't matter anymore...I just...this is gonna sound weird, but don't be a dick about it, okay?"

He laughs and a tear makes its way down my cheek. "No promises."

"Thank you for standing by me all these years, I know I've lied and hid things from you, but just know it was to protect you. You're like my brother, Christopher. I want you to know I love you."

He's silent for a moment before his somber voice says, "You're fucking freaking me out."

I try to lighten my voice. "Sorry man, I'm just high. I'll catch you later, alright?"

"Are you sure you're okay?"

"Golden."

"Well, just so you know...I feel the same. I mean, you're my best friend. You always have been."

I hang up the phone and turn it off before picking up my bag and setting it on the bed. I pull out all the pictures I took off the fridge, kissing her in each one.

"I'm sorry I couldn't be who you needed, I will never stop loving you, Tavin. Not even this can stop that. I just hope he makes you happy and gives you the life I never could. Goodbye, Love."

I tuck the photographs into my lyric book and grab a pen.

Love is darker than hate
When it comes to pain
I need the silence
And the hush to fall like rain

I pull my works kit, a water bottle, and a balloon from my bag before pouring as much powder as I can into the spoon. After pulling the mixture into the syringe, I mix a little more. Surely this is enough to do the trick. I find the vein and take a deep breath.

I know I don't deserve it, but I hope it doesn't hurt to die. Looking out over the view of Shadoebox, I push down on the plunger.

BOOM. BOOM.

CRASH.

The softest silence….

⌐

"My darling boy, what have you done?"

Her voice is sweeter than honey on a comb. She's more beautiful than I ever imagined.

"Mom?"

Her hand caresses my face and it feels like flower petals and her white dress flows around her like wings.

"Oh, my love. With all you have suffered, you have also inflicted pain on others. That's not how you want to leave things is it?"

"But it's too late."

"It's never too late to change, Toben. You can make up for what you've done. Pay your penance and let out my precious little boy that I know is still in here." *Her hand presses against my chest as she smiles.* "Be the man I know you can be. I love you so much and I always have."

"I'm scared. I don't want to live without her."

"She'll never truly leave you. Though she may live her own life, you will always be a part of it."

She's right. I feel it in my skin. This doesn't have to be the end. It can be a whole new beginning. "I want to try. I want to make you proud."

Taking my face in her hands, she kisses my forehead. "Then go, live the life you never allowed yourself to dream of."

"How?"

She leans next to my ear and whispers, "Just...breathe."

The hospital machines *beep* as they pump me full of fluids through tubes. I scrape the bottom of my third lime Jell-O as the cartoons on the TV play.

Tavin clearly was a little unsure of how to feel about what I told her last night, but she'll see. I'm going to make my life mean something. Something I can be proud of. The first thing I'm going to do is go see Nikki. I'm going to explain to her that I don't want to cause her anymore pain. I want her to be free.

The chances are I'm going to see some jail time. The thought still makes me uncomfortable, but I know it's what I have to do if I ever want to try and right all my wrongs. Apparently, Alexander thinks I can get a minimal sentence with our history.

It's not going to ever be easy watching Tavin with him, but seeing her so happy will be worth the ache. I will be her friend however she needs me.

My door opens and I look up and smile expecting to see Tavin. I get to leave the hospital today and she and Alexander are picking me up.

The smile falls from my face when Kyle enters the room. He's wearing a raincoat even though it's a sunny day outside and is carrying a plastic bag. The machine measuring my heart rate *beeps* faster as he shuts the door and makes his way to my bed.

"You really didn't think I'd know it was you?" He reaches into his jacket and pulls out the blade. "He was my only friend. He was the strongest, most intelligent man I've ever known and he was the only person I've ever cared about." My tongue has swollen to three times its size and I'm not able to speak. "From the moment he bought you, things changed between me and him. The only thing I regret, is not being able to make this last."

Suddenly, I can't breathe and trying is excruciating. I open my mouth to speak and instead, I choke, coughing blood splatter onto the white hospital sheets. I look down to see the knife in my stomach. When he twists the blade, my body turns so cold. As if I've been dipped in a tub of ice water. The lights begin to dim and the sounds in my ears become muted. I see the blade going in and out of my body, but I don't feel it and eventually, even that becomes blurry.

The darkness surrounds me before it's overtaken by an explosion of light and I burst into infinite pieces.

"Do you believe in magic?" She asks as she draws on her wall.

She makes me smile. I know she's asking because she wants to believe it, she just wants me to, also. All the horrible things she's seen and been through and she still is able to believe in magic.

"I don't know, maybe…why?"

Placing her pencil on the floor, she gets up to sit next to me on the bed. "Because I think I wished for you before I met you. I wanted a friend for so long. I hoped and hoped and then one day, you came…maybe it was magic."

I wrap my arms around her and pull her closer to me. "What would you wish for now?"

"That we could go somewhere that it's just us. A place where we're never hungry, or dirty, or cold and that nobody could ever hurt us. That it would be just you and me forever."

She makes me smile, even in this horrible place. "Well, you don't need magic for the last part. It will always be just you and me."

Her grin is so sweet when she says, "Forever?"

"Forever and ever."

Cupcakes
PLAYLIST

1. *Black Balloon*—The Goo Goo Dolls
2. *Hush*—Hellyeah
3. *No Milk Today*—Herman's Hermits
4. *Crooked Spoons*—Otep
5. *Beautiful Creatures*—Illenium Ft. MAX
6. *Monster*—Skillet
7. *Mr. Brightside*—The Killers
8. *Comfortably Numb*—Pink Floyd
9. *Heroin*—Lana Del Rey
10. *My Demons*—Starset
11. *I Miss You*—Blink 182
12. *A Million Men*—Melanie Martinez
13. *Ocean Eyes*—Billie Eilish
14. *Dark Side*—Bishop Briggs
15. *Under the Bridge*—Red Hot Chili Peppers
16. *Angel*—Theory of a Dead Man
17. *Cotton Candy Land*—Elvis Presley

HELP LINES AND WEBSITES

RAINN (Rape, Abuse, and Incest National Network):
1-800-656-HOPE (4673)
www.rainn.org

National Domestic Violence Hotline:
1-800-799—SAFE (7233)
www.ndvh.org

National Child Abuse Hotline:
1-800-422-4453
www.childhelp.org

National Suicide Prevention Lifeline:
1-800-273-8255
www.suicidepreventionlifeline.org

SAMHSA (Substance Abuse and Mental Health Services
Administration)
1-800-662-HELP (4357)
www.samhsa.gov

Acknowledgments

Salina Donovan, you were the very first person to ever read my work. This novel was something I was a little worried to share and your response made me feel amazing. I'll never forget that. Thank you so much for supporting me in this and being my friend.

Terry Rains, you were the first to read this story in its entirety. The enthusiasm and excitement you showed, and have continued to show, means the world to me. Thank you for being such a great fan and friend. I'm so glad you and Katrina found each other.

Kween Corie, you have been absolutely incredible. You have helped me promote as well as being among the first to read my writing. Thank you for everything that you do and for being a wonderful friend.

Katrina Rains, I can't express how grateful I am to have you as my friend. You have been a consistent positive light in my life and never fail to make me smile. Your love and support for me and this series is something that will always stay with me.

Lori Lewis, I wonder how many hours you had to listen to me talk about this story and these characters. You were the first one I told about the story while it was still in its infancy. I don't know how I ever would have got this far without you as my soundboard.

Kathi Goldwyn and Maureen Goodwin from Maureen and Kathi read and The Dark Angels. I would never have gotten where I am without you guys. You have not only been invaluable to these books, but you have been great friends. I have had such a wonderful time with you guys and your support, promoting, and encouragement have been such a blessing to me.

Kim BookJunkie, Robin Craig, Elaine Kelly, and Danielle Krushel for reading the book(s) in their early stages and giving me your honest feedback. You all took a chance on an author you knew nothing about and were a huge part in me being able to reach for my dreams. Thank you so much for all your help and encouragement.

My amazing readers and beautiful ladies in the Broken Babydolls, absolutely none of this would be possible without you. You have shown me so much love and your enthusiasm for this story warms my heart so much. Leaving your reviews, posting about the books and talking about them, your participation in parties and giveaways…all these things have had so much more of an impact than you know and I am truly grateful to all of you. You are making my dreams come true.

All the fabulous authors who have promoted me and allowed me in your groups, have participated in my parties and events, and have helped me with their knowledge of the business. You have helped me find my way through this crazy journey that can make me feel lost sometimes. You have given me so much love, support, and encouragement and I am so thankful for each of you.

All the blogs who have posted the covers, release blitzes, and reviews. Thank you so much for choosing my book(s) to promote. It truly is such a huge help and gives me a rush every time I see one of your posts.

My editor, Joanne LaRe Thompson, I don't know where I would be without you. You have helped make these books so beautiful and have led me in the right direction to get my writing career off the ground. Thank you for all your feedback and kindness. Your encouragement has really been a blessing.

Megan with Mischievous Design, for making the most beautiful teasers for this series. You have always been so kind to me and your incredible work has helped me showcase this series in the way I always dreamed. Thank you so much.

Stacey with Champagne formats, you made these books more stunning than I ever could have imagined. You are a saint and your patience with me and my pickiness has been amazing. You made my words look so incredible. Thank you so much for the fantastic job you did with this series.

Murphy with Indie Solutions Cover Design, I had no idea what I wanted with these covers and you created such a unique and beautiful series that went over and beyond my expectations. These covers truly are perfect. Thank you so much for your incredible work.

BOOKS BY
CHARITY B.

The Sweet Treats Trilogy

Candy Coated Chaos
Sweetened Suffering
Cupcakes and Crooked Spoons

ABOUT THE
Author

Charity B. lives in Wichita Kansas with her husband and ornery little boy. She has always loved to read and write, but began her love affair with dark romance when she read C.J. Robert's The Dark Duet. She has a passion for the disturbing and sexy and wants nothing more than to give her readers the ultimate book hangover. In her spare time, when she's not chasing her son, she enjoys reading, the occasional TV show binge, and is deeply inspired by music.

Made in the USA
Monee, IL
01 August 2020

37395680R00225